## "DON'T HURT ME!"

"Hurt you?" Burke was puzzled. "You know what it is I want, Arielle."

But she saw only the riding crop in his hand. She saw that he held it with great familiarity, and paralyzing fear—the kind she'd known for so long—flooded her.

"I will . . . do as you please," she stammered. And Burke watched in utter bewilderment as she began to pull open the long row of buttons on the front of her gown. Her hands were shaking as she nearly ripped off her clothes, so great was her frenzy.

Then she was naked, her fingers unfastening his clothes with amazing speed . . .

*Other Avon Books by*
**Catherine Coulter**
*Coming Soon*

NIGHT SHADOW

AVON BOOKS  NEW YORK

NIGHT FIRE is an original publication of Avon Books. This work has never before appeared in book form. This work is a novel. Any similarity to actual persons or events is purely coincidental.


AVON BOOKS
A division of
The Hearst Corporation
105 Madison Avenue
New York, New York 10016

Copyright © 1989 by Catherine Coulter
Inside front cover author photograph by Jeanette Stringham
Published by arrangement with the author
Library of Congress Catalog Card Number: 88-92109
ISBN: 0-380-75620-X

First Avon Books Printing: February 1989

## To Linda Howard

A wonderful talent and a wonderful friend
She's got a zillion fans
Me included

# ❄❄❄ PROLOGUE ❄❄❄

Rendel Hall, Sussex, England
November 1812

He knew now that he could control her. Oh, yes, indeed he could. She realized that she could count on nothing from her greedy half brother. And her prune-faced maid, Dorcas—a simple threat to that old biddy's well-being and he'd brought her to heel with gratifying speed. He was stupid not to have thought of that sooner. In the future he would simply remind her on occasion that the old woman could be dispatched easily to her maker. Oh, yes, now she would do precisely what he told her to do.

He looked down at her and smiled. His young and tender seventeen-year-old wife. She was naked, on her knees, her arms wrapped about herself, her head bowed. He particularly liked the way her rich, thick hair fell on either side of her face, touching the floor. She was still breathing heavily, her thin shoulders quivering, from memory of his leather belt.

"You have been a bad girl," he said and gently flicked the tip of his leather belt over her shoulder. It licked at a new welt, but she said nothing, nor did she move. It pleased him. She'd tried to fight him, to run from him so many times before. But

1

now he had no doubt that she would stay where he told her to stay, as long as he wished.

"You will never again leave me," he continued. "I was most displeased with you, Arielle. It was an embarrassment for your dear brother, you know, fleeing to him with all your wild tales."

She said nothing. She didn't move.

"No, you shouldn't have done that," he added thoughtfully after a moment. He flicked the leather belt lower, near her waist. She was slender, always had been, but now she was thin, he saw, and he didn't like it. He didn't like seeing her ribs. He liked flesh on his women. "How do you expect me to do my duty if you look like a skinny hag?"

She said nothing.

He frowned. "Look up at me, girl! I am tired of speaking to the top of your silly head."

He watched her stiffen, watched her slowly raise her head and push her hair away from her face. She was still lovely to him, despite her obvious lacks as a woman. That beautiful hair of hers—plain red, his mother would have called it—but he was a poet, and had visited Italy on his Grand Tour, and knew better. Yes, her hair had drawn him to her, and those blue eyes of hers, so light and pure, not a drop of gray or green in them. And they usually held fear, of him. He liked that. He fancied her fear made her pale flesh even more colorless. "I was so happy that you had no freckles, my dear," he said, more to himself than to her. "Most unusual, yes, indeed. Look at me, Arielle, and stop that silliness of yours." She managed sometimes to cloak her fear of him by gazing directly at him, through him. It irritated him no end.

She looked at him, straightly now. He saw nothing, absolutely nothing in that clear stare of hers. Not hatred, not fear, just a sort of blind awareness. He preferred her fear, but he supposed she shouldn't be scolded further; he was certain that she finally understood what she was to him and what she would remain for as long as he wished it.

"Good," he said and smiled at her. "Now, that is enough punishment for your little peccadillo. I give you permission to address me, Arielle. I want you to tell me what you told your brother, all of it, my dear, else I'll welt the beautiful flesh on your buttocks. Why, this time I've scarce marked you at all. I am feeling benign, I believe. You will speak to me, Arielle, and you will tell me the truth, all of it, or I might be tempted to haul that old woman of yours in here and let her have a taste of my belt as well."

She believed him. She was so tired, tired to the depths of her. As for the throbbing pain from the strikes of his belt on her back and thighs, it was proof at least that she was alive. That was the only thing she could say now—she was alive and she still breathed and saw and heard. She only wished she could still feel, still laugh, from the inside.

She said slowly, very precisely, so that he wouldn't accuse her of sullenness and hit her again, "You had hurt me very badly. I could not bear it anymore." She was rather surprised to hear how calm her voice sounded, and she drew strength from it. Before she could continue, he said sharply, "What did you expect? I have taught you how to arouse a man, but you bungled your instructions yet again. What was I to do—praise you for leaving me limp and unsatisfied?"

Wisely, Arielle said nothing.

"Go on," he said irritably.

She watched him move away from her, and she felt herself relax a bit. Her muscles were beginning to cramp from her rigid kneeling position. She watched him sit down in a high-backed chair and wrap the leather belt about his hands, as would a

lady sorting out a ball of yarn. She wondered why
he wanted her to tell him of her meeting with Evan.
Then she realized his motive and again she wished
she could laugh—at herself, at her incredible naïv-
eté. He wanted to gloat, to preen, to strut himself
in front of her, to make her say how very powerful
he was. She forced herself to continue, her voice
quiet, emotionless. In her mind's eye, she saw herself in her bedchamber, felt distantly the now
nearly forgotten pain of that time. . . .

"I cannot bear it further," she'd said to Dorcas
as her lifelong maid and companion gently soaked
the swelled welts on her back with a warm wet
cloth.

"These welts won't last long," Dorcas said. "Lie
still and I'll be as gentle as I can with this cream."

"I hate him. I cannot bear it."

"Then you and I will leave here just as soon as
you are able."

Arielle twisted about, ignoring the jabbing pain
in her back, to look at Dorcas's face. "I have wanted
to run away back to Evan, but you have told me it
wouldn't work. You told me my brother would
laugh at me. You said to wait for Nesta and her
husband."

"Aye, 'tis what I told you, young miss, but now—
well, you've the proof of his cruelty on your back. I
care not for Mr. Goddis, but when he sees these
welts, how can he not do something? As for your
half sister and her husband, Miss Nesta and Baron
Sherard could be in China for all we know. A letter
every three months, but no word when they'll come
again to England. I'll help you—'tis but ten miles
to Leslie Farm."

Arielle pulled herself upright, gritting her teeth.
"I want to leave now, Dorcas."

"No, not yet, my baby. We must wait until he is
in his bed and the house is quiet. Then we'll leave.

Now lie down again and let me finish with this cream. I don't want you to be scarred."

"Scarred? I am already scarred. And I imagine that he enjoys seeing scars, particularly those he inflicts himself." But she eased herself down again onto her stomach. She was naked. She thought briefly of the modest girl she had once been, and a vague sort of hatred for that innocent foolish girl surged through her. It seemed that she had been naked and beaten ever since Evan had forced her to wed Paisley Cochrane, Viscount Rendel. And those other things. She gagged, unable to stop herself. But there was nothing in her belly. If she stayed longer she had no doubt she would even become used to each of his sexual demands.

Dorcas helped her pack a small valise. They slipped out of Rendel Hall at midnight, the witching hour, Dorcas murmured, and Arielle nodded, feeling no desire to jest about any superstition at the moment. Arielle had been raised with horses and she quieted them as best she could, her voice pitched low so they would not awaken anyone. She quickly and efficiently saddled two of her husband's lesser mares, ignoring the pulling pain in her back. She hefted Dorcas, no lightweight, into her saddle.

The November night was clear and cold, the stars brilliant in the sky. They met no one on the country roads.

They arrived at her home, her real home, at one o'clock in the morning. The rectangular Queen Anne manor house was simply called Leslie Farm, after her father's name and a pitiful scant hundred acres that grew some wheat. She hadn't seen the house in nearly eight months. She closed her eyes a moment, and her prayer was simple and to the point: please let Evan help her and protect her.

The old Leslie butler, Turp, a martinet of rigorous habits, stood in the narrow entrance hall, his nightcap askew, and stared at his former mistress, wondering what was wrong to bring her here in the middle of the night, old Dorcas in tow.

"Hello, Turp," Arielle said. "Please fetch Mr. Goddis."

"He is asleep!" Turp blurted out.

"I imagine that he is. However, you will fetch him. He will not be angry."

Angry or not, Evan Goddis came downstairs fifteen minutes later. He joined Arielle in the Leslie library, once her father's pride, now airless and dusty because Evan had only contempt for the hundreds of bound volumes that contained ideas that weren't his and therefore were of no use to him. He stood in the doorway, dressed in his gray brocade dressing gown, and merely looked at his half sister, a thin brow arched.

"Well?" he drawled in that affected way of his that made her back stiffen instantly. "What the devil are you doing here, Arielle? Rather a dramatic entrance, I should say, and your timing is deuced inconvenient. It is the middle of the night, you know. My, my, I don't believe I see dear Paisley."

She spoke in a rush. "I have left my husband. He is cruel and sadistic and . . . not normal, Evan. I have come to you for protection."

"Interesting," he said and moved slowly into the room. He was tall, taller than most men, but he was thin as a stork, his arms and legs appearing too long for his body. His hair was a sandy brown, nearly gone on top. His eyes were the color of thin gruel. Everything about him was thin, she thought, realizing it for the first time. Please, she prayed, watching him with hungry eyes, please don't let his compassion be as meager as his body.

"I have always despised this room," he continued, gazing about at the inset bookshelves, shadowly in the flickering candlelight. "Your father's ghost abides here; I can on occasion feel him. I never cared for your father either, him or his bloody ghost."

"Evan, you must help me!"

Evan came to stand in front of her. "Are you not yet with child?"

Her face went white, and suddenly she began to laugh, a deep, wild, savage laugh. "With child? Oh, God, that is wonderfully funny, Evan! Oh, God!"

He watched her as she rocked back and forth in a chair, listening to that awful grating laugh, then said sharply, "Be quiet Arielle. Get control of yourself. So the old fool hasn't managed even that, huh?"

She shook her head, saying nothing, trying desperately to get hold of herself.

"That was why he wished to wed you, of course," Evan continued, his long forefinger lightly stroking his jaw.

His words brought her attention back to him. "What do you mean?"

"The old fool played all his cards years ago, my dear. Dissolute old reprobate. He saw you, saw your beauty, your extreme youth, and believed you would, er, restore his manhood. I gather that you have failed him?"

"Yes," she said.

"So my little half sister is still a virgin?"

She looked at him, her eyes filled with experience and knowledge she should never have had, and again that harsh laughter bubbled from her throat. "Virgin? Ah, Evan, that is most amusing. A virgin. I should have preferred that very simple act to what he does to me, what he forces me to do to him." She paused, drawing herself up. "He beats me, Evan, and abuses me. I can no longer stay with him. I have come home. You will protect me. You must not let him near me; you must help me."

"You are most foolish, Arielle."

She rose slowly, unfastening her green pelisse as she did so. It slipped to the floor. She then unfastened her gown, turning her back to him. She let the gown fall to her waist, the simple white lawn chemise with it. She pulled her hair over her shoulder.

"This is what he does," she said.

She heard him suck in his breath, but he said nothing. She felt a long thin finger lightly touch one of the welts, pause, then touch others. She waited patiently until his fingers left her.

She pulled her clothing back into order and turned to face him. Odd, she thought vaguely, how there was no resemblance at all between them, even with the same mother. He must resemble his father, John Goddis, a man whom her mother had never spoken of in front of her.

"Well?" she said at last. "Will you keep that perverted old man away from me? Will you protect me?"

Evan smiled at her, then looked down at the finger that had touched her back. "Go upstairs to your old room, Arielle. I shall see you in the morning."

Hope flared in her eyes. "You will help me," she said and threw herself against him. "Oh, Evan, thank you! I knew that Dorcas couldn't be right about you.'

He raised his hands, realized her back must be very painful, and let them fall again. "Go to bed, Arielle."

She looked at him, but he only said again, "Go to bed now. . . ."

Arielle now looked dumbly at her husband. He knew the rest of it. She waited. She saw him strike the belt lightly against his palm.

"The next morning," she said finally, "you were there, in the dining room, eating blood sausages and poached eggs, waiting for me. Evan was with you."

"Yes," Paisley said. "You inconvenienced me, Arielle. That is why I whipped you this time. I will not abide disloyalty. You fail at your womanly functions, but that is different. Oh, yes, very different. At least now you understand how things are." It was his turn to pause, and the smile on his lips made her quiver with fear and disgust.

"Do you call Evan your brother or your half brother?"

She simply stared at him.

"Let us say half brother, for he has no caring for you at all, my dear girl. He despises you, as a matter of fact, for you are the offspring of your mother's liaison with another man. How your father could have been so stupid as to leave Evan your guardian has always amazed me. Well, it hardly matters, really. Did you not realize that he sold you to me? Fifteen thousand pounds I paid to have you for my wife. And this time, Arielle, your dear half brother held you for ransom. When I arrived this morning at Leslie Farm, he informed me that I could have you back for the sum of five thousand pounds. He sold you again. What do you think of that?"

Arielle felt nothing at first. Then she felt the rage building inside her, felt herself flushing with it, losing all control. She jumped to her feet, unable to think clearly now, and rushed at him, her fingers curving like claws, harsh jagged cries ripping from her throat. She was screaming at him. She felt the flesh of his heavy jowls split, felt his blood on her fingers, heard him yelling curses at her. Even when she saw his fist coming toward her, she couldn't stop. She was thrown onto the floor with the force of his blow. Her head struck a chair leg and she

saw brilliant white flashes before she fell unconscious.

## Rendel Hall, Sussex, England
## One Year Later

Arielle was afraid. She wasn't, however, certain
of the cause of her fear. But it was there nonetheless. She looked at her husband's illegitimate son,
Etienne DuPons, son of a French seamstress, now
dead. He bore a slight resemblance to his father as
a young man; even his nose was slightly crooked
and hooked in the same fashion, and his lower lip
was fuller than his upper. His chin was just as
prominent, his gray-blue eyes just as pale, just
as piercing. She was afraid of him, she realized,
and slowly, very slowly, so as not to gain her husband's attention, she laid her fork across her plate.

Etienne had been here for nearly two weeks now.
It wasn't that he appeared to openly admire her, or
to show her any excessive courtesy. But still she
found herself avoiding him. She was aware that on
occasion Paisley would watch her, then his son, and
there would be an assessing look in his eyes. Assessing what?

"The pheasant doesn't appeal to you, Arielle?"

He saw everything, which was strange because
his eyesight was failing. "It is delicious. It is just
that I am not very hungry this evening, Paisley."

"Nevertheless, you will eat your dinner. It would
displease me if you did not."

She picked up her fork and ate the pheasant. He
hadn't whipped her since the second night of his
illegitimate son's arrival at Rendel Hall. Nor had
he forced her to be naked for endless hours in his
bedchamber, hanging by that rope attached to the

hook in the ceiling, or on her hands and knees in front of him, her hands on his body, her mouth caressing . . . She shuddered, feeling herself gag on the pheasant.

She heard Paisley say to Etienne, "No, she doesn't look eighteen, does she? But she is, you know. She's been a wife for nearly two years now."

Why would Etienne care how old she was? She risked a glance at him. He was staring at her. She felt her heart pound, felt her hands grow clammy. "More wine, Etienne?"

*"Non, madame,"* Etienne said easily. He turned back to his father, forcing a pleasant expression across his features as he looked at the filthy old bastard. Surprisingly, he had accepted him with something akin to open arms, asked him to remain, but it worried Etienne because he didn't know his sire's motive. The only reason he'd journeyed to England was because his mother had asked it of him on her deathbed. Perhaps Lord Rendel wished him to kill someone? It sounded melodramatic, but he wouldn't put it past the old degenerate. Perhaps he wanted to legitimize him and make him his heir? Well, that would be something. He wasn't likely to have children by this wife.

"You find her acceptable?"

Etienne looked at the old man's veiny hand resting near his arm. He imagined that hand on Arielle. *"Oui,* she is more than acceptable," he said. "You wouldn't have married her, I think, had she not been beautiful." She was also hearing everything they said. Why was the old man doing this?

"True," said Paisley and returned to his plate.

After dinner, Paisley told Arielle to play the pianoforte. "She is barely tolerable," he said to his son. "Since she is lazy and won't practice, what can one expect? She has a modicum of talent, so I abide listening to her now and then."

The pianoforte was out of tune, the keys yellowed, many of them cracked or sticking. She sat down on the swivel stool and essayed a French ballad. It sounded dreadful, but there was nothing she could do about it. She played until Paisley told her to stop. Upon his command, she immediately lifted her hands from the keys and folded them in her lap. And waited.

Once, she had stopped when she had wished to. He had struck her, not even bothering to look up when the butler, Philfer, had come into the drawing room.

"Let us have tea, my dear girl," he said to her. "Ring for Philfer."

The butler brought in the tea, then looked at his master, not his mistress, for further instructions, which Paisley duly gave him. After Philfer had closed the salon doors, Paisley said, "You will go upstairs now, Arielle. You will have no tea."

Immediately, Arielle rose. "Good night, Etienne. Good night, my lord."

Another night of freedom, she thought, and her steps speeded up. She wanted the safety of her bedchamber. She scarce looked at the closed adjoining door that gave into Paisley's bedchamber. "Dorcas," she called, pitching her voice just right, for her maid was growing deaf. She even smiled at the old woman when she came into her bedchamber.

Within fifteen minutes Airelle was in her nightgown, her hair brushed out, and into her bed. She wanted to lie there and simply savor her continued reprieve, but she fell quickly asleep. An hour later, a light shone into her eyes and she felt someone shaking her shoulder. Paisley's voice said. "Time for you to do as I tell you, my dear. Out of your bed now."

She drew away, unable to help herself. "No," she whispered. "Oh, no."

"Do as I tell you, you little slut, else I'll flay the hide off you! And then I will have your maid fetched. I leave you to yourself for a few days and look at your insolence!"

Arielle rose immediately and reached for her dressing gown.

"No, you will have no need of it," he said and jerked the dressing gown out of her hands and threw it across the room. "Come with me."

Numbly, she followed her husband through the adjoining door into his bedchamber. He was fully clothed. What did he want of her? Did he want her to disrobe him? She'd done it many times before, doing it very slowly, caressing him as she removed an article of clothing, her every motion a ritual he'd taught her. She closed her eyes for a moment and willed herself to obey. Even if she'd learned nothing else during the past two years, she had certainly learned that she had no choice at all when it came to Paisley's demands.

"Is she not lovely?"

Arielle came to an abrupt halt. There, standing in front of the fireplace, his body silhouetted by the leaping orange flames, was Etienne. He was in a dressing gown, his feet bare.

"Yes," he said in his strongly accented English. "She is exquisite."

Paisley laughed. "Well, my dear? Can you guess what it is I wish you to do?"

She turned to him, and her eyes were filled with understanding and hatred, for him and for herself. "No," she whispered. "No, you cannot, please . . ."

"I can do whatever I wish, Arielle. You have failed me. You must bear me an heir. Since Etienne is my son, though his mother was a trollop of little count, I will let him get you with child. He would do it for me even though he were to find you displeasing, which he doesn't. Tonight, my dear girl,

I wish you to show him what I have taught you. I wish him to see your accomplishments. And since you have so few outside the bedchamber, well, I encourage you, my dear, to do your best. You will pleasure Etienne; yes, indeed you shall."

"No!"

She was running when he tripped her, still fighting him when he ripped the nightgown off her, still struggling when he pulled her upright back against him and said, "Well, Etienne, does her body please you, or do you find her too thin?"

"No!"

"She is quite beautiful," said Etienne. "But I have never raped a woman. I do not wish to rape her."

Paisley laughed, his arms squeezing beneath her ribs until she couldn't breathe.

"You won't have to rape her. Tonight she will pleasure you. And tomorrow night, my boy, she will be perfectly calm and willing, and I will hold her whilst you take her. She is a virgin, you know." He laughed again.

"A girl doesn't necessarily become pregnant with but one . . . encounter," said Etienne.

"No, you will plow her until she is with child. You will be amply rewarded, my boy. Oh, yes, indeed you will."

She was sobbing, tears rolling down her cheeks, her nose running, her hair in tangled confusion about her face. Paisley turned her about, raised his hand, and slapped her hard. "Enough, Arielle. Cease your foolish sniveling, else I will whip you. I expect you to show Etienne how very well trained you are. All women are whores at heart, and you are included. 'Tis just that you have had to wait to have your little belly filled. I give you a night of anticipation. Etienne, remove your dressing gown.

I wish Arielle to see your male endowments. Raise your eyes and look at the gift I give you, my dear."

She did. She watched Etienne shrug out of his dressing gown, watched it pool at his feet. His body was well made, she supposed, at least compared with his father's. His member was aroused, thrusting out, and she whimpered. She felt her husband's hand stroking over her breasts. To protest would bring more humiliation, more pain, endless pain, and harm to Dorcas. She forced herself to be perfectly still.

"What do you think, Arielle? Should you like the young stallion to cover you?"

She said nothing.

"No matter. Now, Arielle, I will release you. You will very gracefully see to Etienne's obvious need. Then you will return to your bed and think about what pleasure awaits you."

She did as she was told. It was different because he was swollen and hard and thick. When it was over, she fell back and lay still, her face pressed into the bright green Aubusson carpet in front of the fireplace.

"Very well done, my dear girl. Leave us now."

She was on her feet in an instant, swiping her hand across her mouth. She heard Paisley laughing as she dashed across the room and through the adjoining door.

Arielle ran to the night table and picked up the pitcher of water that sat there. She washed out her mouth, and then she vomited.

It was too much.

She could bear no more.

She looked up at the bars on her window, bars installed by a silent workman a year before, after her mad flight to her half brother. She knew that the door was already locked from the outside. Paisley had taken no chances with her since her at-

tempted escape. Even with his threats against
Dorcas, he **was** still careful.

Surely if she killed herself he would have no reason to hurt Dorcas. Her only problem was how to
do it. She looked at a glass figurine on the night
table. If it were broken, the edges would be sharp
enough. She stared at the figurine, and stared at
her wrists. She didn't move for a very long time.

The next morning her husband ordered Dorcas
from her bedchamber and pulled her from her bed.
He watched her bathe, dress, then accompanied her
downstairs. He didn't allow her to be alone, even
going to the convenience with her.

And that evening at the dinner table, Paisley
Cochrane, Viscount Rendel, choked on a herring
bone and died, his wife and illegitimate son in at-
tendance.

# 1

Battle of Toulouse, Toulouse, France
April 1814

It was the stench that brought him back.

He opened his eyes and gazed up at the starlit
sky, unaware that the stench filling his nostrils and
seeping into his lungs was of human suffering, human blood, and human death. He heard a low moan,
but it didn't quite touch him. It was odd, that was
all.

It took him longer to realize that he couldn't
move. He didn't know why he couldn't move, but
there it was. What was wrong with him? What had
happened?

It occurred to him that he was dead. No, not dead,
he thought, but perhaps near death. He began to
remember the battle in all its detail, as was his
habit. Just as he had never forgotten the screaming
death of Sergeant Hallsifer at Massena in 1810, nor
the memory of how Private Oliver from Sutton-on-
Tyne, a young man of vast good humor and excellent marksmanship, had bled to death. He closed
his mind to it. Later, he thought, if he were blessed
with a later, he would remember.

He wondered vaguely if Wellington had won the

battle. It was doubtful, for if Wellington hadn't managed to bring up the heavy guns, well, there would have been no surrender and the French would have escaped from the city and been halfway to Paris by now. What the devil had happened? He tried again to move his legs, then realized with a start that a dead horse was pinning him down.

He wondered if he had been wounded, but he could feel nothing. His body seemed separate from his conscious mind. Had he been left for dead? No, that wasn't likely. Where were his men? Please, God, not dead, please.

He knew a moment of panic, then forced himself to breathe deeply, to control his fear. It was then that he felt the whisper of pain in his side. He concentrated on that pain. Then he turned his mind inward. He would simply have to wait until Joshua came for him, and Joshua would come.

He focused his mind back in time, back to a beautiful spring day in Sussex. He dwelt on *her*. His memories were still vivid, not vague and blurred with time, which usually happened. No, he could see her smiling face clearly, see the rich gleam of her hair in the brilliant sunlight.

Arielle Leslie, a child really, only fifteen years old in 1811, and he had wanted her more than he'd ever wanted anything in his life.

He could still hear her laugh, high and pure, not some sort of romantic angel's laugh, but a young girl's healthy pleasure. . . .


Sussex, England
1811

He was home that May in 1811 to recuperate from the wound in his shoulder, a deep bullet wound that had left him weak from the loss of too much blood and in steady pain for weeks. But he'd survived and made it home to Ravensworth Abbey. Made it home in time to attend his brother's funeral. Montrose Drummond, seventh Earl of Ravensworth, was laid to rest in the Drummond family vault next to their father, Charles Edward Drummond, and their mother, Alicia Mary Drummond. Not that he deserved to spend eternity next to the senior Drummonds, the stupid ass. Montrose had fought a duel over a married woman and had been shot through his heart by the husband. Bloody stupid fool. It had taken him a while to realize that he, Burke Carlyle Beresford Drummond, was now the eighth Earl of Ravensworth. He remembered the day of the funeral clearly, for it was also the day he had met Arielle. He was in the Ravensworth library, the long, thick draperies flung back to let in the bright sunlight. Lannie's voice was high and distraught, pitched just right to her captive audience.

"What will become of me? What will happen to my poor fatherless little angels? Oh, oh, I shall moan into my pillow, so all alone. Ah, the horror of it. We shall starve. I shall have to sell myself to save my babies." From her tone, the final degradation didn't seem all that appalling.

Lloyd Kinnard, Lord Boyle, was Burke's only brother-in-law, his older sister, Corinne's, husband. Burke grinned, watching Lloyd try to stifle his laugh. It turned into a cough. "Pardon me," he gasped and earned a reproachful look from Lannie.

Burke looked at his sister-in-law and wished she would shut her Cupid's bow mouth. Her plaints were now repetitive, her creativity used up. Sell herself? He wanted to laugh as well, but the choked look on Lord Boyle's face made him hold his mirth. Lannie had never known a day of want in her life.

Surely she could not believe for an instant that he, Burke, would toss her and her babies out on their respective ears.

No one said anything, but Lady Boyle gave Lannie a look that would have crushed her flat had she had the courtesy to pay attention to her sister-in-law.

"I am going riding," Burke said, seeing Lannie open her mouth to begin another round. He strode quickly from the library. His arm was still in a sling, but the pain was only an occasional twinge now.

"Be back by four, Burke," Corinne called after him. "Mr. Hodges will be here to read Montrose's will then."

"All right," he said over his shoulder and kept walking. He heard Lord Boyle say something about a brandy, and smiled as his sister roundly told him that his nose was already too bulbous from drink.

Darlie saddled his big black stallion, Ashes, then offered him a leg up. "You have a care now, my lord," he said, and Burke was startled to hear that appellation.

"I will," he said and smiled at the old man who'd hefted him onto his first pony's back.

He rode to regain the feel of his boyhood home. He hadn't been back for nearly four years, and that visit had been at the death of his father. Not a happy stay and he'd left as quickly as was decent. Now he was back again, this time to bury his brother and to become the eighth Earl of Ravensworth. A damned earldom. It was something he didn't want, had never wanted. He was no longer free.

Burke rode down the long, curving lime-lined drive with its high, immaculately trimmed yew bushes on either side. At least Montrose had kept the estate up. He rode the perimeter of Drummond land, heading unconsciously eastward for the small lake that nestled like an exquisite emerald at the boundary of Drummond and Leslie land. Bunberry Lake was precisely as he remembered it from a good fifteen years before. It wasn't smaller, as things tended to be when one grew out of childhood. In fact, it seemed more precious simply because it had survived, would survive long after Burke had cast off his mortal coil.

He dismounted carefully from Ashes' broad back and tethered him to a maple branch. He breathed deeply. There were lily pads, willow branches dipping nearly to the surface of the still water, and daisies carpeting the ground, blooming wildly under the warm spring sun.

He sat back against the thick trunk of an oak tree. Lazily, he pulled up a blade of grass and chewed on it. He listened to frogs croaking and wondered if it was some sort of mating ritual. He listened to a hummingbird screech angrily at an intruder. And he listened to the sweet quiet that surrounded him, and savored it.

Then Ashes raised his head, sniffed the air, and whinnied.

Still Burke didn't move. So someone was coming. He had no intention of leaving his comfortable spot. He'd been here first, after all.

Then he saw her. She was riding a chestnut mare and she was laughing, at her mare's antics, he supposed, for the horse was prancing and dancing sideways. He could not see her face because a scarlet-plumed hat covered her hair and curved about her cheek. Her riding habit was a brilliant green, and as her mare did a particularly smart side step, he saw a booted foot. He wondered who she was. She had an excellent seat. He waited for her to notice him.

When she did, she paused but an instant, then

waved to him, calling out in her pure, sweet voice,
"How do you do? Are you the new earl? You are,
are you not? After all I can see that you are
wounded and the new earl was hurt, I heard, and
you have the look of a hero, although you are the
first I've ever seen. Yes, well, my name is Arielle
and I am not really trespassing on Drummond land.
Indeed, this brief patch is Leslie land, or at least it
should be if it isn't."

During this guileless speech, Burke rose slowly
to his feet. "Come here," he called to her. He carelessly brushed off the thighs of his buckskin riding
breeches and straightened his dun-colored jacket.

She nodded, the scarlet plume caressing her
cheek. She carefully guided her mare through the
shallow end of the lake some twenty-five yards
away. Then she cantered toward him, coming to a
graceful halt. She looked down at him and smiled,
extending a gloved hand. "I am Arielle Leslie, my
lord."

"And I am Burke Drummond."

"Major Lord Ravensworth," she corrected in good
humor.

"Yes, that's true. Would you care to join me for
a while? We can make it neutral territory for a
time, neither Leslie nor Drummond land."

"All right," she said agreeably and dismounted
without waiting for any assistance from him, to
spare him from using his arm, he realized. It was
when she was standing in front of him, looking up
at him full in the face that he saw that she was
beautiful. But it wasn't her beauty that was making him feel so odd. Burke had known many lovely
women, some more arresting than this female. No,
it was something else about her, and he could feel
his heart pound in slow, steady strokes, feel something change deep inside him. He also saw that she
was young, very young, too damned young. He

couldn't believe it. He knew he was staring at her, but he couldn't help himself. When all was said and done, it was really quite simple. He wanted her. And not as an adult wants to care for a child. No, he *wanted* her.

Dear heavens, what the hell was wrong with him? Had he been too long without a woman? He shook his head at himself. He felt like the hero in a ridiculous novel who falls head over arse in love at the first sighting of a female. It was altogether ludicrous and not a little unnerving.

"Come sit down," Burke said after a moment. "Sorry, but I have no refreshments with me."

"It doesn't matter in the least. All I have is but half a carrot, to give to Mindle if she behaves herself, which she always does. Now Ashes, that is a horse I much admire."

"You know my stallion?"

"Oh yes, but Montrose would never allow me to ride him. He said I was too young and a little female to boot. It is nonsense, of course. I am neither too young nor too little, and I cannot see that being female has anything to do with it."

"Of course you are not and it doubtless doesn't."

"You are laughing at me, I think."

"Not I. I am enjoying you. How old are you?"

She paused for a moment, cocking her head to one side in question, and he looked deeply into her eyes. He was losing and he knew it. He swallowed convulsively and thanked the stars that she was too young to notice his obvious besottedness.

"I am fifteen," Arielle said. "And you, my lord?"

"I am twenty-four."

"I am nearly sixteen, at least I will be in October, so it is not such a great difference."

"No, not in the future, but now it is a gulf—" He broke off appalled at himself. This had to stop.

"Nine years. No, eight and a half years. Well,

nine years ago I was quite a little girl, really, nothing more than a child. Whereas you, my lord, you were already quite the young man."

"Just as at fifteen you are quite the young woman?"

"Exactly so." She sounded perfectly serious, but he chanced to see a dimple quivering in her left cheek. "All right," she said, throwing up her hands, "I must admit that you are quite young now to be all that you are."

"All that I am? I am simply a man, Arielle. And please call me Burke. This sylvan setting doesn't allow for formality, you know."

"That is neither here nor there. You are a major and an earl. I do realize that the earl part had little to do with your mental abilities or your worthiness, but surely the major part—you have doubtless dispatched many French devils to hell, and managed it in an awesomely heroic way. I trust you are nearly well now? Will you return to the Peninsula?"

"Yes, I am nearly well now, and I will return to the Peninsula, soon."

"I do not like pain, but I am never ill, so it is not to the point."

"No, I suppose it isn't. Your hair is lovely, if you don't mind my saying so. It is an odd color."

"My father, Sir Arthur, you know, he says it is the perfect example of Titian, and that is after some rather famous painter who lived ages ago in Italy."

"Yes, I should say he is right."

"It is still red, no matter how one dresses it up. One must always face up to things, don't you agree?"

He started to say yes, he did agree, but that would be the grossest lie of his life because he was quite consciously refusing to face up to his instant and overwhelming intoxication with a fifteen-year-old girl. Was it her beautiful hair? Those clear, pure blue eyes? Dear God, he was fast becoming a half-wit. He didn't want to be infatuated with any female. And this one was a girl, not a woman.

And he'd never loved in his life.

He didn't want to start now. But he didn't seem to have a whole lot of choice.

"No, I don't agree."

"I am sorry, my lord—excuse me, Burke—but I don't remember my question. You have been long silent. Just what is it that you don't agree to?"

"I don't remember either. You have a sister, don't you? I don't remember her name."

"Yes, my half sister, Nesta. She married Alec Carrick, Baron Sherard."

"Good heavens, I know him. I met him in London several years ago. He was very young as I recall but even then he was vowing to remain a bachelor all his days. Amazing. Does your sister look like you?"

"Not at all. As for her baron, well, he seemed to fall head over tail in love with Nesta. From the sound of it, he met Nesta just after he met you, my lord. Oh dear, should I have said that? Perhaps head over toes is more proper?"

"You can say precisely what you want. I shan't mind in the least."

"You are very kind, Burke. Are you certain it is proper to call an earl and a major by his first name? All right, very well, it is your decision, after all. Nesta and her baron left just three months ago for America. I will not see her for a very long time. Now, I also have a half brother whose name is Evan Goddis. I have seen him only rarely. You see, my mother was married once to John Goddis, and Nesta and Evan were their children. Then he died, quite scandalously if one can believe lowered voices when one is eavesdropping, though Mother refused to speak of it to me, you know. In any case, she married my father and they had me. She died two years ago."

"I'm sorry. I didn't know. However, I am thankful that they had you."

"I don't think they had an immense amount of choice in the matter, my lord."

"You forgot. You must call me Burke. I should like for us to become friends."

"All right. And I am Arielle. My dear father has a penchant for romantic, rather flighty names—"

"Your name is perfect for you."

"Flighty, am I? Since there is nothing I can do about it, I should suppose I must make do."

"Is that something else one must face up to? Like your plain old red hair masquerading as Titian?"

"You are stretching the point a bit. Yes, you are right. The most perfect example is dear Lannie. She is such a ninny. Oh, dear, she is your sister-in-law. I was forgetting that."

"She is a ninny. Indeed, the reason I am here right now is to escape her infernal melodramas."

"She is rather good at them, though."

"Not when she has but one subject to draw from."

"Oh, yes, Montrose. Has she told everyone, the servants included, that you, as the new earl, will most likely make her work shuttling coals to the bedchambers, before dawn, mind you, to be able to feed her poor little darlings?"

Burke burst into laughter. "Had she done that, I probably would have remained. No, her main focus before I left was that she would have to sell her body to feed her little angels. You know my sister-in-law well, I see."

"Yes, Lannie isn't really bad, you know. She is just sometimes irritating. I am most sorry about Montrose, as is my father. He doesn't believe in funerals, of course. They are, unfortunately, in the category of heathen orgies, and thus he won't abide them. Forgive us for our seeming disregard."

"You're forgiven," Burke said. He found himself staring at the clean lines of her profile as she turned to look out over the lake. He would not have cared if Sir Arthur had classified funerals as Viking pyres.

"Why are you staring at me?" Arielle asked, turning to face him. Her eyes were alight with laughter and teasing. "It is my nose, isn't it? Mother told me when I was six years old that I shouldn't ever have any pretensions to beauty. It is the Leslie nose, not the Ramsay nose."

"It is a perfect nose. Incidentally, your mother was quite mistaken."

"Ha! Well, you are a very nice man—rather, major and earl. I must go now or Father will be concerned. He is a pet, you know, but since I am his only child, he does fret."

"Shall I see you home?"

"Do you know my father?"

"I met him when I was a boy. It's been at least fourteen years since I've seen him."

"Then you'd best not. He is in the throes of a translation—Aristophanes, I believe—and since he is having some difficulty with a few Greek phrases, he is a bit abrupt with those around him. It is possible he would treat you like an importunate tradesman and that wouldn't do at all! I am the only one he seems to know when one of these bouts overtakes him, and if I am not there, he shouts at everyone. Good-bye, Burke. You will get well, quickly now."

"Of course." He tossed her into her saddle. It hurt him to do it, but he had to touch her. Her waist was very small, as was the rest of her. If nothing else could save him, he could at least be aware that she

had the body of a young girl, all coltish angles and
bones and hollows and straight lines. Nevertheless,
his fingers tingled. He stood quite still, like a besotted buffoon, staring after her. She finally turned
in her saddle, saw him standing there, and gaily
waved good-bye.

The next time Burke met Arielle was over tea at
Ravensworth Abbey. She was dutifully listening to
Lannie carry on.

"Oh yes, indeed, the infamous will! I vow and
declare, Arielle, I was never so shocked in all my
life!"

"But, Lannie," Arielle said reasonably, reso-
lutely keeping her eyes from Burke, "Poppet or
Virgie couldn't become the Earl of Ravensworth.
Unfortunately, girls aren't given all that much
worth.'

"I disagree," said Burke, thinking that Arielle
had more power over the damned Earl of Ravensworth than any human alive.

"You would," said Lannie with charming ambi-
guity, giving him a petulant shrug. "And Montrose
left *him* the guardian of my poor little babies."

Arielle pursed her lips to hold back her laughter.
"Burke will be an excellent guardian, Lannie.
Would you have preferred the myopic Mr. Hodges?"

"Oooh, that miserable old tight-fist!"

"There, you see. Burke will never draw the purse
strings, will you?"

"Not at all," he said. "I am the most generous of
men, Lannie." He gave another glance in Arielle's
direction, trying to be subtle about his infatuation.
She was wearing a soft lavender muslin gown, a
school girl's dress with a high neck and a wide satin
sash about her waist. But her hair . . . He swallowed. Her hair was in loose, thick curls down her
back. He'd prayed that today when she came to
visit, he would see her as he was supposed to—as a

very delightful young lady who should spend most
of her time in the schoolroom, a delightful young
lady, nothing more. But when she'd walked into the
drawing room, he'd felt that same blasted feeling
as on the day of the funeral, save more so. Damn
her, she wasn't even grown. She was by far too innocent and candid for an adult man. He cursed
softly into his teacup.

"Did you say something, Burke?"

"Surely dear Burke wants all that is due to him,"
said Lannie in a snide voice. "He is, after all, the
earl."

"I agree," said Arielle, those innocent blue eyes
as naughty and full of guile as the most practiced
flirt in London. "We must ensure that he is filled
with consequence."

"As in hot air?"

"No, I propose to advance your vanity. You have
not enough. Joshua was telling me that—"

"You know my Joshua? Joshua spoke to you?"
Burke regarded her with frank surprise. Joshua
Tucker wasn't precisely a misogynist, but he had a
very low regard in general for the female of the
species and didn't hesitate to voice this opinion. He
was also as loyal as a tick, and his ingenuity had
saved the both of them several times during the
past five years.

"Certainly," Arielle said. "He was speaking to
Darlie and I introduced myself. He does assure me
that he cares for you to the best of his ability but
that you haven't a vain bone in your major's body.
Er, *major lord's* body."

Lannie gave a shrill laugh. "Really, Arielle, you
haven't a notion of what you're talking about!
Montrose told me about that girl Burke took up
with at Oxford—"

"Enough, Lannie," he said quite pleasantly.

"You see, " Arielle said, "you won't even let Lannie brag about your exploits with females."

"I doubt she was going to brag."

"Lannie is most kindhearted," said Arielle and turned her candid blue eyes on Lady Ravensworth. Lannie had the grace to twitch a bit. Burke sat back in his chair. It was odd, but Arielle held the reins of control at this tea party, not Lannie, and Lannie was seven years her senior.

"More tea, if you please, Lannie." He wondered what Joshua would say about this female.

"Will you resign your commission now, Burke?"

He shook his head. "No, I cannot, Lannie. Not until things are settled."

"I should not resign either," said Arielle, and there was a definite blood lust in her eyes. "I wish I were a man."

"You would still be too young for the army, my dear."

"If you die, cousin Radnor will become the Earl of Ravensworth," said Lannie, her tone both spiteful and appalled.

"That is a crusher," said Burke. "I haven't seen Radnor in a good six or seven years. What has he been doing?"

"He is a vicar," Lannie told him, "but he still has no chin. He grew a small beard to cover it."

Burke stared at her, then burst into laughter. "Rad? A vicar?" It was too much. He choked on his tea and in the next instant felt Arielle's hands pounding his back. When he stopped choking he breathed in her scent and wanted to rip off her silly schoolgirl's gown and fling her to the Aubusson carpet. He wanted. . . .

"Are you all right now, Burke?"

"Yes, sit down, Arielle. I wonder why our cousin didn't come to the funeral."

"He is in Scotland," Lannie said, "ministering to

a great aunt he doubtless hopes will leave him some
money when she succumbs."

"He sounds like a thoroughly unlikable creature," Arielle said.

"He is, most assuredly. Now, Arielle, would you
like to ride Ashes?"

He would never forget that afternoon. It was the
afternoon he, Burke Carlyle Beresford Drummond,
fell in love for the first and only time of his life.
Most inappropriately and helplessly and irrevoca-
bly. It was the afternoon he began making his plans
to return to the Peninsula.

Three days later, he saw Arielle Leslie for the
last time. He visited her at Leslie Farm to tell her
good-bye. He'd met her father, Sir Arthur, again.
She had her father's eyes, clear and steady, a cloud-
less blue like the spring sky.

"Do not forget me," he'd said, intending that his
voice would be light, jocular.

"How could I?" He saw sadness in her eyes, heard
her voice crack slightly. "But you will forget me,
my lord earl. I am a silly girl, whereas you are a
hero and—"

"Hardly silly, my dear. I won't be returning to
England for a time, perhaps several years. Then, if
you wish it, I will call on you."

She gave him her sweet smile and placed her
hand on his forearm. "I shall look forward to it. I
doubt you will have time for me, though. So many
ladies will be flocking about you, demanding you
favors and your attention. I promise I will be among
them, at their fore, if it pleases you."

"Yes, it will please me more than I can say." He
wanted desperately to ask her to write to him, but
that would place him beyond the pale. He noticed
that Sir Arthur was frowning slightly. He didn't
know if it was due to a problem with his Greek
translations or to the obvious besottedness of the

Earl of Ravensworth toward his very young and innocent daughter.

He took his leave. . . .


Toulouse, France
1814

There was that moaning sound again. Burke realized this time that it was coming from his throat.

He wasn't with Arielle. He was lying in a battle-
field near Toulouse, three years later, pinned under
a horse, a wound in his side. The pain was building
now into crashing waves, pulling him clearly into
the present, making him grit his teeth to keep still.

"Major Lord! Thank God I've found you at last."

"Joshua," Burke said, surprised at how weak his
voice sounded. "I knew you would come. A horse
seems to have died on me."

"Yes, I see. Hold still. I will return quickly with
help."

It was a good hour later before Burke was lying
as comfortably as possible on a cot in his tent,
Joshua beside him, seated cross-legged on the floor,
telling his master of the French withdrawal from
Toulouse. Burke was naked beneath a single sheet,
save for the bandage that covered the saber slash
in his side. He listened with but half an ear. Memories and pain still held him in thrall.

"Here, Major Lord," said Joshua, rising to bend
over his master, "the doctor said you was to drink
some laudanum. Lost too much blood and you must
rest to restore it, so don't give me any of your excuses."

"I shan't," Burke said and swallowed the water
with the laudanum in it. Joshua tucked a blanket
about his chest.

Satisfied with his master's comfort, Joshua continued. "Wellington couldn't get his heavy guns into place in time and so the damned Frogs slipped away."

"I thought that was what had happened. Where is Wellington?"

"He should be here to see you very soon. He is quietly furious, if you know what I mean, Major Lord."

"Yes," Burke said softly, "I know." He managed a smile for Joshua, seeing the man's fear for him. "I shall soon be quite myself again. Just keep calling me major lord. It does sound like the top of the heap."

He fell asleep then, thankfully, only to hear Joshua's voice calling to him.

"Major Lord! Major Lord!"

He felt a slap on his face and tried to turn away from it, to return to the past, to Arielle, but it wasn't to be.

"Major Lord! Come, you must wake up now. The duke is here to see you."

"I don't want to," said Burke very clearly.

"Well, your commander doesn't care for your bloody attitude, Ravensworth."

Burke forced his eyes open. Wellington was standing beside his cot, his smile a bit forced, lines of fatigue about his eyes. His uniform was immaculate, as usual, his black boots clear as mirrors.

"Sir," he said and tried to raise his hand.

"Lie still, Burke. I have little time, my boy, then I must be off to Paris. I wanted to tell you in person of the waste of it all. Our battle, all the deaths, all for naught. Napoleon has abdicated, had abdicated before we began."

Burke stared up at him. "You're jesting," he said slowly.

"I wish to God I were. It is something I have

prayed for, but God saw fit to lose nearly five thousand more of His souls before seeing to it. Well, hurrah I say, but I only wish we had been spared. The doctor tells me that you will mend soon, my boy. You will return to England, Burke. It is over now, at least your part of it."

Yes, Burke thought later. It was over at last. Arielle was now eighteen years old, nineteen in October he remembered her telling him. Old enough for marriage. Old enough for him. What if she had formed an attachment with another man?

He refused to accept that. Over the past three years he'd received sporadic though informative letters from Lannie. He wondered occasionally if she suspected his motive for asking her so specifically to write about life at Ravensworth and the doings of their neighbors. He knew about Sir Arthur's death, very sudden and but six months after he had left England, and he'd written Arielle a proper letter of condolence. He'd received no response in return, of course.

What had she been doing since the spring of 1811? Lannie had written of the marriage of every male and female within a fifty-mile radius of Ravensworth. No mention of Arielle. Perhaps she was waiting for him.

It was a notion that pleased him and allowed him to heal more quickly than the doctor had predicted.

# 2

Ravensworth Abbey
June 1814

Burke still felt uncomfortable in *his* home. He was the eighth Earl of Ravensworth and as absolute a ruler here as the Sun King had been in France more then two centuries before. He was responsible for every soul that drew breath on this estate, and he was responsible for providing another male soul who would carry on after he had passed to the hereafter. He looked about the Golden Drawing Room, intimidating as the devil, he'd always thought, with its array of gold-legged chairs, Italian marble insets, and intricate filigreed ornaments set in their place of honor atop a sixteenth-century marquetry table. He hoped devoutly that the elaborate chair that looked too old to hold anything would bear his weight. Surprisingly to him, it did. As a boy, he'd scarcely been allowed in this, his mother's favorite room. It held her stamp, he'd been told, but wondered at it. Somehow he couldn't picture his frail, fading mother in this rich, nearly overpowering chamber.

Burke's sister-in-law sat opposite him, straightening the sash on Poppet's dress. Burke said, "They are beautiful, Lannie. You've done well by them, I see."

Lannie preened a bit, then sharply clapped her hands. Virgie and Poppet's nanny, Mrs. Mack, duly took each little girl's hand and towed them from the drawing room.

Poppet turned at the entrance. "Uncle Burke, will you come to play with us later?"

"Most certainly, Poppet. I shall look forward to it. What shall we do?"

"Soldiers," said Virgie. "I want to be your sergeant and fire cannons and kill Frogs."

"My goodness," said Burke, somewhat stunned by this. "No tea party? No conversations with dolls?"

That earned him a disgruntled look from both girls, and Lannie sighed. "Don't ask me, Burke. I have no idea why the little urchins are so bloodthirsty. Ever since Montrose died, well . . ."

"It's all right, Lannie. I fancy that I have a prayer of winning if we play soldiers." He waved to his nieces, saying nothing until they'd disappeared from sight.

Lannie picked up a small iced cake and said, "I trust you are home to stay, Burke?"

"Yes, all is finished now. Napoleon will bother us no more, hopefully."

"I cannot imagine why Wellington simply did not just shoot him. Spending all that money just to send him to his own island—well, I think it is all nonsense."

Burke merely smiled at his sister-in-law. Perhaps this was where the little girls had gotten their bloodthirsty attitudes. Lannie hadn't changed, not one whit in the years he'd been gone. Had Arielle changed? Of a certainty she'd had to. She'd become a woman. She would soon become his woman.

Burke regarded Lannie over his steepled fingers,

wondering how he could bring Arielle up quickly
in the conversation. She was saying in her petulant
voice, "Well, I do hope you intend to hire a new
steward. Cerlew is a bounder, make no mistake,
Burke. Why, the man is forever questioning *my* ex-
penditures, as if I were some sort of bourgeoise. It
is most annoying."

Good for Cerlew, Burke thought. Actually, the
Abbey looked much better than it had during Montrose's tenure as earl. All was in good repair and
clean and polished. Even Joshua approved.

Burke cleared his throat to take the leap, but
Lannie forestalled him, saying, "Corinne will
doubtless be here to stick her oar in. You did write
her, did you not?"

"Actually, I stayed with her and Lloyd in London
when I returned from France. Jocelyn, you know,
it up at Oxford."

"Yes, a most peculiar boy," Lannie said about
the only son of Lord and Lady Boyle. "I remember
all he did was read, simply all of the time."

"He is a scholar, Lannie. His range of knowledge
is awesome."

"Well, I think . . ."

Lannie continued to think aloud about Jocelyn
and his oddities, the result, doubtless, of Corinne's
overbearing influence, and Burke let his own
thoughts wander.

London had been mad with Napoleon's abdica-
tion. Czar Alexander of Russia had arrived in England on June 6th. Now anything Russian was the
fashion, from ladies' gowns to gentlemen's cravats.
Czar Alexander and his sister, Catherine of Oldenburg, were also given the Regent fits, a happening
that didn't touch Burke one way or the other. It
was always the topic of conversation in the Tory
Kinnard household and at the several balls Burke
had attended as well. He'd smiled and chatted with

the ladies, gravely discussed the Battle of Toulouse with the gentlemen, and thought about Arielle. He'd thought to take a mistress that week, but discovered that he simply couldn't do it. He didn't want another woman. He wanted Arielle and only Arielle.

"Burke, really! Haven't you heard a word I've said? Well, here is Montague with tea."

Montague was the epitome of an old revered bishop, Burke thought. He always had been, his full head of stark white hair as thick now as when Burke had been in short coats. "Thank you, Montague," he said, giving the old retainer a warm smile.

"My lord," said Montague, "I venture to say that you need a spot of rest this afternoon. I believe Joshua is waiting for you in your chamber."

"Here I am a civilian again and still I'm getting my marching orders."

"Yes, Lord Ravensworth is right," Lannie said to Montague. "You really shouldn't—"

"I was jesting, Lannie. Yes, Montague, I do feel a bit downpin. Thank you."

But he wasn't about to leave his sister-in-law until he knew about Arielle. He took a cup of tea from her, sat back in his chair, and tried to look nonchalant. He sipped his tea. "Tell me of our neighbors," he said.

Lannie did, to the point of exhaustion. When she finally paused, Burke said, "The Leslies? I remember you writing me that Arthur Leslie had died."

"Goodness, that was *years* ago!"

"Well, not all that many. What happened to the family?"

"You mean Arielle?"

"Yes," Burke said, and unconsciously, he sat forward, his tea forgotten, his eyes on Lannie.

"I wrote you about it," she said. "I remember that."

"Wrote me about what? When?"

"Goodness, as I said, that was years ago. Arielle married."

The Wedgwood teacup fell to the floor. Burke watched it roll off the Aubusson carpet onto the hard wood. It cracked. He watched the brown liquid seep between the cracks and make puddles on the shining wood. He felt too stunned to think.

"Burke! Whatever is the matter? Does your wound hurt?"

"No, no, I'm fine, just clumsy." Actually, he didn't think he could breathe. He felt such a bolt of deadening pain. He couldn't bear it. He moistened his dry lips. "When? To whom?"

"Well, she's been a widow for some months now, since last year, I believe, though no one ever sees her. She married Paisley Cochrane when she was only sixteen."

Burke just stared at her. Paisley Cochrane! Good God, that lecherous old satyr had been known for his wickedness when Burke was a boy. Married to Arielle? He shook his head even as he said, "Her father allowed such a thing?"

"Oh, no. Her halfbrother Evan Goddis, was made her guardian on Sir Arthur's death. He saw to the wedding. Havey-cavey, all of it, if you asked me, not more than six months after Sir Arthur's death. And then, of course, old Paisley died so mysteriously—everyone was talking about it, of course."

But Burke wasn't listening anymore. "Does she live at Rendel Hall?" Cochrane's estate lay only some ten miles to the east of Ravensworth.

"Certainly, it's hers now. She inherited everything. Unlike me, who has had to live on another's bounty and—"

"That'll do, Lannie," Burke said, not unkindly, as he rose.

"Where are you going?'

"Upstairs for a rest. I will see you at dinner."

When Joshua finished clucking over him, he lay on his bed and stared up at the naked cherubs that cavorted on the ceiling moldings. She had married Viscount Rendel when she was sixteen years old. God, the man had to have been at least fifty! And he'd touched her and caressed her and . . . Burke had to stop this. He couldn't change the past. He had to accept things as they were or forget her. It was really that simple.

And during those years he hadn't known, hadn't considered that another man . . . The one lost letter—it seemed beyond irony. But now she was a widow, so it didn't matter. Nothing mattered except seeing her, courting her, marrying her. He wouldn't allow the past to intrude.

He'd forgotten to ask Lannie if Arielle had had any children. If she did, he would raise them as his own. He asked at dinner that evening.

"No, she didn't," said Lannie. "That was why old Paisley wed her. He was wild for an heir, you know. But there was no issue. Why the interest, Burke?"

"I remember her as being a very nice young girl," he said, his eyes studiously on the Ravensworth silver. "Did you ever see her after her marriage?"

"No, not once. It was most odd, really. She was wed, and then it was as if she were whisked to another country. Not a sight of her. One hears rumors, of course, but I discounted them. This is modern times, after all, not the Middle Ages."

"What rumors?"

Lannie shrugged. "Stupid things, like Viscount Rendel keeping her close to Rendel Hall, not allowing her to go anywhere or see anyone or do anything—"

"But you just said that she wasn't ever seen after her marriage."

"Yes, but the viscount couldn't possibly have held her some sort of prisoner. That is really too silly. Also, I don't know if you ever heard of Evan Goddis, Arielle's half brother, but he didn't and still doesn't have the most regular of reputations. I heard talk that he forced Arielle to marry poor Paisley for a huge settlement. I don't know if there's any truth to it."

"Why do you say poor Paisley?"

"Well, he had no children, did he? Just before he died—so mysteriously, as I told you—his illegitimate son was visiting him from France."

"What do you mean by mysterious?"

"Choking to death over dinner is hardly an everyday occurrence, Burke. According to the servants—you know, Martha's cousin is the under-housemaid at Rendel Hall—well, she said that the illegitimate son and Arielle simply sat there and watched him choke to death."

"That sounds rather unlikely."

"I suppose so. I shouldn't simply sit here and watch you make a spectacle of yourself, believe me!"

"Have you seen Arielle since her hus—since Rendel died?"

"Once, when I was visiting a friend in East Grinstead, Lady Fanchaut, you know. She took me to this marvelous little modiste shop there, just off High Street, and there were the most clever ribbons for my new bonnet and—"

"When was this? How did she appear?"

Lannie finished her vermicelli soup and wondered briefly if her waistline could afford just a bit more. She sighed and shook her head at herself. She motioned to the footman, Robert, to serve her some fricasseed chicken.

"Lannie!"

"What? Oh, yes, Arielle. As I said, I saw her in East Grinstead. She appeared well, I suppose. Well, not really all that well. Different. She was too thin, but then she always was. It was odd. She wasn't wearing mourning." Lannie paused a moment, her head cocked to one side. "Why all this interest in Lady Rendel, Burke?"

Before Burke could come up with an adequate response, Lannie said, "It's quite ridiculous to call her Lady Rendel. She is only eighteen years old, for heaven's sake. Well, when you see her, do say hello. I much enjoyed her company when she was younger."

## Rendel Hall

Arielle very slowly set down her tambour frame. "Where did you hear that, Dorcas?"

"Why, in the village. Mrs. Cranage saw him and she told me he wasn't alone."

"Evan," Arielle said very slowly, her eyes suddenly wide and strained.

"Yes, that's right. Etienne DuPons was with that bounder of a half brother of yours. The only thing I don't understand is why. What would Evan Goddis want with that man? It's not as if he had any money."

"I don't know," said Arielle. "I had thought that Etienne had returned to France right after his father's funeral."

"Perhaps he did, but now he's back. Return of bad garbage, I say."

"Is there ever any good garbage, Dorcas?"

Dorcas raised her head from her tatting at that. "A smile. Excellent, Miss Arielle. You should smile more, you know. Lord Rendel has been dead a long time now. You should get out, go to parties and balls. You should—"

Arielle raised her hand to stem the advice tide. "No, not yet. I will go out when I am ready."

When would that be? Dorcas wondered, returning to her tatting. Poor Miss Arielle; the child had suffered so much at the hands of that monster, and now, well, what was keeping her at Rendel Hall, as if she were still a prisoner?

"Surely you don't intend to mourn him for a full year?"

Arielle looked at the pale yellow of her muslin gown. Hardly mourning. Celebration colors, that was all she wore. She looked over at Dorcas, not only her former nanny and maid, but now also her companion. The old woman was the only person on the face of the earth who cared about her. She still had no idea where Nesta and her husband were. She'd gotten a tattered envelope containing a brief note from Nesta some four months before, from a place called Macau. Nesta had said nothing about coming home.

Arielle rose from her chair and walked to the wide bow windows that overlooked the sloping front lawn of Rendel Hall. It was hers now, all of it. She wasn't wildly rich, but rich enough to do anything that pleased her; at least that was what her estate manager, Mr. Harold Jewells, continued to tell her at their Monday morning meetings. Two Mondays ago he'd hinted that she should go down to London and enjoy herself, and she'd merely stared at him. No, she couldn't go anywhere. Not yet. She was too afraid. She was still too ashamed. People would know if they saw her. They would see the truth in her eyes. She couldn't face it yet.

And she couldn't face men and the way they would treat her, look at her. Even Mr. Jewells, who was thin as a reed, bald, and utterly harmless.

She turned back to Dorcas, forcing a smile. "I think I shall go riding. Poor Mindle has been sitting idle for two days now. At last the sun is out."

"Take a groom," Dorcas called to her back.

"I'll take Geordie," Arielle said, but not for reasons of propriety. She was afraid to be alone. Even on Rendel land. She was afraid of her half brother, a silly fear, really. But she couldn't change her feelings, and now there was Etienne. She was so weary of living with fear. Why hadn't it all magically disappeared when Paisley had died? Why was she still haunted? What, for God's sake, could Evan do to her? Or Etienne, for that matter? Be nasty? That was nothing, nothing at all, but yet the fear remained, that paralyzing fear.

When Geordie had finished saddling Mindle, he helped her into the saddle. "Let me saddle up old Rigby, my lady. Then we'll be off."

"No hurry," she said, looking fondly after her servant. He was a Scot, from Glasgow; short, wiry, tough, and his arms and hands were so strong he could break a man's neck with a snap. And he was hers. She'd dismissed nearly all of Paisley's servants immediately after his death. They'd been loyal to him, not to her. The only one she'd kept on was Philfer, the butler. It wasn't that she was particularly fond of him, because she wasn't. It was simply that he was too old for another position and he had no family.

Invariably when Arielle rode, it was in the opposite direction of her old home, Leslie Farm. Was Etienne staying with Evan? If so, why? She shivered, remembering Etienne just after his father's death. The funeral was over, the will read, and Arielle had faced him in the winter-dark drawing room. Whenever she saw him, she saw herself: on her knees before him, her fisted hands on his thighs, taking him into her mouth. . . .

"You will leave in the morning, Etienne," she'd said.

He'd looked at her and slowly said, "I want you to pleasure me again, Arielle."

She'd stared at him.

"I never got to have you, as my father promised me. Tonight, nay, right now, come with me upstairs."

He couldn't harm her, he couldn't force her. Paisley was dead. No one could force her now. "I wouldn't go to the grave with you."

Etienne looked genuinely bewildered. "But why? I am not my father. You have already pleasured me, and I have seen you. Now I want you beneath me, I want to be inside you. You will enjoy it. My father told me you loved to be fondled and caressed. I want you, Arielle. I want you with me, always. I want to wed you once a decent period of time has passed."

Arielle walked to the bellpull and gave it a yank.

"What are you doing?"

She simply shook her head at him. When Philfer arrived not three minutes later, she said, "Please have Monsieur DuPons' luggage packed, Philfer. Then see to it that he is out of Rendel Hall and off my property within the hour."

"Very well, my lady."

Etienne waited at least until Philfer had left the room, then shouted, *"Non!* You can't do that! This is my home—my father wanted me here. I *want* you, Arielle."

It was too much. Had he really believed she'd been enamored of him that awful night Paisley had forced her to . . . ? She shook her head. "Listen to me, Etienne. I do not like you, and I do not want to have anything more to do with you. Your father made me do those things. I didn't want to. Do you understand me? I never wish to see you again."

"You are thinking of the proprieties. You English are so very concerned about such nonsense and—"

She wanted to kill him. Instead, she said in a voice of surprising calm, "You will leave. Now."

He turned, and his pale eyes glittered at her. She took a step back, unable to stop herself.

"I will have you, Arielle. My father told me I would have you. He promised me."

"Your father is dead! Dead and buried!"

Etienne gave her one last, long look, bowed, and left.

That was another reason, she supposed now, that she was afraid to go into society, even the narrow society of Castlefields and beyond to East Grinstead. Etienne had believed she'd enjoyed doing that despicable act to him. He'd expected her to want to continue with him. Was it something about her, something in the way she looked, or spoke, or held her head? Could he have told others? She heard a small broken sound and realized it was a moan from herself. She had to snap out of this. It had been many months, and she was free, truly free.

"Where are ye going, my lady?"

Arielle forced herself back. "Nowhere in particular, Geordie. Have you a suggestion?"

He gave her a very straight look. "Aye. I should like to beard a mangy lion in his den."

She became quite still. "Any particular mangy lion?"

"Aye, one that's in truth a damned bounder, if ye'll excuse me language."

"The thin mangy lion," she said.

Arielle had never said a word about her half brother to Geordie. Where had he heard about him? She thought about it. She had been a coward, a pitiful coward, for more than seven months now. Laying the shame on herself, feeling the guilty one.

Perhaps, just perhaps, she could exorcise one ghost. "All right," she said, turning Mindle as she spoke. "Let us see the lay of the land. Let us see if Monsieur DuPons is residing with Evan Goddis."

Geordie rubbed his hands together. "Aye, the little weasel." Arielle laughed, an honest, pure sound, but deep down she felt fear turning like sour milk in her stomach.

They rode onto Leslie Farm land a little less than an hour later. Arielle looked about, waiting for homesickness to strike, but there wasn't any. The manor house soon came into view. The place looked rundown, not as if there weren't enough money, but as if the person living here simply didn't care about the appearance of the manor house.

"Miss Arielle!"

"Hello, Jud. How are you? Is Mr. Goddis at home today?"

"Yes, he is, ma'am. I'm fine, as is my missus. You want to see the master?"

"Why not?" Arielle allowed Jud to help her dismount. She turned to Geordie. "I can't very well permit you to come with me, but I would ask that you remain near those windows over there. I shall ensure that I am in that room. You are feeling like Saint George, Geordie?"

"Aye, indeed, my lady."

Geordie watched her walk to the double front doors, her thin shoulders squared, her chin high. Poor little mite, he thought, but she needed to come here and face down that devil half brother of hers. She'd been too long locked into herself. She had to come back to life and deal not only with her own fears but also with the Rendel estate, which was now her responsibility. Then perhaps she could return to a more normal way of life. He remembered six months before, when he'd met a fellow who'd just been fired from Rendel Hall by Lady Rendel.

The man had been full of spite, insults, and information. The next day Geordie had presented himself to Lady Rendel, and she'd hired him
immediately. Don't lose your head, lass, he told her
silently. At least she was showing some backbone.
He watched her disappear through the front doors.
Quickly, he moved to the east side of the house and
saw that the windows were open.

Evan accepted the news from his portly butler,
Turp, that his sister was waiting for him in the
small front drawing room. He frowned. How odd
that after all these months she would come to see
him. He'd been wondering how to get to her, for the
several times he'd visited Rendel Hall he'd been
denied entrance. Let her wait a bit now, he thought
as he reviewed what he had to say to her. He would
keep Etienne out of it for a while. He was beginning to doubt Etienne's real uses in any case, the
devil curse the man.

He walked slowly into the drawing room. "My
dear Arielle. How lovely you look. Not at all a
mourning widow."

Arielle felt herself pale, felt her palms become
clammy. "Hello, Evan," she said, relieved at the
calmness and lightness of her tone. "How well you
are looking. Of course, there is no reason for you
not to appear well-looking, is there?"

He bowed. He was wearing morning clothes, and
his smart superfine jacket hid the thinness of his
chest and shoulders. But his legs in the buckskins
looked like two straws.

"What an honor to see you after so long," he said.

"Yes, I suppose it is." Her gaze went slowly about
the room. "My father loved this room. We played
chess in the evenings by the fireplace."

"Your little charmed circle. Well, it no longer
matters, does it? I have been wanting to see you for

the longest time, Arielle. I have been very concerned about you."

"I believe I shall sit down," she said and seated herself on an Egyptian claw-footed chair and arranged her riding skirt. She sent a surreptitious look out the window, and sure enough, there was Geordie, standing still as a statue in the shade of a yew bush.

"As I said, I have been worried about you," Evan said, his voice even and cool. The little chit seemed different. She was trying to control him, that was it. "You don't seem to believe me, Arielle. You are my sister—"

"Half sister, Evan."

"You have only me, Arielle. Who knows where Nesta is at the moment or when we shall see her and the baron again?"

Arielle looked at him closely. Exorcise the ghost. "Paisley told me what you did, Evan. There is no reason for you to act the loving brother at this late date. I know that you sold me. Paisley said he paid fifteen thousand pounds for me, then five thousand pounds that time when I came here begging you to protect me. He said you were holding me for ransom."

Evan paled, and his hands fisted. "That is a bloody lie! God, you would believe that dissolute old bastard? It's not true, Arielle, I swear it to you."

She regarded him calmly. "It isn't. Perhaps it is perverse of me, but I think it is true. All of it."

"Listen to me, Arielle. I had to let him take you that morning. I had no choice! He is—was—your husband; all the legal rights were on his side. He threatened me. He said he would ruin me."

She didn't believe him. She wouldn't believe him. Slowly, Arielle rose from her chair. "I am vastly sorry that I share your blood," she said and walked toward the door.

"Arielle! Wait! Listen, he swore to me that morning that he wouldn't strike you again. He swore! I made him. I told him what I thought of him and he swore he wouldn't hurt you again."

She said nothing, merely kept walking.

"Stop—you can't leave." She felt his long, thin fingers wrap about her upper arm. She had a moment of horrible, paralyzing fear, then forced herself to be calm until he released her. She would not be afraid. Not any longer. Even as she thought it, she knew it wasn't true. She wondered if she would be afraid for the rest of her life.

"Listen to me, Arielle. It wasn't a question of ransom, dammit! If you would know the truth, Paisley had information, damning information, about my father. He threatened to make it known if I didn't give you to him in marriage. It's the truth. I'm not proud of it, but I love my father and I couldn't allow Paisley to ruin his name. He had sworn to me that he would turn over the information at your marriage, but he lied. He used it again when you came to me. I had no choice!"

"Let me go, Evan."

He did. She said very quietly, "Your father is dead. He was dead then. I wasn't. You cared more for a dead man's name than your own sister's life. You are despicable, Evan. I suppose I came here to say that to you."

Her voice was low, contemptuous, and he retreated. "Arielle, please, you must try to understand."

"I came here to exorcise a bogeyman. I have done that. You are really a quite paltry person, Evan."

"My father isn't dead! He would have met the hangman had I not saved him."

"You're a liar. A long time ago I can remember the servants speaking in hushed whispers about John Goddis and his scandalous life and his sordid ending. But no matter. If you care for me all that much, why is Etienne here?" She waited, but he was silent. "I see you have no answer for that. Good-bye, Evan. I never wish to see you again."

Her hand was on the doorknob, her fingers tightening about the latch, when he said, almost in a whisper. "Etienne DuPons is in love with you. He came to me begging that I intercede for him with you. He hated his father. He never even knew him, you know that, Arielle. He is not like Paisley Cochrane."

She felt a slight stirring of uncertainty, but then she shook her head. She could never forget that terrible night when Paisley had forced her to pleasure his son. She could still hear Etienne's moans, feel his fingers tangling in her hair as he pressed her head against him. She realized she was trembling. "No," she said and jerked the door open. "No, damn you!"

"You have become a cold woman, Arielle," Evan said. "Poor Etienne, he hasn't anything now."

She could only stare at him. "He doesn't deserve anything. Good-bye, Evan."

He said nothing more. He watched her stride across the long, narrow entrance hall, saw her speak quietly to pathetic old Turp, that witless fool, before she left.

Evan wasn't completely cast down. He'd sensed that brief uncertainty in Arielle, and now he would determine how best to make it grow. He whistled as he strode up the stairs, bound for Etienne's bechamber.

"Well, lassie?"

"Paltry," Arielle said with relish. "My half brother is really very paltry."

But, like Evan Goddis, Geordie heard the lack of

complete conviction in his young mistress's voice. He frowned at her profile but said nothing.

"You know what I should like to do, Geordie?"

"Not a clue, lassie."

"I think I shall go to Bunberry Lake. Alone. There is never anyone there, truly. I believe I have some thinking to do."

"Ye mean that little slice of water between Drummond and Leslie land?"

"Aye, you dour old man, that is the one. You make it sound like a tiny, scummy pond."

He said nothing more. She was mocking him and smiling. Not a tremendous smile, but a smile nonetheless. Perhaps she was beginning to heal now that she'd seen that Evan Goddis was naught but a man, and not a very nice one at that. He took his leave of her, watching until she was out of sight.

Arielle slowly guided Mindle to the edge of the gentle blue-green water. When Mindle raised her head and whinnied, Arielle automatically stiffened.

Then she saw a man. She couldn't make out who he was. But she recognized his stallion. It was Ashes.

Burke Drummond was home.

# 3

Arielle was flooded with feelings she'd believed had never really existed; feelings that, if they had existed, had belonged to that other girl, the one with the soft, gentle memories.

That stupid, gullible, naive other girl.

From the distance that separated them she thought he still looked the same. He was standing beneath an oak tree, tall and lean and powerful. Very handsome he was, a hero, a man who'd been very kind to a young girl those three long years ago. That spring afternoon they'd met for the first time, here at Bunberry Lake, flowed through her mind, and she felt a strange sort of inevitability.

She realized belatedly that he was home because the war was over. She'd been so isolated, not only on the estate but in her own mind, that she'd paid little attention to the happenings in France. Napoleon, she'd heard from someone, had been incarcerated on an island somewhere.

Burke was waving to her. "Come here," he called.

His deep, rich voice crystallized the memories. Odd that she should remember that voice so clearly. She touched her fingers to her cheek and smiled at another memory. She was remembering the crimson plume of her riding hat she'd worn that long-ago afternoon. She wondered briefly what had become of it.

Arielle waved back, then directed Mindle slowly and carefully through the shallow end of the lake.

Burke had known, had been certain, she would come. He'd wondered, mocking himself, if this newfound sensitivity of his would prove accurate. This first time he hadn't wanted to go to Rendel Hall to see her. He hadn't wanted to see her in another man's house. He hadn't wanted to call her my lady and acknowledge that she'd belonged to Paisley Cochrane.

Ashes whinnied again and pulled on his reins, nearly jerking them free of the yew bush branch. Burke felt his pulse slowly begin to increase.

He watched her guide her mare through the shallow end of the lake, some twenty-five yards distant; watched her as she neared. It was fitting, he thought, that he should see her here for the first time in such a long time. So many years. If only he hadn't been so bloody noble before. It could have been he who had been her husband. He could have taken her at sixteen. He shouldn't have waited.

She was drawing closer. She looked the same on horseback, her back straight as a rod, her riding skirt flowing about her, an ostrich plume brushing her cheek. It wasn't red, but a pale gray. Odd that he would remember that. He'd wondered, many times, what he would feel at this moment. Would he look at her and laugh at the romantic fantasies of a young man, fantasies that had staled in the intervening years? Would he still want to drag her to him and make love to her until they were both insensiate?

When he saw her, full in the face, he didn't want to do either. She was pale, and her pure blue eyes were wide, the pupils dilated. He wanted to hold her, to press her face against his shoulder, to stroke her rich hair, to pour out all the dammed-up words that were stored inside him.

"Burke."

Her voice was soft, thin-sounding. Burke realized he was holding his breath and released it. He grinned up at her. He felt wonderful. All the questions, the doubts, had disappeared. She was Arielle and she was his. Her marriage to Paisley Cochrane meant nothing. She would belong to him. Forever.

He realized, had realized long before this meeting, that he couldn't rush his fences. She had no idea of the depth of his feelings. Lord knew, he hadn't either, until just this moment. He must go easy.

"Hello, Arielle. Come down and join me." As he spoke, he raised his hands to draw her out of her saddle. To his surprise, she pulled back. She kicked her booted foot free, slid out of the saddle, and tethered Mindle next to Ashes.

"I remember the first time I met you, you wouldn't allow me to assist you, but that was because my arm was in a sling. And this time, Arielle?"

"I am not helpless," she said. She wondered where those words had come from. She wondered why she was here.

"You still have Titian hair."

"What? Oh, that." Her fingertips nervously touched her hair. "Something I don't suppose anyone could change."

"You are taller."

"Yes. I was a bit later than most girls, but I did grow up."

He heard something odd in her voice. "Yes, delightfully so," he said and gave her a warm smile. She didn't smile back, merely stared up at him, as if he were some sort of ghost.

Arielle wished now that she hadn't come to Bun-

berry Lake today. Strange, how many different
things he made her feel. He'd changed; she saw
that. Oh, he was still charming and kind to her,
but his face was more severe, hardened perhaps, as
if he'd seen more than a man should have to see.
He still had the marvelous dimples that deepened
when he smiled, and the thick brows that flared
slightly, giving him a slightly rakish and inquisi-
tive look.

"You're home finally," she managed to say. "It's
been a very long time. How long have you been
here?"

Burke couldn't take his eyes off her. She was no
longer the fifteen-year-old girl, such an open book
to him, so completely guileless. This Arielle was
nervous and uncertain, perhaps even wary of him.
She was also a mystery to him, and she fascinated
him. Her body was much the same, he saw. Too
slender, he was thinking, but he could see the curve
of her high breasts, the narrowness of her waist.
No longer the coltish angles of a young girl, but a
woman's slenderness. But it was her face that drew
him now, as it had three years before. The purity
of her features, the innocence of— He broke off his
thinking, realizing that she'd asked him a question
and that instead of replying, he was staring at her
like a besotted ass. As he had three years before.

"At Ravensworth Abbey? Only two days. Come
and sit down, Arielle."

She plucked at her riding skirt, her nervousness,
her skittishness, palpable. "I—I don't know, my
lord—"

"That girl called me Burke. Don't you remember? Won't the woman do the same?"

Of course she remembered! And what did he
mean talking of the girl and now the woman? She
wanted to leave, quickly. "Very well, Burke. I think
I should return to Rendel Hall."

"Nonsense. You are mistress there. If you are late, will the butler order you to your room without your dinner?"

That made her smile. "Probably not, though he would try to dash me down with one of his looks." *And Philfer would look so sly, so knowing.*

He watched her gracefully ease down onto the grass and spread her blue riding skirt about her. She carefully folded her gloved hands in her lap. He ached just looking at her.

"I trust you aren't wounded this time?"

He sat beside her and was surprised when she pulled away to place more distance between them. "Yes, but nothing much, really. A saber thrust in my side."

She grimaced. "I'm sorry. Have you much pain this time?"

"Not now."

"Will you remain in England?"

"Yes, since Napoleon is out of the way. It is time I did earllike things and earned my title and my keep."

"Surely there is more than enough to occupy you."

*I don't wish to speak of this nonsense,* he thought. He felt frustrated. He wanted to tell her he wanted her to marry him. Now, today.

So, instead, he said, "Do you remember what you told me three years ago, Arielle?"

She cocked her head to one side and stared at him as she sorted through her memories. It was there, of course, there with the feelings she'd felt then, the feelings she'd had after he'd left. She'd told him that she would be waiting for him with all the other ladies. Oh, no, she thought. She began shaking her head. "Why?" she asked.

He chuckled, trying to mask his tension. "You have become a fickle woman, I see."

She had to change the course of this—she had to.
"Is your wife at Ravensworth? What is her name?
Have you children?"

That startled him, and he arched a dark brow.
"Why would you think me married?"

*Because you have to be!* "I just assumed that you
would be. You are the earl and have need of an
heir. You are older now, fully grown, and I—" She
ground to a halt, so embarrassed that she could only
stare at the loose blades of grass that would certainly stain her skirt.

"I was fully grown that first afternoon three years
ago, Arielle. As I recall, you told me so yourself."

"I was a child, a foolish, trusting child. I didn't
know anything."

Her bitterness was a live thing. What the hell
had happened? Was this because of Paisley Cochrane? He said calmly, "I am back now to do as I
ought. You are right. As the Earl of Ravensworth,
I have need of an heir. For that I shall need a wife."
He smiled at her and despite his best intentions,
all the tenderness he felt for her was in his eyes.
"Have you any thoughts on the subject? Any rec-
ommendations, perhaps?"

No, she thought wildly, he couldn't mean what she
thought he did. Oh, no. He couldn't want her, at
least not as a wife. She was used and dirty and . . .
It would mean bedding him, doing all those disgusting things, being beaten again and crying with
the pain, the helplessness. She realized that she was
shaking her head. She jumped to her feet. "No, I
have no thoughts. Well, actually, yes, there are
many lovely ladies who live hereabouts. I am certain you will see them all very soon. I must go now.
Really, I must."

Burke stared up at her. He saw fear in her eyes,
and distaste. He tried to retrench quickly, saying
mildly, emotionlessly, "Don't go yet, Arielle."

"I shouldn't be here, alone with you."

"That didn't concern you when you were fifteen. It doesn't concern me now. Come, stay, and let's get acquainted again. I was sorry to hear of the death of Sir Arthur. I wrote you."

Arielle watched him uncertainly. He seemed controlled enough, calm enough. Perhaps she'd misunderstood him. She had nothing but lovely memories of him. He'd always acted the perfect gentleman, but still, he was a man and thus unpredictable, not to be trusted.

"Yes, I received your letter. Thank you. Of course I couldn't reply."

"I knew that, yes. You were very young."

*Young and foolish and stupid.* "How is Lannie? And Poppet and Virgie?"

At least she's not bolting, he thought. He said easily, "Lannie is just the same, perhaps even more so. I shall probably become her nemesis again now that I am home. My steward, Cerlew, is the current recipient of all her melodramatic wrath. Lannie is very adaptable, as you probably remember. She said she missed you. As for my nieces, they're really quite cute."

"Excellent," said Arielle.

And that was that? he thought. Burke looked out over the placid lake. "I remember thinking that you and I were friends. That is no longer true?"

*Friends.* To be friends with a man was an alien thought. It required trust, a commodity that was elusive, indeed a commodity that was most unlikely in her experience.

"No," she said honestly, "I don't believe it is."

That drew him up short. "Whyever not? I haven't grown two heads, and I am still accounted an honorable man." He'd meant his words to sound light, humorous, but her expression remained grave, withdrawn.

He wasn't aware, would never have guessed, that she was seeing him in that moment as a very real threat to her. She was seeing a large man, powerfully built, so much stronger than she that he could easily break her, easily intimidate her, easily beat her with little effort on his part. As for his good looks, that made her distrust him all the more. A man who had been a young girl's dream hero for months was likely nothing more than a chimera, a foolish fantasy woven from unreal cloth. Then her father had died and Evan had taken control of her life. She'd blocked out the Earl of Ravensworth just as she'd blocked out every other man who'd come into her ken. A gentle breeze lifted his dark brown hair, ruffling it, and he sent impatient fingers through it. His eyes were a dark brown, his eyelashes thick and lush, the envy of a woman. His face was strong, and even without speaking, he held the aura of one born to command, one who was used to being obeyed, one who would not tolerate not being obeyed.

She felt fear, cold and harsh. He was a man. He wasn't to be trusted. No, she wouldn't believe his offer of friendship. She was no longer gullible and stupid.

"Arielle?"

"What?"

"What's wrong? Have I said something to distress you?"

A handsome and charming man, a strong man, could dissemble, could draw one in before springing for the kill. He was holding out his hand to her, a strong brown hand that could hurt so easily, could slap her, could mark her. She ran her tongue over her dry lips. She found herself looking at him, and her fear grew. Unlike Evan, the Earl of Ravensworth in riding clothes was an impressive sight, from his close-fitting jacket of pale blue to his sparkling black Hessians. Then, quite suddenly, she saw him naked. She saw him standing just as Etienne had stood, his back to the fireplace, the flames framing him, casting him in shadowy lights.

She sucked in her breath and leaped to her feet.

"Why won't you tell me what is wrong?" His voice was soft and reasonable-sounding, the voice of an adult soothing a frightened child.

"I must go! Good-bye!"

She rushed away from him and climbed onto Mindle's back. She realized she hadn't untied Mindle's reins and sat there a moment, feeling stupid and afraid.

She saw him rise slowly, brush the soft earth from his thighs. He was coming to her, and she was so afraid that she felt frozen in place.

Burke didn't understand. He felt hurt and angry and confused. Slowly, he untied Mindle's reins. He saw Arielle staring at his hand as he lifted the reins to her.

Her eyes bothered him; her pupils were large and fixed. What the devil was wrong?

"I wish to visit you," he said, his voice formal. "Will you be at home tomorrow?"

"Why?"

He smiled, showing straight white teeth. "To renew our friendship. For whatever reason, I think I've set myself an awesome task. Perhaps you will tell me."

What to say? What to do? "All right," she said, and he felt fury at the ungraciousness in her voice. He wasn't a damned troll, for God's sake. He wasn't ill-looking or old. He had all his teeth; he wasn't fat and didn't intend to become so. He was titled now and he was rich. What the hell was wrong with her? Aloud he said mildly, "I will see you in the early afternoon, then. After luncheon. Good-bye, Arielle."

She looked at him, uncertainty in her eyes. He couldn't do anything to hurt her, not at Rendel Hall. She would make sure that Dorcas was there. She nodded and click-clicked Mindle forward.

Burke didn't move, merely stared after her. He watched her gallop her mare through the shallow end of the lake, sending spumes of spray flying upward, soaking her riding habit.

Their first meeting hadn't gone at all as he'd envisioned.

Indeed, it had been a fiasco.

She wasn't the Arielle he remembered.

This Arielle he didn't understand. He wanted this Arielle even more. He shook his head at himself. Why had God, in His infinite wisdom, created this particular woman and destined him for her?

He patted Ashes' nose. "Well, old fellow, I've got my work cut out for me, hmm?"

Ashes obligingly whinnied.

"What the devil is wrong with her?"

Ashes whinnied again.

"Why did she treat me like I was carrying the plague?"

Ashes was silent this time.

Arielle was cold, so cold her teeth were chattering. She was naked, tied down to the bed, her legs and arms spread wide, her wrists and ankles tied with satin strips to the bedposts. He was there, of course. She saw him standing by the fireplace, his pose relaxed, a riding crop in one hand. He was slapping it lightly and rhythmically against his open palm. He was fully clothed.

She didn't plead; it would do no good. She stared at the riding crop, knowing it would strike her soon, nearly feeling the stinging pain each stroke would bring. But he'd tied her down on her back. Usually she was facedown on her knees on the floor. She swallowed painfully, unable to still her shivering.

The, suddenly, there were others. At least six men were now in the room and they were drinking brandy. She didn't know how she knew it was brandy, she just knew. They were laughing, talking loudly, but she couldn't make out their words. One man looked toward her and made some obscene gestures with his hands. She watched, dumb with terror, as the men came over to the bed, circled it, and stared down at her. They all had riding crops. The man closest to her head leaned down suddenly, grasped her jaw between his thick fingers to hold her still, and kissed her hard.

She tried to pull away, tried to scream for him to leave her alone. She felt all their hands now, touching her, slapping her. She opened her mouth but there was no sound.

Just as suddenly, all the men were gone, all except him—Paisley. He was yelling insults at her, his voice contemptuous, telling her that she was so sexless she couldn't interest any man. He'd even gotten them drunk, he yelled at her, but still they didn't want her. She was a worthless trollop, of no value at all, even as a diversion.

She wanted to scream at him that she was glad she was worthless, glad that no man wanted her, but still she couldn't seem to make any sound. She felt tears sliding down her cheeks, tasted the salt in her mouth. Now he was grinning at her. He tossed the riding crop to the floor and opened his breeches. She stared at him. His member was hard and ready.

Now, he told her, now he would take her. At last. He climbed over her, sitting back on his heels. He leaned down, his hands rough on her body, and suddenly she screamed, loud, piercing screams.

It wasn't Paisley coming into her body.

It was Burke Drummond.

Arielle sat up in bed, fully awake. Unconsciously, she was rubbing her wrists and her ankles, as if soothing them from the straps. It was a dream, she said over and over to herself. But why had Paisley become Burke Drummond?

She'd felt a threat from him, that was why. The poor man had probably not meant a thing, yet her fear of men had made him evil and rough and harsh, like Paisley Cochrane.

She huddled down under the mound of covers, trying to get warm. The room wasn't cold, but she was, and the cold was from deep inside her. She wondered blankly if she would ever be warm again.

"Her ladyship is not receiving today, my lord."

Burke looked at the old man's sly features and knew he could probably bribe any information he desired from the fellow. Why didn't Arielle boot him out, for heaven's sake?

"Tell her the Earl of Ravensworth is here to see her."

"She knew of your visit, my lord. She told me to give you her apologies." Philfur studiously flicked a piece of lint from his black sleeve. "It is possible that her ladyship isn't as ill-disposed as she seems."

Miserable old bastard! Burke hadn't been privy to such a blatant bribery attempt in a very long time. "I trust she is not," he said finally, his voice bland. "Tell her that I shall return on the morrow. My best to her."

"Certainly, my lord."

Burke stood there a moment longer, undecided. He didn't want to leave. He didn't want to give in to this nonsense. He knew she wasn't ill. He knew, deep down, that she simply didn't want to see him. The question was, why? Did he repulse her? For some reason was she afraid of him? Was she still grieving for that miserable excuse for a husband?

He walked thoughtfully toward the Rendel stables, where he'd left Ashes and Joshua. Joshua had asked if he could accompany him and he'd agreed, not really paying much heed to his batman. No, he corrected himself silently, no longer a batman. Joshua was now his valet. When he reached the slate-roofed stables, he saw Joshua in conversation with an older man whose wiry, lean body didn't fool Burke for a minute. The man was as strong as he was, perhaps stronger.

"My lord," Joshua said. "I'd like you to meet Geordie. He's Lady Rendel's groom and the head stable lad."

Now this was odd, Burke was thinking, but he nodded politely and said, "Geordie."

"Me lord," said Geordie, and Burke was aware of being studied and assessed and weighed. He felt at once amused and annoyed.

"We will return tomorrow, Joshua," he said finally, ignoring Geordie.

"Aye," said Geordie. "Tomorrow, me lord. Joshua."

"What the devil was that all about?" Burke asked as they rode down the narrow drive away from Rendel Hall.

Joshua leaned forward and scratched his horse's ear. "Well, Major Lord, I came because I wanted to know what happened to that sweet, mouthy little girl I'd met three years ago. And Geordie, he wanted to know all about you and what you intended toward Lady Rendel."

Burke turned in the saddle, his hand fisting on the reins. "Joshua, have you any idea how very—" Burke stalled. He chewed on his lower lip, searching for words to convey his indignation without insulting his longtime batman and friend.

"Yes, Major Lord. Forward, that I'd call it my-self."

"But you don't like women!"

" 'Tis true enough, but this little one . . . well, I never thought of her as exactly a female, if you know what I mean."

"No, I haven't the foggiest notion of what you mean. Arielle—that is, Lady Rendel—not a fe-male?"

"As I said before, Major Lord, a mouthy little thing she was, but not a mean splinter in her body. And open for all to see."

"As in honest, I presume?"

"Yes. Flat out leveled me, me disliking the fairer sex the way I do. Now Geordie, he'd kill for the lass—that's what he calls her. Told me, he did, that she dished out all the servants right after her husband died. They'd been loyal to him, you see. He heard one of them carrying on about her and what a slut she was, and, well, he said it made him furious as spit. Lady Rendel hired him on and he protects her, you might say."

"You learned all this in the few minutes I was being told by a thoroughly reprehensible butler that I wouldn't be admitted?"

"Yes. Now, Philfer, that's the butler, Geordie said Lady Rendel didn't get rid of him, miserable old fool that he is, because she'd too kind."

"Fine. She should pension him off. He's obnox-ious, dishonest, and hasn't an honorable or loyal thought in his damned brain."

Joshua merely nodded, falling into silence, his report completed. Burke chewed over what he'd been told. Why did she need Geordie to protect her?

Arielle let the lace curtain gently fall back into place. He was gone. He hadn't made a scene. She turned stiffly away from the window, willing the images from the nightmare to leave her. When Philfer told her an hour later that Lord Ravensworth would return on the morrow, she said nothing, merely nodded.

It was that evening that her half brother paid her a visit. Philfer admitted him. Evan was standing in her drawing room before she'd even known he'd come.

She rose slowly, wondering wildly where Dorcas was. She was alone and she was afraid, again.

# 4

"Good evening, Arielle. I hope I have not disaccommodated you overly."

Arielle stared at her brother. "I wasn't expecting to see you again, Evan," she said finally, her voice chill. "How did you manage to get admitted to my house?"

"You are not very gracious, sweet sister. I merely came to see how you were. Your butler—I can't remember the old fellow's name—well, he wasn't at his post and the door was open. I trust you don't mind that I came in?"

She cocked a brow at him, knowing deep down that he was lying. Philfer not available to answer the front door? Impossible; at least she would have thought so. Had Philfer let him in? For a bribe? It was an unwelcome thought.

"I suppose you wish some tea or something?"

"I should appreciate a brandy, if that is all right."

Brandy, she thought, remembering so vividly the nightmare of the previous night.

She nodded and walked to the sideboard. She poured him a drink and handed it to him. She suddenly remembered that night so long ago when she'd escaped to him for protection and his fingertips had traced the new welts on her back. What had he been thinking while he'd been doing it? How much money he would charge Paisley for her return?

"You will not join me?"

She shook her head. "What do you want, Evan? Quickly. I want you out of my house."

He sipped the brandy, looking at her closely. "I already told you. Why would I lie?"

You are a man, she wanted to shout at him. It is natural to you, everything that is awful and deceitful is natural to you, but she said only, "If you wish to hold to that tale, who am I to quibble?"

"So gracious," he murmured.

"I believe I told you I never wished to see you again. I didn't lie, Evan. I want you out of my life."

"And I want you to know how very sorry I am. I really had no idea that Paisley Cochrane was such a—"

"Enough," she shouted.

"Very well. My father isn't dead, Arielle, and I can prove it to you. I can prove that I wasn't lying. I ask you, wouldn't you have protected your father at all costs, even sacrificing me?"

"In an instant," she said, "were it you."

He ignored her words and continued slowly. "He is in Paris, very ill. I must go to him. Here is my letter from him. Read it. Read it and know that I didn't lie to you. I wouldn't have hurt you knowingly, Arielle, I swear it."

Without meaning to, Arielle took the single sheet of paper and unfolded it. The handwriting was spidery, the ink blue-black, the number of words minimal. The letter stated simply what Evan had just told her and was signed "Your loving father."

She handed the letter back to him. "So he is alive. What do you want me to do about it?" She paused, her eyes glittering. "Ah, I see now. How stupid of me. If your father is alive, then my mother was never married to Arthur Leslie and I am thus a bastard. That is it, isn't it, Evan?"

He looked pained. "Surely you can't imagine that I would announce this to the neighborhood. I am not such a blackguard as that."

Ha, she thought. "Then what do you want?"

"I need money," he said baldly.

"For money you will keep silent about my lack of proper parentage?"

"No, that isn't at all what I meant!"

"You are really quite an amazingly paltry person, you know. However have you managed to spend the twenty thousand pounds you got for me in a mere three years?"

He ground his teeth. But then again, what had he expected? She was giving him a look of contempt, and it angered him so much that he wanted to strike her.

"Yes, indeed," she continued when he remained silent. "A pity. I doubt your sire is worth it."

"And your sire, Arielle? Your sire's good name?"

"It is called blackmail, Evan." She smiled at him and said very slowly, "If you wish it to be know that your half sister is a bastard, so be it. Believe this, Evan: I really don't care."

"What the hell is the matter with you?" Damnation, he had thought his silence would be worth something to her, but it obviously wasn't.

"Why, nothing at all. You and your threats are quite ridiculous. Go away, Evan."

"Very well, I will take my leave now. Thank you for allowing me time with you, Arielle."

"I wouldn't have if Philfer had been at his post."

"No, I don't suppose you would have. Well, what could I have expected? To be forgiven for mistakes that I couldn't help?" He sighed deeply, and again Arielle felt a spurt of uncertainty. She shook her head at herself. No, it still came down to twenty thousand pounds. He couldn't lie about that. Paisley had kept records.

"Good-bye, Evan." She turned on her heel and strode from her own drawing room. She didn't look around to see if he followed her. From the corner of her eye she saw Philfer emerging from the kitchen. There was an odd furtive look in the old man's expression, but she paid him no heed as he began to make excuses, and just continued on her way to the small, informal dining room.

To her surprise, Dorcas was sitting there, looking tense.

"Is he gone?"

"I assume so. I am surprised you didn't come in astride your brave charger, lance in hand, to rescue me."

"What did he want?"

"To blackmail me. You see, he's claiming his father is alive, which, if he is, means that I'm a bastard. He wants money to keep quiet about it. I told him I didn't care."

"John Goddis alive? That is absurd! I was with your mother when his body was brought to her, his chest torn open with a bullet wound. He was dead, the filthy bounder. Quite dead."

Arielle frowned down at a chip on her plate. "Why would Evan try such a thing, then? Didn't he know you were there?"

Dorcas shrugged. "I suppose he didn't. Why would he know? He wasn't there, the lying sod."

It was all very interesting, Arielle thought as she took a bite of her braised ham.

Dinner in the stately dining room at Ravensworth Abbey was a different affair. Midway through the boiled leg of lamb, garnished with young carrots and the greenest parsley Burke had ever seen,

Lannie announced that she was traveling up to London in precisely three days.

Burke thought about the silence that would replace the chattering complaints and was hard pressed not to applaud her decision. He managed not to shout for joy and to say politely, "I see. Will you stay at Ravensworth House?"

"No, with Corinne and Lloyd. She has invited me, you know. And the girls, of course."

He hadn't known and was frankly surprised. Even Lannie sounded a bit surprised. His elder sister made no qualms about her feelings. Lannie was a fool and that was that. Why the invitation?

"How long will you stay in London?"

Lannie forgot about her lamb and her boiled bacon cheek and sat forward, her face flushing with excitement. "There is so much happening now in London, Burke. All the foreign royalty and Czars and things! Corinne wrote me that there are balls every night, even though the Season is long over, and there is so much gaiety."

"Yes, when I was there, there was more than I could stomach."

"Ach, you are a man! So tedious. I shall visit my modiste—Madame Giselle is her name. Now, don't screw up your mouth like that, Burke. You won't have to worry that I will be spending *your* money. I have my widow's jointure, you know, and I have been most careful since Montrose died, aware, of course, that my very existence is dependent on your continued good will and . . ."

Burke looked at the gooseberry tart on his plate and pretended rapt attention to Lannie's monologue. He would have Ravensworth Abbey all to himself. He would ask Arielle to visit him. He could see if she admired his home, he could—He broke off those inviting thoughts. What if she refused to see him again?

". . . Corinne wrote me about a gentleman, if you must know the truth of the matter, and I can see that your male curiosity is at its peak. Well, his name, if you insist upon knowing, is Percy Kingstone, and he is, unfortunately, only a baronet, Lord Carver, I believe. However, according to Corinne, he is a catch and quite a charming man, and I shall . . ."

The gooseberry tart continued under study on its plate. No, Arielle couldn't do that. He wouldn't allow it. He loved her and he was going to wed her. His very stubborn jaw set and his eyes narrowed.

". . . and of course I shall take Virgie and Poppet, even though you know as well as I that they get in a fret when closed up in a carriage. It will simply . . ."

I shall treat this just like a military position, he decided, picking up his wineglass. He swirled the ruby-red liquid about, and he saw her hair. That glorious, rich Titian . . . He cursed softly. He would do whatever was necessary.

". . . I *know* you will insist, dear Burke, so I shall have James informed that I will take the carriage. As for grooms and protection, perhaps I should have at least one outrider."

He raised his head and looked at his sister-in-law. He realized that she'd been speaking, nonstop in fact. Having no idea of the subject, he merely nodded, saying warmly, "Whatever you wish is yours, Lannie," and prayed devoutly that, like Salome, she hadn't asked for his head on a platter.

Later in his library, Burke's favorite room in this pile of a mansion, he sat in front of a blazing fire, his legs stretched out, a snifter of brandy cupped in his hands. Odd that it should be so chilly in June. Perhaps his blood had thinned out from all his years in Spain and Portugal. He found himself wondering what Knight was up to. He'd seen him only briefly

in Paris upon his return to England, and he'd been
damnably weak from the wound in his side. After
he wed Arielle, he would invite Knight to visit. Arielle would like him; all the ladies did. He frowned
at that. No, Knight was a man of honor; he would
never poach on another's preserve. Burke remembered suddenly those three blissful days in Portugal when he and Knight had been at loose ends and
looking for an adventure of the tender sort. They'd
found just what they'd sought. Her name was Ga-
briela and she was quite pretty and more than willing to be indulged by two English officers.
Fortunately, she was also possessed of a sister, San-
cha, who was equally toothsome. Suddenly Burke
felt himself growing randy as he thought about
those three exhausting days. He cursed softly at his
obvious reaction and rose.

He wanted Arielle. Damn her eyes.

Burke became cunning in his frustration. He had
no doubt that she would try to avoid him again.
The next day, he instructed Joshua to keep an eye
on the front entrance of Rendel Hall. As for himself, he kept the garden at the back of the Hall under observation, feeling like an utter ass but doing
it nonetheless. An hour later Joshua came to him,
ducking behind trees and bushes like a soldier behind enemy lines.

"Her ladyship is going to the stable, Major Lord."

"Please, Joshua, that sounds very odd now. Call
me anything, just delete the 'major.' "

"Aye," said Joshua, giving the earl a meditative
look. "What do you plan to do with the lass?"

"Lass?"

"That's what she is," said Joshua. "A girl who's
much to young to be what she is, leastwise that's
what Geordie told me."

"I plan to keep her company, that's all," said

Burke. "Did you think I was going to whisk her away to a faraway land and hold her my prisoner?" He laughed before Joshua could respond, then continued seriously. "Go back to the Abbey, Joshua. You've done well."

Joshua nodded, but he fully intended to visit with Geordie after Lady Rendel and his master had left. The earl was tip over arse in love, a phenomenon hitherto unseen by Joshua, leastwise as regarded the earl, and he wanted to find out more about the lass.

Arielle patted Mindle's soft nose. "A bit of exercise for you today, my girl. Thank you, Geordie. I won't need you today. I plan to remain well on Rendal land." No, she thought, staring at Mindle's worn leather saddle, no excursions for her today. No Bunberry Lake, no visit to Leslie Farm. A simple gallop over the north field, that was all she intended.

"If yer certain, lassie."

"I'm certain."

Geordie hefted Arielle into the saddle, then stepped back. He gave her a brief salute and smiled.

"I shall be back in an hour or so. Mr. Jewells will be coming." She clicked Mindle forward, and soon Arielle felt the wind pulling at the pins in her riding hat.

She didn't see him until he was nearly beside her, and then it was too late. For an instant, she thought it was Paisley, then Etienne, and she froze. She pulled Mindle to a halt and tried to find just a shred of composure.

"Hello," she said finally, not meeting his eyes.

"Arielle. I am glad you came out for a ride."

"What do you want?" she blurted out.

"To see you, of course. Just as I wished to see you

yesterday, but you refused me. I really should like to know why."

"I was not well."

He studied her pale face. He could tell her that what she didn't do well was lie. Her hair was a bit ratty from the wind and two thick strands hung down, nearly curling around her right breast. He started to reach out his hand and quickly drew it back. He was losing his mind, what remained of it. "What was wrong with you?"

Lying was a foolish solution because it was no solution at all. "I had the headache."

"Ah," he said. He was aware in that moment that she was trying to pull her mare away from him, and it angered him to the point of fury.

Arielle found herself staring at him. He was indeed handsome, perhaps more so than she remembered, for his features were more finely planed, more chiseled perhaps. He wore his thick brown hair longer now that he wasn't a military man. But his brown eyes were the same, rich and bright with intelligence and deep with expression. He was dressed in a royal blue riding jacket, his breeches the same shade, his Hessians a gleaming black. He looked utterly powerful and in control and ruthless. She was terrified of him, and all because of that foolish nightmare.

Burke realized they were simply staring at each other. Silence hung uncomfortably between them. He said abruptly, drawing on years of measured control, "I should like you to visit the Abbey on Friday for tea."

She almost began to shake her head, then stopped herself. Better to get it over with; then perhaps he would leave her alone. There was nothing at all dangerous for her in visiting Ravensworth Abbey. Lannie with all her chatter would act a perfect buffer. "All right," she said finally.

"That is what you told me before, your exact words, as I recall. Can I believe you this time?"

There was a sting to his words and she drew back. What did he want from her? Her chin went up and her voice was as cold as a January day in Yorkshire. "You may be certain that I shall send word if I contract another illness."

"I thought the headache only brought ladies down once a month."

Airelle jerked back in her saddle as if she had been struck. He was dangerous and he wasn't a gentleman. Without another word, she whipped Mindle away from Burke and lashed her into a gallop.

Burke was caught off guard. He cursed himself loudly for his stupidity and his abominable impertinence. "Arielle! Wait up!"

He saw her turn back at his shout just for an instant, and in that brief period of time, Mindle veered to the left and took a fence mid-stride. Burke felt his blood run cold. "Arielle! Watch out!"

It was too late.

Her scream caught in her throat. Mindle didn't make it over the top rung of the wooden fence. The mare struck her hind legs and twisted frantically in the air. Arielle saw the narrow ditch just on the other side of the fence and stretched Mindle out as far as she could. The mare gained the other side of the ditch, but her front legs crumbled and Arielle felt herself flying over her head. The world was a jumbled blur. She wasn't afraid—everything was happening too quickly.

She hit the rocky earth hard and that hurt her shoulder, a blinding hurt, but only for a moment, because her head hit a rock and she became unconscious.

Burke had never been so afraid in his life. He set Ashes forward, controlling him firmly, and felt the mighty stallion sail over the fence, clearing the opposite ditch by a good four feet. He drew him up and dismounted. Mindle was standing now, her head lowered, blowing hard.

But it was Arielle who held his attention. He realized he was praying as he knelt down beside her. His long fingers sought the pulse in her throat. It was strong and steady, thank God. Slowly, his movements as detached as he could make them, he felt each arm and leg. Nothing broken. But internal injuries. She could be bleeding inside and she could die, and there would be nothing he could do about it.

He shook himself. He removed her riding hat, then began to probe her head. There was a growing lump behind her left ear. He felt himself expel a sigh of relief. Pray heaven that the most she would suffer was a concussion. She would be all right—she had to be. Burke eased down beside her, leaning against the trunk of a maple tree, and gently lifted her head onto his thighs. He touched her nose, her chin, her high cheekbones. Her brows were a bit darker than her hair, he noticed, and absently he stroked a fingertip over them, smoothing them. He stared down at her, mesmerized. He said softly, "I want you, Arielle. Marry me."

She moaned.

He cushioned her head on his open palm and, without meaning to, his other hand lightly caressed her throat. He wanted desperately to touch her and he didn't deny himself. He lifted his hand and laid it on her breast. Her heartbeat was strong beneath his palm. He closed his eyes, his body so filled with the strange lust-tenderness she evoked in him that for many moments he couldn't think a cogent thought. He moved his hand from her breast to her upper arm. He was losing his mind. For God's sake, she was lying here unconscious and all he could think about was bedding her!

"Arielle, wake up. Come on, open your eyes."

He shook her shoulders.

She moaned again and opened her eyes. She stared up at him, at first not understanding.

"It's all right," he said. "You will be just fine. You took a tumble. Does your head hurt?"

Arielle realized she was lying on her back, her head nestled against his hand. It was his fault that Mindle had taken that fence. All was his fault. She said harshly, "Yes, I have the headache."

Burke grinned down at her and held her firmly when she tried to pull away from him. "Hush and be still. You'd best not move for a while."

She saw that movement of any sort was beyond her. A fierce pain slashed through her head and she swallowed convulsively, closing her eyes.

"Shush," he said softly. "Do you need to be sick?"

The thought of retching in front of him was unnerving. She said nothing, merely kept her lips tightly closed and prayed.

"Take deep breaths and don't move." He began to stroke his fingertips over her forehead. It wasn't near the lump, but it did seem to ease the pain a bit.

"You shouldn't have run away from me. I was wrong to be so flippant, but you angered me and I struck back. Perhaps you will contrive to forget it, and to forgive me for my strange lapse. I am usually a gentleman, you know."

At the moment, she wouldn't have cared if he were the devil. "I want to go home," she said. "I want to die in my own bed."

It was a pity they were so close to Rendel Hall. He would have preferred to take her to the Abbey. But Lannie was still there, and a fussing Lannie could easily send Arielle or any sentient human being to the hereafter with a sigh of gratitude.

"All right. Let's stay here just a few minutes longer, until you fell more the thing again."

Arielle said nothing. She felt the warmth of his thigh beneath her shoulders. She felt his left hand on her shoulder, light and gentle. She hated this weakness. She hated the fear that stirred itself to life as if it were a living thing inside her. She hated being dependent on him, even though it was just for a little while. She wasn't aware that tears were streaking down her face.

Burke saw the tears and felt as though he'd been struck. He couldn't bear it. He wiped the tears away, speaking nonsense words to her, trying to ease her.

"It's all right," he said and repeated the words again and again. "You'll be all right very soon now." And even as he spoke, she lurched up onto her knees and lost the little breakfast she'd eaten. She continued to retch, dry heaves, for there was nothing in her stomach, and he held her shoulders to keep her steady, then supported her, knowing the awful weakness that followed sickness. He handed her his handkerchief and she wiped her mouth. He wanted to take her home with him and never let her out of his sight again. He wanted . . .

"I want to go home now," Arielle said, not looking at him. She was drowning in misery and pain, and there was no help for it. "Please, I want to go home."

"All right. Will you trust me enough to let me do what I think is necessary?"

She felt too awful to reply. No, she didn't trust him, but she couldn't see that she had any choice.

She felt his hands slip around her thighs, felt him lifting her in his arms as he himself rose.

Lord, she was light, he thought. Too thin, too

slight. He carried her to Ashes. "Hold on," he said,
and cradling her in one arm, he managed to mount
the stallion. "I'll send Geordie for Mindle. Don't
worry, she'll be all right."

During the short ride back to Rendel Hall, neither one of them said anything. Burke held her very
close, his ears tuned to any sound she might make.

To his relief, Geordie took charge quite efficiently. Burke carried Arielle into Rendel Hall, up
the stairs, and down the narrow hallway to her bedchamber. Something in him stirred as he realized
that it wasn't the master suite. He was aware of
the old woman, Dorcas, dogging his heels, making
false starts and stops, wringing her hands until he
finally said, "Bring me some water. She needs to
wash out her mouth and bathe her face."

Then there was that old ass, Philfer, acting as
though Burke had intruded into *his* domain. He
blessed Geordie, who said to Philfer with great con-
ciseness, "Shut yer trap, old man. Fetch his lordship a brandy and let the doctor in when he comes."

Dr. Mortimer Arkwright, bent and thin as a stick
as he neared his sixtieth year, greeted Burke in the
dour voice that had been a part of him for nearly
fifty of those years. The old man had brought Burke
into the world and for that, Burke was profoundly
grateful. He'd also thought Dr. Arkwright long
dead and blurted out as much.

"Not yet," said Dr. Arkwright, giving Burke a
nearly toothless grin. "I'm retired, but the Rendel
stable lad caught me fair and square. Being I was
so close, I thought it silly to send the lad on for
Mark Brody. You know Brody, don't you?"

"Yes, I met him three years ago when he first
came." Burke then told the doctor what happened.

"Arielle Leslie, poor little girl. Well, lad, let's
take a look. What were you doing with her anyway?"

Good question, thought Burke, but he didn't reply, merely walked more quickly toward Arielle's room.

"She's grown up," said Dr. Arkwright as he stared down at Arielle. "Well, girl, open your eyes and tell me where you hurt."

Arielle said only, "My head. Dreadful. Please make it stop."

Dr. Arkwright grunted. "I approve a woman of few words. Now, my girl, open your eyes, that's it, and tell me how many fingers I'm holding up."

Burke stepped back, saying nothing, watching the old man efficiently treat Arielle. Oddly, Dr. Arkwright turned to Burke after a few minutes, saying, "I can't give her any laudanum just yet. Concussion. Wake her up every couple of hours and ask her who she is and where she is. In eight hours or so, some laudanum. I'll leave instructions."

Dorcas finally regained her senses. "His lordship doesn't live here! He merely brought her home."

Dr. Arkwright looked at Burke, then grunted. "So that's the way of it, hmm?"

Burke found himself leaving with Dr. Arkwright. "You're certain she'll be all right?"

"If I didn't think so, I wouldn't be leaving. Don't be such a fool, my boy. The chit will be singing songs in her bath by tomorrow morning. If you were her husband, you'd be there to sing with her."

"That's true enough," said Burke. "It scared me witless when she flew over her horse's head."

"Natural enough reaction," said Dr. Arkwright. "She's a beauty. I wondered how she'd turn out. Haven't seen her for three years, you know; last time was just before Sir Arthur died. I suppose you'll be back tomorrow to see her?"

Burke nodded. He watched Dr. Arkwright climb into his small brougham and leave.

"Is she all right?"

"Yes, Geordie, she'll be fine. Dr. Arkwright
swears it. You'll keep an eye out, won't you?"

"Aye, that I will. The lass promised me some
haggis, and I'll remind her about it tomorrow
morning." Geordie scratched his head. "Old Philfer
can be got around."

Burke didn't want to leave, but he couldn't find
another choice for himself. Finally he returned to
Ravensworth Abbey and spent a very long afternoon and night.

"Is she singing yet?" was his first question when
he greeted Dorcas the following morning.

The old woman smiled, and Burke saw she was
missing almost all her back teeth. "Very nearly. Do
you wish to see her, my lord?"

Burke couldn't believe it. Everyone in Arielle's
employ seemed eager to promote him. Only Arielle
was fighting tooth and nail. "Certainly," he said,
all calm and confident, and followed Dorcas up the
stairs.

"You were with Arielle since she was a child,
were you not?"

"Yes, a sweetheart she was, open and chatty and
clean of spirit, if you know what I mean."

"A pity she changed."

"What can you expect? It was bound to have happened. Ah, lovey, I've a visitor for you."

She turned in the doorway and motioned to
Burke. He heard Arielle call out, her voice harsh
and wary, "No, Dorcas! Please, I don't wish to
see—"

"Hello, Arielle. It's just me. You look well again.
Does your head feel all right?"

Actually, she looked as awful as Arielle could
look, her beautiful hair tumbled and tangled and
lank, her face as white as the counterpane, an ugly
purple-and-yellow bruise showing at her left temple. She was grasping the covers to her chin, and

her back was pressed tight against the headboard. He took a step toward her and heard her gasp.

She was behaving strangely, and that pulled him up short. For heaven's sake, it wasn't as if she were a young girl who'd never been married. Her reputation was quite safe, particularly since her old, very respectable-looking nurse was here. Why was she behaving in such a missish fashion? He tried a smile and managed a mechanical one. "I was just concerned for you. Will I still see you at teatime on Friday?"

She nodded, mute, but he saw the lie in her eyes before she lowered them. She had changed her mind. Perhaps she was more ill than Dr. Arkwright had thought.

What the devil should he do now? He didn't want to leave her, not yet. "You are supposed to sing in your bath this morning, according to Dr. Arkwright."

"If you leave I promise I shall."

"Have you breakfasted yet?"

She shook her head, wincing a bit.

"Would you like to have something?"

"Yes," said Dorcas, stepping to the bed. "Let me have Bessie bring you some toast and tea."

Arielle didn't realize that Dorcas was leaving until she was nearly out the door. Arielle called after her, but the old woman didn't come back.

"You are safe with me," Burke said, slanting an eyebrow. "It has never been my practice to seduce or ravish ladies who have such colorful bruises on their faces."

She didn't reply, and Burke, at loose conversational ends, looked about her bedchamber. He wasn't certain what he had expected, but this wasn't it. It was nearly a monk's cell, sparsely furnished and those furnishings severe. Not a feminine flounce or furbelow in the room. He found himself staring toward the adjoining door. Was the master suite on the other side? He didn't want to think about that filthy old man opening that door and coming in here, to this bed, to Arielle. He heard himself saying harshly, "Is your husband's room beyond?"

Arielle heard the fury in his voice but didn't understand it. She didn't want to understand it. She wanted Burke out of her bedchamber. He filled it, his scent, his vitality, his *maleness*.

"Please go away, my lord."

He swung about to face her. "I will if you give me your word you will come to Ravensworth Abbey on Friday."

She chewed her lower lip.

He felt his frustration grow.

Finally, very quietly, she said, "No."

# 5

Burke stared down at her, absorbing the consequences of that one simple word. He couldn't recall the last time he'd been rejected by a woman. Whenever he had been, though, he knew deep inside it couldn't have hurt as much as this did. Nor would it have made him so furious he couldn't think straight.

"Why?"

"Please," she said, "please just leave me alone. I don't wish to see anyone or . . . or be with anyone. I am a widow. I wish to remain a widow."

"Your husband is dead . . ." The rawness of his voice shocked him. ". . . how long? Seven, eight months now? For God' sake, Arielle, he was an old man! Don't you want a young man, one who will give you so much more than he could have?"

Arielle wanted to laugh, but when she opened her mouth, an ugly, harsh sound came out. She got hold of herself. He didn't know what he was saying. She would keep her mouth shut. He would leave. But he was made of tougher stuff than she'd imagined.

"You couldn't have loved that old satyr! He was a disgusting old man! Look at me . . . don't you remember how you felt three years ago? How I made you feel?"

She remembered, but the memories weren't hers;

they were that other girl's. She remained silent, her eyes on her clasped hands.

"Damn you!"

He leaned over her, grasped her arms, pulling her against his chest. His mouth was on hers, hard and aggressive, his tongue probing against her closed lips. "Open your mouth!"

She opened her mouth to yell at him and felt his tongue.

"Here's your breakfast, my dear—oh, goodness!"

Burke froze at the sound of Dorcas's voice. Slowly, as if he were a man waking from a dream, he pulled his hands back and straightened to look down at her. "I will see you again, Arielle."

"No!"

"Oh, yes. It's not over between us." He shook his head, a pained expression on his face. "It won't ever be over." He strode across her bedchamber and left.

Arielle was staring straight ahead, toward the open doorway. "He is much stronger than Paisley," she said calmly. "Entirely stronger than Paisley." Then, without another word, she rose from her bed and walked to the wide windows that gave onto the front of the house. She watched Burke walk toward the stable. She leaned forward, her forehead against the glass. It came to her that evening what she would do.

Mr. Gregory Lapwing, Arthur Leslie's former solicitor, seated himself across from his old friend's daughter. He'd known her all of her eighteen years and was as fond of her as an older man besotted with a new, young wife could be. *His* nineteen-year-old wife was certainly livelier, prettier, than this pinched-looking girl.

"I appreciate your coming to me, Mr. Lapwing," Arielle said, giving him her hand.

"My pleasure, Arielle. What is it you wish?"

He thought she looked ill, so pale and thin was she. Was she still grieving for her dead husband? It was the first time he'd seen her since her father's death more than three years before. Strange business, that, leaving the girl in the guardianship of her half brother, but he supposed Arthur had had no choice. Her precipitous marriage to Lord Rendel had shocked him, but then again, it had nothing to do with him, so he had forgotten it. Until now.

"I want to sell Rendel Hall, all the land, and all the furnishings. Everything. Immediately."

Mr. Lapwing didn't blink. He'd perfected the expressionless expression long ago. Nothing a client said could discomfit him. "May I ask you why?" he asked politely.

"I wish to leave the country. I wish to move to Paris. Napoleon is gone and Louis the Eighteenth is on the throne. There is no more danger." She added, a dimple appearing in her left cheek, "I do speak French, you know. Father insisted."

"I see," Mr. Lapwing said, frowning. "May I ask why you wished to deal with me rather than with Lord Rendel's solicitor?"

"I don't know him," Arielle said. It was only a half lie. She didn't trust him simply because he'd been Paisley's man. "Really, sir, there is nothing to keep me here. I wish to travel."

Mr. Lapwing rose from his chair. "It is unusual, of course, for a lady to wish to travel, most unusual. You must be properly protected and chaperoned—"

How ridiculous, Arielle was thinking. I wasn't protected here, in beautiful, just England. Men! They spouted such nonsense. However, she had a goal to attain, so her voice was calm and respectful. "Of course, Mr. Lapwing. Pray don't worry. I will be duly chaperoned."

"But—"

"My mind is quite made up, sir."

"Very well. Who is Lord Rendel's solicitor?"

"Jeffrey Chaucer, of all things. I've heard it said that his late mother was a poetess. Do you know him, sir?"

"Yes," said Mr. Lapwing shortly. "One can't forget him, what with that silly name of his. A poetess, huh? Well, no matter. I will make inquiries immediately, my dear. I will also send a man here to speak to your steward—"

"Mr. Harold Jewells is his name."

"Yes, certainly, and he will also take a thorough inventory. Not only of household furnishings but of livestock, outbuildings, tenants' cottages—you get the idea."

"How soon do you think I can leave England?"

"I don't know . . . a month, perhaps? We can't do very much without a buyer, you know."

So she would have to hide for a month. Brighton, she thought. She and Dorcas could stay there until everything was done. No one else would know. "All right," she said aloud. "Oh, just one more thing, Mr. Lapwing. The buyer mustn't dismiss any of the Rendel tenants or servants, nor may their circumstances be changed."

"It is unlikely that a buyer would do that, but I will make your wishes clear. Ah, doesn't your land march to the east with Ravensworth?"

"Yes," she said, her voice becoming suddenly cold. "Why do you ask, sir?"

"I was simply curious, that's all." That gave Mr. Lapwing an excellent idea, but he didn't want to speak of it to Arielle. It could lead to disappointment. No, he would tell her only if he were successful. He ate an excellent luncheon with her, then returned to East Grinstead. He made an appointment to see the Earl of Ravensworth the following Monday morning. Although he would have few facts

or figures, he could still determine whether or not
the earl was interested.

When Mr. Lapwing entered the Ravensworth library the following Monday morning, George Cerlew preceding him and making the introductions,
Burke wondered what the devil the man wanted
with him. He hadn't long to wait.

He found that he couldn't quite take in what he
was hearing. "I beg your pardon, sir?"

"My lord, Lady Rendel wishes to sell everything
as quickly as possible. Your land marches on hers.
I wished to give you the first chance at it. As of yet,
my man hasn't done an assessment or an inventory, so I cannot provide you with an estimate of
its worth. However, if you are interested, your man
could work with mine."

Burke wasn't attending him. He waved his hand.
"Just a moment, sir. Why does Lady Rendel want
to sell out?"

Mr. Lapwing smiled with understanding. No one
wanted to buy a possible pig in a poke. The earl
was most efficiently trying to determine if the house
had terminal rot of some sort or suffered from gross
mismanagement. "Nothing to do with the property,
my lord. Lady Rendel has been a widow for a while
now. She said she wanted to leave England and live
in Paris since the Bourbon is restored to the throne.
It is probably because of her grief over her husband. It was his house, you know. The memories
must be painful for her. You know how ladies feel
so deeply about things such as this."

"I see," Burke said. He was silent for several
minutes. It struck him cleanly between the eyes
that it was because of him that she wanted to sell
out. She wanted to run because of him. Why? he
asked himself again. Why was she so wary of him?
Mr. Lapwing said nothing, merely watched the earl.

Finally Burke said, "I will buy everything. I will
have my steward, Mr. Cerlew, work with your man,
as you suggested. I will give her a fair price."

"I imagined that you would, my lord. There is
but one condition Lady Rendel places on the sale.
She doesn't want any tenants or servants dismissed."

"No, of course not," Burke said absently.

"Lady Rendel will be pleased to have an offer
coming to her so quickly. I had told her it might be
at least a month before I could find a buyer. She
wants to leave as soon as possible, as I told you."

"I also have a condition, Mr. Lapwing."

Mr. Lapwing raised a brow.

"Lady Rendel is not to know that I am the buyer.
Under no circumstances are you to tell her."

"Most unusual, my lord. How is it to be avoided
when your steward will work with Mr. Jewells?"

"An excellent point," said Burke, frowning. "I
shall have to give that some thought. Nonetheless,
you may proceed."

Mr. Lapwing agreed to proceed, seeing no reason
not to. Why the earl wanted this condition made no
sense to him, but he couldn't see that it would make
any difference. He took his leave of the earl, feeling
quite pleased with himself. He would buy his delicious little wife, Lottie, a lovely necklace with the
commission he would earn. Yes, he thought, emer-
alds. He was whistling as he told his driver to go
to Rendel Hall.

Burke drove to London to see his own solicitor.
His man would handle the entire matter. Then
what? he wondered. *Arielle wouldn't be in his
power. On the contrary, she would have his money.*
What to do about that?

He was surprised at himself. Did he truly want
her in his power, for God's sake? Like some sort of
master with a slave? He remembered their last

meeting. His jaw tightened. Yes, he did, and he would have her.

He visited his sister, Corinne, and her husband, Lord Boyle, and the newly arrived Lannie. He told his relatives of his purchase, not wanting them to discover it by accident. He sounded so detached, he was almost putting them to sleep.

"How odd," said Corinne, Lady Boyle, when he had finished. "A young girl leaving England? Most odd."

"There's probably a man involved," said Lloyd Kinnard, Lord Boyle. "Bound to be."

The gave Burke a start. As for Lannie, she did allow that, knowing Arielle as she did—which was knowing her not at all—it wasn't a man. The girl obviously had bats in her bell tower.

"I do wonder," said Corinne in a thoughtful voice, "why the girl would just want to up and leave."

"I don't know," Burke said finally.

"I trust the property is worth the price you're paying, Burke," said Lord Boyle.

"I don't know the price yet," said Burke. "It should be quite reasonable, though."

Burke turned down his sister's offer of dinner, earning himself one of her looks that could fry an egg at a distance of ten feet, and took himself off to White's. To his immense pleasure, Viscount Castlerose, Knight Winthrop, was there, an impressive pile of bank notes strewn in front of him, three cards remaining in his hand. He waved negligently toward Burke, pointing to the chair next to his, and tossed down a ten of hearts.

His opponent, Lord Lucy, something of a renowned fool, at least in Burke's opinion, was grinding his teeth. Since he hadn't counted, he had no choice but to continue grinding. He tossed a diamond. Knight calmly laid down two more hearts.

"Sorry, old man," he said and began to gather up the pile of notes."

"Another hand, Winthrop?" said Lord Lucy.

"Sorry, but my friend here needs me, don't you, Burke?"

"Indeed."

Lord Lucy whined a bit more until another partner was found for him. It was Lord Davies, and he would most certainly relieve Lord Lucy of every bit of gold he'd ever possessed.

Burke watched Knight stuff the money into his pocket. "You are a shark, Knight."

"The fellow's a bloody fool. Can you believe he didn't keep his hearts? A fistful of diamonds, that's all he had! I was most delighted, as you saw."

Knight Winthrop waved to Henry, one of White's noted waiters, and ordered a bottle of their best French brandy.

"How's your side?"

"Fine. No pulling and not much tenderness anymore."

"Excellent. With Napoleon off France's shores for good, you should be safe from further holes in your hide. Now, what brings you to London, Burke? Gambling? Fleshpots? Drury Lane? Not business, I hope."

Burke studied his best friend for a moment in silence. He said finally with a twisted smile, "I wish I could have a woman right this moment. I am so damned randy I think I would plow her until dawn."

Knight laughed. "At least you're still young enough to make that wish a reality."

"Go to the devil, Knight." Burke sighed and ran his fingers through his thick hair. "Damnation!"

"No, no, you want a woman, a woman you will have. Her name is Laura, she isn't French, nor does she pretend to be. She is warm, loving, and will doubtless enjoy herself with you. Not as much as with me, of course, but enough, I imagine. I will escort you there myself. In the morning, my friend, you and I can meet for breakfast at my house. Perhaps then you will be more yourself."

Burke laughed, his look incredulous. "You are offering me your mistress?" Knight shook his head. "Who is she?"

"My mistress's friend."

"I don't know ... It's true that I'm randy, but that's out of sheer frustration. You see, the girl I want, the girl I've wanted for nearly three years, won't have a thing to do with me." *She's even willing to leave England to avoid me.*

Knight was surprised, to say the least. He gave Burke a pained look. "You know what I think of matrimony, old man. Good God, that you should think of succumbing! It *is* matrimony you're considering?"

"Yes."

"I can't talk you out of it? Convince you to make this girl your mistress instead?"

"No."

"Do you want to tell me the name of this paragon?"

"I don't think so. Not yet, Knight."

"All right. Spend the night with Laura. We will discuss it in the morning. And, Burke, you aren't being disloyal. You aren't yet married to the chit. After the parson has locked you away but good, you can remove the word 'mistress' from your mind and your dictionary forever, if you so wish. But tonight, forget this girl and let Laura, ah, ease you."

Burke said yes. Knight accompanied him to a small, respectable-looking house on Curzon Street. As for Laura, she was everything Knight had promised. She was soft, warm, endowed with immense breasts, and very responsive. Burke didn't believe she was feigning pleasure, but it didn't really matter. He was hurting with need. And when at last he thrust into her, he arched wildly, his head thrown back, and he cried out, "Arielle!"

The shock of release was so great that he lay sprawled atop her, unable to move. He was mildly surprised to realize that he was breathing.

"Have you been living in a monastery, my lord?"

Burke had difficulty raising himself onto his elbows. "I imagine you would think so," he said, smiling down at her. "I am sorry I was so carried away, but—"

She hugged him and kissed his bare shoulder. " 'Tis all right." She moved beneath him and he was instantly hard again, filling her, his powerful body quivering with renewed need.

He gave her a rueful smile and leaned down to kiss her, thoroughly. Everything he did this time was thorough in the extreme, much to Laura's delight.

Laura watched him sleep. He was a beautiful man, a wonderfully normal man in his sexual demands, and he enjoyed a woman's pleasure. Who was this Arielle? His wife? No, she didn't think he was married. He didn't *act* married. Who, then? When he awoke some thirty minutes later, again hard and ready for her, she gave herself to him without hesitation. "I shall cock up my toes, happy now," Burke said on a deep sigh.

Laura giggled and ran her toes up his leg. She looked at him straightly and said without preamble, "I am currently without a protector. I should like to belong to you, my lord."

Burke felt wonderfully sated, his senses dulled and hazy. He hadn't kept a mistress for a good four years. There simply hadn't been the opportunity, what with the army picking up and leaving without a moment's notice. But there was Arielle to consider; he fully intended to marry her as quickly as possible. He knew even as he thought it that he was indulging in a man's inimitable reasoning: he should keep a mistress until his marriage. That would save him losing control with Arielle.

He felt Laura's muscles tighten about him, but thankfully, he'd indulged sufficiently to remain cerebral for the moment rather than corporal. She was lovely, no doubt about that, and she satisfied him sexually, no doubt about that either. He cursed softly and pulled away from her body. He rolled onto his back and cradled his head on his arms.

"I don't know," he said aloud.

"Is it this Arielle?"

He froze, then remembered crying out her name. He cursed again, pungently.

"Forgive me, my lord . . . your wife, perhaps?"

"No," was his harsh reply. Then he sighed and said, "She will be—'tis just a matter of time and, well, ruthlessness, if you will."

Laura didn't understand that, nor did he completely. He knew only that he would do whatever was necessary to have Arielle.

He felt Laura's soft hand stroking down his side. He felt her fingers slide over his belly to find him and caress him. He should have been dead as summer ashes, but he wasn't. "All right," he said and turned toward her yet again. "Until I marry."

Laura was pleased. She was also sore, but she discounted that as unimportant.


Rendel Hall

"No, Dorcas, I won't speak to anyone until I have signed the deed over to whoever it is who has bought Rendel Hall. You know as well as I do that something could change at the last minute."

Dorcas nodded agreement. She watched her young mistress rise from her chair, her embroidery dropping unheeded to the floor. She saw her walk to the front windows and stand staring out over the front lawn. She'd been present when Arielle had spoken to Mr. Jewells two days before, telling him of her decision and instructing him to aid Mr. Lapwing. He'd looked at her oddly. He'd also sweated profusely . . .

"What is the matter, Mr. Jewells?" Arielle had asked.

"Oh, nothing, my lady! Surely you wish to consider, do you not, perhaps—"

"No, I don't. Please don't worry that you will find yourself without your steward's position. That is one of my conditions. The buyer must agree to it."

She didn't care much for Mr. Jewells, a man she regarded as one of Paisley's minions, a tubby man with large spectacles and an oily manner. But he was efficient, as he constantly assured her of that fact. He'd said little more and quickly left her.

She found herself even more surprised when Paisley's solicitor, Mr. Jeffrey Chaucer, arrived. If Mr. Jewells had seemed distracted, Mr. Chaucer seemed fairly frantic.

But now she had a buyer, for everything. She hadn't yet informed Mr. Jewells of this fact, or Mr. Chaucer. She supposed she didn't want more arguments from either man. Coming up the drive was a small carriage. She pressed closer to the window. It was Mr. Lapwing.

He looked distraught, no, more than that, she thought, studying him as he followed on Philfer's heels into her drawing room. He looked as if the world had fallen on his head. She'd heard about his new, very young wife and wondered if that lady were the cause.

"Sir?" she said.

Mr. Lapwing looked at Dorcas briefly, saying, "I should like a word with you, Lady Rendel, privately."

"Certainly," she said.

He didn't speak again until they were alone.

"What is wrong, sir?"

Lapwing drew a deep breath. "Jewells and Chaucer, they've robbed the estate blind. They've fled England."

Aurielle merely stared at him. "But how?"

"You gave Chaucer power of attorney. He mortgaged Rendel Hall and all the tenant property to the hilt. Jewells has taken all the tenant money since your husband's death. There is nothing left. Nothing. My God, this is ridiculous! Didn't you make inquiries? Didn't you—"

"No. I believed what Mr. Chaucer and Mr. Jewells told me. But the money I've spent since my husband's death—"

"Jewells simply borrowed it through Chaucer. They would have continued doing that until the bank foreclosed."

Arielle sat down. "I haven't a sou then, is that what you're telling me?"

He looked extremely unhappy as he nodded. "I'm sorry, my dear. I shall keep the creditors at bay as long as I can, but news of this fraud will circulate soon enough. Then—" He swallowed at the dazed look on her face. "I am sorry."

"Of course you are. I don't suppose that my buyer is still willing. Not that it matters a whit to me!"

"I don't know. I haven't yet spoken to him."

"Who is he? Since it is now academic, I might as well know."

"Burke Drummond. The Earl of Ravensworth."

Arielle sucked in her breath, turning as pale as a human being could be.

"My lady!" Lapwing reached out his hand toward her, but Arielle automatically pulled back.

"Have I absolutely nothing left, sir?"

He shook his head. "Time, is all. I am hopeful that you will have another month, but I cannot be certain even of that."

He wondered what this poor child would do now. He disliked her half brother, Evan Goddis, excessively. He couldn't see her living with that bounder, but then again, where else could she go?

"Do you know the whereabouts of your half sister, Baroness Sherard?"

"No." She didn't meet his eyes for a long time. Then she raised her head. "I have been living in a fool's paradise, I believe the expression is. I never really trusted either Mr. Jewells or Mr. Chaucer, but I couldn't be bothered with it. It is truly all my fault for being a fool."

That was true, he thought, but he didn't want her paying such a heavy price. "I have given this some thought, Arielle. Why do you not marry again?"

She shrank back, turning paler, if that were possible. She said nothing, merely shook her head back and forth.

"I know it isn't a full year yet since Lord Rendel died, but your need is pressing, truly. You are a lovely young lady, my dear. Surely there are many gentlemen—"

*"No!* No, pray don't mention that again, Mr. Lapwing. You will speak to Lord Ravensworth? You can tell him that he will certainly pay very little for the estate now."

"Yes, I will."

"Good," said Arielle. With the news that she was now a pauper, perhaps Burke would leave her alone once and for all. "Please excuse me now, sir, but I have a lot of thinking to do."

* * *

When Mr. Lapwing told Burke of the situation, the earl smiled, rubbed his hands together, and said under his breath, "Now I've got her."

He began making plans even before Mr. Lapwing was out the door.

# 6

Arielle couldn't believe her eyes. She reread Nesta's letter. She wanted to shout with relief. She wanted to dance. Instead, she reread the letter again.

Nesta and her husband, Baron Sherard, were in Boston, Massachusetts, in America! Arielle's letter of seven months earlier, telling them of Paisley's death had finally caught up to them, or they to it, as the case was. They were inviting her to come to America and stay with them.

She offered a prayer of thanks heavenward. She was finally safe. She couldn't wait to tell Dorcas. With the letter clutched in her hand, Arielle dashed out of the drawing room only to come to an abrupt halt in the entrance hall. There was Philfer in close conversation with Evan. She saw money change hands. She'd always believed Philfer an obsequious fraud, and now she saw that it was true.

It didn't bother her in the slightest. The nasty old man would shortly be cast out. Then he would earn what was due him. She called out gaily, "Evan! Welcome! Do come in. I would speak to you of my news."

Philfer jerked about, turned a remarkable shade of gray, but Evan, all aplomb, merely smiled and walked toward her.

"Well, good morning, my dear sister. What is your marvelous news?"

"You will be the first to know, Evan. I am leaving as soon as possible for Boston." At his blank look, she added, " 'Tis a large city in America."

"I know," he said. "Who's in Boston?"

"Nesta. She's inviting me to stay with her for as long as I wish."

"But what about Rendel Hall and all your responsibilities?"

"You mean Paisley Cochrane's home? I am as certain as I can be that it will continue on a proper course."

He said nothing, and Arielle was too happy to care. She wasn't about to tell him of her miserable situation, one rendered inconsequential now. Let him find out in his own time, perhaps when the creditors came and kicked Philfer out. She pictured it in her mind. The old man would huff and hem and haw, and it wouldn't matter. As for the rest of the servants, they would have no difficulty finding new positions. Geordie, now, he was different. She hoped he would agree to come with her to America.

"Well," Evan said finally, "I suppose this is what you wish. Good luck, Arielle. I shall be in charge of things while you are gone, all right?"

She wanted to laugh in his face. His greed was so ill-disguised. "Yes, certainly, Evan. You will see to everything whilst I am away, I'm sure."

"Oh, you can trust me implicitly, Arielle."

It occurred to her then that it might not be possible to transfer power to him without his finding out about Jewells and Chaucer. And she didn't want that to happen until she was gone. "Well, perhaps I shouldn't. No, I don't believe I shall." No explanation for him. She smiled brightly. "Is there anything in particular you wanted Evan?"

He wanted to strangle her with his bare hands.

"No," he said, trying desperately to moderate his voice, "no, nothing really. When will you take your leave? Who will accompany you?"

"I'm leaving for Southampton on Thursday."

"That is but two days from now!"

"Quite so." She'd decided at that very moment. Surely there would be a ship leaving from that huge harbor in the near future. "I shall take Dorcas and Geordie with me, if they wish to go. Now, dearest brother, I am quite busy. I'm certain Philfer will be delighted to show you out. He was obviously quite delighted to show you in, after all."

She turned on her heel and sailed from the drawing room, humming, paying him no more heed.

Etienne DuPons was nervous, excited, and overly warm in the long black wool cloak. He privately thought it ridiculous to dress up as some sort of silly highwayman, but Evan had insisted.

"We can take no chances that you are recognized," Evan had said. "After it is done, then no matter."

Etienne pulled his horse back into the shadows of a giant oak tree. The servant, Geordie, would be riding just ahead of the carriage. He didn't want to kill the man, merely take him out of the game, so to speak.

*Where was Arielle?*

He felt lust just thinking about her. He closed his eyes for a moment, seeing her again on her knees before him, her soft hands caressing him, her mouth touching him . . . His own moan brought him back to the present.

*Where was she?*

He heard a horse galloping toward him. Slowly, he drew the pistol from his wide belt and carefully cocked the trigger. He peered through the thick foliage, holding himself tensely still. Several moments passed. Finally, he saw a man riding toward him, a stranger. He quickly pulled his horse back in the shadows again, cursing softly under his breath.

*Where the devil was she?*

It occurred to Burke as he waited in the shade of a thick-branched maple tree that he had never told Arielle that he loved her, had loved her for three years, and that he wanted to marry her. He hadn't seen her since that Friday morning when he'd kissed her and left her, so furious and frustrated he'd wanted to spit. He'd become a madman when Mr. Lapwing had told him she was selling up and leaving England.

A madman. He shook his head, his eyes still trained on the road, knowing full well that no sane man would do what he was planning. Well, the devil, he thought. When he'd discovered from Mr. Lapwing that she'd been robbed by her solicitor and steward, he had ridden to Rendel Hall immediately. To this moment he still wasn't certain what he would have said to her if he'd been allowed into the house.

It was probably just as well that he hadn't seen her. He might have acted precipitously. His visit to Mr. Lapwing on the previous day played in his mind. If he hadn't gone . . . oh, God, he would never have found out that Arielle was leaving England. But he had gone. . . .

"I see, my lord," Mr. Lapwing had said, turning and twisting a quill between his fingers. "Obviously if you wish the Rendel property, I am certain you can buy it from the creditors at an excellent price."

Burke shook his head. He wanted nothing to do with the Rendel property. It was just that he didn't want Arielle to feel compelled to marry him because she hadn't a sou. No, he wanted her freely because she wanted him. He would find a way to salve her pride by filling enough of her purse.

"It no longer matters, my lord," Mr. Lapwing continued. "Your decision will have nothing to do with Lady Rendel."

"What? I'm sorry, I was thinking of something else. What no longer matters?"

"Any of it, my lord. Lady Rendel received a letter from her sister inviting her to come to Boston to stay. Lady Rendel is leaving tomorrow, I believe. We are still at war with the Americans, but I did manage to locate a Dutch merchant ship for her that will be safe enough."

Burke could only stare at him. To hell with her pride, was the first thought that struck him.

It was still in his mind.

"I am a madman," he said aloud, and Dandy, a huge raw-boned stallion he was certain Arielle had never seen before, obligingly whinnied. He became very still when he heard the hoofbeats coming. That would doubtless be Geordie—and Joshua's problem. He waved a hand and saw Joshua's return wave.

The road was flat and fairly straight, so both of them could see Geordie a good thirty yards before he reached them. When he did, Joshua, a mask over his face, rode from his hiding place, an enormous pistol in his hand.

"Halt and deliver!"

Geordie pulled the bay to a halt and whirled about toward the voice. Stupid fellow! For heaven's sake, he had no money worth speaking of.

A man swathed in a long black cloak, a black wool mask tied about his head, appeared from the shade of the trees, "Don't move, or I'll kill you!"

Oh, God, Geordie thought, the fellow's an amateur. Geordie had no intention of doing anything. "I won't move!" Geordie said quickly, holding himself as still as one of those London actresses doing attitudes.

"Get off your horse and lie facedown on the road."

Geordie did as he was told, one eye on the pistol in the man's gloved right hand. The man sounded familiar, but at the moment he couldn't place him.

Joshua quickly tied Geordie's hands behind him, fastened a mask over his eyes, and said, "All right, let's go now. Don't give me any trouble, else I'll cosh you good."

"Yer mad," said Geordie. "What do ye want with me?"

"Not a thing," said Joshua and shoved Geordie into the woods. He turned, waved toward Burke, and disappeared.

Burke felt the tension mount. His heartbeat quickened; his palms were clammy. Then he saw the carriage, the single driver. Arielle and her maid, Dorcas, were within.

The tricky part, he thought.

He rode to the middle of the road, drew his pistol, and waited.

The driver, Samuel, took one look at the man and the evil black gun pointing at him and stood up, yanking the horses to a halt with all his leveraged strength.

Arielle grabbed for the leather strap and missed. She was flung facedown beside Dorcas on the opposite seat.

"Well, I never!" said Dorcas.

Arielle drew herself up and stuck her head out the carriage window. "Sam, whatever is the mat—" Her voice dropped like a stone into an abyss at the sight of the highwayman.

"What do you want?" she asked, thinking about the one hundred pounds in her reticule, all the money she had in the world. It wasn't fair. Where was Geordie?

"Get out," the man shouted at her.

"No," Dorcas said and grabbed Arielle's arm. "The man's a rogue, he'll hurt you."

"Release me, Dorcas. He will probably just take my money and let us go."

With those words, Arielle opened the carriage door and jumped down to the dusty road. To be robbed in broad daylight was too much. Where was Geordie?

Burke stared down at her. She looked beautiful, but so pale and scared. He didn't want her to be frightened, but he saw no hope for it. His breathing deepened, quickened. "Come here," he said, trying to flatten his accent so that she wouldn't recognize him until he had her.

"Take my money," she said, flinging her reticule at him. "Damn you!"

Burke caught the reticule and weighted it in his palm. "How much have you got?"

"Surely enough for the likes of you!" Arielle said, gritting her teeth.

"I will count it later, and we will see. Where were you off to, sweetheart?"

He saw her go even more pale, if that were possible. "To Southampton, to leave this accursed country!" To his surprise and amusement, she stamped her foot. "Just go away! It isn't fair. What do you want anyway? What did you do with my man?"

"He isn't harmed, I promise you. As for you, well, I do have plans."

As he spoke, he walked Dandy toward her. She took a step back. He spoke again, wanting to distract her. He didn't want anyone hurt in this madman's fantasy. "When does your ship leave?"

"Tomorrow, early morning. Please, I must be there! I cannot miss my chance!"

"And where do you go?" He was nearly close enough.

"To Boston, to my sister. Can you not rob some-one else? I—truly, I haven't much money, and I need it, desperately. I cannot arrive in Boston—"

God, he hated the pleading. One more step and Burke, without warning, reached down, circled her waist, and hauled her up against him. She was per-fectly still for several moments; then all hell broke loose. She was wearing gloves and thus didn't hurt him. She would have scored the flesh off his face had her hands been bare.

"Stop it, now!" he said, squeezing her tightly about her ribs. She gasped for breath and from pain, but continued to hit at him. If he was a madman, she was certainly a witch.

Burke toppled her and she landed stomach-down in front of him. As if from a great distance, Burke heard Dorcas screaming, yelling insults at him that he doubted his salty sergeant had known. As for the driver, he just stared, openmouthed.

Arielle twisted about frantically, trying to lurch up, but Burke's hand came down hard at her waist, holding her still.

"Don't move, Arielle, or you'll just hurt your-self." His words had no effect at all, and he made his voice as mean as he could. "Stop it or I'll knock you unconscious."

She quieted.

A believable threat, he thought. He yelled to Dor-cas, whose furious face was regarding him from the carriage window, "She won't be harmed!" He dug in his heels and Dandy raced forward down the road. He realized suddenly that he'd said her name aloud. He cursed silently.

Arielle felt the breath whoosh out of her at the stallion's pace. "How do you know me?"

He said nothing.

"You called me Arielle. Who are you?"

He kept his mouth shut. He didn't want her to recognize him just yet. When he revealed himself, he wanted the both of them to be in more comfortable surroundings. She would doubtless be more amenable to reason if she weren't slung on her stomach over his saddle.

"Where are you taking me?" She didn't expect him to say anything this time. Her face was pressed against his thigh, and the wool of the black cloak was scratchy. She could feel the strength of him, the muscles bunching and pulling as he guided the horse with his legs. And she could feel her own fear begin to grow at that moment. The palm of his hand was against the small of her back, and it felt hot and strong.

The rocking motion of the horse was making her nauseous. "I will throw up if you don't let me sit."

"All right," he said, frowning a bit. She was small, with not nearly enough strength to overpower him. He pulled his horse to a halt and brought her astride in front of him. Her gown rode up to her thighs and he had a marvelous view of her stocking-clad legs. He swallowed, saying nothing.

He placed both arms around her, holding the horse's reins in front of her. "Don't move or you'll go back down again, and if you retch, well, you'll just have to live with it."

"Who are you? What do you want?"

He said nothing.

"Where are you taking me?"

His arms tightened about her waist. "Keep quiet," he said softly against her left ear.

Arielle sagged. It was too much. She'd been helpless for so long; then she had the first small, sweet taste of freedom. Now it was gone. He would probably ravish her and beat her. He was a man, and all of them did that extremely well. She would have given anything to have a pistol at that moment. Anything.

"What did you do to Geordie?"

Burke said nothing. He heard her fear and it bothered him. He tried to disguise his voice. "He is all right. He won't be harmed, I promise you."

"Please tell me what you want."

"In good time. Why don't you rest? Our ride is long."

Was the stupid man out of his mind? Rest! To their mutual surprise, she fell asleep, leaning back against him. He was relieved. He would have had to blindfold her to keep her from seeing where he was taking her.

"I'm indeed a madman," he said, looking straight between Dandy's ears.

He eased Arielle into the crook of his arm. He now was free to look at her to his heart's content. Her bonnet was a simple affair, pale yellow crepe and ribbons, and the bow beneath her chin was untied, the bonnet now on the back of her head. He couldn't keep his fingers away from her lovely hair. Soft and thick and that incredible color. He wished it were October. He rather thought the shade now more a mixture of brilliant fall leaves. I am become a fanciful madman, he thought. He gently pulled the bonnet off and tied its ribbons around the saddle pommel. He pulled the pins out of her hair, then smoothed out the mane with his fingers. He pictured her hair spread about her face, over his pillow, with him above her, his manhood pressing against her, and she was opening to him, welcoming him, yielding to him.

His own moan brought him out of that damnable erotic dream, and for the time being, he kept his eyes on the road ahead. Dandy moved at a steady pace. They had only about twelve more miles, their destination Knight Winthrop's small hunting box just two miles north of Shepherd Smeath.

When he looked down at her again, it seemed to him that she was regaining some of her color. Her pallor had alarmed him. Her mouth drew him, her lips so soft-looking and full, a pale pink color. And that straight little nose of hers. He could picture her nostrils flaring in anger. Their children would have stubborn jaws, he thought, running his fingertips lightly along hers.

Burke recognized the leaning road sign. It said Rowhams to the left and Shepherd Smeath to the right. He turned Dandy to the right. The road narrowed, and oak trees met over the road in a rich green canopy. He passed old Hookham's farm, situated just where Knight had promised it would be. The hunting box was set back from the road, a small, rectangular, two-story house, covered with ivy and smelling of rich summer rose and hibiscus blossoms.

Burke dismounted, holding Arielle carefully. It would suit him if she didn't awaken just yet. He managed to unlock the door and get her upstairs into the charmingly furnished master bedchamber. He covered her, then left, locking the door behind him. He settled Dandy into the small stable, then took himself back to the house.

When Arielle opened her eyes, she didn't move. She was no longer on a horse. No man was holding her. She kept herself perfectly still. Looking about, she realized she was lying on a bed canopied with rich blue brocade. A single knitted quilt was covering her. She was fully dressed, even her slippers still on her feet.

The man was nowhere to be seen.

Slowly, she sat up. There was no more nausea, nothing. She stood, took a step, and saw that the ribbon on her left slipper was unknotted. She leaned down and fastened it tightly. She straightened and looked around. She had no idea where she was. The room was neither predominantly masculine nor feminine, but the furnishings were expensive, she could tell that much. The armoire was oak and intricately carved, as was the small commode, and the pitcher and basin atop it were fine porcelain. The pale blue-and-green carpet was soft and lush.

The door was locked, of course. What had she expected? To find her reticule with her money still inside and an open door?

Arielle walked quickly to the wide window and pushed aside the draperies. She was on the second floor, but that made no difference to her. She quickly unlatched one window and shoved it outward. She climbed up on the ledge and looked down. It was a good twenty feet to the ground. At the very least she would break something and be in a worse fix than she was in now. Still . . .

The door opened.

Arielle whirled around. She clutched at the top of the window frame. "Burke," she whispered, so surprised that she couldn't think straight.

"Come down, Arielle. I don't wish you to hurt yourself."

"No," she said precisely and put one foot down on the stone ledge outside the window. "You stay away from me or I will jump."

"Why?"

"Why what?"

"Why would you want to jump out of the window?"

"All right. You are quite correct, I am being precipitous. First you will tell me what you want—then I will decide whether or not to jump."

This was sticky, he thought. He'd expected screams, yells, tears, whatever, but not a negotiator on a window ledge. She seemed perfectly calm.

"You wouldn't let me in your house," he said, an awful beginning, but for the moment his brain was betraying him.

"So? It is—was—my house. I didn't allow Evan there either, but he bribed that old fraud butler of mine."

"I wish I had known," Burke said. "I could have bribed him too."

"I repeat, my lord, what do you want?"

"I want to feed you, Arielle. It is late afternoon, you know. When was the last time you ate?"

She cocked her head at that and answered automatically, "An early breakfast."

"Well, then, I'll go fetch our dinner."

She watched him turn on his heel and stride toward the chamber door.

"Wait!" she shouted.

"Yes?" He didn't turn.

"This is ridiculous! I don't want anything to eat. I demand to know what I'm doing here."

"Soon," he said, closed the door after him, and locked it. Arielle was left standing with one foot inside, the other outside, not having the faintest idea of what to do. "This is all very strange," she said aloud, but still left the one foot outside.

Oddly enough, she wasn't really afraid now. Burke was a gentleman and he could be managed. At least she hoped so. But why had he abducted her? She saw him clearly in her mind, saw him pull her against him and kiss her. She felt his tongue against her lips, felt the heat of him. And she knew, of course; she knew what he wanted.

He wanted her to be his mistress. He would treat her as a man treated a woman, and it would be worse because she wouldn't be his wife. A mistress must be treated awfully badly. She put on her mental brakes. No. Perhaps mistresses were treated better than wives. After all, couldn't a mistress simply leave? She wasn't bound legally. Yes, being a mistress had to be preferable by far.

"Well, I won't do it," she said aloud to the silent room. She was already planning to move the armoire in front of the door. It looked strong enough to take a siege. She turned, about to climb back into the room when her skirt caught on the jagged stone edge and she was pulled backward out the window.

She screamed once.

# 7

Hobhouse Hunting Box

Arielle twisted about in the air and stared into Burke Drummond's startled face. Her only clear thought was: I'm going to smash him!

And she did. Burke, at the last moment, dropped the ladder and held out his arms. It didn't help. She landed against his chest, arms and legs churning, and sent both of them flying backward onto the ground.

It had rained the day before, and the grass was thick and springy. Thank God for no rocks, Burke thought. The breath was knocked out of him, but he didn't loose his hold on Arielle. She was locked against the length of him, his fingers laced together behind her back.

Arielle was terrified, not for herself, but for him. She tried to wrench herself free but couldn't. "Burke! Are you all right? Burke!"

He opened one eye to see her face very close to his, and she looked scared out of her wits. That was nice, he thought; she was worried that she'd killed him.

"Why did you jump?" he asked with an air of

great interest and with but the one eye open. He still wasn't able to cope with the other eye.

"Don't be ridiculous. I didn't. Let me go!"

"No, hold still. You're hurting me."

"You deserve it!"

Both eyes were well focused now. "Ha! If I hadn't been here, you silly half-wit, you would have broken a leg, an ankle, your damnable neck!" He moaned then for effect.

"All right, so you saved me from possible injury. Now let me go. I want to leave here. I must be on my way to Southampton. My ship leaves tomorrow and—"

"No," he said succinctly and closed both eyes.

He became aware of her body, sprawled atop him, one thigh between his legs, her breasts flattened against his chest. It would have been wonderful had he not been lying on his back on the ground, looking up at a sky that was no longer clear but filled with ominous, blackening clouds. Without warning or a word, he rolled onto his side, bringing her with him. They were nose to nose.

Consequences were beginning to force themselves into his brain, and the thought that she hated him so much, or feared him so much, that she was willing to jump was enough to give him pause.

"Why did you jump?"

She gave him a look of strained patience. "You are utterly absurd. I told you, I didn't jump. I was going to push the armoire in front of the door to keep you out, but my skirt got snagged on something outside the window and I got yanked out. Oh, God, it isn't fair! What do you want, Burke?

He was so relieved that she hadn't jumped that he wanted to sing. He wasn't as yet certain about dancing. So he said, "I want to get us inside. I just felt a raindrop on my left ear."

He hauled both of them to their feet. "Come along." He held her hand firmly, and when she dug in her heels, he simply dragged her around to the front of the hunting box.

"I must get to Southampton!" She tugged frantically at his hand. "Damn you, you're pulling my arm off!"

He said nothing, merely jerked her through the front door and slammed it.

"What have you done with Dorcas and Sam? Where is Geordie? If you've hurt them, I'll—"

"I would have pushed the armoire away easily enough," he interrupted. He released her then and watched her back away from him. Her hair was a tangled mess, her pale yellow dress ripped beneath her right arm, the ties of one slipper streaming behind her foot. She looked wonderful.

"The armoire is solid oak and very heavy."

"Nonetheless, I am a hero, as you once told me, and heroes can shove armoires aside with little effort."

"I want to leave now!"

He grinned at her. "Do you like this place? It belongs to a friend of mine. It's called Hobhouse. After whom, I haven't the foggiest notion. Rather pedestrian name, I think."

Arielle gave scant attention to the dark-beamed ceiling, the picturesque paneling, the diamond-paned windows. "I like this place about as much as I do you. Now, my lord, I wish to leave."

He took a step toward her and she shrank back. He stopped cold in his tracks. Now he saw fear in her eyes. He hated it. Of course any female of reasonable sensibilities would be feeling none too secure alone with a man who was not her husband in a hunting box that was stuck in the middle of nowhere, and that was exactly where Shepherd Smeath was.

"Don't be afraid," he said gently. "Come into the drawing room and have a sherry with me."

"I want to leave," Arielle repeated, not budging.

"You are not leaving just yet." He held out his hand, continuing in his best military commander's voice. "I will carry you, you know, if you don't obey me."

Obedience, she thought; that was what power brought. She had no doubt at all that he would force her to do whatever he wanted. At least a glass of sherry wasn't the height of humiliation. She shrugged, not looking at him, took two steps, and stumbled out of her slipper.

"Hold still," said Burke. He went down on one knee and tied the ribbons around her ankle. Arielle looked down at his thick dark brown hair. Paisley had had a bald spot directly on the top of his head. She shuddered, then forced herself to hold still.

"Done," said Burke and rose. He gave her his most engaging smile. "Not, of course, that I wouldn't have much preferred carrying you."

She slithered past him into the drawing room. He followed, went to the narrow sideboard, and poured each of them a glass of sherry.

When he handed the glass to her, he felt the chill of her fingers and frowned. "Are you cold?"

"No," she said. She was frightened.

"Very well. Do sit down, Arielle."

She sat. The drawing room was decorated as elegantly and simply as her upstairs bedchamber, the furnishings consisting of a pale blue silk sofa and two matching chairs with tables scattered about. There was but one carpet in the center of the room, and it was a rich rose color.

"I won't be your mistress," she said abruptly, without preamble. "I won't. So you might as well take me to Southampton now."

"My mistress," he repeated slowly, so surprised that his mind shut itself down for a long moment.

"That's correct. I won't do it."

Burke walked to the fireplace and leaned a shoulder against the mantelpiece. He gave his sherry a long meditative look, then said easily, "Perhaps I have missed something here. I've kept in pretty close touch with myself the past weeks, and I'm nearly certain that I've never asked you to be my mistress."

"I would hope that you already have one."

"Well, I do, as a matter of fact, but only until—"

"Excellent. Then leave me alone!" She tossed down the sherry and jumped to her feet.

"Sit down, Arielle."

She knew that preemptory male tone of voice and shivered. She sat, not daring to look at him, her eyes on her folded hands in her lap.

"You believe I am so desperate for a woman that I have to abduct one to satisfy my lust? You are not being remarkably complimentary, Arielle. Nor excessively reasonable."

"Well, no, it is just that . . . I don't know!"

"What makes you think I view you as good mistress material?"

She looked at him then, her eyes wide and confused. "Why else would you indulge in this elaborate ruse?"

"You believe that because you now are poor I wouldn't want you for anything else?"

"So you know about that, do you? Mr. Lapwing has been quite busy, I see."

"Yes, and most desirous of pleasing the Earl of Ravensworth. It was he who so obligingly told me of your proposed flight to America. He has a young, quite beautiful wife, you see, and so to capture an earl in his solicitor's net would make him a more appealing specimen to the lady."

She said nothing, but she knew all about old men and young wives. She couldn't really see Mr. Lapwing beating his wife, but one never knew, not really. Burke was making it sound as if the wife ruled Mr. Lapwing, a concept that was utterly alien to her.

"I *am* poor," Arielle said. As long as he was standing there by the fireplace, a good ten feet from her, her voice was cool and firm and she could attempt to reason with him. "Dreadfully poor. Indeed, that hundred pounds in my reticule is all I have in the world. I am going to live with my half sister in Boston."

"Actually," Burke said, ignoring her words, "Mr. Lapwing also told me about your half brother, Evan Goddis. A true bounder. And also about your dead husband's illegitimate son, Etienne DuPons. It gets complicated, does it not? Did you wish to marry that Frenchman? Did he back out when he realized you were poor?"

She stared at her hands, then at him. "Don't be mad," she snapped.

To her surprise, he laughed, a self-mocking laugh. "I am, my dear, but I cannot help it. Indeed, just today when I held up your carriage, I determined that there was no help for my condition. I've accepted it. But it is all your fault."

Everything a man did that he disliked he blamed on a woman. There was no surprise in that. Arielle didn't bother to contradict him. "I want to leave," she said again.

"I'm sorry, Arielle, but I can't let you go."

"But why not? Why are you doing this? You are a gentleman, are you not? You said you didn't want me for your mistress, so—"

"I can't seem to recall saying anything of the sort, but since you are so very certain, perhaps I don't indeed want you for my mistress. The more I think

about it, the more I'm convinced you're quite right.
I—"

"Stop mocking me!"

"All right," he said, and his voice and his expression were perfectly serious. "No, I don't want you for my mistress."

"Then, well . . . what is it?"

She looked at him, those large clear eyes of hers seeing right into his soul, if only she would really *see* with them. He took a very deep breath and plunged forward. "I want you for my wife."

Arielle drew back, pressing herself against the sofa. *Wife!* "You're mad," she whispered.

"I believe we've already agreed on that. I am serious, you know. I have wanted you since I met you at Bunberry Lake three years ago. I fought against it for a while for the simple reason that you were so damnably young. But you were always there, in my mind, with me in Spain and finally in France. Thinking of you after the Battle of Toulouse saved my sanity." He arched a brow at the word. "Perhaps 'sanity' isn't correct. Let me just say that you kept me whole amidst carnage that could destroy a man's soul. I didn't know you'd married until I came home. It turns out that Lannie's only truly important letter never got to me. But your husband is dead and I'm not and you're free. Marry me, Arielle. Be my countess, my lover, and the mother of a future earl."

Arielle stared at him, through him really, beyond to what he would do to her. She'd already seen him in that nightmare, and she saw him again clearly over her, able to hurt her as Paisley hadn't, seeing herself as the supplicant again, the slave to his master. She blinked and saw him now, his man's body, so tall and strong and powerful. So very controlled and self-assured. Invincible. The pain he would cause her, that was the reality of things, not the words he was saying. She wouldn't be able to ever escape him. Oh, God, the pain. A sob caught in her throat. She turned her head away, rose very slowly, and walked to the door.

"Arielle?"

Her hand closed on the silver lion's head handle.

"Don't go. Come back here."

She shook her head, not turning.

"Come here."

His man's stern voice.

She shook her head again and pushed down on the heavy latch. It clicked down but the door didn't open. His hand was pressed against it above her head. She hadn't even heard him come toward her. She closed her eyes for a moment, trying to get hold of herself. He said he wanted to marry her. It was insane, he was insane.

"What if I tell you that I don't want to marry you?" she whispered. She was terrified at her own words. What would he do? Would he strike her now?

Burke said nothing. He was looking down at her, wishing he could see what was in her mind. "Were you so much in love with your husband?"

She tasted bile. "Why would you think that?"

"You seem still to be grieving for him."

"No, I'm not," she said, and that was all.

"You will marry me, Arielle. I have made up my mind, you see, and if you feel I'm coercing you, well, then, I suppose you would be quite right. Consider yourself coerced. You will not leave until you're wed to me."

"No!" She whirled about as she yelled that one word and struck her fists to his chest. In the next instant, she brought up her knee, but he was faster and her knee struck his thigh. She felt his arms close around her, holding her so tightly that she couldn't move. Why had she done it? she wondered blankly. So stupid, so very stupid. Now he would hurt her. She felt the pain begin inside her, knowing what was to come. She'd not felt this pain for so many months, but she hadn't forgotten. She would never forget. She waited, unaware that she was crying, silently, hopelessly.

Burke slowly moved one hand up to press her head to his shoulder. "Shush," he said, kissing her hair, "it's all right, Arielle. No, no, love, don't cry. Please, don't."

"Let me go."

"Not yet. I have this most inexplicable need to protect my manhood. I am fortunate that you aren't a perfect markswoman."

She didn't understand his jesting, not at all. It was an act, it had to be an act to draw her in. He would turn on her in a flash. It was inevitable.

He was so strong. She had no chance. She didn't struggle, merely leaned against him, waiting. Waiting.

Nothing happened.

She continued to wait, and nothing continued to happen.

"Would you like a cup of tea, perhaps?"

"Yes," she said, praying he would release her. If she could put distance between them again, she'd be safe, at least for a while. She'd learned to think and live in minutes. She'd thought she'd forgotten that habit during the months after Paisley's death. It came back to her, as naturally as breathing.

"I don't understand you," Burke said, but he let her go and led her unresisting back to the sofa.

"Why would you care?"

"The better question is why would you believe that I wouldn't care? I have told you that I care for you mightily, that I wish to marry you."

"No, no, 'tis not that." Arielle waved a distracted hand. "You are a man," she blurted out, "and nothing I could do or say would make the slightest difference to you, so—"

"What? You think your feelings mean nothing to me?"

He seemed truly stunned.

"Very well, then my feelings you care so much about are these: I want to leave. I don't want to marry you or any man, ever. Ever, do you hear me?"

"Yes, I hear you. You are very nearly shouting. I'm glad there are no servants, else they would believe murder being done in the drawing room."

This jesting of his was wearing her down, flipping her about like a sheet hung out to dry on a windy day.

"Arielle," he said and took a step toward her.

She jumped, and paled, and Burke stopped cold. "What is the matter with you? I won't attack you. I have no intention of attacking you."

He was playing this man's game with rules she did not recognize. He was toying with her, something Paisley had rarely done, and never toward the end, simply because she was too experienced in his ways and couldn't be taken in. Burke was looking so sincere, so well-meaning. She shook her head. "Please," she whispered, aware that her body was straining against the sofa back.

He eased down beside her and took her hand. He felt her resistance even though her hand was as limp as it could be in his. "Will you wed me, Arielle?"

He felt the quiver run through her body. Arielle was looking at his hand covering hers. It as large, browned, a sprinkling of darker brown hair on the back. His fingers were long with blunt tips and short, well-buffed nails. Those hands could rip off her clothes and throw her down and slap her. Those hands could wield a whip. Those hands could encir-

cle her throat and squeeze until she fell unconscious.

"And if I don't? What will you do?"

He smiled at her, but she wasn't taken in. She
sat stiff and rigid.

He shrugged. "I will keep you here until you
agree. Or I could take you to France or to Italy. I
can't take you to visit your half sister until you are
legally my wife. My basic madness doesn't encom-
pass that much trust."

She gave him the most pathetically hopeful look
he'd ever seen. "You would truly take me to visit
Nesta and the baron?"

"Once you are married to me, I will take you any
place you wish to go."

She shook her head. "No, no, I know you
wouldn't. You are lying to me.'

"No, I'm not. I do wish you would stop looking at
this as if I were trying to toss you into Newgate
prison. I will take you to your half sister, Arielle, I
promise."

"Would you really? Truly?"

He smiled at the myriad shifting expressions on
her beloved face. It struck him that in her current
state of mind she might even marry him in order
to be able to leave him flat. She was remaining an
exquisite mystery to him. He started to tell her that
he would take her to Boston as soon as he'd gotten
her with child. But no, he kept quiet. Let her make
plans to leave him. He would weave the magic
around her that she'd so carelessly and easily woven around him three years before.

He could do it. He had to. He had to believe that,
or this madness would all be for naught.

He released her hand, leaned back, crossed his
arms over his chest, and crossed his ankles. "Marry
me and we'll start making plans for your visit immediately." He was grinning at her.

You are a handsome man, she thought, willing to give him that much. But you are still a man. "Why don't you want someone who wants you? It is quite absurd, you know, what you've done."

"My only other choice was to follow you to America. I didn't want to take that chance. The two countries are still at war. I didn't want to take any risks with your safety."

She could only stare at him. "To save me you abducted me?"

"That's about it, I expect."

Suddenly, without warning, Arielle saw herself as she had been three years before, her heart in her eyes as she'd looked upon this magnificent hero who'd been, remarkably, aware of her. She was hearing his deep voice, teasing, gentle, mocking— when it suited him. Just as he was now. Arielle shook her head at herself. That girl might as well be on another continent, another world. She no longer existed, the stupid little fool. But what about Burke? She'd been scared to contemplate that he truly had been interested in her; after all, a perfect god such as he caring about a silly girl? Still, she'd nurtured every romantic fantasy about him until her father had died so suddenly that bright fall afternoon.

Then she had learned to grieve. Then she had been married off to Paisley Cochrane and learned the truth of things.

And the truth was that men used women just as they used their horses or their dogs or their servants. They used them because they were the stronger. She said abruptly, "Do you really have a mistress?"

"Yes, but as soon as we're married, I won't. Actually, since I have no intention of ever letting you out of my sight again, I think I'm now disqualified from having a mistress any longer."

*Because you will do all the things to him that she does now.* Arielle nearly cried out.

Perhaps if he kept his mistress, then he would leave her alone more often than not. "What is her name?" she asked, deciding to back into this argument, doing her best to be subtle.

"Laura." He cocked his head at her. "Why the devil do you want to know that?"

She shrugged. "It is a nice name. It would seem to me that you would want to keep her rather than leave her."

Burke couldn't quite believe this conversation. Arielle seemed perfectly serious. It was something of a blow to his self-image, no doubt about that. "No, I wouldn't do that. I don't believe that a married man should be disloyal or unfaithful to his wife."

That was something she couldn't grasp. That girl from three years ago could have, but not Arielle Leslie Cochrane, Lady Rendel. "I cannot see that it is at all important or has any bearing on anything."

"You mean that you would have no compunction, were you my wife, to taking a lover?"

She laughed at that. It was so utterly ludicrous a proposition. She choked. "A lover?"

"Does that mean you would or you wouldn't?"

She shook her head, laughter still bubbling in her throat.

"This is a very strange conversation we're having, Arielle. Will you wed me?"

She stopped laughing. She looked at him, not at all fooled by his negligent presentation, and was afraid to say no again. Surely his man's rules had to veer off into violence quite soon now; they simply had to. "I—I don't know. I would ask you for some time to think about it."

"That's a start," Burke said, smiling at her.

She breathed a sigh of relief. She'd said the right thing. His temper was still in place. She rose very slowly, half expecting to be jerked back down, but he didn't touch her. "I think I should like a nap now."

"You won't jump out the window, will you?"

"No, I shan't."

But she was thinking about knotted sheets.

"Oh, my dear, another trifling matter. Money. I took your hundred pounds. If you do manage to get to the ground intact, without me there beneath you, you will find yourself quite without any means of going anywhere."

She whirled about on a cry. "No! You had no right to steal my money! God, I hate you!" She got the door open this time and dashed upstairs.

Burke didn't move. She'd been going to escape him, or try. He should simply let her go, the objective man said. But he couldn't. He firmly believed that he could make her love him. He had to believe it or truly go mad. He rose and left the drawing room. He would give her a few minutes—not enough to knot any sheets together—then fetch her. He would simply have to keep her in the master bedchamber. The windows were long and narrow, too narrow even for her to squeeze through.

He didn't imagine that she would like that at all.

It was just too bad. He walked slowly up the stairs, picturing her on his bed, her clothing magically strewn on the floor, her thighs parted, her . . .

He frowned at himself and turned his mind from that delightful image. He thought about the conversation in the drawing room, if one could call that disjointed chaos a conversation. Her behavior was inexplicable to him. Cowering one minute, defiant the next. It made no sense to him. He would come to understand her and she him. He would not swerve from his course. He couldn't. Was she lying?

Was she still grieving for her husband? No, he didn't think so. Something wasn't right, and it wasn't simply her alarming aversion to him. Ah, well, he had all the time in the world to discover every thought in her head.

He considered the evening ahead. She wasn't going to like it at all.

"That is just too bad," he said aloud to one of the time-darkened portraits that hung on the wall at the landing. "I'm doing what is best for both of us."

# 8

It was dark early because of the storm. Arielle was sitting quietly on the edge of the bed, looking blankly toward the windows. Rain pounded against the glass. Damp seeped into the room. She vigorously rubbed her arms, thinking that even if she had had sheets to knot, she couldn't escape on a night like this. Arielle sighed and wondered what the devil she was going to do. She didn't really want to sleep on the raw mattress. Burke had followed her upstairs, come into her chamber, and stripped the sheets off the bed. He'd only smiled at her, saying nothing.

She heard his footsteps in the corridor and rose, tensing a bit. The single candle she'd lit on the small table beside the bed was nearly gutted.

"Arielle? Come along, you must have your dinner. I have prepared it, and it is your responsibility to be most impressed by my culinary talent."

She wasn't certain what she'd expected him to say, but that amused voice speaking nonsense wasn't it. He'd abducted her, for heaven's sake! She called out, "A man—an earl especially—doesn't go near the kitchen, nor does a man cook for a woman."

"All right, I cooked dinner primarily for me, but

you may have a bit, if you are very nice. Will you join me?"

"I'm coming," she called. Of course she'd come down. What choice did she have? It was what he wanted, after all. She didn't bother looking at herself in the mirror. She saw no reason to give herself a fright. She smoothed down her gown, looked vaguely at the tear under her right arm, picked up the single candle, and opened the door. He stood in the corridor.

She looked like a ragamuffin and so wonderful that he was hard pressed not to pull her into his arms and kiss her until she was silly. He smiled and offered her his arm.

"My lady? Shall we?"

He'd changed into evening clothes, and looked every inch the lord of the manor. His linen was pristine white, his breeches and form-fitted coat stark black. She said nothing. She saw before her an awesome task. She had to convince him—a man—that he didn't want her, that he should let her go. Her present appearance should have assisted in that goal, but it appeared that either he was myopic or he simply had no sense.

"I made ham sandwiches," he said as he led her into the small wainscoted dining room to the right off the entrance hall. The table sat no more than eight, and the table and chairs, unlike the other furnishings, had a Spanish look, all heavy, dark wood, intricately carved.

"Actually, I sliced the ham and the bread and put the pieces on the same platter, almost a sandwich. And there is turtle soup, a gift from the housekeeper, who lives nearby. I had nothing to do with the wine save uncork it with remarkable precision." He held out a chair for her.

He hadn't seated her at one end of the table, rather at his right. It was too close to him, but she forced herself to ease into the chair. "Shall I serve you some soup? I'm sorry, but it is quite green."

"It is supposed to be," she said and nodded. She was ravenous, and her stomach gave a notable growl.

At last she'd said something, Burke thought, seating himself. She was eating the soup now, hopefully finding it to her liking. He saw her reach for the salt shaker and give it a liberal shake. He tasted his own soup and held out his hand for the condiment. They ate in silence. It wasn't a particularly comfortable silence, but then again it wasn't particularly uncomfortable either.

The dining room was in shadows, all save the table, which held a single branch of candles lighting the turtle soup and the two of them. And her beautiful hair. She hadn't even bothered to comb out the tangles, but Burke didn't mind. He liked her hair wild and free, tumbling down her back.

"It is odd, you know," he said after finishing off his soup, "but it is a most invigorating task to find a topic of conversation that is of acceptable interest to the lady I was forced to abduct. She isn't all that receptive to me as yet, you see, and I have no wish to make her unhappy or frighten her. By any chance, would you have a suggestion?"

"Let the lady leave. She is most discreet, you know, and she will not tell a single soul anything. However, you must also tell her what you have done with her servants so she may fetch them. And her horses and her carriage."

"But I am most concerned about her reputation. After all, she is alone in the company of a man who is not yet her husband—"

"She cares not one whit about her reputation. She could be alone with you for a year and still it wouldn't matter."

That had to be a clanker, he thought, and served himself some ham. "Would you care for some?"

Arielle served herself. There was a pall of silence that lasted through Burke's sandwich.

"Actually," Burke said, picking up his wineglass and swishing the deep red bordeaux about, "the lady is wonderful, albeit a puzzle, and the gentleman wants her to know that and believe he is telling the truth."

"The lady cannot believe it," she said, very quietly, and gave him a quick look.

"Why the hell not?"

"Please, my lord—"

"Burke."

"All right. Burke. The lady isn't that much of a fool. Please, enough of this silliness. Let me go. 'Tis true, I won't tell anyone—"

"Stop talking, Arielle."

She did, instantly, becoming as still as the fork beside her plate.

"I didn't mean for you to turn into a statue on me or stop breathing. I simply want you to cease your Greek chorus, for it will do you no good. I am not going to let you go. I am going to teach you that you can't live without me." There, he'd said it. "I'm going to teach you to love me, and that's all there is to it. You wouldn't give me the chance before, so I've given it to myself."

"Love you," she repeated slowly, turning her head to stare at him.

"That's right."

"That's impossible."

"Why?"

She nearly shouted at him that love was a hoax perpetrated by men to draw women in. But she controlled herself. She had to be logical, convincing. "You are remembering another girl, Burke. You doubtless found her enchanting because she worshipped you so obviously. But that girl is dead. You lost her. She lost herself. Go find another. I am sorry, but I would not lie to you. She is dead."

"That girl, my dear, is sitting next to me. She didn't die, she simply grew up. If you are referring to your loss of innocence, I care not that you aren't a virgin, that you've known another man. I truly don't. Believe it, Arielle. I have wished that I'd married you when you were sixteen, but I didn't and what's done is done. It is ridiculous to don a horsehair shirt and wail about the past. What I want is a future with you, and I fully intend to have it."

"But I don't want you!"

"I can't believe that. I won't believe it. You loved me once, you will love me again."

She wanted to scream at him. Instead, narrowing her eyes, she said, "Not only did I know another man, I knew several. In fact, I have no innocence, none at all. I know quite a lot. Too much, perhaps. Probably more than a mistress knows. I am not a lady wife, not at all an appropriate female for a countess, surely. Go find yourself a sweet innocent in her first season, Burke."

"You had lovers, Arielle?"

"I find that word strangely inaccurate."

"You had other men in your bed, then? Your husband was old, and you were lonely and you were seduced?"

She would disgust him; she saw her way clearly now. She would repel him so thoroughly that he would be quite content to send her on her way. "Not seduced, no. I did the seducing. And you were quite right about his illegitimate son, Etienne. He enjoyed me most thoroughly." That was the truth, she thought, bile rising in her throat. "As I did him." She had trouble getting those words out of her mouth. She hadn't realized it would be so difficult to speak like this.

"Did your husband know of it?" He sounded calm, very nearly disinterested, and Arielle was so caught up in shaping her lie and keeping herself from retching at her own words that she didn't notice his underlying anger.

"Certainly he knew. He . . . approved."

"Why did you marry him?"

*Because I was told to, and I didn't ever imagine that I had a choice, and I was only sixteen and so innocent and grieving about my father and . . .* She could only shake her head. She looked down at the remnants of her ham. The words came out easily enough. "He was rich."

"Not that rich. If you'd wanted money, you should have waited for me. I told you I would come back to you."

"Only a silly idiot would have believed that."

It was indeed curious, Burke was thinking. She was mixing truth with lies, and he wasn't exactly certain which was which. "The bird-in-the-hand theory?"

It had been Evan's theory, evidently. She nodded. Of course, she'd never told her half brother about the Earl of Ravensworth. She hadn't told him much of anything. She'd been married to Paisley Cochrane without so much as a by-your-leave. That pale, sad-eyed girl in the small church, not really understanding, not until that night when he'd ripped off her nightgown and . . . She let out a small cry.

Burke clasped her hand. "What is wrong? What were you thinking?"

"Nothing," she said, and the word came out on a gasp.

"All right," he said. He sat back in his chair and clamped down on his frustration. "You and I have been fencing about for a good while now. I want it to stop. I want you to understand something, Arielle, very clearly. Tonight you will come with me to my bedchamber. You will sleep with me."

She'd never slept with a man. "Why?"

He cocked his head at her.

"Why would you want to sleep with me? That sounds rather curious."

He was confused. "You mean . . . no, forget that. Let me make myself perfectly clear. You will sleep with me after I have made love to you."

He knew he'd get a reaction, but the one he got wasn't at all what he'd expected. She threw her plate with its ham slices at his head. Arielle was out of her chair and in the entrance hall before he had peeled the last ham slice from over his left eye.

"Arielle!" He was out of his own chair, knocking it flat. He saw her tugging furiously at the front-door knob, and it finally turned and she was outside in an instant. He was six steps behind her. He shouted her name again but she didn't stop. If anything, she ran all the faster.

It was still raining hard, thick cold rain that soaked him in three steps. He was furious with her. He was scared for her. He didn't really know what he was. He saw her running toward the stable, her hair flying out behind her, becoming quickly matted to her head, her skirts sodden, dragging her down.

She felt a stitch in her side and ignored it. The stable was dark and smelled of horse, leather, linseed oil, and hay. No light, she thought foolishly. She heard a horse whinny and rushed toward the sound. Then she heard the stable door slam shut.

Burke knew where the lantern was. He felt his way to it and after several frustrated minutes managed to get it lit. He held it up. He saw Arielle pressed against the far wall of the stable. In her hand she held a riding crop. Her breasts were heaving, her nipples taut against the soaked bodice of her gown. But he kept his eyes on her pale face.

"Don't come near me!"

He hadn't expected anything like this. She looked wild, nearly hysterical. "All right," he said mildly, set the lantern down on a bale of hay, and slowly straightened to lean against he empty stall next to his horse's.

"Really, I mean it!"

"I see that you do. Now what is this all about?"

She held up the riding crop and her voice was shaking, from fear, from the cold, he didn't know. "Go away. I am leaving. I will hit you with this if you don't."

"You will? I wonder if you can." Enough was enough, he thought, and pushed away from the stall. He walked toward her, his step purposeful, and she was so afraid she thought she would die of it. Paralyzing fear, the kind she'd known for so long, flooded her. She closed her eyes, and in the next instant, struck out with the crop.

It connected and she heard him suck in his breath. Burke grabbed her wrist and calmly wrested the riding crop from her hand.

"That hurt," he said and released her. He stepped back, the crop still in his hand. He rubbed his arm, and she saw how it had sliced through his coat sleeve.

Arielle was beyond thought. She saw that crop, saw that he held it with great familiarity, and knew that she'd gone too far. She'd lost her head and now she would pay for it. "Please don't hurt me," she whispered, her eyes never leaving the riding crop. "Please."

"You hurt me," he said, wondering what the devil he was supposed to do now.

"I—I will do as you please," she managed.

"You know what it is I want, Arielle."

"All right, please, just don't—"

He watched in utter bewilderment as she began to pull open the long row of buttons up the front of her gown. She was shaking with fear and cold. Some of the buttons were recalcitrant and she ripped them off.

She wanted him to make love with her here, in the stable? Wet? In the hay? He suddenly felt the most bizarre sensation. He was outside himself, looking down on the Earl of Ravensworth and the shaking girl who was nearly ripping off her clothes, so great was her frenzy.

He took a step toward her, and she quickly looked up, throwing her hands out in front of her, as if to ward him off. "I'm hurrying," she gasped. "Please, just another moment."

He watched the ripped, sodden gown fall to her waist, then to the hay-strewn floor of the stable. Her chemise was without any lace, a stout linen. Wet, it showed her breasts and nipples clearly. She was frantic now, ripping the narrow straps of her chemise, pulling free the knots on her petticoats. In another moment she was untying her slippers and yanking off her stockings. Then she was naked and she was standing, holding herself still in front of him, her arms at her sides, her hands fisted.

Burke stared at her.

"Please," she whispered yet again. He watched her walk to him, watched her fall to her knees in front of him. He felt her fingers on the buttons of his breeches. She got them unfastened with amazing speed. He was hard and ready, painfully so, and she was naked, for him, and she was on her knees . . .

He felt her hands slide up his thighs, felt her hands slip into his breeches, cup him, and then she was leaning forward and drawing him out and taking him into her mouth. He froze. His mouth opened, then closed. He couldn't believe this.

"What the hell are you doing?"

She stared up at him, her eyes wild, her pupils dilated. "Please, I will do it as you like, but just give me a moment, please, just give me a chance . . ."

And that other Burke was staring down at the girl he loved, at the girl he'd wanted to marry for so long. He heard that Burke moan as she took him more deeply into her mouth, as he felt the experienced fingers caressing him, felt her tongue and her mouth . . .

He grasped her naked shoulders. "Stop it!"

She fell back on her knees. She started to cover herself with her arms and hands; then, just as quickly, she dropped her hands and rested them, palms down, on her thighs. Her breathing was shallow and harsh.

Burke stared at her, trying to think, trying to understand. His manhood was still throbbing and swollen, still wild for her; and angrily, he straightened himself, and fastened his breeches.

"Why?" he said finally. He saw her shivering violently, and cursed. He reached over for her discarded gown, stopping cold when she burst into frantic speech.

"Please, don't! If you would just tell me what you want, just give me a little more time, I can do it, I swear!"

She was looking, not at him but at her gown, in a wet heap on the straw. Her eyes were nearly opaque with fear and her face was as pale as her white belly. He shook his head and reached for her gown.

She screamed. "No, please!"

"Arielle, I don't understand you. Now what—" He gaped at her. She'd scrambled away from him and was pressed against the wall, her knees drawn up, her arms wrapped around them. She looked like a small wild animal trapped by a merciless hunter.

"Arielle?" If possible, she bound herself into an even smaller ball, but at least she was looking at him. Her damp hair tumbled around her shoulders and down her back. "I was simply going to get your gown for you." He spoke very quietly, very slowly. She didn't move. The small animal trapped and frozen, the eyes watchful, waiting. Then he looked at her, really looked this time, and followed her exact line of vision. He realized blankly that she wasn't looking at her gown but was staring at the riding crop near it on the floor. He felt his breathing hitch up, felt a fury that he couldn't seem to control or understand. "You believe I would whip you?"

A whoosh of air came out of her and she jumped to her feet. "No," she yelled, "no more!" And she ran toward the stable door.

He was closer this time, but still she was slick with rain when he caught her. "Stop it!" It took a good deal of his strength to subdue her. This is insane, he thought, as he half dragged her, half carried her back to the stable. "Stop fighting me, dammit! We have to get your gown and the lantern."

She heard only his irritation, his anger. "You want the riding crop!"

Oh, God, he thought. He grabbed up her gown, wrapped it around her as best as he could, then picked up the lantern only to realize that he couldn't handle both her struggling body and the damned lantern. He doused it and strode from the stable, trying to hunker over her to protect her from the rain.

Burke didn't stop until he had set her on her feet in his bedchamber. She clutched the drenched gown in front of her. Quickly, he fetched his blue velvet dressing gown. He pulled the gown from her and she stood quietly, her eyes on the floor, as he helped her into the dressing gown. He tied the waist and stepped back. "Hold still," he said and left her to get some towels.

When he returned, she hadn't moved. "Come to the fireplace and sit down."

"There's no fire," she said.

"There will be as soon as I can manage it. Here, dry your hair while I make one up."

He found his hands were steady and that relieved him. This entire situation had to be relegated to a bizarre dream brought on by overindulging in snails or something equally as strange. In a few moments, he sat back on his haunches and regarded his handiwork. He wadded up more paper, tossing it in, and the flames stretched and roared upward. "Come closer, Arielle."

He turned as he spoke. She was very calmly drying her long hair, her face expressionless. She wasn't looking at him. It didn't seem to him that she was looking at anything. He rose and stretched out his hand. She ignored him and slipped off the chair, moving to stand by the fire. His dressing gown was long enough on her to be a train on a wedding gown, he thought. He pulled her chair closer, then motioned to her.

She sat down again, still silent. He went to the dressing table and picked up his comb. He pulled a chair close to hers, sat down, and took a long, thick tress of hair and began to comb it. Arielle looked at him now. She didn't understand him. Very slowly, very tentatively, she pulled away and said, "Let me do it, please."

He handed her the comb. "I will change out of my wet clothes," he said, as much to himself as to her. There was no screen in the room. Modesty was an exclusively female preserve. Yet he felt strange about undressing in the same room with her. In fact, it was silly, he knew, but he'd felt not only embarrassed when she'd freed his manhood and stroked him and kissed him, but also, in a sense, violated. He drew a deep breath, seeing that she wasn't really aware of him at all, and took off his clothing. He slipped on his one other dressing gown, a deep burgundy velvet, so old that the elbows were nearly worn through.

She'd finished combing her hair. It was only slightly damp now. He stood over her, wondering what the devil he should do. The enormity of the situation was still seeping into his mind. He felt helpless, completely at a loss.

"Arielle," he said very quietly, "we must talk, but first I'm going to get you a brandy."

When he returned, she was silent and still as a stone.

He came in front of her and eased down on his haunches. She drew back, of course; he had expected that. Even the undisguised fear in her eyes wasn't much of a surprise, but still it shook him profoundly. "Here, drink the brandy. It will warm you." The laudanum he'd put in it should also help her sleep well; at least he hoped so.

She stared at the liquid as if it were the vilest poison on the earth. His eyes narrowed, and she saw that and quickly took the glass. She downed the brandy, coughing and wheezing at its savage warmth.

He took the glass from her. "Now, tell me why you ... well, why you did what you did to me in the stable."

She looked at him as if he were insane, utterly without a grain of sense, and blurted out, "I didn't think you wanted me to take the time to undress you. It was cold in the stable and I didn't think you wanted to be cold. I only did what I thought would please you. You wouldn't tell me what to do and I tried to . . . did you want me to undress you?"

He closed his eyes against her words. He couldn't bear to hear anymore now. "Arielle, enough." There was sharpness in his voice, sharpness he didn't hear, but she did and froze. Burke looked into the roaring flames in the fireplace. "I didn't ask you to service me," he said finally.

"Service you," she repeated slowly. "Does that mean caressing you and taking you in my mouth and—"

"Yes, it does. I didn't ask you to do that."

Again she looked at him strangely.

"Why did you do it?"

"You had the riding crop," she said, as if stating the most obvious fact in the world to the greatest half-wit. He saw that her fingers were pleating and unpleating the folds of velvet.

"No, you had the riding crop and you struck me with it. I didn't do a blessed thing." He unconsciously rubbed his left upper arm. The whip hadn't broken his skin, but it throbbed nevertheless.

Suddenly she looked very young and very lost. "I don't believe you! You would have! You're just trying to draw me in, but I won't do it, do you hear?" She jumped to her feet, took two steps, and tripped on the overly long dressing gown. He caught her and brought her against him.

"You must stop running away from me. I will always catch you, you know, and I always will. Now, I'm going to put you to bed."

She stiffened like a board.

"No, tonight I won't make love to you. You need to sleep, Arielle. We will work all this out in the morning."

She didn't believe him, not for an instant. "I want to go to my own bedchamber."

"There are no sheets."

"I don't care."

"No."

He led her to the bed, pulled back the covers, and turned to her, saying, "Come in between the sheets, that's a good girl."

He tucked her up as he would a child. And she stared at him, watchful and wary and distrusting as she clutched at the blankets under her chin.

"We will work all of this out when you're rested."

He doused the candle, sending the raised bed into shadows, and walked back to the fireplace. And when I'm rested, he added silently to himself. He locked his bedchamber door and pocketed the key. Then he returned to the fireplace, eased his weary body into the chair, and stared into the flames. She'd serviced him with the expertise of an experienced whore. It angered him so greatly that he trembled from the force of it. And that damned riding crop.

It was silent in the room, save for the slashing rain on the windows. He heard a rumble of deep thunder, followed a few moments later by a white slash of lightning. What the devil was he to do?

He was nearly asleep when he heard the muffled sob. He didn't move a muscle. Another sob. Another. Then a low moan, followed by a choked scream.

He jumped to his feet and rushed to the bed.

# 9

Burke quickly lit a candle beside the bed. He'd expected a nightmare, but when he looked down at her, she wasn't tossing or flailing about. She seemed to be sleeping soundly. Then she moaned softly and turned her head slowly to and fro on the pillow. Her face was flushed, her breathing harsh and jerky, and when he lightly laid his palm on her forehead, he felt dry heat. She had the fever. He cursed softly.

"Arielle," he said urgently, and gently shook her shoulders. "Wake up. You're dreaming."

She heard the man's voice and it was him, she knew it. He was standing in the shadows of the stable, and this was the first time he'd spoken. He was calling her name clearly, then mumbling things she couldn't understand. He was smiling at her and reaching out his hand to her. His other hand was behind his back.

"Arielle."

He was calling her again. She wanted to believe him, wanted to run to him. Suddenly he brought his other hand from behind his back. In it he held a riding crop. Then he was laughing and telling her that she must be punished for her clumsiness. *Why are you laughing?* she screamed at him, but she could hear no sound from her throat. She saw the whip come down, and saw her naked body as if from a distance, but no, she didn't feel the whip, the ripping pain. Still, she screamed, cowering.

"Dammit, wake up!"

He was shaking her, and she fought like a wild thing.

Burke eased into bed beside her and pulled her against the length of him. She continued struggling but he held her still, one of his legs holding hers immobile.

"Hush," he said, cradling her head between his two hands. "Hush, love."

She felt his hands on her and his warm breath against her ear. It wasn't a dream. He was holding her and he would hurt her and she was terrified.

"Please," she whispered, "please don't hurt me."

Burke closed his eyes a moment against that awful emptying pain her words brought. He wished that Paisley Cochrane weren't dead. He wished he were right here so he could kill him. It would give Burke the greatest pleasure. "No, Arielle, no, I won't hurt you. I swear I will never hurt you."

She didn't believe him, but his voice sounded gentle, sincere. He was lying, he had to be. She realized in that moment that she didn't feel right. Her head felt heavy with thudding pain; her throat was raw, her chest tight.

"Please go away."

"Your forehead is hot. You have a fever."

She felt his warm breath against her left temple, felt the wonderful heat from his body.

Burke sighed. "It would help if you would trust me."

"Go away."

He did. He fetched a discarded towel, dipped one end of it into the water in the basin atop the commode. "Hold still," he said and began wiping her face.

The wet cloth felt glorious, and unconsciously she

searched it out, pressing her cheek into its coolness. He continued, knowing he should rub down her body as well, but he didn't. He didn't want her fighting him again.

Finally she fell back asleep. Lightly Burke touched her forehead. She was cool. He hoped that now she would be all right. Just a slight cold perhaps. He added more blankets, tucked them all under her chin, and stood over her, wondering what the hell he should do now. Sleep, he thought, and climbed into bed beside her. He didn't touch her.

When he awoke, it was light. The rain had stopped and sunlight poured through the long narrow windows. He turned his head on the pillow. Arielle was still sleeping.

For a moment he smiled, thinking that this was the way it would be for the rest of their lives. He would sleep with her and wake with her every morning. Then he remembered.

Slowly, he rose, careful not to disturb her. After he'd bathed and dressed, he returned to the bed and again felt her forehead. She was burning up.

"Oh, God, no," he said to the silent room. He stood quietly for but another instant; then, his decision made, he strode from the bedchamber.

Close to an hour later, he led the barrel-chested Scotsman, Dr. Armbruster, into the room.

"Ye said yer wife became ill quite suddenly, my lord?"

"Yes," Burke said and stood on the other side of the bed. "I kept wiping her face with a cool cloth until the fever was down. When I woke up this morning, as I told you, she was like this."

Dr. Armbruster was leaning over her. Arielle opened her eyes, saw the strange man, and screamed. She was weak, but she managed to pull her arms free of the covers and strike at him. Dr. Armbruster grabbed her wrists, saying to Burke,

"I daresay, my lord, that she wasn't like this or you wouldn't have left her. She's locked into her mind with the fever. Delirium. Hush, my lady, hush. Come here, my lord, and hold her for me. I need to listen to her lungs."

Burke did as he was told. He'd never been so afraid in his life. He tried to soothe her, calm her, but it was no use. She had no idea who he was, but in her mind, he wasn't a nice man. He was beginning to believe that there was no such thing as a nice man. He continued speaking to her, nonsense really, anything to distract both Arielle and him.

Dr. Armbruster straightened. A Scot, he was fond of saying, might not know what ails ye, but he'll ne'er kill ye with remedies. "Here is what we must do, my lord." He gave Burke exact instructions, adding, "I will ask the housekeeper for Hobhouse to return; also the maid. I can have a local woman come and nurse her."

"No, I will do that," said Burke. "She will be all right, will she not, sir?"

Dr. Armbruster was a straightforward man, usually blunt to a fault, but the desperate fear he saw in the young earl's eyes made him moderate his speech. "She is young, and despite her rather fragile appearance, I think she is strong. We will see, my lord. I shall come back late this afternoon."

As he left Hobhouse, Dr. Armbruster decided to have the vicar visit. It couldn't hurt.

Two hours later saw Mrs. Ringlestone, the cook and housekeeper, and Ruby, the maid, installed again in Hobhouse.

"She's either freezing or burning up," said Mrs. Ringlestone as Burke came into the bedchamber after leaving briefly. "Poor little dear. Try to see if she won't drink some of my beef soup. She won't for me."

Burke nodded and sat beside her. "Arielle," he

said sternly, knowing that she wouldn't respond to a cajoling voice. "Open your mouth. Come now."

She made no sign that she'd heard him.

"Open your mouth, girl! Do as I tell you!"

She did this time, without hesitation, and he managed to pour a good half cup of the soup down her throat. If Mrs. Ringlestone thought him rather rough, she didn't say anything. After all, he got results.

" 'Twill be a long night," she said.

It was, as a matter of record, the longest night of Burke's life. He decided toward dawn that Arielle was going to die. And there was nothing he could do to save her, nothing Dr. Armbruster could do. One moment she was thrashing about, completely out of her mind; the next, she was so pale and still and limp he nearly choked on his own tears. He finally fell into an exhausted sleep, his fingers over her wrist, feeling her pulse to reassure himself that she still lived.

"Why is she giving up?" Dr. Armbruster spoke more to himself than to Burke the following day. "I don't understand it. She is young, beautiful, and not long married, I fancy. Why?"

In that instant, Burke made a decision. He spoke at some length with Dr. Armbruster. The doctor left to pay his overdue visit to the vicar. While Burke waited, he sat beside Arielle and began his ritual of stroking the cool, damp cloth over her face.

He spoke of the past, as he usually did. It passed the time and it seemed to keep her calm. On some level, he was certain that she heard him and understood. "My brother, you know how he was, Arielle, all bluff and good-natured, loved jests as much the dozenth time as the first. Well, he also had the most stubborn streak you can imagine. I was usually the recipient of it. He made up his mind about something, and nothing I could ever say or do would change it. I remember once—Lord, that was so long ago—Father gave me a pony. Victor was his name. He was dun-colored, strong as the devil, and he ate his head off. Well, my brother wanted Victor. The instant he saw him, he wanted him. Strange as it may sound, the pony wanted my brother just as much. But he was mine. And I would be damned before I gave him up. Do you know what my brother did?"

"My lord, the vicar is here." Burke momentarily ignored Mrs. Ringlestone.

"Well, no, my brother didn't call the vicar, not that time." Burke quickly rose to face the frail old man. He was very slight, with scraggly hair and a gentle, tired smile. He smiled at Burke now and shook his hand. "It is good of you to come, sir," Burke said. "Please sit down. I have something very important to ask you." He told him what he wanted.

The vicar, seeing nothing at all amiss with the earl's analysis of the situation, nodded, saying, "I must ask my bishop, of course, my lord, but—"

"You realize that time is of the essence. She could die anytime."

"Oh, dear, of course you are right. What shall I do?"

"Simply perform the ceremony. I myself will speak to the bishop later, after she is well or . . ." He couldn't say the word. Finally he managed to continue. "Surely the bishop will agree. It is an emergency, after all."

"It is most irregular, my lord, but still . . . I can't think it bad, no, not at all. Perhaps we can get the special license later."

"I shall fetch our witnesses."

"But her responses, my lord—she won't be able to say that she agrees or not."

"Of course she will," Burke said. "Please prepare

yourself, sir. I will bring the women here immediately."

Thirty minutes later Burke was seated on the bed beside Arielle, holding her hand. She was delirious, but that was just as well for the moment.

Dr. Armbruster stood on the other side of the bed. Mrs. Ringlestone and Ruby stood behind the vicar.

"Dear beloved," the vicar began. "We are here for an act of mercy and an act of grace and goodness. We will unite this—"

"It wasn't like that!" Arielle suddenly yelled.

"No, I know it wasn't." Burke's voice was pitched low. "Hush now, love. You're getting married."

"He won't get away with it!"

"No, certainly not. I shan't let him. Trust me."

The vicar cleared his throat. "Well, let me see . . . this man and this woman will unite their lives, God willing, and—"

"Father, please don't leave me!"

"I'm sorry, love. No, Arielle, I won't leave you. Never."

". . . what the Lord our God has ordained, let no man put asunder."

"Amen," said Burke.

"Now, Lady Rendel, you must repeat after me. "I, Arielle Leslie Cochrane, do solemnly take you, Burke Carlyle, ah, Beresford Drummond, for my wedded husband—"

"She can't do that," said Burke. "When you wish her to say 'I do,' tell me."

"I will not go with you! Never!"

"No, sweetheart, I wouldn't expect you to."

" '. . . till death do us part.' She should say 'I do,' my lord."

"Arielle, listen to me. No, damn you, listen!" He grasped her chin between his fingers and held her still. In his hardest voice, he instructed, "Say 'I do,' Arielle. Say it now, or you will regret it."

"I do."

"Excellent. Well done, my dear."

"How odd," said Dr. Armbruster. "She does respond well to harsh tones."

The vicar was wondering what the devil was the relationship between these two. "And now you, my lord. Oh, dear, this is so very irregular."

Mrs. Ringlestone sniffed at that moment. Ruby looked bug-eyed and weepy.

Burke calmly repeated his vows after the vicar. He was smiling down at Arielle as he said "I do."

"I pronounce you man and wife, my lord. Oh, dear, is she conscious?"

"Yes, barely," said Dr. Armbruster. "You have done very well, my lord, yes, indeed."

Mrs. Ringlestone and Ruby left the bedchamber to fetch the small cakes and wine. "Though 'tis not a proper wedding breakfast, my lord, still we must do something!"

"Yes, my lord," said the vicar. "If the young lady, ah, doesn't make it, well, she will pass to our dear Lord a virtuous woman. You are all kindness, my lord." He suddenly looked worried. "Both of you must sign the wedding papers. How—"

"Fetch them," Burke said, "and I will see to it that she signs her name."

Dr. Armbruster didn't doubt for a minute that the young earl would have the paper signed. He watched as Burke lifted his countess against his chest, placed the quill between her fingers, and told her in a very stern voice to sign her name. The vicar sucked in his breath, surprised that the young lady instantly did what she was bidden. He took the paper and saw that her name was quite legible. He shook his head. "Most unusual," he remarked yet again.

Burke wanted to laugh, but didn't. He was too

frightened. Arielle was quiet now, ominously so, sagging against his chest. He gently laid her down.

"She's sleeping," said Dr. Armbruster, and he sounded both surprised and relieved. "It is sleep, I promise you. Perhaps you were right and her lack of will was because she wasn't your wife and thus felt herself damned. As your mistress, she felt guilty. When she became pregnant out of wedlock, her feelings of guilt and hopelessness were intensified. By wedding her, my lord, you have expiated her guilt, made her feel worthy again, given her safety and refuge. And thus she regains her will to live. It is an interesting theory, one that I shall discuss with my colleagues in London."

Arielle's supposed pregnancy, Burke thought, had been a fine and, in his opinion, necessary touch. It had certainly brought the vicar around much more quickly.

"You have paved your path to heaven," continued the vicar, "by lifting this fallen young woman from her ditch of sin. The good Lord will look kindly upon your fine deed."

"It was I who seduced her," said Burke, who couldn't stand this utter nonsense another moment. "Aren't I the one to be judged harshly?"

"You are a man, my lord," said the vicar without a blink. "If you will recall your scripture, you will remember that the woman, the temptress, holds the power of evil. A man may be weak, my lord, but not many men would perform such a noble service as you have this day. I will pray, devoutly, that the young woman becomes deserving of the honor you have bestowed upon her."

No hope for it, Burke thought. When Ruby and Mrs. Ringlestone came back into the bedchamber bearing trays of cakes and wine, he was profoundly relieved.

She was his wife. She didn't know it, but that
was all right.

Now she had to live.

"Please pray for her, sir," he said to the vicar as
he helped the old man on his way. "I love her, you
see, and I don't want to lose her now. I don't think
I could bear it."

"Since she has both Armbruster and our good
Lord on her side, I venture to think she will survive, my lord. I will visit tomorrow."

Burke, elated, weary, and so scared he could
scarce think straight, resumed his vigil by his wife's
bed.


Arielle opened her eyes. She felt lazy and
strangely at peace. However, she soon realized she
hadn't the foggiest idea of where she was. She
slowly looked about, noting the long narrow windows whose draperies were tied away, admitting
weak rays of sunlight; the few pieces of furniture;
the single wing chair that was drawn up next to
the bed. And the heat of the room. A fire was blazing enthusiastically in the fireplace. She realized
she was sweating and she wondered why the devil
her maid had built up such a blaze.

It was summer, wasn't it?

"Dorcas," she called out, but nothing emerged
from her mouth save a flat croaking sound. "Oh,
dear," she whispered. She wanted to sit up, but the
pile of blankets covering her wouldn't allow it.

Why was she so weak? She raised her hand and
pushed the hair off her forehead and realized that
someone had braided her hair. The thick braid felt
lank, heavy and oily.

She lowered her arm and tried to think. "Paisley," she whispered, thinking he'd brought her
here. She felt that awful fear wash through her.

No, he was dead, a long time ago, months ago. A lifetime ago.

"Hello. Is that really you, Arielle?"

She turned her face toward the sound of the voice. A man's voice. Deep and calm. Burke's voice. What was he doing here? She tensed.

"No, no, my dear, don't be frightened. You are all right now—at least I think you are. Your eyes certainly look bright. Welcome back." That wasn't even close to what he was feeling at the moment, but there was no reason to frighten her by yelling aloud and dancing about the bedchamber. His smile grew wider. She was all right, truly, finally.

She opened her mouth and this time, with great concentration, she managed to say, "What are you doing here? Where is here?"

"I will answer everything. First, would you like something to eat? Drink?"

Her mouth watered immediately. He smiled and walked away from the bed.

She heard him calling outside the chamber door to someone named Mrs. Ringlestone. When he came back, he held out a glass of water. "Here, let me help you. Don't be alarmed."

He held her up while she sipped at the water. She couldn't seem to get enough.

"Very good," he said and gently eased her back down. "Mrs. Ringlestone—she's our cook—she'll bring up food. How do you feel?"

"Fine," she said absently. "Just weak."

"No wonder. You've been very ill. You've had me so scared I promised years and years of devout rectitude if you would but come back whole."

"How long was I ill?"

"Eight days. You came down with an inflammation of the lung, the result of your mad dash into the storm. Do you remember?"

She frowned, trying to recall, but it only made her head throb.

He saw the sudden tensing of pain and said quickly, "I'm sorry. Don't try to remember. Just relax and get well again."

"You've lost weight, Burke."

He grinned, knowing that he had and strangely pleased that she would notice.

"You shouldn't have. You're too thin now."

He made a vow not to give her a mirror. Not only was she as skinny as his malacca cane, her skin was pasty and her glorious hair was dull and lifeless.

"But you," he said, "look wonderful."

She stilled at his words, and he cursed himself silently for rushing his fences. "Ah, Mrs. Ringlestone, some food for our patient. Arielle, my dear, this is our cook, Mrs. Ringlestone."

"My lady," said Mrs. Ringlestone.

"Hello," said Arielle.

Burke lifted her against the pillows. Mrs. Ringlestone had prepared some hot barley soup and warm bread piled high with butter. There was also a small crock of honey.

"Thank you, Mrs. Ringlestone. I'll watch to see that she doesn't spill the soup on her lap."

Arielle didn't think to protest that comment; she was too busy getting a spoonful of soup into her mouth.

Burke watched her, a slight smile on his lips, and quickly eased down beside her when he saw she was too exhausted to continue.

"More?" he asked as he took the spoon from her.

"Please."

She seemed to fall asleep shortly thereafter. Burke removed the tray, only to almost drop it when she said, very clearly, "Where is that little man with the scraggly white hair?"

So she did remember something.

When next she awoke, it was nearly dark. Burke had sent Mrs. Ringlestone and Ruby on their way an hour before, and he was sitting in a chair next to Arielle's bed, reading a book of John Donne's poetry. He wasn't particularly interested in the poet, but Knight's library downstairs didn't have a great selection. One moment he was half attending to a poem about men not being islands when he sensed she was awake. He didn't know how he knew, but he just did.

"Hello," he said before she even raised her eyes.

"May I have some water?"

"Certainly."

She downed an entire glass. Surely she would have to relieve herself, he thought, and wondered what the devil he should do about it. He doubted she had the strength to handle the task herself. He said, "Are you hungry? Mrs. Ringlestone left some food for you."

She nodded and said nothing more. When he left the bedchamber, she looked about for the chamber pot. I must make myself move, she thought.

She did, barely. She couldn't imagine being this weak and shaky. She also didn't think she would manage, but she did. When the door opened again to admit Burke and her dinner tray, she was half standing, half sitting at the end of the bed, clutching the bedpost. Her nightgown was bunched up about her knees and she was breathing heavily.

She looked pale and sweaty. Burke didn't say anything. He merely set the tray down on the table next to the bed. "Let me help you back into bed."

Her chin went up. "I don't need your help. I just need another minute to—"

She felt herself being scooped up and gently placed in bed.

This time she managed to feed herself a good deal

before she became too tired and allowed Burke to
feed her the rest of the chicken breast. She gave a
sigh of contentment afterward and leaned back
against her pillow.

"Did I almost die?"

He placed his cup of hot black coffee on the tray.
"Yes," he said, "yes, you did almost die. You scared
the hell out of me. But you're fine now."

"You'll let me leave, then?"

He shook his head. "It wouldn't do at all. Not
now."

"What do you mean by that?"

"I spent all your hundred pounds on the doctor."

"You *what?*"

He gave her a crooked grin. "I didn't have any
money with me. I had to give the doctor yours."

"You will certainly pay it back!"

"I had fully intended to provide you with a generous quarterly allowance. You needn't worry."

"Burke! Now you listen to me. I won't hear any
more of this nonsense, and I have no intention—"

"Hush. Would you like a bath? Your hair is a bit
on the edge."

A bath sounded so marvelous that she forgot her
grievances for the moment. "Yes, but you can't
stay."

"You'll need my help, Arielle."

She said neither yea nor nay to that. When at
last the tub was filled, Burke helped her out of bed.
She was so thin, he thought, so fragile. Except for
her will, thank God.

He helped her to the tub, then turned her to face
him, holding her firmly against him. "Now attend
me. I have taken care of you since you became ill.
I did everything for you. There is no reason for you
to feel embarrassed with me now. You can't do this
alone. I will help you into the tub, then I'll wash
your hair for you. All right?"

She said in a low, pained voice, "Everything?"

"Everything."

"Why?"

"I'll tell you why later, when you're back in your bed."

He helped her off with her nightgown, efficiently and matter-of-factly. Once she was in the hot water, he unbraided her hair and brushed out the tangles.

"Let's wash your hair first," he said. It was quite a chore, something he wasn't at all used to doing, but he managed. Once he'd gotten all the soap rinsed out, he said, "I'm going to change your bed now. You wash the rest of you, all right?"

Arielle was beyond embarrassment. She was shaking with weakness, but she didn't say anything.

Burke rose and looked down at her for a moment. Her breasts were covered by the water, but he knew their shape, feel, and texture quite well. Lovely breasts, almost too large for her slender torso, and he'd cursed himself every time he'd taken care of her because his body had become hard and throbbing instantly. He forced himself even now to tamp down thoughts and images so lustful that he nearly trembled, and headed for the messed bed.

He'd just finished changing the bedding when he heard a cry behind him. He whirled around to see Arielle trying to climb out of the tub, a towel in one hand, the other hand flailing about wildly. She lost her balance and went tumbling to the floor before he could move.

# 10

Arielle lay on her back, her arms and legs sprawled, feeling like a great fool.

"Arielle!"

She saw the fear and worry in his dark eyes and quickly said, "I'm all right, just clumsy." She wanted to cover herself, but she hadn't the strength. It was too much. She turned her head away from him and choked back a sob.

He gathered her and the towel and lifted her into his arms. He carried her to the fireplace and sat down in a chair. He began to dry her. Instead of fighting him, she was pliant, her head against his shoulder. He tried to keep his hands off her, but it was impossible. His fingers lightly stroked over her left breast. I won't look, he thought. I won't respond. I won't be a damned animal. But he couldn't help himself. He looked and saw that her nipple was taut, and it nearly did him in.

He pretended he was going into battle, reaching for the cold, emotionless control that had kept him alive more times than he cared to think about. He didn't linger, was nearly rough, until he got to her feet. They, at least, were safer than the rest of her, but even there he found beauty. Her feet were narrow, finely arched. He was looking at her toes when he said, "You are too thin. We've got to feed you ten times a day."

He hadn't intended to say anything, particularly something so inane. "Nice toes, though," he added, trying for some vagrant humor and not finding any. He sighed and began to dry her hair.

But it was simply too much. The wretched towel he'd wrapped around her wasn't enough. It was torture, and there was no chance he was going to make her any less wary of him than she already was. He carried her to the bed and got her into his dressing gown, wrapping it twice around her and tying the belt securely. She made no protest during this operation. He knew that she would have fought him to the edge if she'd had the strength. She said not a word when he carried her back to the chair by the fire.

By the time her hair was only slightly damp, his arm was aching from combing out tangles and holding her. He eased her down and arranged himself more comfortably. Her long hair was hanging loose over his arm, nearly to the floor. She was well covered, the fire was well stocked and hot, and soon both of them were sound asleep.

Burke awoke to a dark room. There were only glowing embers in the fireplace. He felt cramped, his neck sore, and his left arm was numb. Arielle was nestled against him, still deeply asleep, her body so relaxed that it quickly gave rise to more errant erotic fantasies.

He brought her closer, breathing in the sweet scent of her. My wife, he thought; she is finally my wife. It was deep in the middle of the night. He heard the sounds of the house, the groans and the quiet creakings, the gentle swishing of tree branches against the windows. He felt at peace and pleasantly hazy in his thoughts. Reality did not intrude.

"Let's go to bed, wife," he said and smiled at his words. He truly was happy with the sound of that.

It was Arielle who awoke first the following morning and she was wonderfully warm. It took her a moment to realize that the warmth was from Burke. She was lying against him, her head on his chest, her leg thrown over his thighs. One arm was holding her firmly against him. She could hear his even, deep breathing. She flattened her palm on his chest and stilled. He was naked. Crisp hair was between her splayed fingers.

"Burke?"

He mumbled something in his sleep and tightened his hold on her. Slowly, very slowly, she managed to pull away from him. His dressing gown gaped open down her front and she quickly drew it tightly against her. She was nearly free when she heard him say easily, "Good morning. Did you sleep well?"

Her cheeks were flushed, her hair in tangles about her face and down her back. He could have told her that she was the most exquisite creature in the world to him.

They stared at each other, she at a stranger, he at his wife.

"You have whiskers," she said.

"Men usually do in the morning."

"You also have hair on your chest."

"Just about everywhere, I'm afraid, except for my back. I'd just as soon not shave my body, if you don't mind. I hope it doesn't offend you too much."

This was ridiculous, she realized. "I want to leave now."

"This very moment? Wearing my dressing gown?"

She lowered her head. He was teasing her, sounding gentle, but it made no difference to her fear. It made no difference to the reality of things. He was lying in bed with her, naked, ready to do whatever pleased him. "I feel much better," she said at last, moving a few inches away from him.

"Good. So do I. Now I will remove myself for a while. Become presentable and all that. Will you be all right until I return?"

She nodded.

"I believe I can even find a nightgown for you."

"A nightgown? Where did a nightgown come from?"

"I bought one for you." There, he thought; face a bit of reality, Arielle. "In London, when I was planning to abduct you. I couldn't be worried about bringing any baggage from your carriage, so I had to buy you a few things. Had you looked in the armoire in the other bedchamber, you would have found several gowns, slippers, and undergarments. No bonnets, though. That was beyond me. I'm sorry. Actually, I bought you just one nightgown and you wore it all during your illness. I'm not certain if Mrs. Ringlestone has laundered it."

Whether she faced reality or anything else, he didn't know, for she said nothing.

She continued to say nothing until he left the bedchamber. She turned away when he'd gotten out of bed. Nor did she turn to face him even when he told her he was well covered. Burke gave her a long look from the door, then left, gently closing it behind him.

Burke didn't want to leave her alone too long. He knew the moment of reckoning was very near now. After all, Mrs. Ringlestone and Ruby couldn't be expected to keep their respective mouths closed around her. He would have to tell her and he would have to put the plain gold band back on her third finger

When he entered the bedchamber, he found her sitting by the fireplace, a blanket over her legs, her head against the cushion. She'd brushed most of the tangles from her hair, pulled it back, and wrapped a thick strand of her own hair about it to hold it in place. Her eyes were very large in her thin face and he thought her the most beautiful woman he'd ever seen, certainly the most beautiful woman he'd ever loved. He was smiling at his foolish and pleasing thoughts as he said easily, "Mrs. Ringlestone will be bringing our breakfast soon. Are you hungry?"

"Yes. At this rate I shall be fat as a flawn by winter."

"Good, I'm partial to overweight flawns. Now, Arielle, there is something we need to discuss."

"I want to leave."

"Something other than that."

"I don't want to talk to you about anything else."

"A pity, but you must. Remember I told you that if you married me I would take you to Boston to see your half sister?"

She frowned at that, not trusting him an inch, but intrigued by his question. "Yes. Why?"

He drew a deep breath and pulled the wedding band from his pocket. He took her hand, and before she knew what he was about, he had worked the ring over the knuckle of her third finger. It was tight, which was just fine with him.

"We're married," he said.

Arielle stared down at the ring. She tried to pull it off but failed. She kept shaking her finger, yanking at it. "Don't be ridiculous! Of course we aren't married. Why, I—" She looked panicked, and uncertain, and stricken. "That mangy little man . . . that other man who had the oddest accent . . ."

"The mangy one is the vicar. He married us. The other is Dr. Armbruster. He's a Scotsman, thus his accent."

"That's impossible! A woman must agree, I know that."

Burke leaned down, placing one hand on each chair arm, his face only inches from hers. "You must listen to me, and I will tell you everything." He straightened and leaned against the mantelpiece. "It's really very simple. I thought you were dying. In your delirium, you spoke of many things. But over and over you said you wanted me. You said you couldn't bear your life the way it was, the way it had been. I asked you to marry me and you said yes."

"That's a lie! I would never—"

"In your delirium, Arielle. In any case, I felt it was what you wanted, deep down somewhere in your mind, so I spoke to the vicar about it. He agreed. He married us. I have since taken care of the bishop, the special licenses, and all that. We are legally married."

"I can't remember anything!"

He hated the panic, the fear, in her voice, hated the necessity for the lie about her sentiments. "Arielle, I could not force you to marry me. But you said 'I do' quite clearly when the vicar asked you if you would take me for your husband. There were three witnesses. You signed the marriage papers. It is done."

"It cannot be true."

"It will be good between us, you will see."

She gave him a bitter look. "Aren't you afraid that I will murder you just as I did my dead husband?"

"No. Did you? Murder him, I mean."

"Yes," she said, her voice vicious. "Yes, I did, and I'll murder you too!"

She was hurting so much. He wished there were something he could do, something magical he could say. "I will try to make you happy, Arielle."

"Will you?"

"Why would you think I wouldn't? I love you, after all. Why would I want to make the woman I love unhappy?"

There was a light knock on the door. Burke called out impatiently, "Come in, Mrs. Ringlestone."

The older woman came into the room, smiling widely. "Och, I knew you'd be much better this morning, my lady. His lordship ordered a breakfast grand enough to feed a battalion. Yes, he did, and I agree that . . ."

Arielle was looking at Burke, paying little attention to Mrs. Ringlestone's ramblings. Her husband. Burke now owned her just as Paisley had. He would possess her completely in any fashion he wished, and he had every right to treat her any way he pleased. She saw clearly, starkly, the dream she'd had before. Paisley had become Burke, and he was over her, and naked, and he wasn't impotent, as her husband had been. She'd seen the future and it had happened.

She wasn't aware that tears were falling slowly from her eyes and silently running down her cheeks. Mrs. Ringlestone saw them and was so startled and dismayed, she stopped talking, staring helplessly at Arielle.

"Please leave us, Mrs. Ringlestone," Burke softly ordered.

When she had left, Burke took Arielle in his arms and pulled her onto his lap. She didn't protest. She didn't say anything. She seemed distant and sealed off from him.

He couldn't stand it. "Tell me why you're crying."

Her head went back and forth against his shoulder.

"You will tell me now, Arielle."

It was his meanest voice and he hated using it with her, but yet again, it worked.

"I won't do it! I won't!" She was trembling, with rage, fear, he didn't know what.

"What won't you do? Answer me, damn you!"

"That awful dream, it's come true, but I won't let you hurt me, I won't!"

"Tell me about the dream."

It didn't occur to her not to tell him. He was using his man's voice and she responded to it instantly. "The night after I met you again, at Bunberry Lake, I dreamed. There were Paisley and other men as well and they all had ... and then Paisley became you and you were in my bed and forcing me. I couldn't stop you. You're too strong. Don't you see?"

"Yes," he said quietly, "I do see. But why was I forcing you? That makes no sense."

"You're a man!"

"A man who loves you."

"That is stupid, it doesn't matter, and you're lying."

Burke leaned his head back and closed his eyes. His hand began stroking her upper arm. Her tears stopped. She supposed she cried so little because tears meant there was some sort of hope. She had none. And he'd ordered her to stop, so she did.

Burke wanted desperately at that moment to tell her that he knew the truth, but he wasn't certain that she could take it. Finding out she was married to him was quite likely more than enough for her to absorb, at least for the present. He admitted too that he was wary about telling her, frightened about his reaction to what she would tell him, if she told him anything. Never for as long as he lived would he forget the helpless rage that had consumed him when he'd realized the truth. His beautiful, innocent girl, abused by that monster.

Never would he forget that moment, never. It was as clear in his mind now as it had been then. It was late at night, their wedding night, actually. Her fever had risen as it always did at night and her breathing was heavy, labored. He'd been bathing her, quite efficient at it now, thinking vaguely that in all his fantasies about her, he'd never envisioned this one for his wedding night. Finally, he'd turned her onto her stomach and tossed her thick braid over her shoulder. He began stroking the cool, damp cloth across her back, over her hips, and down her long legs. His rhythm was steady, the pressure light, and he was silently reciting Latin declensions in order to control his own desires. The candle gutted suddenly and he paused to light another. He held it up for a moment. And then he looked at her, really looked, with the light strong and steady, and he grew very still.

He shook his head automatically. It had to be a trick of the candlelight. But it wasn't. He brought the candle nearer. He lightly touched a fingertip to one of the thin white marks. Then to another. There were so many. He looked at her buttocks and thighs. More white lines, and he wanted to howl, to scream, but he didn't. It wouldn't help. It would make no difference. She'd been beaten, often and thoroughly. He closed his eyes, unable to handle the reality of those marks. Her father? Her half brother? He was shaking his head even as he thought that. No, her husband, of course. That was why she was terrified of men, and why she hadn't wanted to marry him.

The enormity of the situation struck Burke squarely between the eyes. He continued to run the cloth over her until finally she cooled and once again her fever was down. Gently, he turned her over. He saw now several of the faded white lines on her breasts and on her belly. He swallowed convulsively. He climbed into bed with her then, holding her tightly against him, trying to think things through. To beat a sixteen-year-old girl. And not just any girl, but a young lady of quality. The truth strained credulity, and he wasn't certain he would have believed it if the proof weren't before his eyes.

While he'd been thinking about her during the past three years, weaving fantasies that had run the gamut of intensely erotic to tenderly sweet, she'd been naked, beaten, and on her knees in front of her husband, taking him in her mouth and servicing him, learning to do it with the expertise of the most accomplished courtesan.

Dear heavens, he couldn't bear to think of it, but he did, of course. She'd been broken so completely that she'd even accepted him when he'd merely held the riding crop. He remembered her urgency, her frantic movements to strip off her clothes. She believed he was going to beat her if she didn't hurry.

He wondered if Paisley Cochrane had given her to other men. He wouldn't have been at all surprised.

If only he'd married her three years before, he thought again and again. To hell with scruples for her youth, to hell with everything.

What was he going to do now?

He looked up, aware that he'd been locked into his thoughts. She'd begun to eat her breakfast. He tried to smile, but it was difficult. How to deal with it?

He helped her into bed once she'd finished. He set the tray outside the chamber door, then returned to sit on the end of her bed.

He realized in that moment that he didn't want to tell her that he knew. He couldn't begin to imagine her reaction. No, he thought, his decision made, he would have to make her trust him first.

And sexual intimacy between a husband and wife? He didn't know. He knew only that he would make her accustomed to him, to his body, to his touching and holding her.

"You are very strong," she said suddenly, surprising him.

Everything she said now had new meaning to him, but he wouldn't let her know. Not yet. He said easily, "Yes, and that strength is for your protection. Don't ever fear my strength, Arielle, but be glad for it."

"You are very fluent, Burke."

He paused a moment, then said the truth of her vague words for her. "As in all men are liars and cruel and ravening beasts?"

"Yes." Her chin went up, but he saw the fear lurking in her eyes even as she gave voice to her small defiance. He rose and she shrank back.

He ignored her reaction and said, "When you are well enough, we will go to Ravensworth Abbey. Your servants are doubtless there, waiting for their mistress."

"I want to go to Boston. You promised."

"Yes, and we shall." *As soon as you are pregnant.* And that, he knew, was probably going to be a formidable task. The lie for the doctor and the vicar had been as far from reality as Burke could ever have imagined telling. "As soon as the war between the two countries is over," he continued. "This fall should see the end to it. Now, would you like to rest for a while?"

She nodded, and he thought, Anything to be rid of me. So be it, he decided, and left the bedchamber.

"What are you doing?"

Her voice was thin-sounding, shrill.

He smiled at her and continued unfastening the buttons on his breeches. He pulled down his breeches and his undergarments and stepped out of them. He stood there, naked, still smiling at her. He wasn't particularly aroused, but if she kept looking at him, he soon would be.

"I'm going to bathe," he said easily. "Would you care to join me?"

"No! Please, can you not go into another room?
Or let me leave this one?"

He walked toward her and her eyes fell from his
face and he knew that she was looking at him and
every masculine feeling in him responded and he
felt himself swelling and thrusting outward. Well,
she wasn't an innocent. She needed to know that
he desired her as a woman.

Then he saw her fear and he stopped. He calmly
reached for his dressing gown and slipped it on.
He'd accomplished a little bit. Next time he was
naked, she wouldn't react so strongly; at least he
hoped she wouldn't. She would become accustomed
to him. He knew her body as well as he knew his
own. He had no intention of remaining a physical
stranger to her. She would learn him; she would
become used to him.

"Would you like to have a conversation with
me?" he asked, arching a brow at her.

"I would like to dress and leave this room."

"All right. Dr. Armbruster will be coming
shortly. If he says you are well enough, I will carry
you downstairs."

Then he calmly stripped off his dressing gown and
stepped into the tub. He sang as he washed himself,
watching her from the corner of his eye. Her expression was pained. From his singing or the threat
of his man's body?

Dr. Armbruster wasn't particularly surprised
when the earl kept him downstairs for several minutes. No, he agreed, he would say nothing to her
about her pregnancy. Certainly he understood that
she would be embarrassed.

Merciful heavens, Dr. Armbruster thought some
five minutes later, she is afraid of me! He was the
bluntest of men, but this girl, clasping her arms
over her breasts, her eyes haunting and never leaving him for an instant, made him want to use all

his skill to reassure her as he would do for a deathly
sick child.

He backed up a step and sat himself in a chair.
He smiled at her. He would go very, very slowly.
"You are looking as fit as old Mr. McGee, who can
now dance a jig with his wooden leg. How do you
feel, my lady?"

"All right, sir."

She had a lovely voice. He just wished there were
no fear in it. He looked over at the earl, her husband. His face was expressionless, but Dr. Armbruster wondered what he was thinking. Did he
recognize her fear? The doctor needed to listen to
her lungs. He started to rise but stopped himself.

"You had a very worried husband, my lady. He
has also been an excellent nurse. Both of you are
looking a bit peaked. I recommend a lot of rest."

"When can she travel?" Burke asked.

"Tomorrow, by the healthy looks of her." Dr. Armbruster rose slowly, aware that she was watching him
warily. "May I listen to your lungs, my lady?"

He saw her swallow convulsively. He didn't move
until she nodded and said, "All right."

He didn't pull up her nightgown. He didn't touch
her with his hands. It was difficult, but he leaned as
close to her chest as he could without touching her.
Her lungs, thankfully, were clear. Unable to avoid it,
he lightly touched his palm to her forehead. He felt
her flinch even though she seemed not to move.

He moved away from her. "Yes," he said to
Burke, "tomorrow, but in easy stages. Where are
you going?"

" 'Tis not far. Only to Sussex, near East Grinstead."

"Your estate is there, my lord?"

"Yes. Ravensworth Abbey is just on the edge of
Ashdown Forest."

Dr. Armbruster saw that she was relaxing and

said, "A beautiful spot, Ashdown Forest. I was visiting in the Weald not too long ago. I've a sister in Hammerwood."

"A lovely little hamlet," Burke agreed.

"Will you ride with her in the carriage, my lord?"

"Certainly. If she tires, we can stop. I will take very good care of her, Dr. Armbruster."

Dr. Armbruster nodded, then turned to Arielle. "Do as your husband bids you, my lady. He's endowed with nearly as much common sense as a Scotsman."

Arielle didn't care about that. She wanted to ask him if she was indeed married to the Earl of Ravensworth. He saw her evident distress and asked her gently, "Is there something wrong? Something you would like to ask me?"

She looked at Burke, and he realized with an awful start that she was afraid to ask the doctor anything. She was afraid of him, afraid he would become angry with her and beat her. He said easily, "Arielle, do you want to ask Dr. Armbruster about our wedding ceremony?"

She looked both alarmed and surprised. "If it's all right. It was over a week ago?"

"Yes, and very nice. The vicar said the right words, as did you and your husband. Now I must be off. If anything happens before you leave, my lord, just send for me. Good-bye, my lady." Dr. Armbruster strode to the door, then stopped and turned. "You have an excellent husband, my lady, yes, excellent. I hope both of you are happy."

Arielle stared at him as if he'd suddenly announced that he was the new King of England. He pinned on a smile and left, a very thoughtful man.

Nothing untoward happened for the rest of the day, at least in Burke's view. He taught her to play piquet that evening and she proved adept, both at strategy and at keeping count of her cards.

"I won only five thousand pounds," he said, sitting back. "Soon it is I who will lose my fortune to you."

She'd forgotten about everything but the game. She'd even laughed several times, and he'd swelled inside at the wonderful sound. He said abruptly, "Would you like another game?"

She agreed quickly, but he saw that she was tiring. "No, better not. You're looking a bit like a lovely rose that's just beginning to droop on its stem. You need to rest if we are to leave tomorrow."

She watched in silence as he carried the deck of cards and the table away from the bed. Then he began calmly to strip off his clothes. When he turned, naked, she gasped out, "No! Please, I don't want you to stay here, please!"

He simply shook his head at her. "I am just a man, Arielle. Nothing new. I am also your husband. I imagine you'll see me unclothed every day for the next fifty years. Get used to me, all right?"

He didn't really expect an answer. He walked to the bed and eased in between the covers. She quickly moved to the far side, so close to the edge that he imagined her crashing to the floor during the night.

He could feel the nearly tangible waves of tension coming from her but didn't know what to do about it.

"You never did tell me what your brother did to get Victor."

For a moment he didn't know what she was talking about. "Good heavens, you remember my telling you about the pony?"

"Yes, certainly. So how did Montrose get Victor? Or did he?"

"If you kiss me good night I'll tell you."

He heard her sharp intake of breath. He came up, balancing himself on his elbow. "Well?"

"No," she said, her voice as thin as watery gruel. "Please, just stay away."

"As you wish," he said. He did. Until the middle of the night when a storm blew in and the temperature plummeted. He woke to find Arielle sprawled over him, both her arms about his neck. Her nightgown was bunched about her waist. His left hand was on her naked buttocks. It was wonderful and he was still half asleep. Her skin was smooth and soft. He began dreaming about loving her and his fingers made his dream real. Her legs were slightly parted and his fingers slipped between her thighs. And he touched her woman's flesh. She was warm and soft and he thought he would explode.

The dream continued. His fingers continued. He wanted to feel more of her and slipped his finger inside her. So tight she was, and hot. He moaned softly and his finger moved in her, deeper.

His thumb eased through the soft folds of her flesh to find her, and he wanted more, he wanted to hear her moan and yell for him, he wanted . . . He groaned, and that groan brought him awake. Instantly and completely awake.

"Arielle," he whispered, feeling her, not quite understanding, and not wanting to. He felt her stir; then she came up on her elbows. He could barely make out her features in the darkness.

She moaned and he felt her hips move.

"Arielle," he said and, in a swift movement, turned her onto her back and came down over her.

# 11

It was dark and the darkness cloaked his mind, giving his desire free rein, holding him away, but only for a moment. Her nightgown was still bunched about her waist. His hands took in the feel of her, the smooth softness of her legs and belly. It was too much when he heard her small cry, a pleading cry to his ears, a wanting cry. He pushed himself against her, wanting desperately to come into her body. He reared up, his breathing hard, intent upon his task, when she suddenly became rigid.

"Arielle," he said, his voice hoarse and raw, "I want to come inside you. I want you to belong to me, all of you." His voice was none too steady and he realized the depth of his lust for her. He had to stop. He mustn't frighten her. Slowly, he eased off her and onto his back.

"Go back to sleep," he said. "But, Arielle, dream about me, all right? Perhaps that's what you were dreaming when I touched you. You did feel desire for me. I want to fill your life with desire and pleasure." Odd how it was easier to speak of things like this in the middle of the night, in the dark, with no face to see to give away thoughts and doubts. "I want you to be happy. I will make you happy if you will give me a chance."

The strange feelings centered low in her belly had

181

faded, now hollow echoes from something vague and
disturbing, something she didn't understand, didn't
want to understand. She heard his deep voice and
wondered at his words. He sounded so terribly sincere. But she wasn't a fool. She wouldn't ever be a
fool again. He could have taken her but he hadn't.
Why? He'd come over her just as he had in the
dream.

Aloud she said, "I don't understand you."

"Trust me, and understanding will come."

More men's glib words. "Oh, no, I shall not do
that, my lord."

Burke let that go and said, "At least you are lying next to me in bed and we are married and we
are speaking to each other in the middle of the
night. Strides, I call it, Arielle. Very impressive
strides."

He had something there.

"Your nightgown is up about your waist."

He felt the bed give as she straightened the gown.
"Are you cold?"

"Why?"

"I'll hold you."

"No," she said. And that, he thought, was that.

Her face was white with fatigue. She leaned
against him, her head lolling against his shoulder.
He kissed her temple. He held her firmly, saying
softly, "Almost home, my dear. You'll be all right
soon now."

In the past whenever Burke had returned to Ravensworth Abbey, he had felt a sense of intense be-
longing, of homecoming. This time, all his attention
was focused on Arielle. The carriage, driven by Tom
Acre of Shepherd Smeath, turned into the wide
drive, and Burke greeted Toby, the gateman, with
a nod. The drive was long and winding, and he
knew every oak tree, every maple tree, every lime

tree. Their foliage was thick and lush, a riot of greens in midsummer. He kissed his wife gently on her forehead, believing that she had fallen asleep.

She hadn't. She pulled away from him, took her bonnet from the opposite seat, and set it on her head. "Just a bit crooked," he said, smiling at her, and adjusted it. She then tied the bow beneath her left ear.

"Very smart, although the bonnet does look the worse from wear." It was the one she'd worn the day he'd abducted her. One side was nearly smashed in. "The servants will be pleased to see you here as their mistress, Arielle. My man, Joshua, is even enamored of you, and in the normal scheme of things, he isn't at all fond of the fairer sex. I don't want you to be worried about anything. You'll be tucked into your bed very soon. Your maid, Dorcas, is here, and if you wish, you can keep her with you."

Arielle looked out the window, then said quietly, "I didn't want to come here, my lord. I am afraid."

"Of what?"

She shrugged. "I am not what I was before. I wish you had believed me. You will come to dislike me, and then what will you do?"

Tom Acre pulled the carriage to a halt at that moment in front of the Abbey, sparing Burke from having to answer. His butler, Montague, was standing in the open doorways, as stately as any self-respecting monarch. Burke knew that all his instructions would have been followed to the letter, in all likelihood with more efficiency than in the army.

"Do you feel well enough to walk?"

"Certainly," she said, not knowing if this was true or not. She felt weak from the inside out, which didn't make much sense, but it was the case.

A footman, Charlie, decked out in Drummond liv-

ery of royal blue and crimson, opened the carriage
door. Burke jumped down and turned to help Arielle. Her face was pale, and he flinched at the fear
he saw in her eyes. He clasped his hands about her
waist and lifted her out.

"You are the Countess of Ravensworth," he said
quietly. "Don't ever forget that. All right?"

" 'Tis not that," she said, and that was true.

Then she saw Dorcas rushing out of the house
toward her, crying out, "My baby! You're here, at
last!" Dorcas came to a breathless halt, remembering herself, and gave Arielle a deep, age-creaking
curtsy. "My lady," she said. She cast a quick look
at the earl and he nodded.

"She has been a bit under the weather, Dorcas,"
Burke said. "I will help her upstairs. Montague,
have one of the footmen fetch Dr. Brody."

"Please, no, Burke," Arielle said, touching her
fingertips to his sleeve. "Please."

"But I want to be certain you're all right."

"I am. Just tired, that's all. Please."

He would never, he thought, be immune to her.
He studied her face, and without another word, he
lifted her into his arms. "It will be as you wish. My
only request," he added quietly, "is that you don't
fight me."

"No," she said, "I won't."

Arielle had the impression of a great many servants crowded in the entrance hall of the Abbey.
Burke spoke to Mrs. Pepperall, his housekeeper,
and to Montague. They greeted Arielle warmly. Everything was as Burke wished. He nodded to the
servants as he carried his bride upstairs. The huge
master bedchamber was at the end of the eastern
corridor, and next to it was the countess's bedchamber, a room that his mother had decorated in shades
of peach and the lightest of lavender. He'd debated
whether or not to keep Arielle with him, and still

he wasn't certain. He supposed it was Dorcas and his natural perversity that formed his decision.

"In here, my lord," Dorcas said and stepped aside for him to bring Arielle into the countess's bed-chamber.

"I think not," he said and walked down to the next large oak door. He opened it and went inside. "You've never been upstairs before, have you?"

Arielle shook her head against his shoulder. He kicked the door shut with his foot, wondering if Dorcas had followed him and was standing staring at the closed door at this moment.

"Just another moment, and you'll be in bed."

Very matter-of-factly, Burke set her on her feet beside the enormous bed in which he'd been born, and took off her clothes. She leaned against him and he was pleased. He stripped her down to her chemise and petticoat, then sat her on the edge of the bed. He went to his knees and pulled down her stockings and slippers. "There, that wasn't so very awful, was it?" he said with a touch of humor as he rose. He helped her between the cool sheets and smoothed the blankets over her.

"No," she said, a bit of surprise in her voice. She was asleep within five minutes.

There was a sharp rap on the door. Dorcas was standing there looking a bit militant. "She's sleeping," he said. "Let us leave her be."

"But—"

"If you wish to sit beside her, you may. Just don't awaken her, Dorcas."

The old woman gave him a look that would have soured the sweetest chocolate. "I know her. She wouldn't have married you."

"Well, you're wrong."

"You did something to her!"

"Actually, I didn't. Now, I have other things to do besides argue with you."

He walked quickly away, leaving Dorcas to stare at his back, her own bristling.

Burke wanted to speak to Geordie. He found him with Joshua in the stables. Geordie gave him a speculative look, then touched his fingers to the lock of hair that fell over his forehead. "Milord," he said.

Without preamble Burke said, "I didn't harm her in any way, Geordie. You care for her, and I wanted you to hear that from me. She married me. She became ill but is recovering now. Everything is all right. I will do everything in my power to make her happy with me."

Geordie nodded and said to Joshua, "Tell his lordship."

"Tell me what?"

"That French dandy, Etienne DuPons, came sniffing around here."

"The illegitimate son of Cochrane?"

"Aye, that's the one, the bleedin' bugger," said Geordie. "He didn't find out a thing, ye know, but I wondered and wondered, so I followed him when he left."

"Where did he go?"

"To Leslie Farm. To Evan Goddis, her ladyship's half brother. I, ah, slipped around the house and put my ear to the library window. Ye'll not believe it, but DuPons had planned to kidnap her ladyship and force her to marry him. He was furious and talking out of turn, and Goddis told him to clamp up his trap. He told Goddis he knew that you'd stuck in yer oar, what with me and Dorcas being here. And Goddis told him that he'd done it and good riddance to him because he was a fool. He'd had his chance and Goddis wouldn't help him again."

Burke pictured in his mind his position on the road, waiting for Arielle's carriage. Evidently Etienne DuPons had been waiting as well; it was just that Burke had been the first. It was ironic and funny and frightening. "Good God," he said and ran his fingers through his hair. "This situation has more twists and turns than that damned Richmond maze."

Joshua, with something of a lopsided grin on his face, said, "I've instructed the lads to keep a sharp eye, my lord. Now that you and her ladyship are here, we don't want to take any chances."

"DuPons would come here even if he knows she's married to me? I find that difficult to swallow."

Geordie looked from Joshua to the earl. He wasn't certain what to do. Damnation, he had to protect the lassie. "He wanted her powerful bad," he said at last. "Powerful."

Burke looked at him, waiting.

"Aye, my lord. He, well, he lived at Rendel Hall some weeks before his father died, ye know. I'm not sure just what the old man made her do, but . . . well, her ladyship kicked him out right and proper after old Cochrane snuffed it, and he started spewing off his mouth and saying things that were filthy and—"

"I understand," Burke said, turning pale with rage. He took a deep breath. "Thank you for telling me, Geordie. I will protect her, you may be certain of that."

"Er, well, there is something else, milord. Her half brother, Goddis, he sold her to Cochrane. Fifteen thousand pounds. When she ran away and went to him to protect her, he sold her again. Five thousand pounds that time. He isn't a nice man, my lord. What I think is he was behind DuPons to marry her; then he'd take even more money."

"But she didn't have anything. Her steward and solicitor had stolen everything."

"Goddis and DuPons hadn't found out about that, I imagine."

"Well, they must know by now. Surely they wouldn't still act—it wouldn't gain them anything. I won't ask how you know these things, Geordie. Is there anything else?"

Geordie shook his head. Both he and Joshua watched the earl stride back toward the Abbey, his head bowed in deep thought.

"Perhaps ye were in the right of it, Joshua. He's a good man."

"The very best," said Joshua. "Now that she belongs to him, he'll keep her safe."

"Stubborn as hell he is, I'll wager ye as well."

Joshua grinned. "That he is, laddie. But fair, the major lord has always been fair."

"Sounds odd, that title does."

"Fits the man."

"He wouldn't hurt her, would he?"

"I've told you twenty times, Geordie—his lordship ain't like that."

What his lordship was like at that moment was furious. He found himself hoping that both DuPons and Goddis would come here. He wanted to kill both of them. He went to his study, bade his steward, Cerlew, a brief hello, ignored his mournful look and the pile of papers he was holding, and dismissed him. He pulled out paper and pen and wrote an announcement to the *Gazette* of his marriage, then letters to both Knight and his sister, Corinne. This done, he went upstairs to see his wife.

He opened the door quietly, not wanting to awaken her if she were still sleeping. He heard voices and stopped in his tracks.

Dorcas was saying, "Geordie was fit to be tied, but that man, Joshua, he calmed him down. It took some doing, I can tell you that, Miss Arielle. I still can't believe you married him. But he's rich at least."

Arielle's voice was weak but sharp: "I didn't

know I'd married him and I care not if he owns the
whole of England! Oh, Dorcas, enough. I don't wish
to speak of it anymore. It's over. He will take me
to Boston, though. He promised. I think that his
lordship is one who keeps his word. Once in America, I will be able to get away from him."

"What if he beats you, forces you to—"

"Please, Dorcas. If he does, I will bear it until I
can escape him. I don't want to, but a woman has
very little choice in life." Her voice was not bitter,
it was accepting, and that made Burke even an-
grier. "Men own women. I know that. He hasn't yet
shown his true colors, but he will. If I disagree with
him, he will strike me, perhaps use a whip. It will
happen, despite all his assurances now that he's
the sweetest of angels." She paused a moment and
sighed deeply. "I don't know why he is still being
kind to me. After all, I am his wife now and there
is no reason for him to pretend anymore. I don't
understand him."

Burke heard Dorcas speak again, but she'd lowered her voice and he couldn't make out her words.
Slowly, he pulled the door closed and walked back
downstairs to his study. He sat in a very old wing
chair in front of the Corona marble fireplace and
stared at the empty grate.

Burke had dinner brought to the master bedchamber that evening. He and Arielle ate compan-
ionably until she said in a tentative voice that was
striving to sound strong and sure, "I should like to
move into my own bedchamber. It is not proper that
I stay in here."

"Why not?"

"A husband and wife don't share the same bedchamber. It simply isn't done."

"Do you not wish to begin a new fashion, my

dear? Husbands and wives who want to sleep in
each other's arms should share—"

"No!" She looked with misery at the remaining
peas on her plate.

He said very gently, "Arielle, don't speak of this
again. This is our bedchamber. We are husband and
wife, and we will sleep together every night."

Arielle ate the rest of her peas. They were fresh
and she said, "Does the Abbey have its own garden?"

"Yes. If you're interested, I'm certain Mrs. Pepperall would be delighted to show you everything.
You are mistress here, you know. You can do anything you wish."

Arielle took a thoughtful bite of her partridge. It
was excellent, tender and spiced just right. So he
was giving her permission to do anything she
wished. She didn't believe him. She had been Lady
Rendel for too long to believe that. Every servant
toadied to the master, not the mistress. Any and
every servant would quickly betray the mistress if
the master wished it.

Burke said very casually, "Shall we invite your
half brother, Evan Goddis, to visit? Perhaps to dinner? I've never met him."

Her fork clattered to her plate. "No! That is, he
and I are not very close. Indeed, I didn't even know
him until after my father died. Then he became my
guardian." I mustn't sound so odd, she told herself.
"Perhaps he can pay us a visit in the future sometime," she added more calmly.

Burke merely nodded. Her dislike was healthy
and he wasn't about to discourage it. If she'd
cringed when he'd mentioned Evan Goddis's name,
he would have proof that the man had hurt her and
he would have ridden to Leslie Farm like an enraged bull. He buttered a thick slice of bread, say-

ing, "Didn't you have a stepson, Arielle? Etienne something?"

He was studying her beneath half-closed lids. Her reaction was clear enough: The pallor, the dilated eyes, the small quivers that shook her hands. This man had done something to her. Burke watched her carefully set her fork down. "Yes," she said at last, and her voice was smooth, calm. "His name is Etienne DuPons. He is Paisley's illegitimate son. His mother was French and he took her name. I trust he is well and far away from the area now."

"No, as a matter of fact, he isn't. I suppose you knew he was staying at Leslie Farm?"

"How do you know of that?"

'Whatever concerns you now concerns me. Don't forget that, Arielle. Did you know?"

"Yes, I knew. I just hoped he would be gone by now. I don't like him excessively.

"Why? Was he threatening your position at Rendel Hall?"

She laughed, a harsh, grating sound. And she kept laughing, almost hysterically. Once she regained control, she lay back against her pillows and closed her eyes.

So, Burke thought, DuPons had done something to her. Had her husband given her to his son? "You never had children during your marriage."

"No."

"Were you ever pregnant?"

"No."

Burke was thinking that his train of thought was a bit melodramatic. But it could have happened like that. Old Cochrane could have been sterile, after all. If he had been unable to sire a child, could he possibly have forced Arielle to have sex with his son to get her pregnant? No, it was absurd.

"Would you like some tea, Arielle?"

She sighed and nodded. "You have no more questions?"

"Not for the moment. Tell you what, my dear. Why don't we play piquet? Then a long night's sleep for you." And, he thought as he fetched two decks of playing cards, a hellish night for me.

It wasn't as bad as he feared it would be. He'd forgotten that the bed was so damned immense. Lying on his side, he would have to reach out his arm to even touch her side. He lay naked, his member swelled, and he forced himself not to move.

As for Arielle, she stared toward the dark ceiling. What to do? she wondered for the dozenth time. All those questions of his! It was impossible that he would know anything, surely. Then, suddenly, she saw him. She closed her eyes, but his image remained stark and real in her mind. As was his habit since their marriage, he'd very calmly begun stripping off his clothes even as he was speaking to her of the most mundane topics. And she'd looked at him, pointedly, until she regained her senses and turned her back to him. The flames had framed him and he'd looked like a golden god, all lean and strong and beautifully formed. But he was a man, and all that lean strength could hurt.

"Arielle?" he'd said earlier, before getting into bed.

She hadn't wanted to, but she turned to face him. He was still quite naked and he was smiling at her. His member was thrust outward. "Can I fetch you anything before I come to bed?"

"A dressing gown!" she nearly yelled at him. "For you!"

He chuckled. She watched him as he walked to the branch of candles on the table beside her side of the bed. He efficiently doused them.

The room was dark and she heard him climb into

the bed, felt it give under his weight. "Please," she whispered, "please don't make me do—"

"I won't," he'd said.

She listened now to his deep, even breathing. She jumped when he said mildly, "I am going to kiss you now, wife. Just a little kiss, nothing to alarm you. Don't struggle or leap out of bed, all right?"

"I don't want you to."

"Sorry, but I don't give a good damn what you want at the moment."

He rolled over, and even though he wasn't touching her, she could feel the heat from him. She felt his fingertips touch her chin, her throat. "The first and only time I've ever kissed you, I was equal parts enraged and feeling awful about everything. I was rough with you. I won't be now. Hold still, wife."

She felt his warm breath on her cheek, felt her chin held in the palm of his hand so she couldn't jerk away from him. Then she felt his mouth pressing ever so lightly on hers. "Very nice," he said against her closed lips. "Part your lips just a bit, Arielle. It is your duty to kiss properly."

She did. She was afraid not to. He was speaking in the calmest, most gentle voice, but she couldn't allow herself to be drawn in. She wouldn't allow it. She felt his tongue sliding over her bottom lip, then between her parted lips.

"This is even nicer," he said into her mouth. "No, don't draw away. I'm not hurting you." He was quiet then, his kiss deepening.

"You're so frozen and hurt," he said, once he'd left her mouth.

She could see his outline, his face just above hers. She wished he wouldn't speak like this. It terrified her.

"You have a beautiful body, Arielle. No, don't poker up on me. I took care of you all the time you were ill. I think I know your body as well as I do my own. I didn't ravish you, did I? And I could have. I could now if I wished to."

"Then you don't wish to," she said, "because if you did you would. You're a man and you don't care if—"

"Hush. Kiss me again and then let's get some sleep." This time he eased his tongue deeper into her mouth. He wondered vaguely if she would bite him. She didn't. Perversely, he wished she would. Then he would be certain that she wasn't terrified that he would whip her for doing it. He enjoyed kissing her immensely. It hurt, but it also felt wonderful. "Great strides," he said, gently kissed the tip of her nose, and rolled away from her.

"Sleep well, sweetheart."

Arielle turned very slightly to see his form beside her. He was already sleeping. She remembered then that he'd spent so many years in the army and supposed that as a soldier he'd had to catch his sleep whenever it was possible to do so. He began to snore, and despite herself, she smiled.

Arielle wasn't smiling the following morning. Her face was strained, her mouth in a taut line.

# 12

"She'll be all right, Arielle," Burke said gently to his wife as he led her to a chair. "I promise." He rubbed her cold hands, standing in front of her. "Just stay here, all right? That's good."

Arielle stared up at him. "But, Burke, she was—"

"Yes, I know," he said quickly. "I'll take care of it."

Arielle watched the sobbing Mellie, an upstairs maid, being led from the room by Mrs. Pepperall. The girl had a blanket covering her, for her clothing had nearly been ripped off. She walked, Arielle thought blankly, as if she were a broken doll. Tibbens, the old laundress who had found her, was saying to Burke, her deep voice hoarse with concern, "I wasn't in time, milord. He moved away too fast. I wasn't in time."

Burke spoke in his most soothing voice to Tibbens. After a moment she continued, her voice more steady. "I heard her screaming and ran toward the sound. He'd just, well, finished with Mellie when I saw him. He was fastening his breeches, standing over her, you know. When he saw me he ran toward the woods."

"You didn't recognize him?"

Tibbens shook her head. "He wasn't particularly

tall or short. Just a man, my lord. Maybe on the heavy side. He was wearing a hood over his head. Poor little Mellie doesn't know who he is either."

After getting as complete a description of the man as possible, Burke dismissed her. He instructed Cerlew to get a dozen or so men together for a search. He walked back to Arielle and came down on his haunches in front of her. He took her hands in his. Of all the things to happen, and here at Ravensworth.

"I must leave now, Arielle. We are going to look for the man who hurt Mellie."

"He raped her," she said, her voice hard. "That is much more than hurt."

"Yes, it is. When we get him, he will be punished."

"By whom?"

That made him pause a moment. "There must be laws, very stiff punishments, for rape."

She looked at him remotely. "A man can do anything he pleases to his wife. I would think that a man can do just as he pleases to any woman, except perhaps kill her. Men have made the laws, after all. Why would they want to punish each other for what they consider to be their right?"

He said nothing, for he had a horrible suspicion she was right. He rose, lightly touched his fingertips to her pale cheek, and left her.

There was no trace of the man except for a small square of dark brown wool snagged on a low branch of a maple tree some twenty yards from where Mellie had been raped.

Burke rode to Sir Edward Pottenham's manor house, situated just three miles east of Ravensworth Abbey. Sir Edward was a garrulous old man, fascinated by butterflies, and it took all Burke's verbal facility to avoid seeing Sir Edward's colorfully gruesome collection. He did, however, accept a brandy.

"Now, my boy, what brings you here? I fancy it isn't just for chitchat."

And Burke told him.

"Oh, dear," said Sir Edward when Burke had finished. "No idea who the man is, then?"

"No, but we did find this small square of wool. He probably ripped his coat when he was running toward the woods. We're fortunate to have this much. If Tibbens hadn't come so quickly, he very likely would have gotten away without a trace."

"Yes, probably," said Sir Edward. "Well, 'tis a pity, to be sure. We will hope the girl isn't with child. No man would marry her. A pity."

Burke heard Arielle's words in his mind. He heard himself say, "If I catch the man, what will happen to him?"

Sir Edward guffawed. "Well, if he isn't married, we'd force him to wed the girl."

"He raped her. He forced her against her will. He hurt her. I sincerely doubt she'd want him for a husband."

"Ah, well, just a girl's hysterics, my lord, probably because she got caught at it. The man is most certainly her lover, you know. That, or she was encouraging him, teasing him, I daresay. You know how these girls are. Butter wouldn't melt in their mouths until they're caught. I'll wager you fifty pounds the girl knows him." He laughed and slapped Burke on the back. "Now she knows him even better, huh? More brandy, my boy?"

It isn't right, Burke was thinking as he rode back to Ravensworth Abbey. What if it were Arielle who'd been raped? A lady, as opposed to a serving girl? No, it wasn't fair or right, or just.

But it was the way things were. He prayed the girl wasn't pregnant. He went from cynicism to shock when Mrs. Pepperall asked to see him privately upon his arrival to the Abbey.

"How is Mellie?" he asked.

"She is fine, given the circumstances. It's not about her that I wished to see you, my lord." Mrs. Pepperall paused a moment, then pressed on. "Her ladyship is resting now. And she is ... well, she's so young and unworldly, despite her being a married lady. She isn't strong yet, and I feel, my lord, that it is best handled by a man in any case."

"What, Mrs. Pepperall?"

"Mellie, of course. She must be dismissed, naturally. We can't have this sort of girl here. It would be a horrible example to all the other girls."

Burke stared at her. She was completely serious. "Shall I dismiss her, my lord?"

"Where is she now, Mrs. Pepperall?"

"In her bed."

"But it wasn't her fault. The man raped her."

"That's what Tibbens said," Mrs. Pepperall said, and she actually sniffed.

"I have no reason to disbelieve her. The girl was a victim. You saw her clothes, nearly ripped apart. She was in no way to blame for what happened to her. Has Dr. Brody been to see her?"

Mrs. Pepperall looked affronted at that. "Certainly not, my lord. Whatever for?"

Burke looked the older woman straight in her outraged eyes. "He might have harmed her internally. He might have ripped her. Have Dr. Brody fetched immediately."

Mrs. Pepperall just looked at him. All of this was so silly. "If he does, this ... this outrage will be all over East Grinstead by nightfall."

"Excellent. Perhaps we will learn the identity of the man who raped Mellie. Incidentally, tell Dr. Brody I wish to speak to him after he's seen to Mellie."

"Yes, my lord," said Mrs. Pepperall.

"Another thing. Mellie won't be let go. I will say it just once, Mrs. Pepperall. The rape wasn't her fault. You are not to blame her. You are not to allow any of the other servants to abuse her or blame her. I will speak to Montague. He will speak to the menservants."

"You could have knocked me down with a breath," Mrs. Pepperall was saying a few minutes later to Montague. "Can you imagine that little slut staying here after what she did? It's absurd, that's what it is!"

Montague said nothing. He wasn't certain if it was absurd or not. He knew only that the earl was furious. He was also afraid that the man who had raped Mellie was one of the footmen. He spoke to the men and warned them roundly. There were snickers and lewd comments from Charlie, the second footman, a brawny lad from Wendicoe in western Ireland, and Montague told him to mind his own affairs and leave the girl alone. He added for good measure that his lordship had said anyone bothering the girl would get the boot on the spot. Charlie stopped snickering. Montague gave him a long look.

Burke was on the point of going upstairs to see Arielle when Dr. Brody followed Montague into the estate room. Mark Brody was a slender young man with a pallid complexion and fierce blue eyes. He was only a couple of years Burke's senior and had been in the area for the past three years. He lived in West Healthy with his mother. Burke liked him.

Burke shook the man's hand. "A long time, Mark."

"Yes, indeed. Welcome home, Burke. Congratulations on your marriage to Lady Rendel. A lovely young lady."

After a few minutes of amenities, Mark Brody

said, "I examined the girl, Mellie. The man who did this in fact injured her internally. I'm not certain whether or not she was a virgin, but she was quite small and the man was brutal."

"Mellie should have been a virgin. She is only fifteen years old."

"Not so very young in the country, Burke. In any case, I got the bleeding stopped. She's very weak from the loss of blood, but she's a healthy girl. She will survive this. Did you catch the man responsible?"

Burke shook his head, then said quietly, "Do you think he should be punished for what he did?"

"I would say yes only because I saw the girl. She didn't encourage him. She was brutalized. No human being should be treated like that without adequate retribution for the one responsible."

"Well, that is something at least," Burke said. "You will come back to check on her?"

"Certainly." Dr. Brody took his leave and Burke headed upstairs.

Arielle wasn't in bed. She was dressed in a pale blue silk gown and seated by the window. Her hair was in a braided coronet about her head. She looked lovely, too thin, and sad.

"Hello," he said, leaned down, and lightly kissed her cheek.

She flinched only slightly. He was pleased. "Mellie will be all right. I spoke to Dr. Brody." He wasn't about to tell her any of the rest of it.

"That is a relief," she said. She looked up at him. "It is an awful thing, Burke."

"Yes, I know."

"To be helpless, weaker than someone else . . . no, weaker than half the human beings on the earth. It is a fearful thing."

He clasped her about her shoulders and lifted her from the chair. "I know," he repeated and pulled her against him. He gently pressed her cheek against his shoulder. "I will find the man, sweetheart. And I will punish him." Surprisingly, he meant what he said. There would be no punishment for the man under the law. So he, Burke, would have to be judge and jury. He was, after all, responsible for everyone living on Ravensworth land. He'd failed here, and it was his duty to set things right.

He lightly stroked his hands up and down Arielle's back. "Most men wouldn't consider doing that," he said. Most women, too, he thought, remembering Mrs. Pepperall's words. Both she and Sir Edward Pottenham readily blamed the woman, not the man; blamed the victim, not the rapist. How would he himself have reacted if he hadn't been so completely sensitized by Arielle? Indeed, if Arielle hadn't been abused, would she still feel so strongly? He prayed his reaction would have been exactly the same.

Later that afternoon, Burke and Arielle went to the west lawn, where the small gazebo stood, a frothy structure built by Burke's grandfather. He imagined the gazebo had been the spot for many trysts. Still was, probably. Perhaps soon he could seduce Arielle here, Burke thought. That would be nice, very nice.

The sun was low in the west, the air redolent with the scents of freshly scythed summer grass. The slight breeze was warm and Burke felt good. He watched Arielle raise her face to the sun.

He fetched a blanket from the gazebo and spread it beneath a sprawling-branched oak tree. They sat in companionable silence. But she tired so easily. Eventually Arielle ended up with her head on Burke's lap. She stared at the shafts of sunlight through the leaves. "This is beautiful. Nothing bad could happen here."

"I wouldn't let it," he said and leaned back against the trunk. "Are you comfortable?"

"Hmm."

He thought she'd fallen asleep, until she said suddenly, "It is difficult to take this waiting, Burke. It seems interminable to me."

"We'll catch the man, Arielle. I told Cerlew to hire a Bow Street Runner. I understand from military friends that those fellows are more tenacious than lice in the hills of Portugal."

"That's not what I meant."

Her voice sounded dull, emotionless. Very gently, he said, "What, then, is difficult? What are you waiting for?"

"For you to demand that I see to your needs. Are you waiting until you're certain I am well?"

"Why do you bring it up? You make me think you want me to act against you."

"I have become a realist. I simply would like you to tell me when to prepare myself. Not knowing when you will . . ." Her voice trailed off.

Perhaps she did want him to act against her. Then she could escape him, a brute, with a clear conscience. Well, she would be in for a surprise. He picked a loose tendril of her hair and wrapped it around his fingers. "Your hair is very soft." He let his fingertips trail lightly over her throat. She was so smooth and white.

"I find our situation somewhat strange, Arielle. Here we are, lying at our ease on a blanket, the picture of two perfectly relaxed, happy people, and you are asking me when I intend to begin abusing you and when I shall insist that you begin to service me. It jolts the picture, you could say."

"When can we go to Boston?" she asked, ignoring his words.

"I told you. When the war is finally over. Also, even though Cerlew is a most scrupulous fellow, it

wouldn't be fair of me to simply pick up and leave.
There are many decisions to be made about the estate. We could leave in the early fall, perhaps. But
we will wait until it is safe. I hear that peace talks
are gong well. It shouldn't be too much longer."

"But Baron Sherard and Nesta are English and
they live there."

"Yes, but we don't, and I won't take any chances
with your safety."

Arielle had nothing to say to that. He was a complicated man, and slippery. Just when she thought
she understood him, he changed like a shadow hand
against a window shade. He was concerned about
her safety, yet he had abducted her. It was all very
confusing. She felt fatigue pulling at her. She hated
this weakness, this proof of her body's betrayal.

When Burke looked down he saw that she was
asleep. He smiled and touched his fingertips to her
slightly parted lips. So soft. He decided to take her
to London when she regained her strength. He
wanted to take her everywhere and introduce her
to all his friends. His sister would remember Arielle with fondness—at least he hoped so. And Lannie. He must find out when she was planning on
returning to Ravensworth. Although he wanted to
have Arielle all to himself, it didn't occur to him to
ask Lannie to remain at his sister's. Burke thought
about his last night in London, the night before he
had left to kidnap his bride. He'd dined with Knight
at his town house.

Over brandy, Knight had remarked, "I say, old
fellow, isn't there an easier way to get a woman to
marry you?" He had been tossing playing cards
negligently on the table between them, some landing faceup, others facedown.

"Probably, but not this one." Burke raised his
brandy snifter. "Let's drink to my wife, Knight.

And to that wonderful hunting box you are providing for the honeymoon."

"Don't you mean *pre*-honeymoon? Ah, three jacks up, Burke. That will be hard to beat. You intend to keep her there until she agrees, don't you?"

"If I have to." Burke sighed, then gave his friend a crooked grin and began tossing the cards from his deck. "Sounds as if I've gone round the bend, doesn't it? Perhaps I have. I just know that I have to have her."

"I look forward to meeting this paragon of all that is wonderful," Knight said and grinned when he tossed the fourth jack faceup on the table. "Wonderful for you, that is. As for *this* man, he firmly intends to remain unshackled until he's old and gray, and the night before it is his fate to be dead or impotent or both, he will beget a legal heir."

Burke choked on his brandy, but within a very short time, managed to turn up three queens.

"I trust, dear fellow," Knight drawled as he closely scrutinized the queen of hearts, "that this is an omen of good things for you. But I don't know, Burke. Women can be the very devil, you know." After wishing him luck, Knight had left his own house, whistling, to visit his mistress.

Burke now smiled down at his sleeping paragon. She had loved him once; she would love him again.

Arielle dressed for dinner that evening. She chose a simple muslin of pale green from her own trunk, not from the gowns Burke had purchased for her. Dorcas fastened the final button and stepped back. "The neckline comes to your chin," she said, slapping down an errant fold in the skirt. "You hope to keep him away from you," she added matter-of-factly.

"Yes," Arielle admitted.

"You look like a girl still in the schoolroom. A decent man would stay away from you."

Arielle wasn't at all certain just how decent Burke was. She said nothing, however.

When she entered the drawing room some thirty minutes later, Burke's expression told her that she could wear a rag and he would still want her, desperately.

He smiled at her, his sweet smile, one that made her feel quite strange and warm at the same time. She pulled herself together. How would he look at her in a month? A year? Five years? That thought brought back the chill of an empty future.

"You look wonderful," he said, and before she could move, he kissed her wrist, then her mouth. "Are you ready to be a glutton?"

She nodded and said as she quickly stepped away from him, "You're a very handsome man, Burke. I've always thought that, but I—"

"Let's have our dinner. And thank you for the compliment."

Over her fresh mushroom soup, Arielle asked, "What has happened to Rendel Hall? Do you know?"

"No, and I don't really care."

"You were willing to buy it, Burke—the house, all the land, everything."

"Only because I was making plans to have you even then." He robbed his words of threat for her by smiling broadly. "It doesn't make too much sense now when I think about it. How could I have had you in my power if you had so much money?"

"What you did is not amusing, Burke."

"No, but then again, I was dead serious."

Montague came into the dining room, two footmen on his heels, each carrying huge silver trays. Burke said nothing more until all the food was served; then he nodded dismissal to Montague.

Even as he did it, he realized Arielle should do the dismissing. She was the mistress, after all. He would have to discuss it with her. He didn't wish her to feel a visitor in her own house. He wanted her to *know* that she was truly the mistress here.

Both of them did full justice to Cook's offering of lamb cutlets and fresh peas. Arielle looked down at her lemon cream dessert and made a face at it. "I can't hold another bite. It was delicious, all of it."

"You must tell Montague so he can inform Cook of your delight."

She nodded, then looked about the massive, dark oak wainscoted walls. The chandelier overhead could, if it fell, slay a good twenty people. It was dusty. She started to say something, then shook her head at herself. Why should she care? She looked at the bank of three long windows that gave onto the front lawn of the Abbey. The draperies were thick, dark blue velvet. Too dark, and the velvet was shiny with age. She pictured pale yellow draperies, perhaps, to make the room airy. Again she shook her head at herself. It didn't matter if the room looked like a tomb.

She glanced over at Burke and saw that he'd been watching her, his expression intent. "What are you going to do tonight?" she asked, pleased that her voice sounded as calm as a summer pond to her sensitive ears.

"You will see," he said.

She paled at his words, but he held his peace. He wasn't in any hurry to adjourn to his bedchamber. He asked Arielle to play the piano for him and she did, singing several Italian ballads that were soft and soothing and sad.

When Montague entered with the tea tray, Burke gave a start. He didn't realize the time had passed so quickly. He nodded to the butler and said to his wife, "That was lovely. Thank you. Come and have some tea now, before we retire."

Arielle didn't want to retire, ever. She fiddled with her teacup, crushed a moist piece of raspberry-and-currant tart on the gold-edged plate. "My father sang quite well," she blurted out.

"He taught you?"

"Yes."

"I sing, too. Perhaps we can try a duet soon."

"Do you play?"

"Not so well anymore. When it was decided that I was to be armybound, my father said I shouldn't be bothered with such nonsense. A pity. I much enjoyed playing."

"You could begin to play again."

"Yes," he said easily. "Here we are once more, the picture of two relaxed, happy people. Only one of them is terrified that her husband will rip off her clothes and do unspeakable things to her. The picture is awry, Arielle."

She ignored him and said, "I think I shall retire now, Burke. May I use my own bedchamber?"

"No. Pray don't ask that of me again, Arielle. That 'no' will still be in effect in fifty years."

"Good night," she said and rose.

"Wait for me, my dear. I will come with you."

He saw that she'd moved a screen into his bedchamber. It was a Chinese affair that he thought particularly obnoxious, but he didn't say anything. Within a month, he would be able to destroy it without any demures from her. At least he prayed that that would be so. When she emerged, swathed from neck to floor in a white lawn gown, he was already lying in bed, seemingly engrossed in a fascinating book about the Borgias.

He was naked; he was determined on his course.

"Come here," he said, putting the book on the bedside table and patting the bed beside him.

Her step lagging, her eyes down, she neared the bed. Burke took her hand in his. "Very good. Now, Arielle, I would like you to take off the nightgown."

Her head jerked up and he saw the stricken look in her eyes. His expression didn't change. He saw her tongue glide over her lower lip.

"Shall I help you?"

She shook her head then and quickly, frantically, pulled open the ribbons and unfastened the myriad of buttons. He watched her lift the gown over her head, watched it pool at her feet. He said nothing, merely looked at her. She stood very still, as if she were used to this scrutiny. "You look lovely," he said at last with great but inadequate sincerity. She didn't flinch when he reached out his hand and gently cupped her left breast. "Come sit beside me, here."

She sat, her hands on her thighs, her legs slightly parted. How many times, he wondered had Paisley Cochrane forced her to do this? Her hands were on her thighs because obviously her former husband hadn't wanted her trying to cover herself.

In the dim light it was nearly impossible for Burke to make out the faint white scars. "Look at me, Arielle."

She jerked. That was something she wasn't used to, he thought. Slowly, she raised her head. Her expression for just a moment was pain-filled before she managed to mask all expression so he wouldn't know what she was thinking or feeling. Very gently he clasped one of her hands. He felt the warm smoothness of her thigh beneath his hand. Long slender legs, she had, sleekly muscled.

"How do you feel?" he asked.

"All right."

"Come into bed now. I don't want you to take a chill."

He pulled the covers back. She looked undecided,

but then slowly, she crawled over him and burrowed under the covers.

He turned on his side to face her. "Now, you told me you couldn't bear the waiting anymore."

She nodded, her eyes tightly closed.

"I am sorry to disappoint you, love, but I don't feel like a ravening beast tonight."

Her eyes flew open and she sucked in her breath, blurting out, "Why are you toying with me like this?"

"Shush," he said, leaning forward to kiss her. He could feel her fear of him, taste her bloody fear, damn her, hear the small, gasping breaths. He said slowly, "I intend to toy with you until you don't want me to stop."

"Can I not simply . . . do it? I will try, truly I will."

"Tonight," he continued, ignoring her words as he stroked his splayed fingers through her hair, "I'm going to love every inch of you. I'm going to learn you, memorize you."

She looked at him as though he'd lost his mind. Since he'd already decided that there was little enough left, he couldn't blame her.

"You have the cutest ears," he said, kissing the shell of her ear, then nibbling lightly on her earlobe. "Soft and small and very feminine." He saw the tiny hole and continued. "I shall have to buy you some jewelry. Actually, there are the Drummond jewels—heirlooms, the lot of them—I'll fetch them for you and you can decide what you would like. There must be pierced earrings. If you don't like any of it, I will buy you what you wish."

She gave him a disbelieving look. Paisley had allowed her to wear his first wife's jewelry on occasions when there were guests. A rather ugly emerald bracelet had fallen off her wrist one time, and he'd beaten her soundly for her carelessness.

Burke was still toying with her and she hated it. She felt off balance, and she was frightened.

His tongue glided again over her ear, then made a light foray into the inside. It felt odd. She shivered. Perhaps he would give her jewelry, then accuse her of losing it. "I don't want any jewelry," she said.

"Why not? Don't you look well in jewelry?"

"I—I might lose it. And you would be displeased."

"I see," he said, and he did indeed understand now. "Now, where was I? Ah, yes, your right ear. I think while I pay attention to that part of you, I should like to feel your breasts against my chest. There, that isn't so bad, is it?"

# 13

Burke didn't think he would be able to sleep, but eventually he did. She was tangled against him, held to him tightly, his arm firmly around her back. He wasn't concerned that she'd felt his swollen member against her belly. He wanted her to know that he desired her. He wanted her to realize, eventually, that no matter how much need he had, he wouldn't force her.

What she'd realized to this point, of course, was that he wasn't behaving the way a man should. She was waiting, waiting for him to turn on her, to beat her, to force her to her knees. Time, he thought yet again, and patience and consistency, praying that he was right.

How very strange, he thought, on the point of sleep, that things had turned out this way. A wife terrified of her husband. It was certainly a situation he'd never considered.

When Burke heard the scream he was calmly retreating his troops into the hills of Portugal, back, back, away from the French, who were coming ever toward them. He was waiting for Major Lufton and his men to arrive from the rear and entrap the French between them. He shaded his eyes against the ferocious noonday sun. Where the hell was Major Lufton?

There was another scream and he bolted upright in bed.

Arielle whispered, "What is that?"

"Stay here." Burke was quickly out of bed and into his dressing gown. It was just after dawn, and the light in the corridor was pale and indistinct.

He dashed down the corridor, coming to a halt when he saw Mrs. Pepperall standing at the top of the stairs, staring downward, her hand covering her mouth.

Burke walked quickly to her. He looked down to see the girl, Mellie, swathed in a white nightgown, lying in a pool of blood. From here he could tell that her neck was broken.

He felt a wave of sickness, but his voice was calm with authority. "Fetch Montague, Mrs. Pepperall, and tell him to send a footman for Dr. Brody."

An hour later, Burke, Arielle, and Mark Brody were seated in the drawing room.

"I'd say she died some five or six hours ago," said Dr.Brody between sips of strong dark tea.

"Then why wasn't there a candle anywhere about?" Arielle asked. "Burke remarked on that immediately. What was she doing there without any light to guide her?"

"It is an interesting point," said Burke. "In any case, we must call in Sir Edward Pottenham, since he is the local magistrate—not that he will be one whit of help to anyone."

Mark Brody said, after darting a quick glance at Arielle, "Mellie was bleeding profusely. Do you think possibly she awoke, saw the blood, and tried to find someone to help her? Perhaps she was too frightened to think of lighting a candle."

There wasn't an answer, of course. Sir Edward was told the story several hours later. He sat quietly for a moment, then slapped his hands on his thighs and said, "Well, perhaps it is for the best.

The girl was ruined, of course, no future at all for her. Her death was an accident, or suicide. For the best."

Arielle couldn't help herself. She jumped to her feet, the abrupt movement making her dizzy. But she held her ground, clutching at the back of a chair. "For the best!" she cried. "An innocent young girl is dead, her neck broken, and you think it's a good thing? God save us from all men! I hope you fall down some stairs and break your neck—then *I* can say it is a good thing!"

She gathered up her skirts and ran from the drawing room. Burke regarded Sir Edward from beneath half-closed lashes.

"Well, I say! Your new wife, my lord, well, hysterics in women, one must put up with it, I suppose. I daresay she's breeding. Women are such strange creatures and—"

"Actually, Sir Edward," Burke said as he rose, "I quite agree with my wife. I don't think Mellie died by accident or took her own life. I think she was deliberately lured out to the stairs and pushed. Do you still believe it's a good thing if the girl was murdered?"

Sir Edward was miffed. He wanted to be left in blessed peace and get back to his butterfly collection. "So who did it? You, my lord?"

Burke smiled at his snide tone. "No, but perhaps the man who raped her is a servant in this house, a possibility that makes my skin crawl. He feared she would remember something and identify him. He killed her."

"A theory without substance. And exactly how will you find out who this mythical man is?"

"I haven't the foggiest notion right now, but I will have a Bow Street Runner soon. Then we'll see. There is a flaw in that theory, however," he added thoughtfully. "Even if he'd been caught, nothing much would have happened to him for rap-ing Mellie. Murder is a lurid extreme."

"Not given your attitude, my lord! The fellow must have believed that if you found out he was the so-called rapist, you would cut his throat. Well, there it is. Now I have more important things to do."

"I shall show you out, Sir Edward," Burke said. So, he thought, it is my fault that Mellie was mur-dered. Well, hell.

The day after Mellie's funeral, Burke was called from his study by Montague, who was looking somewhat bewildered. "My lord, you have com-pany. Not entirely company, but some of one kind and some of another. Many of both."

"Very clear, Montague. I will be there immedi-ately."

He saw Montague's problem when he came into the entrance hall. Lannie had returned with her two children, Knight, and a gentleman Burke had never before seen.

"Well," he said. "Welcome, everyone."

"Uncle Burke! Uncle Burke! We're home and we brought you a present!"

Burke caught both little girls in his arms and kissed them soundly. "And I've a present for each of you, Virgie and Poppet."

"It's our new aunt, isn't it?" said Virgie, two years older than Poppet and thus more of a can-did speaker. "Mother told us you married a girl who had killed her husband, and she couldn't understand it because the poor old man hadn't a son and—"

"Oh, dear," said Lannie, having the grace to blush. "I didn't say it *exactly* like that! Girls, let go of your uncle. Ah, Mrs. Mack, take them to the nursery. Your uncle will visit you later, girls—won't you, Burke?"

"Certainly." He kissed both girls again, to their giggling delight, and gave them into Mrs. Mack's long-suffering patient care.

"Burke," Lannie said, "this is Percy Kingstone. Percy, may I introduce you to my brother-in-law and the master here, Burke Drummond, the Earl of Ravensworth."

The men shook hands. So, Burke was thinking, the wind sits in this direction, does it? The man seemed unobjectionable to Burke, somewhat stout, a bit of a dandy if the truth be told, but his expression was pleasant, his eyes intelligent. He smiled and remarked on the excellent condition of the roads from London. Burke turned to Knight.

"May I ask what wrenches you from London, old fellow?"

"I'm here to see your bride, of course," Knight said. "I told Lannie I would be delighted to play propriety, so I sat between the two of them for four hours."

Percy Kingstone, Lord Carver, grinned and took Lannie's gloved hand. "He did indeed, my lord, and he snored for three of the four hours."

"A gross untruth," said Knight.

Lannie, who had been looking about her, said abruptly, "We got your letter and then saw the notice in the *Gazette*. Corinne was furious, Burke, simply outraged that you would wed without having the family present. You know how she is."

"Yes, I do." He gave Lannie a sweet smile. "Montague will see to everyone's luggage. I assume this is to be a visit?"

He assumed correctly, Knight told him. It was a good thirty minutes later before Knight and Burke finally found themselves alone in Burke's estate room, the only room in the Abbey that guaranteed them privacy.

"Where is your bride?"

"Asleep, I hope. She still isn't completely well yet and tires easily."

"I didn't realize she had been ill."

"Yes, she became quite sick at your hunting box. She is much better now."

Knight wandered over to the fireplace and leaned his broad shoulder negligently against the mantelpiece. "I don't suppose you will tell me what transpired at Hobhouse? Other than your bride's illness, of course."

"Her illness is at the root of the business, if you would know the truth. I married her really without her knowing about it. I daresay that if she hadn't been ill she never would have married me. She is hurt, Knight. I have an odd marriage, I suppose you could say."

Knight regarded him, saying nothing.

Burke gave it up without a whimper. He and Knight had been through too much together for him to even consider dissembling now. "Her first husband abused her dreadfully. If you saw the white lines on her body—" He paused, and Knight frowned at the fury and pain he saw in his friend's eyes. "He beat her. Often. Obviously with great pleasure. There, now you will understand. I ask that you be gentle with her. I'm glad you're here. We've had some nastiness, and your presence will take Arielle's mind off it, hopefully."

A houseful of guests certainly did distract Arielle. She went so far as to laugh at dinner at a comment made by Lord Carver. She'd thought him rather like a stuffed, very well garbed sausage until she discovered he was near to overflowing with a keen wit. And he appeared kind.

"That was too absurd," Lannie said, taping her fork on his hand, "and I won't believe a word of it."

"That Daisy kissed the dowager duchess or that the footman pinched Daisy's, ah, her . . . well, you understand."

Burke watched her laugh and felt something warm and sweet fill him. He wished at this very moment that he could touch her, nothing more, just feel her warmth and softness. And, of course, she would look at him, trying to control her fear, trying desperately to discover what it was he wanted so she could do it to keep him from striking her.

It was better in the dark when she was lying beside him in the big bed. He couldn't see her fear, her wariness, perhaps even her revulsion. But he still knew that after each kiss she expected an order, expected him to hit her, to yell at her. But nothing save more kisses and caresses followed. He wondered if his behavior was still driving her frantic.

There was a brief lull in the conversation as Montague directed the footmen to remove the green-pea soup and the stewed trout and serve the entrées of venison, scallops of chickens, and tendons of beef.

Lannie, not waiting for the footmen to remove themselves, said with a meaningful look toward Burke, "So, my brother-in-law, this very romantic fellow who Corinne says slew at least half a dozen ladies during his visit to London, comes back to Ravensworth, takes one look at you, Arielle, and marries you. It is vastly romantic, don't you agree, Percy?"

"To be swept off one's feet, my dear, is that what you mean? Sort of like swimming off Dover at high tide?"

"You are provoking! Now, Arielle, did you set your cap for Burke?"

"I suppose you could say that, Lannie."

Burke gave her a warm smile. Arielle didn't return it. She felt very alone at that moment, felt indeed something of a fraud.

"I suppose he is passing handsome. At least that's what the ladies whispered to me whilst I was in London. And, Burke, you naughty man, I heard Lord Donnovan tell about your mistress, Laura Something-or-other. Oh, dear, really, forgive me—I didn't mean, truly, 'tis just that—"

"Your mouth is filled with nonsense rather than the venison, Lannie," Burke said easily. "Eat and amuse yourself by counting the peas on your plate."

Knight, a diplomat of the first order, said in a thoughtful voice, "I say, Burke, that painting just above your left shoulder, is it an ancestor?"

"Yes, my great-great-grandfather, Hugo Everett Drakemore Drummond." As he spoke, Burke looked toward Arielle. Her head was down. He felt a wave of anger at Lannie for her damnably loose tongue. He glanced over to see Knight regarding him, a question in his eyes.

When Arielle said quietly, "If you will excuse us, gentlemen," and rose, it took all Burke's resolution not to go to her and drag her away to explain. He watched her walk gracefully from the dining room, Lannie beside her.

"Well," Lannie said brightly, looking about the drawing room, "You haven't changed anything, I see."

"No," said Arielle.

"How odd it is to have another lady here as mistress. Not that I mind, Arielle, for I truly don't. It just feels rather strange. Even after Montrose died, I was still the mistress. Yes, very strange."

"Lord Carver seems a nice gentleman."

"Yes, I fancy that I shall marry him. He is very smart, you know." She added a bit uncertainly, "He is, I am told, much admired for his wit."

Arielle smiled at that negligent bit of praise. "Yes, he is most amusing. Do Virgie and Poppet like him?"

"They are most indiscriminating. They rally around any male who comes into their ken, including Percy. Percy's first wife died in childbirth. He didn't believe, so he told me, that he would ever find another lady he could love." Lannie turned a pale shade of pink at her words. "I think we will deal well together."

"I think so too."

"Now tell me about poor little Mellie. I couldn't believe it. Mrs. Pepperall told me, you know. Killing herself like that!"

Arielle's expression turned hard. "Mellie was raped. She didn't kill herself, Lannie. I am sorry to say this because it is frightening, but someone killed her, probably the man who raped her. You see, she went down the stairs in the middle of the night. There was no candle anywhere about."

"But Mrs. Pepperall told me that Mellie was struck with guilt and—"

"Guilt? About what? She was raped, Lannie! She didn't do anything! She was fifteen years old!"

Lannie gave her a long look, then said, "I think I shall play a French ballad for you."

The gentlemen soon made their appearance, and good manners dictated that Burke play the attentive host until all his guests were ready for their beds. It was close to midnight before he closed his chamber door, drew a deep sigh, and began to take off his clothes. Arielle had excused herself a few moments earlier. She was in bed, the covers drawn up to her eyebrows. He could see her outline from the light of the single candle on the table. He knew she was awake. He gritted his teeth and said in his major lord's voice, "Arielle, get up now. I wish to see you."

There was no response from the bed. he held his breath, hoping against hope. "Arielle, I said to get up. I don't wish to tell you again."

He was naked, and as he was reaching for his dressing gown, he saw her sit up in bed and look toward him. He guessed she wanted to plead with him and he waited. She said nothing. She slipped out of bed. She was wearing a nightgown.

"Take off the nightgown. Now. I thought I told you never to wear one."

Her hands fluttered to the long row of buttons, paused, then began to unfasten them.

"Hurry."

He felt that damnable pain as he watched her become frantic, pulling and prodding at the tiny buttons. Finally she jerked the gown over her head and stood perfectly still in front of him. He reached out his hand. She didn't move. Her eyes were closed.

"Open your eyes!"

She did, without hesitation. His fingers lightly stroked over her breasts. He watched her carefully. Because he was coming to know her so well, he saw the fear building even though she tried to keep her features expressionless. Slowly, he ran his hand down to her stomach. She was so incredibly soft, so smooth. He let his fingers tangle in the fine curls that covered her, curls just a bit darker than her beautiful Titian hair. He heard her suck in her breath, felt her near desperation to flee. She didn't move. He was hard with need but ignored it. Gently, he picked her up an carried her to the bed.

When he laid her down, he saw a flash of pure anger in her eyes before she masked it. Her hands were at her sides and were fisted against the linen sheets. She made no move to cover herself, waiting, knowing herself to be helpless.

Burke sat on the bed beside her. "Arielle."

She didn't want to, but she looked at him.

"What are you feeling? Right now?"

She stared at him as if he'd lost his mind. She ran her tongue over her lower lip and appeared completely bewildered.

"Are you feeling desire for me?"

She couldn't hide her reaction. She shook her head, a small cry escaping her throat.

"I see. Do you feel anger toward me?"

"No, no, truly, I am . . . tired! Forgive me, just tell me what you wish and—"

"I wish to hold you and fall asleep holding you." He followed action to words, shed his dressing gown, and slipped into bed beside her. She was trembling. Damnation. He pulled her against him and settled her. Patience, he thought. Patience. "I'm too tired to kiss your beautiful ears. Forgive me."

He thought she'd fallen asleep, when she said abruptly, "Laura who?"

He felt an excessive spurt of joy. He said easily, "Laura Hogburn. Not a romantic last name, I grant you, but what can she do?"

"She could change it!"

He smiled into the darkness. Acrimony. He was delighted.

"What did you do to her?"

Now what, Burke wondered silently, did she mean by that? He said aloud, "Do you mean, did I pay her money?"

"Yes."

"Certainly. Do you mean, did I visit her?"

"Yes."

"Not since I left London to come after you. I already told you that, remember? Do you mean, did I beat her?"

"Yes, damn you!"

"No."

"But what—"

"I had sex with her. It is what one usually does with a mistress, you know."

"Then she was used to doing and being exactly what a man wished her to be."

"I suppose so," Burke said. "After all, she makes her living by pleasing men. Mistresses do that quite willingly, and hopefully with sufficient skill to earn enough money for their needs."

Arielle fell silent. She'd been right. Mistresses weren't beaten, simply because they were free to leave whenever they wished. Men had no legal hold over them. They weren't at all like wives, who had no choice about anything.

She sighed and closed her eyes. She was very aware of Burke's lean body against hers, the crinkly softness of his hair against her cheek. Her hand lay as still as she could keep it on his muscled belly. She was terrified that she would touch him by accident and that he would lose control. When he'd taken off his dressing gown, his member had been hard, thrusting forward, ready. She made a small, distressed sound, unable to help herself.

"Shush, sweetheart. Go to sleep. Someday you will believe me, you know. Someday you will trust me. Many men have told me that I'm quite the adequate friend, and perhaps you will come to think so as well." He heard another small gasp. "All right, tell me what's wrong."

"I'm afraid. Your manhood is—" Her voice dropped like a stone from a cliff.

"My manhood is what?"

"Big and hard."

He felt his insides clench at her words. "I cannot help it, you know. I want to be inside you, very much. It's the way I am made, Arielle."

"Then why haven't you?"

"Come inside you?"

"Yes."

"You haven't asked me to," he said simply. He heard her suck in her breath, and he smiled into the darkness.

Suddenly, without warning, she reared up, jerking away from him. "You are cruel! You mock me, and taunt me, and—" She paused, and he knew that she was terrified of what she'd done. He waited. "Why can you not just be done with it? I—I cannot bear it. Please, Burke, just be done with it!"

He hadn't expected this assault. She was so disbelieving of him, so uncertain of him, that she wanted him to force her, just to have it done and over with. She was so far from feeling desire that in dark moments, he feared of ever reaching her. Even if he were gentle, he knew she would hate it, feel that he was violating her.

"Lie down, Arielle."

His voice, cold and imperious. She tried to control her breathing, control her fear. Slowly, she uncurled her body and eased down beside him, her eyes shut. At least it would be done and over with soon. But if he didn't like her, what would he do? He will beat you, you half-wit, she told herself. That's what he will do. But it was better than not knowing. It had to be better.

She felt his large warm hand stroke over her breasts, downward over her ribs, and come to rest in the hollow of her belly.

"Part your legs."

She did.

She felt his fingers searching, felt the warmth of him as he touched her. Then he kissed her mouth. She wanted to scream and run, but she didn't move.

"You want to know what I'm going to do to you, Arielle?"

She said nothing.

"I'm going to slip my finger inside you. There, how does that feel?"

She said nothing, but he felt her stiffen.

"You're very small," he said, and she heard pain in his voice and wondered at it. She was frozen, rigid, waiting. "Even my finger is stretching you."

"I can't help it," she finally managed.

His finger went deeper, and he wondered if he was hurting her. He hadn't expected this smallness. He had expected that she wouldn't make a sound even if he did hurt her. "What can't you help?"

"Paisley," she said, turning her face into his shoulder.

"Paisley what?"

"He couldn't . . . go very far . . . couldn't . . ."

Burke stared into the darkness, his thoughts tumbling wildly against one another. No, it wasn't possible, was it? "Are you a virgin, Arielle?"

"A virgin? How could I be a virgin? No, well, I don't know."

"Did your—did Paisley come inside you?"

"He tried, but . . . yes, a bit, but . . . he said I wasn't a woman, that I was too skinny and he disliked my body. I couldn't arouse him properly, and he forced me down on my knees, so he wouldn't have to see my face, he said, and he tried and tried and . . . God!"

Burke took his finger out of her and gathered her into his arms. "It's all right," he said, over and over until her trembling lessened. "He didn't let Etienne take you?"

"He would have, but he died first. He made me be naked in front of his son and made me take him in my mouth to show Etienne how obedient and well trained I was and—"

"I understand. It's all right."

"He wanted me to be pregnant, so he told Etienne he could have me until I was."

The words were awful. They were, hopefully, also

somewhat cathartic. Burke clamped down on his rage and said in a light, cool voice, "How wonderful that the damnable old bastard died. What a sick old bedlamite. Don't you agree?"

She was surprised at his words and his tone, and realized suddenly that it was indeed most fortunate. "Yes," she said. "You're right about that." She was silent for just a moment, then added, "If I hadn't been such a coward, I would have murdered him. I thought about it, you know, but in the end I was just too afraid."

No, he thought, she'd been too well trained, terrified not to be obedient. A possession didn't turn on its master.

"I would have murdered him too. Now, kiss me and let's go to sleep."

To his utter delight, she did. Shyly, her lips closed, but it did rank as a kiss.

# 14

"Oh! Lord Castlerosse, forgive me. I didn't mean to interrupt you and—"

"You aren't, Countess," Knight said easily, turning away from the long windows to face her.

He looked at her closely. In but a brief moment, he saw her hesitation about coming into a room that held only a man; saw her decide that no matter what the man tried, he couldn't hurt her because of the servants close by, and finally attempt a smile to put him at ease because, after all, he was her guest.

He was a good friend of Burke's, Arielle was thinking. It was important to be nice to him. She'd realized the previous evening that he was a handsome man, not as handsome as her husband, but still ... That wayward thought brought her up short. He had the blackest hair imaginable, thick and a bit too long for fashion, she suspected, and eyes a golden sort of brown, a fox's eyes. He exuded power, strength, and dominance, both physical and mental, just like Burke, and that scared her. She stopped cold.

Something, Knight thought, had made her hesitate yet again, and he said in his casual drawl, "Won't you join me, ma'am?"

227

"All right," Arielle said. She felt like a fool, behaving like this, and came into the room.

Knight was beginning to feel like the gallows. He wished she'd realize that he wasn't going to be her executioner. "Your gown is lovely, if you don't mind my saying so," he said. "I wouldn't have thought that that particular shade of yellow would complement your hair, but it does."

"Thank you, my lord."

"Do you think you could call me Knight?"

"Your name is unusual."

"I suppose so. My mother was infatuated with King Arthur, you see. She was realistic enough to know that Lancelot or Galahad or Gawain simply wouldn't do, not in modern England, so she decided I could simply embody all of them."

"Arthur isn't bad."

"I remember once telling her that. Her reply to me was that she didn't think I'd prove worthy enough to bear that exalted name. Behold a man who is all and none, a concept, a designation."

Arielle smiled. He was charming and amusing. He didn't seem at all threatening. "My father was a scholar. He thought Arielle sounded poetic and ancient enough for his tastes."

Knight chuckled. "I tease Burke that his is a most pedestrian name. He naturally tells me that he was named after Edmund Burke, but I know that's a corker. What has he told you?"

"Me? Oh, nothing. Would you like a cup of tea, perhaps?"

"I don't think so. Actually, I was just admiring the prospect from the windows. It is lovely."

"Yes, I think so too. I've rather taken over this room, I suppose you could say. It is so bright and airy, and the prospect onto the western garden is, as you said, quite nice." She added, a frown furrowing her brow, "I suppose I should ask Burke if he doesn't mind."

"Why should Burke mind?"

"It is his home. His orders and wishes take precedence."

"Well, Burke has his estate room and the library. If he said he wanted it, I would suggest you tell him smartly that he simply can't have it."

Saying such a thing to a man who was her husband and her legal owner was such an outrageous notion that she had to laugh.

Knight laughed with her, although he wasn't certain of the jest. He then saw that there was a chair between them. It made her feel safe, he realized with a start. Knight made no move to come around that small barrier.

"Burke tells me that he met you when you were still a young girl. Fifteen or something close to that age?"

"Yes," she said, her voice becoming clipped. She hated to be reminded of that silly little girl, that gullible and stupid twit who'd known nothing about anything and believed the world to be her own private preserve of all things wonderful.

Knight wasn't daunted. He was charming when he applied himself, and he was in a full application attitude with this woman. He wanted to find out all he could about her. Burke loved her beyond anything, if he didn't miss his guess. Her wariness made Knight feel extraordinarily protective, a feeling he wasn't at all used to. It frankly surprised him. He wondered if Burke felt the same.

"Your husband is a fine man, Arielle. We have known each other since we were boys in short coats. I think perhaps he is a bit at loose ends, as am I. We were both in the army for so many years, you know."

"Yes, I know."

"Don't get me wrong. We all wanted peace. It is just that it is difficult to adjust to a life without the regimen and challenge of the army. Even the endless frustration with the War Ministry. Burke was wounded in his side at Toulouse."

"Yes, I know," she said again. She's seen the scar but hadn't said anything to Burke, as well as the scar on his upper arm and on the outside of his thigh.

Hell, Knight thought, he wasn't gaining much ground.

Arielle wasn't stupid. As she'd realized she was being silly to be afraid of this man, she also saw now that he wanted to know if she was worthy of his friend. He wanted to protect Burke. It was a novel idea. Truly novel. She laughed, unable to help herself.

This time Knight was totally at sea. His dark left eyebrow shot up. "I beg your pardon?"

"I was just thinking how unusual this is, my l— Knight. If you would like to continue singing your friend's praises, I will not cavil." And she smiled at him.

It was a lovely smile, albeit sarcastic. Knight brushed a small bit of lint from his coat sleeve. "Burke won't see any other woman now that you are his wife. He is honorable and faithful."

"Poor Laura What's-her-name," Arielle said, and her voice sounded wonderfully flippant even to her own ears.

She was still congratulating herself when he added, "He was wild for you when he was in London before you wed. He was, I guess you'd say . . . well, he was hurting, the way a man hurts when he, well . . . It was I who offered him Laura."

"You *offered?* Goodness, do you own an entire string of women, sir? Sort of like a horse stable? You *offer* mounts to your friends?"

"I didn't mean it like that," Knight said and he felt a fool, something he truly detested experiencing. "What I meant was that I knew of this woman and I suggested to Burke that—"

Arielle slashed her hand through the air. "I don't want to hear about his mistress. Honestly, I have heard quite enough, both from you and from Burke. It is absurd."

"What precisely is so absurd?"

"All of you."

"All of you what?"

"Men, my lord. Even the noble Burke Drummond, your very dear friend, is still a man. That won't ever change. Not ever. If you will excuse me now, I must see Mrs. Pepperall."

Knight held his temper. "There is really no reason for you to be afraid of me, Arielle."

That drew her up short. What had Burke told his friend? "I am not afraid of you, sir. However, I don't like people who dissemble."

"I've never assumed that all women were cunning, treacherous bitches," he said mildly. "I think it rather unreasonable for you to assume that all men are creatures of deceit."

"I don't agree with you. You were waiting here, hoping I would come, were you not? Well, let me reassure you. I will not stick a knife into your friend's heart, if that is what worries you. I did not, as a matter of fact, murder my first husband. Now, have you any other questions you would like to put to me?"

"No, but I would like to say that I hadn't meant to frighten or anger you. I wanted to begin trying to become your friend."

She stared at him. Another novel concept. "No, that is impossible."

"Because I am a man?"

"As you hinted, this is a very odd conversation,

Knight. Understand that you are a guest at Ravensworth Abbey. You will be treated like a guest, with all due deference. Now, if you will excuse me."

Knight watched her leave the room. He made no move to stop her. She was quite perceptive and intelligent. He hadn't been expecting that, but he supposed he should have. After all, Burke didn't easily tolerate stupidity in anyone, neither man nor woman. She was also lovely. When Burke had tried to describe her to Knight, he hadn't been that able to put the Titian hair with the blue eyes with the slight figure. But she seemed to hate men, all men. Poor Burke. In love with a woman who not only was afraid of him but despised him as well. Given that her first husband had abused her, Knight supposed he understood. But to paint every man with the same brush, that bespoke pain that went very deep.

Arielle leaned back against the closed door for many minutes, her eyes closed. She hadn't believed her feelings were so close to the surface. But Knight had drawn her out in a matter of minutes. She had to be more careful. What if Knight told Burke of their conversation and Burke became angry with her? She hadn't been at all gracious; indeed, she'd been rather sour-tongued. She opened her eyes finally to see a sharp-featured man dressed in footman's livery watching her. She'd never seen him before. He was thin, nearly scrawny, his uniform baggy. His hair was sparse, a circle around his head with the top sporting two long strands. He had a sharp, jutting chin and very dark eyes.

"Who are you?"

The man smiled, showing a space between his front teeth, and bowed to her, a rusty movement, one that he wasn't used to doing. "Me name's Trunk, milady. Ollie Trunk. The earl 'ired me, said 'e needed me. I'm the new footman."

"Very well, Trunk," she said. "Welcome to Ravensworth Abbey." She gave him a brief nod and walked away. A very unlikely-looking footman, she mused, wondering what Montague thought of this new addition to his staff. Trunk! What a name.

She spent the remainder of the morning with Virgie and Poppet, enjoying herself immensely as she drank five cups of imaginary tea. Luncheon passed well enough. Lannie excused herself soon after to prepare herself for the evening, and the men adjourned to Burke's library. Arielle felt tired, but she wouldn't give in to it. She called Dorcas to help her change into her riding habit.

"You look peaked," Dorcas said without preamble.

"Just a bit."

"You've been too busy with all these people in the Abbey."

"Well, Lannie and the girls live here. As for the Lord Castlerosse and Lord Carver, I doubt they will prove much trouble."

"Still," Dorcas began, but she didn't continue because she was concentrating on braiding Arielle's hair.

"I just met a new footman," Arielle said. "I think he is someone Burke hired to find out who killed Mellie. A Bow Street Runner, perhaps."

"You've still got that bee in your bonnet," said Dorcas, her voice sharp. "The girl was a little slut and she felt remorse, unusual for a female with no moral fiber, but sometimes it does happen. She did herself in, nothing else."

Arielle couldn't believe her ears. Not Dorcas too. "I'll admit I didn't know the girl, but, Dorcas, Mellie was only fifteen years old!"

"Well, I did know her. Don't matter, not a whit. I can't see that his lordship would want a stranger poking about the Abbey, all because of Mellie's death. Does it make you feel safe to believe a murderer lives here?"

"No, of course not."

"It is all balderdash," said Dorcas and placed a final fastener into Arielle's hair.

Arielle stared into her mirror, seeing Dorcas's face reflected behind her. "Do you also believe me a slut, Dorcas? Paisley didn't rape me, but only because he wasn't able, but he beat me and forced me to do unspeakable things. Do you believe I wanted it? That what I got was all my fault? Do you believe I really asked for it? Should I have killed myself?"

"You were always a lady, Miss Arielle, always. Certainly you didn't ask to be beaten. You would never give in, never flaunt yourself, not to Lord Rendel, not to that Etienne DuPons, not to Lord Ravensworth. Whereas Mellie did ask for that man—whoever he is—to take her. There, you hair is finished. Go along with you now."

Arielle went along, and she felt very confused. She heard the men's voices coming from the library and kept going. She wanted to be alone for a while, to think, to feel the fresh air against her face. While Geordie was saddling up Mindle, Arielle found herself looking at each of the stable lads. Had Jaime, perhaps, raped and killed Mellie? He was rough-mannered, she knew, a large, muscled young man. Or perhaps it was Lambert, a silent, dark-spirited man who rarely said anything to anybody. But none of these men could get into the Abbey.

"Shall I accompany ye, milady?"

"No, thank you, Geordie. I'm only riding to the lake. It's a lovely day, you know."

"Aye, I do," said Geordie. He gave her a leg up and watched her canter Mindle down the winding drive.

She was thinking about the previous night, lying in Burke's arms, the night dark and heavy, telling him everything, even of Paisley's plan to give her to his illegitimate son, Etienne. She shivered now, remembering. He's said nothing of it so far, but then again he did have guests to entertain.

She tied Mindle to a low branch on a maple tree by the lake. It was a glorious summer day. The water was calm and clear, the air sweet with the smells of thick grass and flowers. She sat down near the edge of the water and leaned her head back against the trunk of a maple tree. Insects buzzed around her head.

"Do wake up, dear sister."

She was dreaming and she didn't want to. She never wanted to have anything more to do with Evan, even in nightmares.

"Arielle! Wake up!"

She came awake with a start. Evan Goddis was standing over her, dressed in riding clothes, a riding crop in his right hand. He was nudging her shoulder with it. She shivered because he was blocking out the sun.

Why hadn't she brought Geordie? Fool, a hundred times a fool! But Evan wouldn't hurt her; he had no reason. She pulled herself together. "What do you want, Evan?" She straightened as she spoke but didn't rise. Nor did she crane her neck to look at him. She kept her gaze on the smooth water.

He dropped to his haunches beside her. "I wanted to see you, sister dear. Etienne was most upset, you know. Poor fellow. I told him that you were a smart little chit. Pretending to travel out of England, and all the time you'd made an assignation with the earl. However did you manage to talk him into marrying you? I've always believed you clever, Arielle, so come, tell me. How did you trick him?"

His reasoning was wonderfully convoluted, and she admired it aloud. "I am excessively talented, I suppose, and cunning and ruthless. What do you want?"

"So that was truly the way of it. Do you know that Etienne was waiting on the Southampton road? He was going to be a romantic fellow and abduct you. He would have plowed your little belly until you wed him."

She could only stare at him. She hadn't had a chance. If Burke hadn't taken her, Etienne would have.

"How much was he going to pay you, Evan?"

"Five thous—oh, no, you don't, my dear. You're too clever by half now, Arielle. But it is quite true that I should receive some settlement. You really should have told me about your solicitor and steward. Rendel Hall, much to Etienne's distress, is going to be sold. You should have told me that you hadn't a sou."

"I wish that I had. It would have kept *poor* Etienne from waiting for me on the Southampton road, wouldn't it? It would have stopped you cold as well. There is no money for you now, Evan, so what do you want?"

"I don't agree with you. Just think of all the opportunities now that you've wed the Earl of Ravensworth. Yes, there are many. I am your half brother. I will visit the earl and talk of settlements and the like. Since I am your former guardian, I will see to it that he treats you fairly. For instance, does he give you an allowance? No, of course he doesn't. He is mistreating you."

"Paisley didn't give me an allowance either."

Evan eyed her. She was different. He'd seen the fear in her eyes upon awakening, but it was gone now. She had become confident. It galled him no end. "You need a man like Paisley, I think," he said, and he purposefully slapped his riding crop against the ground beside him. "He kept your shrew's tongue in your mouth, didn't he? He kept you docile and obedient. He wouldn't have allowed you to speak to your brother this way."

"Half brother," she said, and he saw her eyes flicker to the riding crop. Perhaps she wasn't yet all that confident.

"Does your earl beat you, Arielle?"

She said nothing.

"Do you pleasure him enough with that lovely mouth of yours?"

Arielle rose to her feet. She shook out her skirts. "I'm leaving, Evan. You're not welcome at Ravensworth. Good-bye."

He grabbed her arm, pulling her back. He was breathing hard and his breath was hot on her face. "You little harlot, you will do as I tell you." He flung her away from him. She landed on her hands and knees. She heard the riding crop swish through the air, then felt its sting on her back.

She rolled away, coming up onto her knees. He was smiling, a smile of anticipation, of pleasure. His expression was just like Paisley's when he'd beaten her. "I like this. I never thought of doing it before. Yes, I like it."

"You're insane," she whispered, her eyes on the riding crop.

But Evan raised it again, feeling the strength of it, of himself, and his power.

"He will be quite dead if he doesn't drop that riding crop this instant."

"Burke!"

Evan whirled around to see the earl standing some six feet behind him, a pistol in his hand. "She is my sister," he said, his teeth gritted. "She was never disciplined by her father, she is willful and spoiled . . ." He raised the riding crop. ". . . a harridan, a—"

A shot sounded, harsh and stark, and Evan cried

out. The riding crop dropped to the ground, Evan
grabbed his hand, and Burke placed his pistol back
into his jacket pocket. He walked up to Evan, looked
at him very closely, and said, "You are really quite
amazing, you know that?"

"How did she get you to marry her? Did she seduce you? Is she pregnant? Paisley taught her a lot,
but with her whore's skills I would have thought
you'd have made her your mistress, not your—"

Evan said nothing else. Burke's fist landed
squarely against his jaw. He crumpled to the
ground, unconscious.

Burke didn't take a step toward Arielle. He said
calmly, "I'm sorry I didn't arrive sooner. Are you
all right?"

She nodded, but he saw that she was staring, her
expression fixed, at the riding crop.

He wanted to curse, to hold her and soothe her,
but he didn't. "Turn around and let me see your
back."

She rose and turned her back to him. She heard
Burke curse luridly.

Her riding jacket was neatly sliced through, as
was her lawn blouse beneath it. "Let me help you
off with the jacket, Arielle."

She was obedient to his suggestion.

The riding crop, he was relieved to see had barely
marred her skin. It hadn't drawn blood. He drew a
deep breath. "Do you want me to kill him?"

She lowered her head, saying nothing. He helped
her put on her jacket.

"I think I shall," Burke said. "I'll challenge him
to a duel. That would be fair enough, though the
scum doesn't deserve to be treated honorably."

"Don't," she said at last, turning to face him. She
was surprised at his expression. It was coldly furious. Because Evan had struck her? "He isn't a nice

man, Burke. He is treacherous. I don't want to see you hurt."

That made his anger die a quick death. She did care about him. He clasped her chin between two long fingers, bringing her face up. He was smiling. "Do you mind if I wake him and hit him again?"

"No, I don't mind. Actually, I should like to be the one to hit him."

Excellent, he thought. He couldn't ask for much more from her than that. He picked up her hand, fisted it, and made a thorough study. Then he felt the muscle in her upper arm. "All right," he said, smiling. "Let me get him up, and you, my dear, can plant him a facer."

Burke dragged Evan to the water's edge and stuck his head under. He had to dunk him three times before Evan begun spluttering and fighting him. He jerked him to his feet and shook him.

"Do regain your senses," Burke said and shook him again. "All right, Arielle."

Arielle walked up to her half brother, drew back her arm, and slammed her fist into his nose as hard as she could.

Evan howled. Burke released him and he staggered to a tree, holding his nose.

"Well done," Burke said to his wife. "Now, Goddis, you try to see her again and I will kill. Do you understand me? I will kill you."

Evan was hunched over. He said nothing at all, but eventually he nodded.

Burke turned to Arielle. "Come, my dear, let's go home."

"I hope I broke his nose," Arielle said, wonderful spite in her voice.

"It's a distinct possibility. You were perfect." He was very proud of her.

"He wants some sort of settlement from you. He believes it's due him since he was my guardian."

Burke grinned down at her. "Somehow I doubt
that he will broach the topic with me now."

"He also told me that Etienne was waiting for
me, just as you were, on the road to Southampton.
He was going to abduct me, just as you did. He said
that Etienne was gong to give him five thousand
pounds for his assistance."

Burke tried to look suitably shocked, but of course
he'd already known about Etienne. The vagaries of
fate, he was thinking. The blessed vagaries of fate.

He walked behind her into the Abbey. He didn't
want anyone, guest or servant, to see the diagonal
slash across her back. He nodded to Montague and
spoke briefly to Ollie Trunk. When they reached
his bedchamber, he locked the door. "Now, please
take off your jacket and blouse, Arielle. I want to
doctor your back."

"No, Burke, I am all right."

"Do it, Arielle, now."

With that tone, she said nothing more. He helped
her off with the jacket and blouse, then slipped the
narrow straps of her linen chemise off her shoulders. She started to cover her breasts, then dropped
her arms to her sides. He stood behind her, looking
at the long reddened streak diagonally across her
white back. "Does it hurt?"

She shook her head. "No, not really."

"It didn't break the skin, but I'd better cleanse
it anyway."

He left, returned with a soapy washcloth. Her
head was lowered, her back bare to her waist. He
closed his eyes a moment. God, he was supposed to
protect her, and look what had happened. Gently,
he washed the long slash, then lightly patted her
dry. "Do you have a chemise without all the lace
and ribbons? One that is plain and soft and won't
hurt you?"

She nodded.

"Stay here and I'll fetch it for you." He didn't want her to tell him not to bother. He opened the adjoining door and strode into her bedchamber. Dorcas was there.

"My lord," she said.

"I need a very soft, plain chemise, Dorcas. Now."

He saw that the old woman was bursting with questions, but he said nothing more. None of it was her business unless Arielle chose it to be. He took the chemise from her and returned to his room. He lifted the other chemise over her head, replaced it with the soft one.

"How is that?"

"It's fine. Thank you, Burke."

"Again, I'm sorry I was so late, Arielle. I wanted to see you and went to the stables. It was Geordie who told me where you'd gone."

"Why did you want to see me?" she asked, turning around.

"I missed you and wanted to see your lovely face, that's all."

Arielle picked up her blouse and jacket. She was on the point of going to her bedchamber when she thought to say, "Mr. Ollie Trunk introduced himself to me this morning. He is a most unlikely footman, Burke. Is he a Bow Street Runner?"

"Yes, he is. You're quite right that he's an unlikely type for a servant. Montague doesn't know how to react. I had to take him into my confidence, but no one else. If you have a chance, I would appreciate your ordering some livery for him that fits."

"All right. Does Mrs. Pepperall know what to do?"

"I assume so. Do you mind his being here?"

"No, but it is disconcerting to think that the man who killed Mellie very likely lives in the Abbey."

"Ollie will soon discover his identity. Arielle?"

"Yes?"

"I will make certain that Goddis never gets near you again."

She gave him an uncertain smile. "Thank you for letting me hit him in the nose."

"That was my pleasure."

"I did make him sorry, didn't I?"

"I've never seen a sorrier man."

# 15

If Burke believed that the French-painted doll Virgie pronounced was his present was a bit unusual for a man, he didn't say so. Nor did he ask what had become of the girls' more bloodthirsty army pursuits. "I swear to you," he whispered to Arielle, "the last time I played with them, I was the enemy and they turned their cannon on me."

"I suppose," Arielle said, "that this is just another stage."

"You, my dear, know about as much about these matters as I do. Goodness, look at this doll's face. If you painted yourself like this, I think I should flee to the Continent."

The doll's face was dead white with scarlet lips and black slashes for brows. Its shiny black hair stuck up in clumps from the scalp. "What shall you name her, Uncle Burke?"

He looked thoughtful, then said to Virgie, "What do you think of 'Wellington'?"

"Uncle Burke! Really!"

"All right, then, how about 'Josephine'?"

Virgie beamed and nodded vigorously. "Yes, that will do her quite nicely, I think." She fidgeted a moment, then said, "If you like, Uncle Burke, Josephine could stay in the nursery with me, and you could play with her here."

"You think she would feel more at home here rather than in my bedchamber?"

"Oh, yes, Uncle Burke."

"What do you think, Arielle?"

Arielle struck a thoughtful pose. "I don't know, Burke. Imagine how Josephine would look arranged artfully against your pillows."

Burke ruffled Virgie's pale curls. "You win. Here she stays." He gave the doll into his niece's eager arms. "Now, you two imps," he continued, taking Poppet in, "it's time for you to play with my present to you."

"What is it? What is it?" the children clamored.

"I don't know, though. Perhaps, what with these dolls and all, you won't be interested."

"Uncle Burke!"

Burke got down on his knees and opened the large box. It was filled with soldiers in colorful and opposing uniforms, and there were cannons and horses.

Virgie stared. "We're not boys, Uncle Burke! Uck! Let me see that cannon, Poppet! Be careful, you silly little girl, you might break it!"

"Oh, look," Arielle said, coming down beside Burke. "Is this supposed to be Wellington?"

"No, that's me. Dashing creature, aren't I?"

Soon the two girls were examining the soldiers and arranging them into proper formations according to Burke's instructions.

"Cavalry in the back, in a sort of wedge. That's it, Poppet. All soldiers holding bayonets go in the front."

It was a good hour before the English army—commanded by Virgie and Poppet and Arielle—thrashed the French soundly. Burke tumbled his cannons to their sides and groaned, clutching his chest and sprawling, arms and legs spread wide, on the floor.

"What Lannie will say about all this, I have no idea," Burke remarked to Arielle later as they walked down the stairs from the third-floor nursery.

"I think it wise for girls to know what it is men do. Now when they hear talk, they will have an idea of what happens."

"I doubt that," said Burke with a grin. "But they can certainly impress all their friends under the age of ten."

Arielle giggled, and Burke felt something expand within him. "Have I told you today that I think you're wonderful?"

"You might have."

"Well, I do. And now I fear that we must see to our guests. Are you ready to pour tea for everyone?"

"Yes," she said. "And I even remember that you like only one wedge of lemon in your tea." They were nearing the second-floor stairs when she asked, "I was with Knight for a few minutes this morning. Did he tell you?"

"He said he'd spoken with you and that you were the most beautiful, the most gracious—"

She punched him in the arm, then drew back, blank fear emptying all expression from her face."

"My arm's not broken, Arielle," he said lightly. "It's true, though. Knight thinks you're the most perfect, most wonderful woman—and he remarked that you even appeared to be housebroken."

A very tentative smile appeared. "You're making that up," she said.

"Not I." Actually, Knight had told him much of their conversation. And that had been why he'd wanted to see her. Now it didn't seem all that important, not after the incident with Evan Goddis.

Lord Carver and Lannie were huddled in close conversation in the far corner of the drawing room, leaving Knight to his own devices. His device appeared to be watching the pair, a sardonic expression on his face, sardonic bordering on acute disgust.

"Thank God," he said upon the arrival of Burke and Arielle. "Now I can eavesdrop on some intelligent conversation!"

"Unkind, Knight," Percy called out. "You're just jealous."

"It is a possibility, I suppose," said Knight, "but not much of one. Come along, you two, and be civilized. Grown people cooing at each other is most disconcerting. Our hostess is here to fill our gullets with tea."

Burke watched his wife. He realized that this social setting was new to her, despite the fact that she'd been married before. Had Cochrane kept her alone and locked away? It seemed likely. He thought of the new mark on her back, how it stood in relief against the other faint white lines that crisscrossed her flesh. At least this mark hadn't drawn blood, so there would be no scar. He could envision her on her hands and knees, her slender back bloody. He felt the familiar rage building within him.

"Burke? Really, old fellow, you shouldn't leave your upper story so blatantly unattended."

"Thank you, Knight. I'll have you know I was thinking the most profound thoughts imaginable."

"What are those, pray tell?" asked Arielle, grinning at her husband.

His smile never slipped. "Dinner," he said. "I was thinking about the goose Cook is making for our dinner."

Arielle arched a disbelieving eyebrow at him, then said to Lannie, "I don't suppose Burke will tell you, but Virgie and Poppet are now the proud possessors of military battalions and cannons and horses, everything needed to defeat the French."

Percy brightened at that. "Excellent, Burke. I feared I would be drinking tea out of tiny cups and oohing over little dolls and the like. Soldiers!" He rubbed his plump hands together.

Arielle found herself looking at Percy's hands, wondering how he would treat Lannie once they were married. She certainly seemed besotted with him. Did this mean that she didn't mind what he would do to her after her marriage? Arielle simply didn't know. She couldn't see herself asking the other woman. Perhaps he wouldn't do anything at all to her. She became aware at that moment that Burke was staring at her. Quickly, she asked, "More tea for you, Lannie?"

"Yes, thank you, my dear. How odd it is to have another lady doing this! Not that I mind, because I don't. I am pleased that Burke has married. He needs to start his nursery. Have you initiated bridal visits yet, Arielle?"

Bridal visits! Arielle shook her head.

"Perhaps in another week or so," Burke said easily.

"Well, nothing at all new for you, Arielle," Lannie continued, "since you were married before. It's odd, though. I can't seem to remember being invited to Rendel Hall when you were first married to Paisley Cochrane and—"

"Do have a crumpet, my dear," said Knight and shoved the gold-edged plate under Lannie's nose.

"Why, thank you, Knight," Lannie said. "Incidentally, Burke, I have met the most outrageous new footman. He speaks with a cockney accent, and when I told him to do something, he said that it wasn't his job and anyway, that I looked to be a strong enough missus and I could jolly well do it myself!"

"That would be Trunk," said Arielle, laughing at Lannie's description. "He is something of a character, I admit. I think Burke hired him because he says the unexpected and is vastly amusing. I hope you weren't too upset with him, Lannie."

"No, she chose to be amused," said Percy.

"Corinne wouldn't be amused."

"We will trust that Corinne chooses to remain in London for awhile," said Burke.

Montague appeared in the doorway at that moment, his eyes fixed on Burke until Burke walked over to him. "What is it?" he asked in a low voice.

"There are guests, my lord. I've never seen them before. The gentleman says he's Baron Sherard, and he says his wife, the lady with him, is her ladyship's sister."

"Good grief! Well, let me tell Arielle."

"But how can that be possible?" Arielle said after he told her. "They're supposed to be in Boston."

"We will find out everything in due time, I'm sure."

Arielle gave a small cry at the sight of her half sister and flew into her arms. "Nesta! Oh, how glad I am to see you!" She hugged her, stepped back and exclaimed some more, then hugged her yet again.

Burke paused a moment, waiting for the reunion to complete itself. Nesta Carrick was a small woman, her hair a soft blondish brown, her eyes a very pale blue. He remembered her vaguely from years before. He looked at Baron Sherard and thrust out his hand. "We have met. It was in '09, I believe. In London."

"You're right, of course. It was at White's." Baron Sherard stepped forward to shake Burke's hand.

"Didn't I lose some money to you? Piquet?"

Alec Carrick, Baron Sherard, grinned. "Not likely. I am a miserable gambler. I think it was a wager about a gentleman who owned a dozen pigs and wanted to race them. I can't seem to recall the outcome."

Burke shook his head. "Neither can I, which is probably just as well."

Arielle finally came out of Nesta's arms. "Alec, how wonderful to see you!"

The baron took both her hands in his large ones. "And I you, little sister. I see you've married your neighbor. This man is an excellent choice. He is fond of both animals and children, I believe. Pigs, most certainly!"

Arielle cocked her head to one side. "Pigs?"

"Never mind. A worthless jest, that's all. You have grown up. Hasn't she, Nesta? A woman now."

"A very lovely woman. You have much the look of Mama, though her hair wasn't such a glorious shade of red as yours."

Arielle waved that aside. "Nesta, you're pregnant! I thought you felt rather thick, but—"

"That is why we've returned to England," Alec explained. "I want my child to be born on English soil."

"But you wrote asking me to come to Boston! I very nearly sailed," Arielle said.

"I wrote that letter months ago," Nesta said. "You just received it?"

"Yes," said Arielle.

"Well, when we didn't get a response and I discovered that I was with child, Alec decided we would come home."

"How did you know where to find Arielle?" Burke asked.

"We went to Leslie Farm," said Alec. "Goddis wasn't in fine fettle. He has a broken nose and a bandaged hand." He paused a moment, then said in a meditative voice, "I do wonder what happened to him. He wouldn't enlighten me. Indeed, he was rather churlish, even more so than when I first met him over five years ago."

Arielle giggled. The sound so startled Burke that he stared at her, a wide smile on his face. Alec and Nesta looked puzzled, but before they could comment, Burke quickly invited them to remain at the Abbey as his guests for as long as they wished.

The baron gratefully agreed. "Thank you," he said. "Nesta is exhausted, I fear, and perhaps it would be better to give her some time to rest before traveling to my estate in Northumberland."

"I shall take my sister upstairs now, Burke," Arielle said. "You, brother-in-law, can accompany my husband. We have other guests, so you won't have to endure just our tedious company."

"I'd forgotten them," said Burke. "You know Knight Winthrop, don't you? And Percy Kingstone?"

"Good grief, yes," Alec said. "This is a reunion of sorts. You go rest, Nesta." He patted his wife's pale cheek.

Arielle showed Nesta to a large, airy bedchamber across the corridor from the master bedchamber.

"It is lovely, Arielle. Just fancy it—you're married to the Earl of Ravensworth. I was terribly in love with him, you know, until Alec came along. All the local girls were in giggling raptures over him."

Arielle hugged her again. "I'm so glad you're here, Nesta. Here we are, going on and on, and you're exhausted. Let me get you a maid and we'll tuck you up."

Close to an hour later, Arielle left a sleeping Nesta. She was looking thoughtful when Burke met her on the stairs. "Anything wrong?" he asked.

She looked up, startled. "Oh, Burke. I was just thinking about Nesta. She doesn't look at all well. Shall we ask Dr. Brody to come see her?"

"We can mention it to Alec."

"But he isn't the one who is pregnant and exhausted!"

Burke gave her a very steady look. "But he is her husband, Arielle."

"Yes, it always comes back to that, doesn't it?"

Burke ignored that. "Did Nesta say anything further about Evan Goddis?"

"Only that they had been told in East Grinstead that Rendel Hall was being sold, so they went to Leslie Farm to find out where I was. She said that Evan was very vocal in his dislike of you and me. She also said that another man was staying there. Probably Etienne DuPons."

"Interesting," said Burke. "Well, it seems Alec and Knight are off somewhere reminiscing, and Percy and Lannie are off somewhere, oozing on each other."

Arielle laughed.

Such a sweet sound, Burke thought. He grabbed her hand and lifted it to his mouth. She stilled as his lips touched her palm. He felt her straighten, stiffen. To hell with it, he thought, and leaned down, lightly grasped her shoulders, and kissed her. It wasn't a demanding kiss, but it was a mark of possession, and he knew it. He wondered if she did.

She blinked when he finally released her. He said nothing, merely smiled at her, softly touching his fingertips to her cheek. Arielle drew a steadying breath and said the most unexpected thing: "Do you know that I thought Alec Carrick was the most handsome man I'd ever seen in my life until I met you?"

"Is that true? You had excellent taste even as a young girl."

"Now I am not so certain that I like light-haired men even if they look like bronzed gods, which Alec does."

"Ho, have I just been insulted?"

"And his eyes are such a bright, clear blue, don't you think, Burke? Like a Viking, a Viking chief, of course."

"His eyes are much like yours, Arielle."

"Mine are boring. I think I much prefer deep brown eyes, like yours. Much more intelligent, you know."

He hugged her. "Let's go downstairs for a while. Unless you need to rest?"

"Oh, no, I feel fine."

Arielle led him to the small room where she'd met Knight that morning. In a careless voice that didn't fool Burke for an instant, she said, "I very much like this room, Burke. May I use it?"

"I don't know," he said slowly, looking around him. "I think I should like to add it to my collection. I really only have the library and the estate room. I believe I should like to have this one as well. It is more open than the others. The view is more pleasing. Yes, I shall take this one."

She'd started to nod when she remembered Knight's words. What she intended to come out smartly just emerged as woefully diffident. "Do you think perhaps that you could change your mind?"

"Why should I? It's my house, and you don't really have anything to say about what I want to do. No, you can't ever come into this room again. I forbid it."

"But—but that isn't fair!"

"Isn't this my house?"

"It's my house too. Isn't it?"

"So you think you're the mistress here, do you?"

She gnawed on her lower lip. "Well, yes, perhaps I think I am."

"More definite, Arielle. Try again."

She raised her chin. "I am mistress here."

"So what? What rights does that give you?"

"The house and servants are my responsibility. I like this room and I want to use it. You don't need another room." She paused, pleased, until she saw him frowning ferociously. "If you wouldn't mind terribly," she added.

He leaned down and kissed her hard and quick on her closed lips. "I don't mind, you silly widgeon. Even if I did mind, it wouldn't matter. You could even boot me out of the estate room if it pleased you."

She could only stare at him. He'd done this just to make her stand up for herself? "I don't understand you," she said, and her voice was an odd mixture of wistfulness and uncertainty.

"I don't despair," he said lightly. "Come along now. Let's go for a walk. Perhaps I can even convince you to kiss me underneath the magnolia tree yon."

She gave him a quick look, then lowered her eyes. "I shall think about it," she said, and her voice was demure and teasing.

He wanted to shout, to kick his heels together, perhaps even to burst into song.

It was a chaste, quite shy kiss beneath the beautiful thick magnolia, but it *was* a kiss. And it was offered freely.


"Miss Nesta is the same, or perhaps more so," Dorcas said as she helped Arielle into her evening gown.

"What do you mean?" Arielle asked.

"I mean that she isn't happy. Not with him, she isn't."

"Baron Sherard? Why shouldn't she be?"

Dorcas shrugged. It was a sign that the old woman had no intention of answering and couldn't be made to.

"Sit down and let me arrange your hair."

Arielle sat. Dorcas worked quickly, parting her hair into thick sections, then braiding them loosely. As she wrapped the braids in a circle atop Arielle's head, she said, "I saw your riding jacket and the blouse. He finally beat you."

Arielle met her eyes in the mirror.

"I knew it was a matter of time. He tried to take you, to force you, didn't he, and you resisted him. You said when he did we would leave. But where will we go? Your sister isn't in Boston any longer. You don't have any money, do you? Does he give you any money?"

"Burke didn't touch me, Dorcas. It was Evan. He caught me alone by Bunberry Lake. Burke saved me."

To her surprise, Dorcas merely grunted, a particularly noxious sound. "He will do the same, just wait and see."

But suddenly Arielle knew he wouldn't. She couldn't say just how she knew he wouldn't, she just *knew.*

Dorcas was dusting her face lightly with powder when Burke came into her bedchamber through the adjoining door. He was carrying a narrow velvet box.

"You've done well," he said to Dorcas. "Her hair is beautiful. You may leave now."

"I will see that Miss Nesta is all right," said Dorcas and left the room.

Arielle eyed the box. Her eyes were sparkling, but he saw that she was trying to act only mildly interested in an effort to control her excitement. He felt the shaft of pain in his gut.

"It is yours," he said abruptly, thrusting it into her hands. "It belonged to my mother and to her mother before her. If you don't like the setting, we will have it redone."

He watched her slowly open the box. She gasped

as she stared at the incredible array of diamonds and sapphires. "Oh, it is too beautiful! I've never seen anything to compare with it! Oh, God, Burke . . . no, no, I can't accept it. What if I lost it or broke it or—" She pressed it back into his hand.

"Then I should have to replace it for you."

She stared at him, perplexed. "Let me put it on you." He fastened the clasp and gazed at her in the mirror. She looked mesmerized by her own image, her eyes glittering.

"The sapphires are brilliant, but not as brilliant as your eyes." His hands were touching her shoulders lightly. She could but stare at herself, mute. Never had she worn anything of such beauty. She remembered the emerald bracelet Paisley had insisted she wear once. It had fallen off and he'd beaten her. She knew that the clasp had been defective and she knew that he'd known, deliberately waiting, hoping the bracelet would fall off. But Burke wasn't like that.

"Thank you, Burke." She lifted her hand and placed it over his. But then she thought: What will he want for it? What will he demand?

Burke saw the shifting expressions and wondered at them.

Arielle enjoyed herself thoroughly that evening. Cook had outdone himself, serving his specialties of roast lamb and rump of beef à la jardiniere. The raspberry-and-currant tarts melted in every mouth they entered. Arielle knew she was being too quiet, not at all a perfect hostess, but her guests were all in tearing spirits and vying with one another for the most attention. It was amusing, and she was quite content to sit back and listen to the rapid-fire barbs.

Even Nesta had recovered her color and laughed at the jests flying back and forth between Burke, Knight, and Alec. And Percy was in fine fettle, too.

The major topic of conversation was the ton in London and all its incalculable vagaries. Every so often, Arielle was aware of Burke looking at her intently from the head of the long table. Her fingers consciously went to her necklace around her throat. Was he regretting giving it to her? Well, if he did, he would simply take it back. She would take great pains to see that nothing happened to it.

In the midst of all the hilarity, Arielle felt a lump of unhappiness settle in her throat. She swallowed convulsively. She wanted the necklace. She didn't want him to take it back. She didn't want to have to worry about it. But the necklace wasn't the point, not really. She didn't know what was.

She became aware that Lannie was clearing her throat and nodding toward her. Burke was smiling. "We won't be long, my dear," he said. She rose quickly, not waiting for a footman to assist her. "We will be in the drawing room," she said, turned, and left.

Nesta and Lannie were soon in a very detailed maternal discussion. Arielle listened with but half an ear until Lannie inquired after Nesta's health.

"Oh, I am all right," Nesta said in her sweet voice. "The crossing was difficult, what with my nausea and all that, but it wasn't too bad. Alec was very solicitous."

"I hope so," said Arielle. "He is the one responsible, after all."

Lannie looked a bit taken aback, then she laughed. "That is certainly the truth! Do you wish for a boy?"

"Certainly. It is what Alec wants, you see."

"Not even Alec can control that," said Arielle. "I think you should have a little girl, Nesta."

Nesta grinned even as she shook her head. "Perhaps another child can be a girl. But this first one must be a boy."

She sounded tremendously serious, and Arielle frowned. "But what does it matter? Lannie has Virgie and Poppet. I wouldn't want either of them to have been boys. They're darling and perfect just as they are."

"Montrose wasn't all that pleased with them, Arielle," Lannie said. "It is most odd about men in that regard. It seems that their part in the entire situation must be made even bigger, even more important, thus this demand for a boy."

"And, of course, our laws," Arielle said. "They hardly favor girls. How I should like to see a lady inherit an earldom."

"But surely you have done quite well for yourself," Nesta said. "Wed very young to a rich man who left you all his wealth, then wed again very soon to another one."

"What little Lord Rendel left, Nesta, is long gone," Arielle told her. "Indeed, I understand that everything, the house included, will be sold shortly."

"Oh, dear, I'm sorry," said Nesta. "I had no idea."

"Neither did I," said Lannie, sitting forward in her chair.

Arielle decided on the truth. Why not? "Nor did I. You see, my first husband's solicitor and steward robbed the estate, even mortgaged the house and all the land, and left England when I made it known that I wanted to sell out and leave England as well. So no, Nesta, there was nothing left of his so-called wealth. Had I come to you in Boston, it would have been with only a hundred pounds in my pocket."

"But you met Burke," Nesta said brightly.

"Yes, I did."

The gentlemen were laughing when they entered the drawing room. Burke immediately sought out his wife. He said nothing, merely took her hand in his and sat beside her. Percy went to stand by Lannie at the pianoforte. Alec leaned down and kissed Nesta's cheek. Again Knight found himself the lone man. He grinned ruefully and shook his head. "This is a most discomfitting feeling," he said to no one in particular.

"Hie yourself to the altar, old fellow. Then you won't find yourself ignored at dinner parties," Burke said, grinning.

It was nearly eleven o'clock when Alec said, "It is time for Nesta to find her bed. It is late, you know."

All the guests dispersed shortly thereafter, and Arielle followed Burke to his bedchamber. She stood in the middle of the room, wondering what she was to do. The Oriental screen had been removed that morning for repairs. She just stood there, knowing she was being a fool, but unable to simply walk into the other room.

Burke finished lighting the logs in the fireplace. He rose and stretched, leaning his shoulders against the mantelpiece, staring at her intently. "Did you enjoy yourself?"

"Oh, yes, very much."

"I'm glad. Now, Arielle, take off your clothes. All of them."

# 16

She stared at him, unwilling to understand his words. She'd been so happy, so relaxed, and now . . .

His voice grew sharper. "Are you having difficulty with your hearing, Arielle? I said to take off your clothes. I want to see you naked."

*Paisley's orders, Paisley's words.* Her fingers fluttered to the top button of her gown. She felt the smooth silk, felt the ribbed thread that framed the buttonholes. She saw the buttons parting, saw herself naked and vulnerable and helpless. Her hands dropped to her sides. "I don't understand why you're doing this. You were so nice to me—"

"You think that since I am nice to you I will forgo my pleasures?" He straightened to his full height and took a step toward her.

She made a small, frightened sound, deep in her throat, and her fingers raced to unfasten the long row of buttons.

"After you're naked, I think I want to see you on your knees, dear wife. Perhaps you will take me in your mouth tonight, as you did that evening in the stable. I remember that you were quite well trained."

She stopped and her hands fisted over her breasts. She looked at him, at his set face, his cold eyes. The

259

events of the day careened through her mind. She was shaking her head at his words, at what she was thinking, feeling. "Why are you doing this?"

"Your little whisper isn't tremendously affecting, Arielle. Are you going to do as I tell you, or shall I get the riding crop?"

She watched him stride to the far side of the bedchamber, open a drawer in the armoire, and pull out a riding crop. She stared dumbly at it.

"No," she said. "No!"

"No what?"

He was slapping the riding crop against his palm.

"You won't hit me."

"Won't hit you? Whyever would you believe that I wouldn't hit you? All men are the same, Arielle. We all enjoy hurting those unable to defend themselves; we positively relish humiliating our wives, giving them pain. Surely you know that."

"No, no, you're not like that."

His gaze was intent as he took several steps toward her, the riding crop still slapping rhythmically against his palm.

She didn't move. She wasn't looking at the riding crop, only at his face. "You're not like that," she repeated with more conviction. She sounded as if she really believed what she was saying, not merely hoping it was true.

"You believe that, do you?"

"Yes, I do. You're not that kind of man, Burke."

"Take off your clothes, Arielle."

"No, I shan't. I won't let you shame me like that."

"You will defy me? Disobey me?"

"Yes, if that is what I'm doing."

He walked up to her and took her chin between two long fingers. She did not draw back. He lifted her face. "I can beat you whenever I wish. I can draw blood. I can make Evan Goddis's little mark on your back appear like nothing at all. I can make you do whatever I want."

"Yes, you can." She drew a deep breath. "But you won't. You love me."

"You believe that? I'm a man, Arielle. Don't you believe all men to be deceitful bastards, cruel and sadistic animals?"

She never looked away from his face. "Not you."

"Well," he said, looking down at her pale face, "what do I have here? A wife who finally believes in me? A wife who finally trusts me?"

Her eyes darkened, dilated, the pupils black. It was fascinating to watch. Her voice was shaking as she said, "You've done it on purpose."

"What are you talking about?"

"Since we've been married," she said slowly, "you've done all of it on purpose."

"What? Can't you even answer sensibly?"

"You've pushed me and pushed me and pushed me until . . ."

"Until you pushed back?"

"Yes!"

"And what happened when you did, Arielle!"

"Nothing, because you won't hurt me. You would never have hurt me, despite what you threatened."

"Fancy that," he said and smiled at her.

She grabbed the riding crop and flung it across the room. "You and your damned prop!"

He laughed, a rich, deep sound. He couldn't contain himself. He caught her about her waist and lifted her high. She stared down at him, grabbing his upper arms.

"Now all I've got to do is fatten you up. And then—"

"Then what?"

"Why, I'll have perfection in a wife, that's what."

"Being that you're already perfect, of course, it is only fair that your wife swim in the same pond?"

"A charming metaphor. Yes, we shall swim together." He lowered her to her feet but still held her close against him.

She rested her cheek against his shoulder and wrapped her arms about his waist. "You've scared me so very much."

His arms tightened about her. "Will you forgive me?"

"I don't know. I still—"

"You wonder if sometime in the misty future I will turn on you? I won't. I want you to be happy, Arielle. I want you to be happy with me."

She sighed deeply, and he wondered what she was thinking.

"Let's go to bed, all right? And no, you don't have to take your clothes off in front of me unless you want to. And no, you don't have to even kiss me unless you want to. And yes, you can dress and undress behind that noxious screen once it's mended."

He kissed her softly on her closed mouth and stepped back. He began humming, a particularly graphic ditty popular in the army some three years before. He undressed, neatly folding his clothing, as was his wont. He didn't look at her.

Arielle watched him. Then she smiled. She took off her own clothes and fetched herself a nightgown from the armoire. As she was tying the ribbons at her throat, she noticed how he was watching her. He was simply standing there, naked and lean and powerful, and she looked away, but not immediately this time.

He stretched, the orange fire behind him creating planes and shadows on his body. "I'm gong to bed," he said. "Come when you wish." He lay on his back, the covers pulled to his chest. She climbed in beside him.

"If you would like, Arielle," he said, not turning to face her, "you may give me a good-night kiss."

She did. It was a bit more enthusiastic than the one beneath the magnolia tree.

George Cerlew, a young man of immense sincerity and regular and conscientious habits, stepped into the estate room. Thank God the earl was here, he thought.

"My lord."

"Yes, George? You have more interminable work for me?" Burke saw that his steward was nearly trembling with excitement.

"No, my lord. That man, Ollie Trunk, he wants to speak to you. He said it was urgent."

Burke rose from his chair. "Get him immediately."

Ollie Trunk was looking smug. "I got 'im, milord," he said without preamble. "The little bastid what did in that poor little girl."

"Who was it?"

"One of the stable lads. Arnold is his name."

"Good God," Burke said. "Are you certain, man? Why, Arnold has been here at least six years. He's conscientious, quiet, and—" Burke stopped, shaking his head.

" 'E was braggin' about it, the stupid sod," Ollie said with disgust. "Braggin'! I'd matched up the bit of cloth you'd found, milord, with one of Arnold's coats. It matched, perfect. So I got 'im drunk over at the Duck and Drake in Nutley, and off 'e went with 'is braggin', about 'ow all the girls couldn't keep their 'ands off 'im, damned dumb cove."

"We have a problem here, gentlemen," Burke said to George and Ollie.

"I don't see—" George began, only to be cut off by Ollie.

" 'Tis obvious as the wart on your nose, if you 'ad one. 'Ow could Arnold get into the Abbey to do away with the girl?"

"He raped her but he didn't kill her," Burke said, more to himself than to the other men. He cursed softly and fluently, earning himself a bit more respect from Ollie.

"That's the way of it, milord." He shrugged. " 'Course, it could 'ave been an accident after all."

"No, I think not. Good work, Ollie. I must give this some thought. I wish you to remain, all right?"

"You're the bloke what's payin' me to sniff," said Ollie.

"Keep sniffing," said Burke. "Concentrate on all the people who live here. Have Joshua and Geordie go with you, Ollie, and fetch Arnold here to me. Now. I will deal with him."

Burke had given thought to what he would do when the man who'd raped Mellie was discovered. He felt calm and coldly furious. When Alec Carrick came into the estate room, he said, "You can stay if you wish. But here is what is going to happen."

When he'd finished, Alec said in some astonishment, "My God! And I'd remembered the English countryside as being rather a bore. This is incredible. I will help you if you will allow me to. Any man who would do such a thing deserves everything he gets."

That sentiment, Burke thought, would most certainly please his wife.

By the time Arnold, one arm held by Ollie, the other by Joshua, entered the estate room, Knight had joined Burke and Alec.

"I won't have this, my lord!" Arnold shouted as he was shoved into a chair. "This scum here, well, he's making it all up. It ain't true, none of it."

"Is that so?"

"This is 'is jacket, milord," said Ollie. "And the piece of cloth found near the girl."

"I fear it is a perfect match, Arnold," Burke said.

"It weren't rape!" Arnold shouted. "It weren't.

Little Mellie, well, she and me, we've played here and there, me plowing her for a good long time now, mainly at the gazebo. She was just mad at me, that's all."

"Why, then, Arnold, were you wearing a mask?"

"I told you, she were mad at me! I didn't want her to go blabbin' it around that I was the one who done it. Somebody might've listened to the little trollop."

"Arnold, Mellie was fifteen years old."

"So? She and me, we've been fucking for over a year now. Hot little bit, that Mellie."

"You raped her. Your forced her against her will. No one harms a woman or a girl who is under my protection. Now, do you want to know what is gong to be done with you?"

"Nothin'! I don't deserve nothin'! She was just a little slut, that's all." Arnold saw the murderous rage in the earl's eyes. Suddenly he jerked away from Joshua, sent his elbow into Ollie's stomach, and dashed toward the estate room door. He jerked it open and fell into the hall at Arielle's feet.

"Arnold! What is wrong? Why are you here in the house?"

The men erupted from the estate room. For several minutes there was utter pandemonium.

When Arnold was again securely held by Joshua and Ollie, Burke said, "Take him back into the estate room and keep him there." He waited until all the men had left before he said to Arielle, "Arnold raped Mellie. Ollie discovered the truth."

"Oh, no. Did he kill her as well?"

"I'm not certain," he said. "Go along now, Arielle. I will finish with Arnold."

"What will you do?"

Burke grinned. "Arnold, my dear girl, is going to become a proud sailor in our Majesty's Navy. For a term not less than five years."

"But that doesn't sound bad, not really."

"It is hell, worse than hell. It is a better punishment than Newgate. Trust me."

Arielle stayed outside the estate room door, listening. Suddenly she heard Arnold's yell and knew that Burke had told him. Well, it served him right. Her step was lighter, but niggling at the back of her mind was still the question of whether or not Arnold had murdered Mellie.

The question was answered late that afternoon. Burke told Arielle to remain when Ollie asked to see him again. They were in her favorite room. Arielle was telling him how she wished to redecorate it.

"It's over, milord," Ollie announced.

"What's over exactly, Ollie?"

Ollie looked sideways at Arielle, and Burke said quickly, "You can speak in front of my wife. Out with it, man."

"I found the key, milord. Rusty and old, but it works on the small door to the servants' stairs."

Burke felt as if a great weight had been taken from his shoulders. "Where?"

"In the stable, near the tack room. Arnold, naturally, says 'e knows nothing about it, but the lad's crazy if 'e don't deny it."

"Yes," said Burke.

"It's over," said Arielle. She stuck out her hand to Ollie Trunk, who stared at it as if it were a snake to bite him. "Thank you so much. You are an excellent detective, sir."

To Burke's delight, Ollie blushed. "Well, now, your ladyship, it's just that I . . . yes, good I am. Now, there's thing to do, milord. I can still take old Arnold over to this Cap'n Mortimer so's 'e can be a good sailor. But as it appears 'e might have croaked the girl, do you want 'im 'ere?"

Burke was silent for several moments. Finally he

said, "No. We have no real proof that he murdered
Mellie. The key wasn't in his things, it was simply
in the stable, where anyone could have seen it and
used it. It is, of course, probable that Arnold did
kill her because she threatened to tell everyone he
raped her, but we'll let the Navy keep him from
now on."

Burke handed Ollie the letter he'd written to Ad-
rien Mortimer, the toughest captain to sail under
England's flag. He shook Ollie's hand. "My thanks
also," he said.

"It's over," Arielle said again. She turned to her
husband and found herself smiling shyly up at him.
"Did I tell you today that I think you're wonderful?" she asked.

"No," he said. "Not today."

"Perhaps I shall." She laughed. "It is teatime,
sir, and our guests will wish to know what has happened."

Arnold and his fate were discussed over tea, then
over dinner.

Alec Carrick said, "A pity that the war between
America and England is nearly resolved. We could
have had the Americans impress this Arnold into
their navy. That would have cooled all unaccept-
able instincts in him."

"That poor girl," said Nesta.

"She was a slut, no morals at all," Lannie said
to Nesta. "At least that's what I heard. And Mellie's mother, well, she was a harridan and a thoroughly wretched woman. She couldn't keep a man
near her, husband or otherwise."

"It doesn't matter," said Arielle. "I know men
who are sluts and they don't get raped. Or murdered."

That, Arielle thought as soon as the words were
out of her mouth, was like a cannon firing into the
mist.

There was complete silence for a very long time; it seemed at least an eon to Arielle. Then Burke said: "She's right, of course. Not only are men the stronger, but they can't conceive of a man being raped. That is, no man I know could even begin to understand rape in regard to himself."

"There is another point," Knight offered. "Once women were willy-nilly thrust up on that pedestal back in medieval times, what with the Virgin Mary cult and all that, purity was their main claim to everything that was good in a woman. If they weren't pure, they weren't good. Unfortunately, that notion still persists. Thus, if a woman has lovers, she is bad. If a man has mistresses, he is all the more enticing and exciting, both to women and to men."

"Being a rake," said Percy, "is not my way. I'm one of those men who enjoys keeping himself safe and true and loyal. Indeed, I am a domesticated creature."

Lannie gave him a droll look. "Oh, dear, and I so wanted excitement in a husband, not some sort of pet. Are you tame, sir?"

Nesta laughed and waved her fork toward Arielle. "Remember that little boy who didn't want to play with us?" She continued to the table at large. "Arielle and I locked him in a shed. He wasn't trained, as it turned out."

"After six hours I should think not! Oh, that poor child. I hadn't thought of him in years."

"I wonder," said Burke, "if you two didn't ruin him in some way for life."

"It boggles the mind to think of what possible directions his ruin could have taken," said Knight.

"What kind of husband were you hoping for, Arielle?" asked Lannie. "Does Burke suit you?"

*Actually, dear Lannie, the last thing I wanted in my life was another husband.* "With proper attention I suppose he will suit," she said, aware that Burke was smiling at her. "Eventually."

"Like Percy," said Burke, taking another helping of crimped salmon, "I am a faithful being. Hearth and home and a loving wife, and I count myself content."

"Alec doesn't like home or hearth," said Nesta. "He likes excitement and travel and change."

"You make me sound like the most unlikely husband material, my dear," said Alec. "Surely I am more acceptable than that. I have been as domesticated as you could wish for nearly five years now."

"But all we've done is travel! Seven months ago we were in Macau!"

"Actually, Alec," said Arielle, grinning at him, "you sound more and more like a stray dog. A very *interesting* stray dog, but nonetheless . . ."

"Help me, you three," said Alec, giving a mock frown to the gentlemen.

"Not I," said Knight. "I'm not married. I don't intend to indulge in it—forgive me, ladies—"

Arielle interrupted him, blurting out, "Why should you ask our forgiveness? I didn't wish to wed either, and I didn't ask any gentleman's forgiveness—"

"Until she met me," Burke said easily. "Then she begged me to escort her to the altar. She said she would die without me, fade away, swoon with every other breath. I simply had no choice in the matter."

Arielle retreated without another word behind a fork holding a goodly bite of braised ham.

"Well, in any case," Knight continued, "let me just say that if ever a female does manage to entrap me, I shall immediately revert to being wild and unmanageable."

"There sits a conceited, quite arrogant fellow,"

said Lannie. "Arielle is in the right of it. You men think everything circles about you, us ladies included."

"Perhaps I spoke prematurely," said Knight, giving her a baiting grin. "I am twenty-six years old. I shall marry when I am forty. For an heir. That's what my father did, and he recommended that I follow his footsteps in the matter. He assured me that I should ignore everything else he said or did, except for that. I am a dutiful son, that is all."

"I suggest that you not announce your intentions to the ton in London," Burke said. "You would become the challenge of every lady in town."

"Or he might get done away with for his abominable arrogance," said Lannie.

"Not by the ladies," said Knight and saluted her with his wineglass.

"Oh," said Lannie, "you are provoking, Knight Winthrop!"

In the drawing room some thirty minutes later, Arielle asked her half sister, "When is the baby due, Nesta?"

"I am but three and a half months now. A long time. Forever, it seems."

"You look beautiful. Do you still wish for a boy? Or is that just Alec's preference?"

"Oh, I don't care. Of course, as I told you before, Alec wants an heir. All men do. As if a woman could determine the sex of her child," she added on a sigh.

"Burke wouldn't be like that," said Arielle.

Lannie gave an I-know-all-about-that kind of smile. "A bride speaks," she said, "not a wife. A bride, I add, who didn't want to marry until she saw Burke Drummond."

Arielle knew when she was in a six-foot hole she herself had dug. "That's right," she said and thrust up her chin.

"Have you ever asked Burke, Arielle?" Nesta said. "About children or preferring a boy?"

"No, I haven't," Arielle said, "but I know Burke. He is good and kind and wise—"

"Goodness," said Lannie, bursting into merry laughter. "This is my brother-in-law, my dear, not some sort of Greek god or revered patriarch! You make him sound like a gray-bearded old man who pontificates in a cave somewhere."

"That," Arielle said, "he doesn't do." She laughed. "I shall now imagine him with that beard and in a long black robe."

"Oh, dear," said Lannie. "I think I shall play the pianoforte. Please don't tell Burke what she said, Nesta, or he will replace Knight as the most arrogant, conceited male here."

Nesta grinned at Arielle and patted the seat beside her. "Come sit with me, love."

"That necklace looks lovely on you, Nesta."

Nesta fingered her beautiful opal necklace. "Thank you. Alec gave it to me on my last birthday."

Lannie launched into an ambitious Mozart Sonata in F Major, but the two sisters were still able to chat quietly.

"You've been married nearly five years now, Nesta. I remember Alec then. You were giddy about him."

"Yes," said Nesta. "More than giddy, I daresay. I would have slain dragons for him had he asked. Do you remember how beautiful he was then? And he just seems to become more beautiful every year. It is occasionally most provoking." She lowered her eyes a moment. "I am afraid, Arielle," she whispered.

Arielle blinked her surprise. "Of what?"

"I am growing bulky. In a couple of months Alec

won't be able to . . . well, you know what I mean. He will become quite bored with me."

"But that is silly. Alec loves you."

"He is also a man who is very physical. He needs intimacy. I can't see him going without . . ."

"Intimacy?" Arielle said.

"Yes," said Nesta. "He won't go without. Perhaps I shouldn't be speaking like this to you, but you are, after all, a married woman. Goodness, Burke is your second husband. It is an odd realization, you only eighteen years old." Nesta sighed. "But there it is."

"I know," said Arielle.

"Even now, whenever Alec shows his face, the ladies swoon in his path, hoping to gain his attention. It happened everywhere we went, even in Macau! And you know Alec, he simply doesn't appear to notice all these felled females. How he can be so oblivious of all the quickened heartbeats in his vicinity is a constant source of wonder to me."

"Well, you will keep him safe and oblivious in the country, will you not?"

"We will go to his estate in Northumberland shortly. I hope he won't be too restless there."

"Alec restless?" said Arielle. "Whyever for? He hasn't been there in years. He will have plenty to occupy him. But what about you? You are the one I worry about."

"I am fine. I just wish it were over and the child born healthy."

"Nesta, may I ask you something?"

"You are my sister. It is proper for us to speak of everything together."

"Does Alec ever . . . hurt you?"

"Hurt me? What do you mean?"

*Does he beat you? Does he force you to your knees and humiliate you?*

"I—no, never mind. Lannie plays beautifully, doesn't she?"

"Yes," Nesta said, a thoughtful frown puckering her brow, "yes, she does. As I recall, so do you, Arielle."

"You seem sad, Nesta. Alec is an honorable man, isn't he? I mean, he won't leave you or anything?"

Nesta gave a pained smile. "He is, yes. I lied to you, Arielle. Alec was bored with me three months after we were wed. I hold him with . . . oh, dear, I am becoming more and more indiscreet by the moment. Forget all that, my dear."

How can I? Arielle wondered, but she said no more. She wasn't stupid. She knew, of course, that Nesta was going to say that she held her husband with sex. That, Arielle thought, was something she simply couldn't imagine.

When the gentlemen came into the drawing room not long thereafter, Arielle's eyes went to her husband. He was laughing at something Percy said. *He* was the beautiful one, she thought. And he was kind and good and wise, despite the fact he didn't sport a long, tangled beard and a dirty robe. He wouldn't hurt her, ever. She rose and walked over to him. He smiled at her and laced his fingers in hers. He laughed again when Percy came to the end of his jest. "I see," Percy said, glancing at Arielle, "that you want me elsewhere. I shall turn pages for Lannie."

"The man is wonderfully perceptive," said Burke. He tightened his hold on her fingers. "Hello, my dear."

"Nesta told me ladies swoon in Alec's path to get his attention. Do you think that's true?"

Burke looked startled at that artless disclosure. "Well, I fully expect you to faint before the end of the week. At least once."

Her sweet laughter warmed him. He felt hopeful.

An hour later, as he climbed into their bed beside her, he felt randy, so randy he hurt.

Then he felt stunned.

"What did you say?" he asked.

# 17

He sounded so incredulous that for a moment Arielle felt too intimidated to say it again.

"What, Arielle? Come, what did you say?"

He sounded more like himself now, but there was still that edge of bewilderment in his voice. "Well," she said, glad it was dark and he couldn't see her face, "I just wondered if you wanted children."

"I see," he said, not seeing a damned thing. "I think I told you once that I did."

"Do you think you would insist upon a boy first?"

"I could probably insist until cows swim the Atlantic, but it wouldn't do much good."

"Would you be disappointed if it weren't a boy first?"

He was growing randier by the second. Did she have any idea what she was doing to him? Probably not. He sighed. "No, I wouldn't be disappointed. Didn't I once tell you that I wanted a little girl who looked just like you?"

"You were just being nice."

"Well, I am nice. I'm delighted you've finally noticed. Of course I would like one of our children to be a boy. One of our children needs to be a boy. Unfortunately, girls can't become earls. Equally unfortunately, girls have to take their husband's names. Our girls would cease to be Drummonds."

"Yes, that's true. Lannie once told me that Montrose didn't speak to her for two weeks after Poppet was born."

"Montrose was a fool."

"I'm beginning to think Lannie didn't like him very much."

"Many wives don't like their husbands. And vice versa, I might add."

Arielle didn't say anything to that bit of wisdom. She heard Burke turn and knew that he was on his side now, facing her. She didn't move.

"Burke?"

"Hmm?"

"You didn't ask me to kiss you good night."

He sucked in his breath. His eyes glittered. "Arielle, are you teasing me?"

"I don't know what you mean."

"Of course you do. I can hear it in your voice."

"All right. Burke, will you give me a baby?"

One blow right after the other, he thought blankly. Had he been standing, he would have been reeling. As it was, he way lying down and he was still reeling, figuratively at least. He heard himself say in the calmest voice imaginable, "Are we having this discussion because Nesta is pregnant?"

"No! Well, that's not entirely true. I probably wouldn't have given it too much thought right away if it weren't for Nesta and Virgie and Poppet. While you gentlemen were with your port after dinner, Nester, Lannie, and I were discussing children. I do love Virgie and Poppet. Don't you think I would be a good mother?"

*Getting* to the mother part was uppermost in Burke's mind at this moment.

"Yes, I think you would be a wonderful mother."

"You think you would be a good father?"

"I would be a wonderful father," he said firmly. "The very best, in fact."

"Then you'll consider it?"

"Arielle, you do understand fully how one becomes a mother?"

"Yes, of course. I'm not stupid, Burke."

"The thought of me touching you, caressing you intimately, my member coming inside you—it doesn't repel you? It doesn't frighten you?"

He heard her draw in her breath sharply and added, "I hope you don't mind my plain speaking, but I want to be certain that you understand everything."

"I'm not stupid," she said again, but he heard the *thinness* in her voice.

"All right, Madam Brilliance, do you also know that I will . . . no, forget it. That, my dear, takes demonstration, not explanation."

"What does?"

"You'll see, hopefully." The thought of caressing her with his mouth, every inch of her, nearly made his muscles go into spasm.

"Then you'll do it?"

He was smiling into the darkness, a grim, very tight smile. "I don't see why not," he said finally. And he chuckled. He fell onto his back, laughing deeply now. Good God, he thought, talk about the vagaries of fate.

"What is so funny? I thought this would be excessively serious, you know. Men always—"

He rolled over to her and she felt his fingertip touch her lips. "Shush. No more *men always,* all right? You know very little about men, good men, at least."

He was certainly right about that. She fell silent.

"What is wrong, Arielle?" he asked finally. "You lose your nerve?"

"I guess so. I don't want to be hurt anymore. If you do that to me, it will hurt, won't it?"

*Will you always twist the knife in my guts?* She

couldn't know, of course, that when she said things like that, he wanted to howl in helpless rage and strangle a man already well dead.

"I won't ever hurt you. I thought we'd settled that once and for all. Except—" He paused. No, he thought, he had to. She was a virgin. He said very gently, "Listen, Arielle. Did Cochrane ever—oh, God, this is damned difficult."

"I don't mind."

"All right, did he ever come into you far enough or put anything inside you that made you bleed?" He could practically hear her sorting through one confusing, completely incorrect conclusion after the other. "Let me add to that. Just once, Arielle. Make you bleed just one time?"

"No, she said at last. "The other times . . . well, never mind."

So, Burke thought, his hands automatically balling into fists, Cochrane had humiliated her in that way as well.

"That means your maidenhead is still intact. It will hurt just a bit the first time I come inside you. Then no more pain or discomfort, ever. I promise."

"All right."

"Just like that? All right, Burke? Get started now, please? Get it over with?"

"You needn't be sarcastic just because you're losing *your* nerve. I don't mean to make you feel like you have to, Burke. I'm sorry. Please don't be angry with me. Can we go to sleep now?"

"I'm not angry with you," he said. "Actually, I feel I'm very close to making something we call a tactical retreat. You see, wife, I love you—something I've told you many times now—I care about you and your feelings, and I want, really want, to make love with you. I desire you. Very much. Just looking at you makes my body hard. And you, of course, have no concept of what desire even is. Now you want me to give you a baby, which means making love, and you make it sound like ordering a new gown or asking the cobbler for a new pair of shoes. It isn't, Arielle. Not for me, at any rate. Do you understand?"

"This is very difficult. I would like to think about it, if you don't mind."

"I think you should," he agreed, wanting more than anything to bury himself inside her this very instant.

Burke discovered some silent minutes later that he didn't like going to sleep on a serious note. "Why don't you give me a good-night kiss?"

She rolled over immediately, placed one palm on his naked chest, and kissed him, missing his mouth, then finding it after a giggling exploration. A nice, very firm kiss. Of course her lips were tightly closed.

"Good night, Arielle." he said.

"I don't mind kissing you, Burke."

"That's a good start. Why don't you try it again, only this time part your lips just a bit."

It was dark, it was late at night, she couldn't see his face or he hers, so she did. His tongue touched hers. She drew back, but not before she was aware of a brief, very sweet, very warm feeling deep in her belly.

He was wonderfully aware of that exquisite reaction in her.

Arielle stood outside the door of Nesta's bedchamber the following morning, her hand raised to knock.

She paused at the sound of strange noises from within. She heard a woman's moan. Oh, dear, was Nesta in pain? She pressed her ear to the door and heard Nesta cry out, "Oh, God, oh!" Was she losing the baby? Without hesitation, Arielle flung open the door and rushed in. "Nesta! Is something wrong? Are you all—" Her voice fell like a stone from a cliff. She stood stock-still and stared.

Nesta was on her back, naked. Alec, equally naked and looking every bit as beautiful and powerful as a savage Viking god, was over her, between her parted legs, inside her body. His back was arched, his head flung back. Then Arielle's voice and her presence penetrated his brain.

He was looking at her now, his eyes glazed, his expression utterly bewildered.

"Arielle!" Nesta began to struggle against her husband.

Alec said very calmly, "Get out, Arielle. Nesta is quite all right. Out!"

"Come along, my dear," Burke said, coming up behind her and quickly pulling her out of the bedchamber. He closed the door firmly.

To Arielle's surprise, she heard Alec's bark of laughter, then Nesta's wail of embarrassment.

Arielle pressed her palms against her cheeks. "Oh, dear," she said. "Oh, dear."

"I agree," Burke said, and then he laughed. He drew her into his arms and laughed and laughed. "I don't suppose you were expecting that when you dashed into their bedchamber."

"Oh, dear," Arielle said again, burying her face in his shoulder. "Oh, dear."

"At least Alec was laughing instead threatening to strangle you."

"You are horrible!"

"Not I. I am but an innocent bystander. I was simply walking down my own corridor to my own bedchamber when I chanced to see my wife standing in a bedchamber, her mouth agape like a village half-wit's, staring at her sister and brother-in-law making very passionate love."

"I thought Nesta was in pain. I heard her moaning—"

"I do understand." And he burst into laughter again.

Arielle drew back her fist and punched him as hard as she could in his stomach. He grunted, grabbing her fist. But still he was grinning, an unholy grin, and at her expense. Then he touched his fingertip to the tip of her nose. "I venture to say that we would look as enticing as Alec and Nesta did. Are you interested?"

Arielle closed her eyes tightly. "I've never been more embarrassed in my life."

"I'm sure your sister and brother-in-law probably feel the same way."

"Nesta said that Alec was a man who had to have . . . well, a man who needed . . ."

"Most of us blighted specimens are like that."

"You as well, Burke?"

"Good Lord, yes."

That earned him a very wary look. "But you haven't done—that is, you haven't made me think that you would—"

He cupped her face between his hands, leaned down, and kissed her, hard and quick. His voice was rough and deep as he said, "I want you nearly all the time. Don't ever think that I don't. I look at you and I want you. I smell that special lavender scent of yours and I want you. I hear you talking and I want you. I eat Cook's crimped salmon and I want you."

"Stop that! You're making all that up!"

"And I'm supposed to sleep next to you every night. And you used to sleep naked, in my arms, pressed against me. Can you imagine how I felt? I survived on very little sleep, I can tell you that."

"Oh," she said.

"Not *oh, dear?*"

She punched his shoulder. Then she stared at his coat buttons. They were brass, highly polished, and really rather nondescript, if the truth were told, but her look was one of fascinated interest.

"I want to know what you're thinking, Arielle. But first, I think we should remove ourselves from the corridor. Would you like to take a stroll with me?"

The morning was warm, the light breeze warm. The scent of roses and hibiscus filled the air. They saw Joshua and Geordie in close conversation, and Arielle waved. Burke just shook his head when Joshua, that misogynist, grinned at her like a fool and waved back. Burke took her hand. "There is something I wish to discuss with you, but first, what were you thinking about before in the corridor? When you were staring so fixedly at the brass buttons on my coat."

"I was thinking about how handsome you are and how well you are formed. That's all."

"That's *all?*" He felt himself expanding on the spot. To hear her say that, it was more than any man could hope. It was certainly not what he had expected. He grinned at her as foolishly as Joshua had. "Thank you, Arielle." He guided their walk toward the maple grove, a thicket of trees so dense and private that Burke had no doubt that every young set of lovers used it as a trysting place. "Now, let me tell you what *I'm* thinking. It's serious, Arielle. Maybe too serious for right now. But you want me to give you a baby. And I think we have to resolve that before we begin our parental endeavors."

He always mixed his speech with humor, she'd come to realize, even when he was at his most serious, and she warmed to it.

"You had no choice about our marriage," he said after a moment. He didn't look at her. "You were very ill and I decided that I wanted to marry you.

Even if you died, I wanted you to be my wife if only for a little while." He heard his own voice crack as he spoke and paused, trying to regain his control. "When the vicar needed your response, I ordered you to say 'I do.' *Ordered,* Arielle. You responded immediately to my stern tone, to my man's command. I knew that you would. If I had been kind and good and gentle, you wouldn't have responded to anything the vicar asked you. So, to get what I wanted, I used your fear against you. I used on you what Cochrane had used. Don't misunderstand, I feel bad that I did it, but I'm not sorry. I wanted to wed you. I want you to be my wife until I die. But you had no choice in the matter. I want you to know that I won't touch you sexually until you want me to. This, at least, is *your* choice. As I told you before, even when I was threatening you sexually, I had no intention of ever forcing you to do anything. I want us to be married in the most real sense of things, Arielle. But it is your decision."

"Would you remain celibate forever if I didn't wish you to touch me?"

He looked at her then. One brow arched upward a good inch. "Forever? Merciful heavens, you do know how to strip away the layers of things, don't you?"

"Well, there was Laura What's-her-name in London."

"That was before we were married."

"Well?"

"Probably not. Probably I would try everything in a man's repertoire to seduce you. Wine, brandy, perhaps opium, diamonds, rubies, maybe even a puppy—"

She laughed. "Do stop that! You know I don't want things like diamonds and rubies. As for opium, that's awful! If I were drunk or drugged, I wouldn't know what I was doing. I can't imagine that would be any fun for you."

He gave her a look so filled with hunger that she swallowed and quickly looked away at the small cluster of bluebells beside the path. She said, her eyes fixed on the toes of her shoes, "It's very warm today."

"Yes, but there is a light breeze."

"Yes, there is. You know I am ugly."

That drew him up. "What?"

"Ugly." She looked up at him, straightly. "You've seen me without my clothes enough times to know how I look."

He was tempted to pretend ignorance, to assure her that he thought her the most beautiful and perfectly made of women, which was indeed what he did think, but that wasn't the point now. He had to go very carefully and, he knew, very honestly. "You mean the faint white lines from all the beatings Cochrane gave you?"

"Yes. You can see the—the marks if you look *closely*."

"It's difficult for me," he said. "I see you naked and I see those marks and I feel such rage toward that old bastard that I would like to search him out in hell and kill him again. Then I look at you and I see the years of pain in your eyes, I see how deeply he hurt you, and I want to hold you and tell you no one will ever hurt you again, that you're mine now, you belong to me. I want you to believe that the past is just that—in the past—and that you and I are together and we are the present and the future and it will be what we make it. That's what I think about your so-called ugliness."

"Why," she said very quietly, her voice low and somehow distant, "didn't you take me away with you when I was fifteen?"

He brought her tightly against him. "God, I wish

I had, Arielle. I've thought it so many times, regretted so many times acting the noble and, I believed, honorable man. But I simply assumed that you would be here, a woman instead of a girl, yet still miraculously the same as you were at fifteen, and I would smile at you and we would wed and that would be that." He shook his head at himself. "But it didn't happen that way, and we cannot change the past. But we can look at it, then firmly put it where it belongs—behind us, and if not forgotten, at least no longer important."

He kissed her then, a very gentle kiss.

He felt her breasts soft against his chest. He felt her arms go around his back. Then, to his besotted delight, he felt her lips part very slightly. He didn't deepen his kiss, nor did he thrust his tongue into her mouth. Very slowly, he ran his tongue along her lower lip. Her taste was sweet, seductive, and he was hard and trembling with need for her. But he was a man, not an uncontrolled boy.

He felt the instant she responded. He felt her body change. It was as if something deep inside her loosened, opened, and he knew in that precious moment that she was no longer wary of him, that she no longer feared any part of him. Her lips parted more fully, and he nearly moaned with the pleasure of it when her tongue tentatively touched his.

"Arielle," he said, his voice warm and deep.

Her arms tightened around his back. She rose onto her tiptoes to fit herself better against him. He felt her soft belly pressing against his member, now hard and straining against his breeches. And he thought: She trusts me. At last she trusts me. And his kiss deepened and grew more possessive. She took his passion, his vibrant and urgent need, and gave herself over to it, giving him not only her own need but the suppressed feelings of that young girl so long ago.

Arielle had never before known that a kiss could
be like this. Changing and deepening, teasing for a
while, then so sweet she wanted to cry from the
wonder of it. She felt the power of it in her heart,
making her want to know him—his taste, the planes
and angles of his body, the softness of his flesh, the
hard muscles of his belly, all of him—and mixed
with those elusive feelings were the stark, pounding sensations burgeoning in the pit of her stomach. It was a kind of ache, a strange compulsion to
press herself against him, not to just know him but
also to feel all of him, his maleness, to bring him
into herself. And there was no fear, no hesitancy,
only her sense of wanting and of discovery.

She moaned, softly, and both of them started. He
raised his head just a bit and smiled down at her.
"That is the most beautiful sound I've ever heard
in my life."

He kissed her again. She felt his hands sweep
down her back, drawing her even closer. She felt
his hands cover her hips, then cup her and lift her
and rub himself against her. It left her feeling hollow with near frantic urgency. She drew in her
breath and moaned again.

He was kneading her hips, pressing and moving
her against his member, and she jerked, unable to
help herself, and dug her fingers into his back.

"Burke," she murmured, her voice thin and excited and banked with barely leashed passion.

He kissed her chin, her eyes, her lips, then lifted
her into his arms. "It's time I had my way with
you," he said, and she laughed and hugged her
arms around his shoulders. He felt her head on his
shoulder. He felt her trust flowing over him. He felt
like a god, a king, and better than even that, he
felt like a man and her husband.

He walked deep into the maple grove. It was silent and the leaves were so thick overhead that the

sun could only penetrate in thin, glittering slices,
cutting the still air in silver arcs.

He stopped finally and eased them both down,
letting her feel the length of his body, his hardness, his size. "It is your decision. Do you want me,
Arielle?"

She said nothing. He felt her fingers on the buttons of his shirt, then on his bare chest, gliding
over him, learning him. She smiled up at him. "Just
a moment," he said and nearly ripped his coat jerking it off. He spread it on the soft mossy ground.
"Clothes," he said. "So many wretched layers."

They undressed each other, or at least they tried
to, with awkward movements and clumsy attempts
that made them laugh. Burke thought, as he fought
with some buttons on her gown, that he was a fool
not to wait until they were in bed. He was still
wearing his breeches, his boots tossed haphazardly
atop her petticoat when she was naked. He stopped
cold. He looked at her, all of her. Slowly, he reached
out his hand and gently cupped her breast. He
closed his eyes a moment, lifting her breast, feeling
her. "So lovely," he said. Then he cupped both
breasts, smiling at her, his thumbs lightly caressing her nipples.

He held her tightly against one arm, his other
hand moving downward, searching, and he found
her, and her woman's flesh was hot and soft and he
groaned.

"I feel funny," Arielle said, clutching his shoulder. "I feel very funny."

She raised her face for his kiss and he obliged
her. He tasted her rising desire as his fingers
stroked and caressed her. He felt her move against
his fingers, and it was natural and giving. When he
was breathing so heavily he couldn't bear it, he removed himself from her. She looked at him, her
eyes slightly glazed, her lips parted, her breath

coming in short gasps. He wanted her to know that he would still stop if she wished it. She stared at his face, saw the tenderness in his eyes, his urgent, naked desire for her. "Burke," she said very quietly and opened her arms to him.

"You won't ever fear me," he said, leaning over to kiss her. As his tongue gently slipped between her lips, his fingers again began to caress her, and she cried out, her hips jerking upward.

He knew then that no matter how urgent his own need, he would control himself. He kissed her breasts and felt her response. "You like that," he said, his breath hot against her flesh.

"Just a little bit," she gasped. Then he took her nipple and suckled, and she thought she couldn't bear it. The feelings were too much, too strong, too intense. She cried out yet again into his mouth. His fingers were now rhythmically stroking her and she found herself moving naturally against them, pressing upward, showing him what she wanted. When her body bowed, arching desperately, when the sensations were nearly painful, she cried out his name, lost in the pleasure of her body and the pleasure that was in him as well.

He watched her as she climaxed, watched every reaction, felt her release flow through him. She'd looked so surprised. So wondering. She was his now. Forever.

When her body quieted from its violent tremors, he lifted himself over her and without a word, without warning, came into her in one powerful, full stroke. As he broke through her maidenhead he kissed her, clasped her tightly against him, and absorbed her cry of surprised pain. When he was deep inside her, when she sheathed him, held him tight and warm, he eased down on his elbows above her. Her skin was slick with perspiration and he breathed in the air, feeling it swirl through him,

the smell of the sweet mossy ground, the smell of
the maples leaves, the smell of their sweat, and the
smell of sex.

"Look at me," he said.

She opened her eyes.

"No more pain."

Arielle raised her hand and lightly traced her fingertips over his face. "No, there isn't any. You're
beautiful, Burke."

He quivered, his eyes closing against the incredible feelings she roused in him. She was so tight
and small and ... He gritted his teeth. "Don't
move. Please, don't move."

"All right. Burke?"

"Yes?"

"You are so deep inside me. This intimacy business is a very strange thing."

"Oh, God," he said, trying desperately to control
himself, but it was too late, far too late. He'd
wanted to try to bring her with him again, to give
her more pleasure, to give her more of himself, but
he felt himself heaving and jerking in his need, felt
himself shattering over her and into her, pouring
his seed deep inside her and giving her all that he
was, promising her all that he would ever be.

And she took him and held him and welcomed
him.

# 18

"Burke?"

Her voice was sweet and soft and vulnerable. He tried to gain control of his breathing and managed to grunt.

"What happened to me?"

He came up on his elbows, relieving her of his weight. Her hair was tangled about her face, her eyes were luminous and vague, and her mouth looked so tender he leaned down and kissed her. He balanced himself on his elbows and tried to ignore the very real fact that he was deep inside her and he wanted her again.

He saw her brow furrow.

"What happened to you? You seduced me."

She smiled at that and moved just a bit to accommodate him more easily.

"Don't!" He sucked in his breath. "Don't move like that, Arielle. It does things to me."

She tightened her arms around his back. "And that would mean, then, that you would do more things to me."

"Exactly."

"Please, what happened to me? Those feelings . . . it was like pain, only it wasn't, and I wanted more and more and then I felt like everything inside me just blew up, and I wasn't really me anymore but you were there and with me and part of me, and it was, well, it was wonderful."

He couldn't speak for a moment. Finally, as he stroked her hair from her forehead, he said, "That is what lovemaking is supposed to be like between a man and a woman." He thought of the succession of women whose beds and bodies he'd visited, and shook his head. "No, not really like that, not really so very intense. But that is what it is supposed to be like between us, Arielle, because there is love. Never pain or humiliation or dominance or any of those things. Just giving and taking pleasure and more pleasure, like some sort of magical bonding. Now, I don't want to squash you into the moss." He eased out of her, feeling her flinch slightly.

She raised her hand and pressed it against his chest. "Even sweaty you feel marvelous." She breathed in deeply. "And the smells. The smell of man, the smell of Burke—"

"And the smell of Arielle, lavender and sweet and sweaty and earthy and covered and filled with the smell of me."

"Yes," she said. She missed him, the fullness of him, the sweet pressure of him. Then she felt sticky and wet, and she brought her thighs together.

"Hold still, sweetheart." He reached over and pulled a handkerchief from his coat pocket. He cleansed her, holding himself back with all the inner strength he possessed. He had to wait; he had to give her time. She'd responded so wonderfully to him. He hadn't expected it, at least not before he'd begun kissing her, and after he'd begun, he simply hadn't thought about it, which was probably just as well. If he had thought about it, he would probably have been so worried about hurting her that he would have frozen up and been anything but natural. But they'd both been natural. He thought of the fantasies he'd had of her for three long years,

those sometimes stark images that were replete
with the intense sexual pleasure she would give
him, and now, now that she was his, it had happened and it was so. But what he hadn't imagined
was the searing, nearly violent need deep inside
himself, the core of himself that he hadn't known
was lacking until she filled it with her real self, not
with the girl of his fantasies and dreams who had
merely sustained him for those three years.

He said, his voice deep, so deep and tender that
it filled her, "Will you stay with me now?"

She looked away from him, over his head, at the
glittering spears of sunlight. She told him one
truth, one that neither of them could deny. "I would
have no place to go to. Nesta and Alec are no longer
in Boston."

"True, but they will be traveling soon to Northumberland, to Carrick Grange."

"No, I wouldn't go with them. I shouldn't like to
be a poor relation, and since I have no money, that
is what I would be."

He waited. She looked up at him finally, and her
eyes were questioning. Of herself, of him he didn't
know. "I think," she said at last, "I think I want
to stay with you."

He reached over, his fingertips lightly touching
her breast. It was soft, silky soft, and slowly, he
lowered his head and took it into his mouth. He
suckled and caressed until he felt the answering
response in her. He smiled and blew gently on her
heated skin, looking intently at the taut nipple.
Taut with pleasure from him, from her feelings for
him.

"Do you know something, Arielle? If I had taken
you when you were fifteen, married you—doubtless
against your father's wishes, and you can be certain you would have felt very guilty about that—
and brought you with me to the Continent to be an

officer's wife, you and I would have been vastly different with each other. You would have been open and loving and sweet and very, very young, and I probably would have acted something like a benevolent parent, loving you certainly, yet seeing myself as responsible for raising you and thus ordering you about and treating you more like a child than a woman and a wife.

"I can't imagine that you would have liked that very much, at least after a while. Who knows? Perhaps you would have kicked me out, taken my horse, and left me with just the tent and Joshua."

She laughed, once again appreciating how he could mix lightness and humor with the most serious thoughts.

"No," she said, her eyes luminous upon his face, "I shouldn't have left you. Deborah—she would have been our little girl, you know—and you and I would have stayed in your officer's tent, and I would have continued cooking and mending for you and fending off the other officers, who, of course, would have fallen in love with me."

"And they would have. And I would have been obnoxiously possessive and jealous, and you would have rapped me on my head, thrown your delicious cooking in my face, and doubtless left my shirts unmended and tattered."

"I wish you weren't right so much of the time. And yes, she would have felt overwhelming guilt about leaving her father."

He heard the bitterness in her voice. "Her?"

"I occasionally think about that silly, stupid, guileless little fool."

"No! Dammit, Arielle, she is you, part of you, and whenever you laugh, it is her laughter, your laughter. That very sweet, innocent young girl is still there, but you're a woman now and you've tempered her, made her grow and become someone special, someone I love with all my being."

He leaned over and kissed her. He wanted to kiss her until he had banished all the pain in her, all the bitterness and hurt. "You are my wife," he said. "You are mine."

"Yes," she said and cupped his face between her hands.

He kissed her again, feeling the heat of the sun on his back and the heat of her against his heart.

Burke watched Arielle closely when she walked into the drawing room that evening. He wasn't entirely successful in keeping the amusement from his face. As Arielle's bad luck would have it, only Nesta and Alec were there. She was embarrassed, he knew it, but she managed to smile at Nesta and make an easy enough greeting. As for Alec Carrick, she couldn't meet his eyes.

Alec, on the other hand, wasn't at all leveled by embarrassment. He said in the blandest voice Burke had ever heard, "Lovely day, wasn't it, Arielle?"

"Yes," Arielle said, her eyes on Burke's boots now instead of on her own slippers.

"And it was a lovely, quite memorable morning as well, don't you agree, little sister?"

That brought her head up, and she opened her mouth only to shut it again when she saw the mocking expression of Alec's impossibly handsome face.

"What's this?" Percy said, coming into the drawing room, Lannie beside him. "Trouble in this paradise of couples?"

"Alec is being a cad," said Nesta. "Nothing out of the ordinary."

"A common ailment among gentlemen," said Arielle.

Lannie giggled. "Since Percy isn't yet a husband, I shan't put him properly in his place."

Percy groaned. "I was going to propose soon, fall at your dainty feet, and offer you my hand and my house and my carriage. Now I am not so certain. What do you think, Burke? Would you marry Arielle again?"

"Unfair," said Alec before Burke could respond. "He's been leg-shackled but a very short time. He's still existing in a fog of marital and sexu—well, never mind that. You should be asking an old married man like me. Merciful heavens, nearly five years now. I teeter near the grave. There was a gray hair in my head this morning, and I have yet to see twenty-seven."

"As I said," Nesta remarked to the drawing room at large, "a cad."

Arielle blurted out, "But you are still existing in that . . . well, you've been married a very long time, and evidently that fog doesn't go away—at least it hasn't with you and Nesta and—" Arielle's voice broke off, and she felt herself hugged very tightly by a laughing husband.

"Celibacy is just around the corner," Alec said, giving Nesta a mournful look.

"What is all this?" Knight asked from the doorway. He looked immaculate and fit and, Burke thought, eyeing him more closely, immensely pleased with himself.

"Nothing of import," Burke said. "Just the usual marital bickering. What is going on, Knight? You look like the cat who had his pick of the cream pots."

"Well, my dear fellow, the gentlemen will be off to a little town called Chiddingstone on Friday morning. There's a mill, and I've bespoken rooms for us at the The Gooseneck Inn. I ran into Rafael

Carstairs and Lyon Ashton, and we decided to make a party of it." He beamed at everyone.

Burke almost shook his head, but he paused when Arielle said, "A mill is fighting, isn't it? Between two men? With their fists?"

"Yes, ma'am," said Percy. "I say, Knight, well done!"

"Ugh," was Lannie's comment.

"You will enjoy that, will you not?" Arielle asked Burke.

"I, well, yes, I guess so. But I don't want to leave you."

She smiled at him. "I am not your mother to tie you to my skirts. Nor am I an invalid, Burke."

"No, what you are is a bride and—"

She heard Alec laugh from behind her and quickly placed her fingertips over Burke's mouth. "You will survive it, I am certain, my lord, as will I. I, also, you will notice, have two ladies to keep me company. We will enjoy ourselves immensely, I promise you."

He caught her hands in his. "You're certain?"

"Another symptom," said Alec. "He's in such a fog he can't see the world outside his bedcham—"

"That is quite enough," said Nesta.

"Who are the fighters?" Burke asked.

"The champion, Cribb, and Molyneux. Molyneux's the heavier, I heard—and his arms, Lord, they're a good two inches longer than Cribb's—but neither of them is over fourteen stone. I'm for Cribb, of course, but Molyneux isn't to be dismissed lightly."

"Why would you be for Cribb when Molyneux has such long arms he could hit Cribb and not be hit?" asked Arielle.

"A matter of science," said Knight. "Experience and intelligence and cunning and ruthlessness."

"That about covers it," said Burke.

Lannie shot a comic look at Arielle and Nesta, heaved a martyr's sigh, and asked, "What do you think would happen if ladies became fighters?"

"I don't know," Arielle replied thoughtfully, "but I think we are endowed with goodly amounts of this science Knight was talking about."

Montague cleared his throat in the doorway. "Dinner is served, my lady."

"An important part of science is good and regular eating habits," said Percy and offered his arm to Lannie.

"Another important part of science is a sweet kiss before every meal," said Burke, kissed his wife, then lightly tapped her chin. "It's good for the digestion."

"The final important part of all this science," said Knight, his tone one of amused tolerance, "is the ability to keep oneself sane when surrounded by all these very tedious mating rituals."

"Your day will come, old fellow," said Alec.

"Never," said Knight with a goodly amount of vehemence. "Not I. Not a chance. Never in a million eons. I'm starving."

"In bed at last, where we belong. Do you realize I've never made love to you in a bed?"

Arielle thought of the sweet smell of the leaves and grass and moss, and the tingling shafts of sunlight that had struck her bare flesh. She thought of the hardness of his body over hers, and she knew she would remember until the day she died the feelings he'd ignited in her that first time.

"It was nice," she said with great inadequacy, "in the maple grove."

"Oh, yes," said Burke, his voice very deep. He slowly drew down the sheet and bared her breasts.

"Burke, I hadn't expected things to be like this."

He'd been studying her breasts, but now he

looked at her face. "You mean pleasure, with me, a man?"

"That, I suppose, and feeling good about being me, and not being afraid anymore."

Again he experienced that wrenching feeling deep inside him that made him nearly frantic with need and love for her. He stroked his open palm over her breasts, slowly, back and forth. He said, wanting to be honest with her, "But it is still a very fragile feeling, isn't it, Arielle?"

"I don't know." Her breathing was a bit jerky and he smiled, knowing what she was feeling.

"You are so very soft," he said and bent his head down to take her breast into his mouth.

He felt her fingers tangling in his hair, pulling him closer. "Very nice," he said, lightly touching his fingertips to her taut nipple. "Very nice indeed."

"You're nicer," she said and tugged at his ear. He kissed her mouth then, as she wanted, deeply and thoroughly, giving and giving, offering her everything that he was, willing her to accept him and to understand him.

She felt his finger slide into her just as his tongue eased into her mouth, and she cried out with the explosion of feeling it caused and the images it created in her mind. Her hands were all over him then, feeling him, kneading him, pulling him closer, hugging him to her with all her strength.

His breath was hot in her mouth and she took him and responded to him, her own breath gasping.

He felt her legs part for him, and that simple gesture from her, her giving, her openness, made him tremble. He couldn't slow now. He was between her spread thighs, looking down at her, his fingers urgent as they stroked and parted her, and then he came into her, one full, deep thrust, and she cried out.

He was wild with his own desire, beyond himself, and when he felt himself explode inside her, he cried out her name and felt himself falling blindly, freely, until he realized that she was with him, holding him and loving him and urging him. And then he knew oblivion, and it was perfect.

Arielle finally opened her eyes. He was still deep inside her, his breathing hard, his head on the pillow beside hers. She smiled, lightly stroking her fingers over his cheek. Then she froze.

No, she thought, oh, God, no!

Burke felt her tense. Immediately, he rolled off her. "What is wrong? Am I too heavy for—"

She was shaking her head and rising. "Dorcas!"

Dorcas! Burke tried to regain his wits. What the devil was going on here?

"She was standing there, in the shadows by the door. She was watching us, Burke. Watching!"

Burke rolled off the bed. "Stay here. Please," he said as he put on his dressing gown. He pulled the belt tightly about his waist. He walked barefoot to the adjoining door, opened it, and went into her bedchamber.

Arielle didn't understand. Was it possible that Dorcas had heard them and thought perhaps that Burke was hurting her? Yes, that was it. That would be the only reason the old woman would do such a thing. Oh, God, how long had she been watching them?

She heard Burke moving about in the other room; then he called out, but she couldn't make out his words. Finally he rejoined her. "I couldn't find her," he said.

"I know why she came in," Arielle said. "She must have thought that you were hurting me. It's the only possible explanation."

He looked worried and angry. She heard him

curse very softly, some of his words so lurid that she laughed.

. He grinned at her rather sheepishly. "Sorry, but that's the outside of too much. Now, my dear wife, let me bathe you. Stay still and I'll fetch a cloth."

While he was running the warm, wet cloth over her, he was saying, "Do you hurt?"

"Just a bit sore, that's all."

"I was excessively enthusiastic. Here, does this make you feel better?"

He was pressing the cloth firmly against her, and she felt embarrassment. It was silly; after all, he was her husband, and she imagined that he knew her body every bit as well as she knew it herself, but still . . . "Yes," she managed to say.

He patted her dry, and before she could respond, he leaned down, parted her with his fingers, and kissed her.

"Burke!"

"Hush."

He was caressing her, his tongue probing and stroking, and she was so embarrassed that she jerked upward, pulling away from him. He looked up at her flushed face and smiled. "You're beautiful," he said simply and that, she supposed, was that.

"My face?"

"That too."

"Oh."

"Back to one syllable, I see. I do that to you, my dear?"

"I didn't know that . . . well, I'm not certain that you should do what . . . oh, dear!"

He laughed, gently kissed her again, lightly stroked his fingers over the rich red curls, and came up to lie beside her. "Now let's talk. I can manage five minutes of talk, I think."

She ducked her face into his shoulder. She hadn't

imagined that a man would do that. It was disconcerting, it was . . . Then she thought about herself, on her knees, taking a man's member into her mouth, and she choked back a sob.

"What is this?" Burke felt a stab of concern. He'd expected her to be embarrassed, but this? "Come, sweetheart, what's the matter?"

"I was just remembering how I would be on my knees and how I would—"

She didn't finish. He hugged her to him. "I know. I know. It's all right. Hush now." He sighed deeply and kissed the top of her head.

"Do you want to speak to Dorcas tomorrow, or shall I?"

He felt her become alert at that. "I'll speak with her, Burke."

"Perhaps she came in because she heard you moaning with pleasure and she couldn't believe it."

"That," Arielle said starkly, "is a possibility."

Burke doused the candles. "Let's sleep now, before I am overcome with lust for you again."

He heard her soft laughter in the darkness and he smiled. . . .

It was barely dawn, soft gray light settling into the bedchamber. Burke turned in his sleep, leaving the warmth of Arielle's body, and felt the air, cool on his flesh, and came awake.

He opened his eyes and looked up into Dorcas's face.

# 19

It was her eyes—vague, the pupils pinpoints of light in the dimlit room—that made Burke come awake in an instant. He saw her raised arm, saw the knife in her hand. It was aimed at Arielle. He shouted, striking up at her arm as he rolled over Arielle to get to Dorcas. The blade slid into his flesh. He felt a shudder of cold where the knife had struck, then a blessed numbness. The knife was jerked out of his flesh, its way smooth, even slick, leaving its path frozen. He'd experienced this before, knew what it meant.

Arielle came awake under Burke's weight and his yell. She looked up.

"Dorcas! No!" She saw the knife, saw the tip of it dripping blood. She saw the old woman lift her arm, saw the knife coming down. Burke again was trying desperately to cover her, and she felt the stickiness of his blood, knew he was hurt. With a strength she didn't know she possessed, she slid up, away from him, raised her pillow in front of her as the knife descended. It ripped through the pillow to its hilt, missing Arielle's throat by an inch.

But Arielle wasn't afraid for herself; she was terrified that Burke was going to die. She screamed in fury when Dorcas tore the knife from the pillow. She lunged at the old woman, smashing her against the night table next to the bed. The knife flew out of Dorcas's hand and went skidding across the wooden floor. The old woman was yelling now, fierce, obscene curses. She was panting heavily, her fists flailing at Arielle.

Arielle heard Burke behind her, but she paid him no heed. She brought her leg up and slammed her foot into the old woman's stomach. Dorcas screamed, doubling over. Arielle rammed her fist into Dorcas's jaw, and the old woman crumbled to the floor.

Arielle stood over her for a moment, breathing hard, the insane strength and purpose still holding her in its grip.

"Arielle!"

She whirled about and saw Burke standing beside the bed, one hand clutched to the bedpost for support, the other holding his injured shoulder. Blood flowed from from between his fingers, down his chest. She stared, unable for a long moment to take it in.

Then she quickly grabbed her dressing gown, thrusting her arms into the sleeves as she dashed into the corridor yelling at the top of her lungs, "Alec! Knight! Percy!"

She shouted their names again and again, and within seconds, Alec, shrugging into his own dressing gown, flung open the door opposite her.

"What the hell! Arielle!"

"Quickly! It's Burke!"

Arielle ran back into their bedchamber. Burke was now leaning against the bedpost. His chest and hand were crimson. There was a pool of blood on the floor. His foot, she saw blankly, was splattered with blood.

"Oh, my God! What the devil happened?"

Arielle felt a strange calm come over her. She didn't recognize it as shock, but Alec did. He took her hands and began to rub them rhythmically. She said slowly, as if she were a child reciting a piece for an adult, "Dorcas tried to kill me. Burke saved my life. He is hurt. Ah, Knight, there you are. Please have one of the men fetch Dr. Brody immediately. Thank you."

She turned, stepped over the unconscious old woman, and walked to her husband. "Sit down," she said. Then she went to the basin, moistened a towel, and came back to him, pressing the folded towel against the wound.

Alec said very gently, "Let me to that, Arielle. I'm stronger, and we need to get the bleeding to stop." He didn't add that she wasn't pressing in the right place.

She looked up at him, and he felt his guts twist at her lost expression. "It's all right, little sister. He'll survive. He's a tough specimen, you know. Why don't you sit down, too? Burke needs you to be strong now."

She did as she was told. Burke gathered her against his good side, hoping his ability to make that gesture would help reduce her shock.

Nesta, Lannie, and Percy rushed into the room, staring silently at the unconscious Dorcas and at the people who stood over Burke by the bed. No one remarked that the earl was quite naked.

"What happened, Arielle?" Nesta asked.

Arielle carefully repeated what she'd told Alec.

Percy gingerly picked up the bloody knife. "My God, is she insane?"

"It would appear so," said Burke, trying desperately to focus on anything outside himself. The pain had come suddenly alive. The blessed period of numbness was over. Throbbing, burning heat had taken the place of the deadening cold. He knew what was to follow and he didn't like it at all. The irony of being stabbed in his own bed after surviv-

ing years of fighting the French wasn't particularly
amusing at the moment.

Knight came back into the room. "I sent Geordie
for Dr. Brody. Joshua is here, as well as every servant in the Abbey."

Burke tried to get hold of himself. He had to keep
control; he had to tell them what to do. But the
bloody pain was drawing at his senses. Then, to his
astonishment, he heard Arielle say in a authorita-
tive voice, "Please have Joshua come here and take
Dorcas away, Knight. He can lock her in the sew-
ing room at the end of the east corridor. Tell Montague to have Mrs. Pepperall watch her. Dr. Brody
will see her after he takes care of Burke. As for the
other servants, please have them dress and go
downstairs. We will start the day. I doubt any of
them would wish to return to their beds. Oh, yes,
have a fire set in this room immediately."

My God, Burke thought, striving to keep the pain
from swamping his brain, she is acting the mistress
here. How wonderful! "Now, Burke," he heard Alec
say, "I want you to lie down on you back. Arielle
will help you. I will keep applying the pressure.
Percy, come and assist me."

Burke moaned—he couldn't stop himself. "Arielle," he whispered and reached for her hand.

"I'm here," she said, gripping his hand. "You will
be all right, Burke. I promise." She paused then:
"Lannie, please have Cook prepare some coffee and
tea for everyone, and whatever else you think
proper. Thank you. Now, Burke, take shallow
breaths. That's it. Excellent."

Alec lifted the towel and saw that the bleeding
had slowed considerably.

"Please continue, Alec," she said, looking down
at the wound. "It's almost stopped."

He smiled. She was holding herself together with
admirable aplomb. She needed to. Burke would

need her to. He was beginning to believe all of Ravensworth Abbey needed her to.

Arielle gently eased the sheet up to Burke's waist, smoothing it across his belly, wanting to *do* something, anything. He'd saved her life. He'd cared enough about her to die for her. She felt a crumbling inside her, a slow release of long-embedded memories, dark memories, bitter memories. For an instant, she saw an odd image in her mind. It was a candle and it was lit, but its flame flickered as it was buffeted by the wind. The wind grew stronger, but that flame didn't flicker out. It didn't die. The wind was a gale now, but the candle grew brighter. Then suddenly the wind died. It was gone, over. And the candle burned brightly. In that same moment, Arielle felt warm and strong. She felt herself smiling slightly as she said to Nesta, "Please light candles. It is too dark in here for Dr. Brody when he arrives. And fetch fresh hot water, Nesta, as well as towels and bandages."

Nesta quickly left to follow her instructions.

"I'm proud of you," Burke said and tried not to crush her fingers when a wave of pain silenced him.

She didn't know what he was talking about, but it didn't matter. She lightly stroked her fingertips over his jaw. "You need to shave," she said, and he smiled, albeit a very slight one.

"There," said Alec. "The bleeding has stopped. Now, old fellow, don't move. Brody, is that his name?" At Arielle's nod, he continued. "When the fellow comes, I want him to be impressed by all our respective handiwork. I need your cooperation in this, Burke, so don't move."

"He will be impressed," said Burke, then winced, his mouth closing over his moan. He heard Arielle's voice, so soft and comforting, whispering to him, and he found that if he concentrated on the sound of her voice, it did ease him. He remembered that April afternoon and evening after the Battle of Toulouse, when he'd lain trapped under a dead horse. He'd thought about her then, relived every moment they'd shared in order to escape from the horror that surrounded him. "Thank you, Arielle," he said. He saw her smile; then she leaned down and gently kissed him.

"You will be all right, I swear it. You are my husband, and I won't let anything happen to you."

*Arielle's husband.* He liked the sound of that; indeed he did.

All of Arielle's orders had been carried out by the time Mark Brody arrived. Knight told him what happened as the two men climbed the stairs.

Burke was lying quietly, his wife seated beside him on the bed. He managed a ghost of a smile. "I need patching up, Mark."

"Let's take a look." Mark lifted the towel and probed as gently as he could. "I remember well that saber wound in your side. You healed miraculously fast, Burke. Ah, the stab wound doesn't appear to be all that deep, thank God. I think you're a lucky man. Nothing vital has been injured, and the muscles look all right. About the only thing I should do is clean it well and set in a few stitches. We'll keep bascilicum powder on it. You heard that, Arielle?" At her nod, he continued to Burke. "I'll look at the old woman after I finish here, but I don't understand much about this sort of thing. I can drug her and keep her relaxed and calm. Insanity, you believe?"

Arielle answered. "It's very complicated, Doctor. I've been thinking a lot about it and I fear she has been going mad, very slowly. I would just as soon not talk about what pushed her to do what she did." She paused a moment, and Burke was appalled at the pain he saw in her eyes. "Burke and I will discuss it," she said at last, "once he is feeling better."

The doctor nodded and, in silence, numbed the wound, then put in the stitches. Finally he liberally sprinkled on bascilicum powder. "There, old man. Now for a bandage." When it was done, Mark said, "Let me give you some laudanum. Sleep and rest are the best things for you. Don't get up or you'll begin bleeding again. Can you keep him in that bed, Arielle?"

"Certainly. He isn't stupid. He will obey me."

Alec chuckled and Burke groaned.

"I'm a betting man, and my groats are on Arielle," Knight said.

It was late afternoon, damp and drizzling. The bedchamber was as gray and gloomy as the out-of-doors. Knight sat in the high-backed wing chair beside Burke's bed. It had been two days since the old woman's attack, and Burke was mending well.

"Ah, you're finally awake. Get your wits together, then tell me how you feel. Or if you don't feel like conversing, you can close your eyes and drift off again."

Burke felt light-headed and vague. The damned laudanum, he thought, shaking his head just a bit. The abrupt movement sent a slice of pain through his shoulder, and he quickly sucked in his breath and held himself still as a stone.

"I'm all right," he said at last.

Knight grinned at that overstatement. "I do hope this is your last wound, Burke. You'll look like a scarred warrior, and we both know it's just because you're so clumsy that you got wounded at all."

"Thank God for such good friends! I think I'll go back to sleep!"

Knight lightly touched his friend's arm. "Shall I get you something to drink?"

"Yes, brandy—"

"Sorry, that isn't amongst your choices. Arielle's orders. It will have to be lemonade."

"Surely you're jesting. Lemonade? I don't want that damned child's pap!"

Knight paid him no heed. Burke watched him with vague eyes as he rose and walked to the bedside table. He poured the lemonade, leaned down, and helped Burke drink it without spilling it.

"Good," Burke said when he'd finished the glass. "That's damned good. I had no idea."

"That's what your wife said. She said you would kick and fuss but you would drink it if you were desperate enough and you would like it."

Burke smiled. He felt his head begin to clear. His shoulder was throbbing steadily but the pain was tolerable. He wanted no more laudanum, for the moment at least.

"Sit down, Knight, and tell me what's happening. How long have I been out of things?"

"It's Sunday afternoon. The old woman stabbed you at dawn on Friday morning."

"Ah. You poor devil—you didn't go to the mill."

"There will be other fights, I fancy." Knight paused, seeing Burke was looking thoughtfully toward the fireplace.

He waited.

Finally Burke said, his expression suddenly fierce, "I must get well enough to get out of this damned bed. It's Arielle, you see. I can't leave her to face all the servants and all this damnable nonsense—it would simply be too much for her."

Knight laughed. "Didn't you hear me tell you that it was your wife who ordered the lemonade for you?"

"So? Lemonade, for God's sake, that's nothing, Knight!" That outburst brought a jab of pain that made him draw in his breath sharply. He closed his eyes and his lips became a thin line.

Burke finally managed to get hold of himself.
"Listen to me, Knight. Arielle isn't ready yet to
take control, she's so vulnerable, you know that."

"Just a moment, Burke. Let me tell you a little
story. No, hold still and keep quiet. Now, it was
yesterday afternoon, just about this time, the
weather as gloomy as it is now. George Cerlew had
a problem and he asked if he could speak to her. Do
you know that your wife went with him without
hesitation, to the estate room, and closed the door?
I very nearly interfered, but thank God I didn't. I
happened to see them walk out and she was giving
him very precise, very intelligent orders. Also, I
heard one of the maids earlier on Saturday tell Mrs.
Pepperall that she needed to speak to Lannie about
something, and Mrs. Pepperall sniffed and told her
that it was *her ladyship* who would handle the matter. Montague began by hovering protectively over
her, and now that old curmudgeon is at her beck
and call, awaiting her orders. It's been an incredible change, Burke. You have no need to worry."

But Burke was shaking his head, unconvinced.
"It's shock, Knight. When she comes down from
that, she'll be terrified and helpless."

"I think not. She's quite calm, not like she was
when you were first wounded. She was in shock
then, but not now. Now she is mistress of Ravensworth Abbey."

Burke fell silent. He was thinking and thinking.
It was incredible, if it were indeed true. He tried to
piece together his life during the past two and a
half days. All he could remember, besides the pain
and the periods of vague dimness, was Arielle's face
and her soft, sweet voice. He remembered the feel
of her cool hands on him, how she held his head so
he could sip at liquids.

"But she was with me all the time," he said.

"Much of it. On Friday morning she called all the

servants together and gave them a lecture on the care and maintenance of a wounded earl. She's a general, Burke. She's tough. Believe it. I wouldn't lie to you."

"Incredible," Burke said and lapsed into thoughtful silence again. It had taken him to be felled before she lost her fear. But it appeared that she had lost it. He remembered how she'd always been exquisitely polite to George Cerlew and had avoided him, just as she'd left the reins of the Abbey management to Mrs. Pepperall. "Well, well," he said. "How is Lannie taking all this?"

"Lannie, my dear fellow, is deferring completely to Arielle as if Arielle were the matriarch of long-standing at Ravensworth. Indeed, given the behavior of both Arielle and the servants, you'd think she was at least fifty years old and has been in charge for the past forty-nine of those fifty years. Percy, as you can well imagine, is being most supportive of his beloved, a profound relief for the rest of us, I can assure you."

Burke was still grinning when the door to his bedchamber quietly opened and Arielle entered. She was followed by Dr. Brody, whose presence brought a grimace to Burke's face.

"You're awake, I see," she said. She sent a suspicious look toward Knight. "You didn't wake him, did you?"

Knight raised defensive hands. "No, ma'am, acquit me of anything so reprehensible. He came to himself and insisted on telling me all sorts of questionable jests. I have dutifully laughed. Now it's your turn."

Arielle nodded, smiling only slightly, and then she leaned over Burke. He watched her expression change from one of severity to the softest, sweetest look he'd ever seen.

"Hello," she said and gently smoothed his hair from his forehead.

"Hello yourself, sweetheart. I see you allowed that flesh torturer to follow you up."

"Yes, but he won't hurt you, I promise. He must simply look at the wound and change your bandage. You mustn't worry now, Burke. I'll be here."

He was so startled by her poise that a moan of pain that he should have contained had he been paying attention, slipped out of him when the doctor chanced to unwittingly jerk up a corner of the bandage. Arielle said sharply, "Do pay heed, Mark! Are you all right, Burke?"

"Yes," he said, giving her a bemused smile. She took his hand between her two smaller ones.

She continued speaking to him as the doctor worked, and although Burke knew what she was doing, he still appreciated it. "Yes, indeed, your color is much improved today. I think I will shave you if you wish it. I like you with a beard, though. Well, not quite yet precisely a beard."

"Prickly whiskers?"

"But very handsome prickly whiskers."

She felt him tighten his fingers around hers at a jab of pain and she said quickly, "Mark says that if your stomach feels all right, you can have something more than just soup. Would you like that? Perhaps some rice pudding and toast? Cook has already prepared them for you. I will join you for dinner, naturally."

"Rice pudding," Burke repeated in a voice of loathing.

"I tasted it and had Cook add a bit more vanilla. It now tastes delicious, I promise."

When he was done, Dr. Brody said, "Excellent progress, Burke. You'll be back to your full activity in about two weeks, I'd say. Another three or four days in bed. Then I'll take out the stitches a couple of days after that. You will see that he obeys me, Arielle?"

"Certainly. The earl is a reasonable man."

Knight laughed at that. "Only because he's been unconscious!"

Burke just smiled, saying nothing. He watched his wife walk with Mark from the bedchamber. Her walk was different, of all things. She was straighter, her shoulders back farther, her head held in a confident way. Everything about her bespoke confidence. It was odd and it was exhilarating. "I should have done myself in sooner," he said softly to himself.

Knight heard him. "It has turned out remarkably well, hasn't it? Not that I approve of your lying flat on your back, of course. But Arielle, well, she's got guts, Burke."

"Yes." Burke said. "Guts."

"Before Arielle returns," Knight said quickly, bringing Burke's attention to him, "the old woman, Dorcas, she's still here, locked in a room on the third floor. Arielle has someone with her all the time. She's utterly batty, Burke. She keeps raving about harlots and sluts and trollops. When I saw her once yesterday, her language was so foul that even I was shocked. She thought I was you and she called me evil and Satan and other assorted nasty names. You do know why she tried to kill Arielle, don't you?"

"Yes," said Burke. "It's really very simple. She came into this bedchamber that night and saw us making love. She saw that Arielle wasn't being forced or abused. She saw her little victim much enjoying herself. In her mind, I guess a female was supposed to hate men and their appetites; a good female was never supposed to submit willingly. She was to be beaten and abused instead. Arielle was prefect for her until she married me; until, finally,

she came to me. Then she became like the others—
a slut and a whore, a creature to be destroyed."

"My God."

"Yes. It is probably more complicated than that,
but that is the gist of it, I believe." He looked up
as he spoke and saw Arielle standing just inside the
door. He hadn't heard her enter. She was staring
at him, her face pale, her arms crossed defensively
over her breasts.

He said very matter-of-factly, "Hello, sweetheart.
Have you come to force some vile medicine down
my throat? I should prefer a kiss, truly, but if something vile it must be, then I'll put on a properly
brave front."

Knight started at Arielle's expression and
Burke's nonsense, then carefully arranged his expression into none at all.

Arielle shook her head, forcing a smile. "No
ghastly potions for you, my lord."

"Good. Come here and sit beside me. My head is
aching."

His voice rose to a near whine and she cocked her
head at him. Knight blinked at that tone but firmly
kept any opinion to himself. He did give Burke a
rather stunned look.

"It's all right," she said and seated herself carefully beside him. "Just close your eyes and I'll mes-
sage your temples."

"It hurts," he said.

Knight, shooting another bemused look toward
Burke, said only, "I will see you later," and quitted
the bedchamber. He laughed softly. Soon, Knight
thought, it would be all right for him to leave Ravensworth Abbey.

"Is that better?"

Her voice was soft and warm and her lightly
pressing fingertips were sheer magic, even though

his head wasn't aching at all. "Just a little," he said.

"I heard you speaking to Knight about Dorcas and her motives. I wish you hadn't been so very, well, open about it, but I believe you are right."

He cocked an eye open, looked at her closely, and said, "Please don't be embarrassed, Arielle. Knight and I have known each other since we were eight years old. We met the first time the summer of 1794. All we could talk about—we were blood-thirsty little hellions—was Madame Guillotine, of course. Robespierre was killed that year, executed. We reveled in that, as you can imagine. Knight is, I suppose, like a brother, more so than Montrose ever was. We even gained our commissions at the same time."

"He knows all about me, then, doesn't he? You've told him everything."

Her voice was quiet, strained, and he said easily, "Yes, enough. He is very fond of you, of course. I think he'd already guessed a lot of things about Dorcas. I value his opinion and I hope that you will come to do so as well."

"She couldn't accept that I would enjoy letting a man touch me, make love to me, that I would be a willing partner."

"I believe so. Ah, don't stop, that feels wonderful."

She smiled at him even though she still felt swamped with embarrassment about Knight. Burke's cheeks were rough with whiskers, his hair tousled. The stark white bandage contrasted sharply with the dark curling hair and the smooth olive flesh of his chest. The sheet came only to his stomach. She looked at him, below his waist, seeing the outline of him through the sheet, and she felt a softening deep inside her, a wanting, a burgeoning of need. It surprised her. For the past two and half days she and Joshua had taken care of him, taken care of all his needs. She hadn't seen him as a man, not really. He'd been Burke, certainly, her husband, but he'd been her patient. Now, though . . . She drew in her breath and tried to force herself to concentrate on her massage.

"Arielle, would you please scratch my belly?"

She jerked back, wondering if he'd seen her watching him. But no, his eyes were closed. That wasn't possible.

Very lightly, she laid her palm just above the sheet line. Tentatively she began to scratch.

"Lower."

Her fingertips slipped beneath the sheet.

"Ah, yes, just a bit harder. That's right. Don't stop."

His flesh was so warm, she thought, and so smooth. Her fingers went just a bit lower, tangling in the thick hair. Her scratching became more like caressing.

"God, that's wonderful." He sighed deeply. "I can't do anything about it, though."

Arielle pulled her hand away and stared down at him. He was looking exceedingly mournful—that was the only way to describe his expression.

"Even though my body wants you this very instant, it's only that part of me that's showing true wisdom. The rest of me is deader than a century-old goat. I'm truly sorry. For you, but even more for me, I think."

"No, no," she said, "I'm the one who's sorry. I didn't mean, that is . . . oh, you're doing this to me on purpose, and it's so very ridiculous!"

"No, it isn't ridiculous and we're both sorry. I know what you can do. At Dr. Body's next visit, you can ask him how long it will be before I can make love to my wife."

He thought she would choke on that outrageous

suggestion. He was also aware that the pain was becoming increasingly difficult for him to control. He didn't want it, but he knew that rest and more rest were required for him to heal. He needed some laudanum. He asked Arielle for it. When he'd drunk the drugged lemonade, he said, "Until I fade away from you, tell me about our guests."

Arielle spoke softly, telling him of how Alec, in a spate of pre-fatherhood practice, had played for thirty minutes with Virgie and Poppet. He'd emerged from the nursery, she said, looking a bit dazed, shaking his head. Cannons and battalions and bayonets, he'd said, all handled by two little girls in pigtails and frilly dresses. And a doll named Josephine had been on the sidelines giving strategical advice to Wellington. Josephine, he'd been told, was in truth Uncle Burke's, but he—Uncle Burke—had allowed her to remain in the nursery. Alec had looked at Nesta's stomach, shaken his head again, and gone riding. Knight had mocked Alec mercilessly. When applied to about his feelings toward fatherhood and offspring, Knight had drawled in that way of his that he would take another page from his father's book: Ignore your children. They'll be better off without all your bad habits. He had no intention of having anything to do with his vague, mythical heir, who would make an appearance—if Knight had his way—in the next century.

As for Lannie and Percy, their courtship was proceeding with rapidity since the party was shattered and they'd been left to their own devices. Arielle even imagined that they'd spent Saturday afternoon in the gazebo, doing what, she couldn't imagine. She didn't speak of Dorcas again, which was fine with Burke. He was too woolly-headed to be intelligent in any case.

He fell asleep with her soft hand against his cheek.

It was a cool Wednesday morning. Joshua very quietly closed the door of Burke's bedchamber and just stood there. He looked aggrieved. Arielle came up at that moment, looked at him, and said. "What is wrong, Joshua? Is his lordship feeling poorly?"

"His lordship," said Joshua, his voice biting, "is behaving like an ill-bred mongrel pup! He threw the gruel at me! At *me!*"

Arielle frowned. Burke had begun behaving in the most impossible fashion since he'd awakened the previous day. He'd been demanding, irritable, and rude. But to throw his gruel—not at all awful, for Arielle herself had tasted it—at Joshua. It was too much.

Arielle became militant. "I will speak to him, Joshua."

He looked suddenly worried. "He's in a foul mood, my lady. I don't know if you should—"

"He is just behaving like a spoiled little boy. Don't worry. If he throws something at me, I shall simply throw it back. Him and his interminable headaches! I'll give him a headache!"

Arielle, unaware that her new behavior was still something of a shock to those who knew her at all, walked into the bedchamber, her stance definitely aggressive. She stood beside Burke's bed, her hands on her hips, her shoulders thrown back, a frown furrowing her forehead.

Burke cocked an eyebrow and said, his voice nasty, "What do you want?"

"You are being rude. You have been rude since you woke up yesterday morning. I won't stand for it. It will stop."

Burke's eyes narrowed on his wife's face. *"You* are giving *me* orders in my own home?"

"You shouldn't have thrown the gruel at Joshua. He was most perturbed. Nor, my dear, should you have yelled at poor Joan 'to get the hell out of your bedchamber before you boxed her ears.' She was nearly in tears and I had an exceedingly difficult time calming her down. Now, as for your behavior with poor George, yelling at him to go stuff a sock in his ear, and to take those damnable papers and stuff them in his . . . well, I can't begin—"

"I'm thirsty."

"I will pour you some lemonade after I've told you about how George feels. Your thick-skinned, thoroughly asinine behavior with him—"

"I want a brandy."

"My dear . . . Burke, you can't have—"

"I want brandy! You get it for me, else I'll get up and get it for myself!"

She stood undecided. He was irascible, to say the least. He was behaving atrociously, to be sure. She could not buckle. Finally, she shook her head. "No, not yet. Dr. Brody will be here shortly. You may ask him then."

"You are *refusing* to get me what I want?"

She merely smiled at the most menacing voice she'd ever heard out of him. "Do be good, Burke. I know you must be feeling helpless and bored, but you will be well soon, I promise you."

"Stop treating me like a half-wit!"

He was becoming flushed. She sat down beside him and placed her palms against his chest. She gently pushed him back against the pillow, leaned over, and kissed him. It surprised him as much as it surprised her.

He scowled at her. "You're trying to take advantage of a helpless man."

"Yes," she said, "I suppose I am." She kissed him again, very lightly. She felt his lips part and his tongue stroke over her lower lip.

"Burke," she said, lifting her head again, "you mustn't do that."

"Why the devil not? I'm bored to tears and here you are offering yourself to me, knowing that I can't do a damned thing about it!"

She grinned and kissed him again. "Do you really believe I could be so very cruel?"

# 20

Knight took his leave two mornings later, accompanying Lannie, Percy, and the girls back to London to Lady Boyle's.

He said privately to Burke before his departure, "You've had enough nonsense. Time for you to enjoy peace and quiet and whatever else you feel up to doing with your beautiful bride."

"Your perception, Knight," Burke drawled, shaking his old friend's hand, "needless to say, floors me. So unexpected."

"Same to you, Burke!"

Burke laughed, then immediately sobered, holding his right arm very still over his chest, his lips a thin line, until the pain eased.

"Incidentally, old man," Knight continued when he saw Burke had controlled the pain, "I've much enjoyed your whining invalid performance for Arielle's benefit. She, I suppose, had no notion that you've been a complete and utter ass on purpose?"

Burke grinned. "Have I been that obvious?"

"Only to someone who has known you for twenty years. I was surprised that Joshua didn't catch on sooner, but he has now and he told me yesterday, all the while scratching his head, 'Aye, the major lord is a wily one, that he is! He had Lady Arielle running in rings around him, taking charge, giving *him* orders, aye, more than that, and she just might strangle him!' Of course, I assured him that you knew exactly how far to push your lady before that fate could befall you."

Burke chuckled, very restrained this time, and he was rewarded. The pain wasn't at all awful, to his profound relief. Mark Brody had removed the stitches the previous afternoon, but Burke still had to stay in bed for another day. He was going mad, his act with Arielle and all the servants becoming less an act as each tedious hour dragged by.

"Thank you for accompanying Lannie and Percy back to London, though I doubt they'll know you're even along. Are you to look after Virgie and Poppet?"

Knight looked a bit disgusted. "Someone has to go with them, else they'll end up in a ditch and not even notice. Good Lord, the way they're acting is enough to turn one's stomach. I'll see to it that Lannie and the girls are duly installed at your sister's house, then take myself off. I suppose you'll be coming to the wedding in September?"

"I'm glad it is in September. I wouldn't doubt that Lannie is already pregnant."

"If the vacuous grin on Percy's face is any indication, she must be. Merciful heaven, save me from such a half-witted fate!"

"A sated man," Burke said mildly. "Well, there's a goodly bit to say in favor of it, Knight." He gave a deep sigh.

"Don't you dare overdo anything until your shoulder is healed!" Knight said quickly.

"Somehow," Burke said, "I think my shoulder will be just fine by tonight."

Knight merely shook his head. "You will take good care of Arielle."

"Naturally. She's mine."

Knight gave him an odd look, then shook his head again. "Oh, one other thing. I believe Alec and

Nesta will be leaving for Northumberland shortly. Alec doesn't want to wait until she is too far into her pregnancy. So you'll be alone with your bride at long last."

"Amen to that," said Burke, then added with a twinkle in his eye, "Not, of course, that I haven't enjoyed this visit by all of you immensely. So *many* good friends to keep me company!"

Knight gave his friend his opinion very concisely, in the most lurid of prose, shook his hand, and took his leave.

Arielle visited her husband not thirty minutes later, a snifter of brandy—if his eyes didn't deceive him—in her hand.

"Yes," she said, laughing at his hopeful expression, "it is brandy and it's for you. You've been wonderful, Burke, and I decided you deserved a reward."

"A wife both beautiful and compassionate."

He downed the brandy, sighed blissfully, and laid his head back against the pillow. "You really think I'm wonderful? Even after the way I've moaned and groaned and carried on and driven you nearly to terminal strangulation? Of me, that is."

She gave him the most loving smile. It made him swallow. She sat beside him and smoothed the covers over his chest. "You were just bored and didn't know what to do with yourself. So active and physical a man can't be expected to perform in a saintly manner when he's wounded as badly as you were." She leaned over and began kissing him.

He found himself momentarily without words. It still surprised him, her kissing him, her taking the initiative. Of course, it was only a kiss. She wasn't seducing him, for God's sake. More's the pity. He kissed her back, then said in his patented complaining voice, "I want you to rub my back. It hurts from just lying here like a damnable lump."

"All right," Arielle said agreeably. "Let me get

some of my cream." She didn't mention that it was the cream Dorcas used to rub into her back after Paisley had beaten her. She supposed there was no need to. Burke wasn't stupid. She was, however, relieved that he didn't say anything about it.

When he was on his stomach, the covers pulled only to his waist and her hands smoothing the cream into his back, Burke decided there couldn't be a better way to spend a morning. He moaned with pleasure. Her hands made sweeping motions from his shoulders to his waist, over and over again.

"Lower," he said.

Arielle paused only a moment, then pulled the sheet down a bit farther.

"Ah," he said. "I will be your willing slave if you will do that for the next fifty years."

Without conscious decision, Arielle leaned forward and kissed the base of his spine. She felt him start, then shudder. She kissed him again, her tongue lightly caressing him.

"Arielle . . ."

He sounded as if he were in pain. She straightened, flushing a bit, and began her massage again. She loved the feel of the deep muscles, the smoothness and warmth of his flesh. He was glad that he was on his stomach.

He moaned again as her fingers found a particularly tense muscle and massaged it deeply.

After a few more minutes, she said, "My hands are getting tired, Burke, but I'll do this again this evening, all right?"

"Thank you," he said, his voice muffled into the pillow.

"Shall I help you turn over?"

"No," he said, and he sounded as if he were enduring the most onerous torture.

She was concerned and it sounded in her voice. "Would you like some laudanum?"

"No," he repeated, trying to calm himself. "I think I'll stay like this for a while."

She lightly ran her hand down his back once more. "I must go now. There is so much to see to. I'll return to have lunch with you." She didn't move for a moment. She was staring at him. Slowly, not really wanting to, she pulled the sheet up his back.

Then she lightly patted his rear end. His eyes widened with shock. He couldn't think of a word to say. He heard her skirts, the tapping of her slippers on the hardwood floor, the sound of the bedchamber door being opened and quietly closed.

She'd been so natural with him. She'd patted his butt! He couldn't believe it. He was still smiling ten minutes later. He was whistling when she returned carrying their lunch tray.

Burke watched her in silence as she picked up her nightgown and adjourned to behind the now-mended screen in the far corner of the room. Damned ugly thing, he thought, then sighed, knowing Dorcas's attack had set them and their burgeoning intimacy back a bit. But she'd kissed him, not only on his mouth but at the base of his spine. That had to count for something. For a lot, as a matter of fact.

"Arielle!"

"Hmm?"

"Hurry up. I'm bored and lonesome."

It was his patented whining tone, and she did hurry. A few minutes later, she emerged in her virginal white lawn gown, ribbons tied in cockeyed bows to her chin.

"I like the way you look," he said. Actually, if she'd been wearing medieval armor, he would still have liked the way she looked. "Take your hair down. I enjoy watching you brush it."

"All right." Arielle began removing the pins as

she spoke. "Would you like me to rub your back tonight?"

"Yes, I would like that very much." His mind nearly went into spasms at the thought.

He watched her brush out her hair. The beautiful Titian color, such a rich, deep red, glistened in the candlelight. His fingers itched to touch it, to touch her. He waited, fidgeting only a bit, and forgot to whine.

Soon Arielle joined him, sitting beside him on the bed. "I should look at your shoulder and change your bandage." She kissed the tip of his nose. "I'll be very careful."

He suffered in silence, and it wasn't from any pain from his wound. That lavender scent of hers smelled so sweet. She leaned close, examining the wound, gently touching the surrounding flesh. "There is no swelling and the flesh looks healthy to me. You heal remarkably fast. I'll put only a light bandage over it."

When that was done, he looked at her hopefully. She grinned. "All right," she said, completely mis-understanding his look, "I'll massage your back for you now. Let me turn you over. Slowly, Burke, slowly."

He grunted as he rolled over. When she pulled the sheet down to his waist, he felt himself tight-ening, waiting for her hands on his body.

He continued to wait.

Finally, in a voice so soft he could have spread it easily on his breakfast toast, she said, "You are so beautiful, Burke." And then she started rubbing his back.

He groaned with the pleasure of it.

Her voice was a bit lighter now, teasing. "You are a hedonist, my lord!"

"Indeed," he said on a blissful moan.

"I've been so worried about you." Her fingers

were caressing him now, not massaging. "I was scared that you would die and I couldn't have borne it, you know. I was so angry at you that you had saved me, because I knew that if you died it wouldn't have been fair. You are a much better person than I and—"

"What the hell did you say?" He twisted up onto his side.

"Shush, please lie still. Please, Burke."

"Don't you ever say anything so stupid again! Dammit it, woman, you're my wife, and I just happen to love you more than anything in this bloody world, including myself? Do you understand?"

There was complete silence.

She leaned over and began kissing him at the top of his spine. She worked her way down, very slowly and very thoroughly.

"Oh, God," he moaned, his hands fisting.

He felt her hands pulling away the sheet, down to his knees. The air cooled his hot flesh. "Arielle," he managed.

"Just be quiet."

And she continued kissing him. Her hands preceded her, stroking over his buttocks, lightly roving over his thighs.

His breathing was jerky and he felt his body swell and throb, his muscles tighten, his stomach knot.

He felt her hands stroke down his legs, then up. Her slender fingers slid between his thighs, lightly, ever so lightly, touching him, making him wonder if he wouldn't soon shatter into a thousand pieces.

She kissed his buttocks, then his thighs. "So very beautiful," he heard her whisper and felt her warm breath on his inner thigh. "So different from me. I don't have all this hair, you know."

"Yes, I know. Arielle!"

Her fingers had slipped between his legs and she

was touching him lightly. He nearly jumped off the bed, his healing shoulder forgotten.

He felt her fingers leave him, felt her shifting on the bed. "Let me help you onto your back, my lord."

"Why?"

"Because I want to look at the front of you. I want to kiss you."

He couldn't believe his ears. Surely he must have misunderstood her.

When he was on his back, his arms at his sides, his chest heaving with his harsh breathing, he watched her look at every inch of him. When he knew she was staring at him, swelled and throbbing and thrust toward her, he said, "Do you find me ugly?"

She shook her head, her lips slightly parted. "Oh, no." Then she touched him, tentatively, took him in her hand. "You're warm, Burke, very warm and alive and so beautiful."

He said nothing, words beyond him. He watched her watch him. When she lowered her head, he sucked in his breath. He couldn't believe this. He didn't want her to feel that she had to do this, he didn't . . . Her soft mouth closed about him and he groaned. He hadn't imagined that anything could feel so good, so intensely fine. Her hair was spread over his belly and his thighs. He wished he could see her face, see her caressing him.

She had to stop, else he would lose all control. He clutched her hair in his hand and tugged. "You must stop," he said, and he was appalled at the harshness in his voice. "Please, Arielle. Please."

She lifted her head. "Why?"

"I want to be inside you, that's why. Would you come on top of me, please?"

She just looked at him, her head cocked to one side, and he realized she wasn't certain what he wanted. "Do you want me to become a blanket?"

"Sort of, but not quite."

"That is not particularly clear, Burke."

She was still holding him, lightly running her fingers over him. It was difficult to think, much less speak coherently.

"Well, actually, I want you to sit on top of me and let me come inside you. You will be the rider, as it were, not me."

"Oh, What an interesting idea! I'm getting quite used to being in charge." She gave him a wicked smile accompanied by a show of white thigh as she swung over him. Her virginal nightgown settled about both of them.

"You feel wonderful," Burke manage. "I need to touch you, though, love. I don't want to hurt you when I come into you."

"You won't hurt me," she said and stretched out over him and began kissing his mouth. He could manage with one arm, he thought, and brought it up to tangle in her glorious hair. Then he led his arm glide down her back over her buttocks. He found the hem of her nightgown and moved upward, his fingers on her warm flesh. When he found her, she jerked, and he smiled. She was ready for him, all warm and damp.

"Arielle, I . . . take me in your hand and guide me into you. I think you should sit up, though."

He didn't realize he was capable of speaking so many words that made sense. He was really quite beyond rational thought.

"Like this, Burke?"

"Oh, God!"

He was coming into her slowly, so slowly he swore he would crack apart with the wanting of it. He felt her fingers tightening about him, releasing him so gently, so little of him at a time, that he wanted to yell.

"Burke, that feels wonderful, but—"

"But what? Oh, God!"

"I want you to . . . touch me."

He didn't hear embarrassment in her voice. He wasn't listening. He was feeling and he knew, would swear, that it was all over for him. Then all of him was seated deep into her. "Sit up straight, Arielle. Let's get you out of this nightgown."

Arielle pulled off her nightgown, wadding it up and tossing it to the floor. Then he was so deep inside her that he could feel her womb. It made him crazy. He brought his good arm up and stroked over her breasts, then roved down over her belly to find her.

"Now, come with me, love." He was bucking up against her, but Arielle realized that she was in charge. It didn't really matter, for she felt his marvelous fingers make her begin to spiral out of herself and she arched her back, crying out.

"Arielle!"

She was plunging, taking him, then straightening, all the while his fingers driving her beyond herself, toward him, toward her pleasure. He watched her face as she climaxed, felt her muscles tighten about him, and he moaned, he couldn't help himself. It went on and on and it was something he couldn't believe.

Arielle lay sprawled atop her husband, her hair a mass of tangles spread about her head, onto his face, onto his pillow. His hand was gently stroking her back.

He was still deep inside her. She quivered at the feel of him, and heard him groan at her instinctive movement.

She finally managed to raise herself above him. He was looking at her, his beautiful eyes dazed, his mouth slightly open, his breathing still harsh.

"Thank you, Burke."

"What?"

"I thanked you. That was such pleasure, almost too much. I hope I didn't hurt you."

"You nearly killed me and I loved it."

She flushed, then, to his delight, laughed and gently poked him in his stomach. "Well, we won't take any chances."

Before he could voice a protest, she slipped away from him and lay down beside him.

He grunted in sated bliss. "Pull the covers over us, sweetheart."

On her way to find the covers, Arielle paused at his belly, lightly stroking him, kneading him. Then her fingers threaded through his hair to the thicker hair at his groin.

"The covers," he said, and heard a voice that sounded like a thin reed, if a thin reed could speak, of course.

She kissed his mouth, saying, "Certainly. I don't wish to overwork you, my lord, a mere man!"

He softly slapped his palm over her hips.

She giggled. He felt wonderful. He'd succeeded. She hadn't flinched. And, just minutes before, she'd actually caressed him with her mouth and taken him in her hand and brought him inside her body. She hadn't hesitated. She'd come to a climax. He felt like the luckiest man in the world.

"Life," he announced to the shadowed bedchamber, "life is having Arielle for my wife and loving her until she's silly with it and having her take care of me. Speaking of care, now that you've had your way with me, would you massage my back?"

She laughed.

It was Mrs. Pepperall who entered their bedchamber the following morning. Arielle was just waking up, and the sight of the formidable Abbey housekeeper made her instantly and completely alert.

Burke still slept, and Arielle quickly held her fin-

ger to her lips. She quietly eased out of bed, grabbed
her nightgown from the floor, and pulled it over her
head. She wasn't angry at Mrs. Pepperall's un-
timely intrusion. She knew that it meant trouble.

Arielle put on her slippers, then, after taking one
final look at her sleeping husband, slipped out of the
bedchamber, closing the door quietly behind her.

"What has happened?" she asked without preamble.

"Oh, my lady! I . . . oh, dear, what shall we do?"

"Tell me what has happened."

"The old woman, your old nurse, Dorcas, she's
gone, escaped from the Abbey!"

That news was unexpected, and Arielle was silent for a good while. Finally, she asked, "When
did you discover her missing? And how did she
manage to get out of that room?"

Mrs. Pepperall, wringing her hands, told Arielle
of going to the room herself moments before. Charlie, one of the footmen, was lying unconscious just
inside the door, a lump on the back of his head.

"So," Arielle said slowly, "Dorcas lured him into
the room somehow, then struck him. Is Charlie all
right?"

"Oh, *him!* Serves him right, I say. Always ogling
the females and never minding his own business,
and now this! Stupid, careless man!"

"Of course you're right, Mrs. Pepperall. Still, does
Charlie need Dr. Brody?"

Mrs. Pepperall, more in command of herself now,
snorted. "No. He's all right, my lady."

"I want you to have one of the footmen fetch Geordie. We must find Dorcas. If Charlie was still unconscious, she can't have been gone long. I will meet
Geordie in the drawing room in twenty minutes."

Arielle dressed in her own bedchamber and was
downstairs waiting for Geordie within fifteen minutes.

He came in, Joshua and Montague with him. She quickly told them what had happened. "We must find her. She is very ill. She could harm herself; she could harm others."

Geordie muttered something under his breath and Arielle said in a loud voice, "She is not to be hurt! Her illness, well, it's not her fault. Now, please hurry!"

She looked up, a worried frown on her forehead, to see Burke standing in the open doorway. He was wearing a dressing gown and slippers. She hurried toward him, scolding words on her lips.

He smiled down at her and held up his hand. "No, today I'm allowed to get out of that cursed bed. However, I should like to have a cup of tea. Would you join me, Arielle?"

It was over eggs and a rasher of bacon that he said, "Now, tell me about Dorcas."

Arielle related what she knew. "So Geordie and Joshua should find her soon. I pray so."

She turned at the sound of a cough coming from the doorway. "Mrs. Pepperall, what is it?"

"Agnes found this, my lady."

Agnes, a singularly dim-witted upstairs maid, was standing in the hallway outside the dining room. Arielle accepted the necklace from Mrs. Pepperall. It was old, and the garnets were smooth and quite lovely. "Where was it? Whose is it?"

"Agnes found it in Dorcas's things. It belonged to Mellie, my lady. I'm sure of it."

Arielle closed her eyes. "Oh, no," she whispered.

"It had belonged to Mellie's grandmother. She was so proud of it. Claimed it was her dowry and any man worth his salt would be proud to accept it."

Arielle felt tears sting her eyes. She heard Burke say, "Thank you, Mrs. Pepperall, for bringing it to us. I know Mellie had one aunt still living. The necklace should go to her."

"I'll see to it, my lord," Mrs. Pepperall said.

"That is all, thank you."

Burke rose and came over to his wife. "I'm sorry, sweetheart."

Arielle raised her face. "She must have killed Mellie, Burke. She must have believed all that malicious gossip about her being a slut. I remember now that she was quite certain about it. I was surprised at her attitude—indeed, I was angry at her for being so close-minded. Oh, God!"

"Shush," Burke said. "We'll find her, then—"

"Then what? She's ill. No one can help her—you heard what Dr. Brody said. Just a crazy old woman wandering about by herself."

"We'll find her, Arielle," he repeated firmly.

She pressed her face against his side.

"Come, love, here's Alec and Nesta."

"What the devil!" Alec said, coming into the dining room. "Montague is outside wringing his arthritic hands and Mrs. Pepperall is looking positively pale."

"The two of you take a seat and we'll tell you."

"Should you be out of bed, Burke?" Nesta asked.

He grinned, that stone-melting grin that could gain him anything he wished, Arielle was certain of that. "Nesta, my wife pulled me out of bed by my ear. Lord knows, I'm still very weak. She called me a lazy, shiftless clod and—"

"You're awful! Now stop it and tell them what's happened."

He did, and all grins disappeared.

# 21

Alec and Nesta left Ravensworth Abbey on Friday morning. It promised to be a clear day, not too warm; a perfect day, Alec assured his wife, for travel.

"So you say," Nesta said, looking inside the carriage with a jaundiced eye. "You will ride in the fresh air and I will be stuck inside this stuffy thing!"

"Yes," said Alec in his deep voice as he lightly touched his hand to his wife's swelled belly, "but you will have my son with you."

"Some company he will be, this so-called son of yours. I think, rather, that we've a little daughter. I will speak to her of fashion and how to handle arrogant, quite conceited fathers."

Burke and Arielle stood on the lower steps of the Abbey and waved until the carriage had passed from sight around a bend in the drive.

"Alec seems content, don't you think?" Arielle said.

"Content? With what?"

"Oh, with Nesta, with her pregnancy, I don't know—with life as he has it on his dish."

Burke put his arm around her waist and squeezed her against him. "I will tell you the truth, at least from my perspective. Alec is restless. He must be experiencing new things, visiting different places. He must be *doing*. He isn't one to sit in his library and contemplate the vagaries of the philosophers."

"Like my father?"

"Yes. Alec was on the go even here, examining every aspect of our operation. I must admit he gave George good advice whilst I was recovering. I have no doubt that he will throw all his energies into Carrick Grange in Northumberland and have it running like clockwork in no time at all. Unfortunately, then he'll need something new to occupy his mind and his hands."

"There will be his child."

"There will also be Nesta, a nanny, a nurse, a governess or a tutor."

"Do you think he loves Nesta? Like you, she agrees that he values change, and sex. She told me that was how she held him."

Burke threw back his head and laughed deeply. "She was teasing you, Arielle. Alec is an honorable man. He is also a gentleman. He would never leave his wife."

"No," Arielle said quietly, staring after the vanished carriage, "but he could stop loving her."

"Did you see any evidence of that? Any at all?"

Arielle shook her head. "You're right, of course. It's just that I am worried about her, Burke."

"I know that Alec will do his best to see that everything goes well. He said he would send a messenger to us as soon as the child is born." He realized that she was looking a bit downpin. "Why so sad, little one? You'll see Nesta and Alec again soon. And you'll be an aunt when you do."

"Yes, I shall, shan't I?" she said, brightening a bit. She relapsed into silence for a moment, then said, "Actually, I was thinking about Dorcas, wondering where she was. Do you think she's still alive, Burke?"

"If she weren't, we would have found her body by now. Yes, she's alive. We'll continue the search until we find her."

Arielle wasn't to be troubled by thoughts of any sort later that morning. She lay on her back, her legs sprawled wide, Burke over her, his fingers caressing her, his eyes on her expressive face.

"Arielle."

She stifled a moan of pleasure and opened her eyes.

"This, my love, is something I insist that you will like. In fact, you will very shortly be so beyond yourself that—" He simply stopped, clasped her hips in his large hands, and lifted her to his mouth.

His tongue, raspy and warm, brought all feeling to a single point. It was sharp and sweet and very close to pain. And she knew she'd die if he stopped. But he didn't slow or change his rhythm. And then she cried out, quite unable to help herself, and her fingers dug into his shoulders. He reveled in every cry, in every convulsion of her body, and when at last she quieted, he came into her deeply, fully, and she cried out yet again, and this time he took her cry into his mouth.

"Oh, heavens," Arielle said.

"Yes, I agree." He clasped her more tightly to him, only to wince at the pulling in his shoulder. "Damn, let me rearrange you just a bit. There, that's better now."

"You mustn't be so very enthusiastic about . . . things."

He chuckled. "You would be disappointed if I weren't, now admit it."

Instead, she kissed his shoulder and snuggled against him. She said, her voice vague, "I don't know, Burke. Sometimes I think I'm living in a dream. I'm strong and sure of myself, arrogant perhaps, and I'm filled with more than my share of confidence. And then—"

He felt her shake her head against his shoulder. He simply waited, his hand lightly stroking her hair. "And then I'm afraid—deep inside—and I know that the fear is what's truly real and I am nothing but a sham, a coward who's weak and inept."

"Next I hope you say you think of me."

"You, my lord? Very well, and then I think of you."

"And just what do you think when you think of me?"

"You're more difficult," she said thoughtfully. "I don't know if you're part of the dream. You probably are. A man in the real scheme of things would never allow me—a mere woman—so much freedom, encourage such independence of thought and action. No, you, my lord, are part of my dream. You have given me a perfect dream. I thank you for that."

His voice became rougher. "And when my seed grows in your womb? Will you say that our child is also part of this dream?"

She came up over him and he felt her breasts press against his chest. "I don't know," she said, giving him light kisses on his mouth. "A child— that's both of us. That sounds very real, doesn't it?"

"Particularly when the baby wakes up and starts screaming for his food. Stop moving against me like that, Arielle. I'm very near the shattering point and—"

"All right."

"What?"

"Shatter, my lord. I wouldn't want to deny you such an experience, or myself, for that matter."

He came into her as they lay facing each other, and the deeper inside her he pushed, the closer they came together, until her breath, warm and sweet, was his, and his flesh, heated and taut, was hers.

When she moaned into his mouth, her arms so tight around his back that he knew his shoulder would ache like the very devil afterward, he poured himself into her, his teeth clenched, his body glistening with sweat. And he heard what she told him, told him so softly that for a moment he'd doubted his ears. "I love you, Burke."

It was all because of that god-awful goose, Geordie thought, wiping his palms on his trousers even as he cursed floridly. Miss Arielle had ordered a dozen of the swarmy creatures, six geese and six ganders, not wanting to be unfair to the females by forming any kind of a harem, she'd announced to him; and now, after only one day of residence at Ravensworth Abbey, a gander with a high opinion of himself had herded two geese ahead of him—all of them as quiet as could be—and escaped the wired-off area.

Geordie heard a loud squawk, turned, and cursed even more fluently at one of the other ganders, who looked ready to jump the fence in a more dramatic escape than his brother's or his cousin's or whatever.

"Get back, ye bloody varmint!" Geordie yelled, waving his hands. "Hellfire, shut yer stupid trap!"

Arielle burst into merry laughter. Geordie turned, his frown severe enough to curdle the milk, but Arielle just laughed harder.

"It 'tain't amusing," said Geordie, his arms crossed over his chest.

"I know," Arielle said, trying to catch her breath. "At least you're here safe and sound, Geordie. His lordship is out with a search party beating the brush for Hannibal and his ladies."

"Hannibal?"

"Well, a long time ago it was a case of elephants. Now, in modern times, it's a case of fowl. You don't like the name?"

"Seems to me, Miss Arielle, that ye'll never be able to give the word to wring the necks of any of them for yer dinner, not if ye give 'em all names."

"That's what the earl claims. I fear you are both right. Now, it's my turn to go do some searching. Do fetch Mindle for me, Geordie. I daresay she's become so fat she'll wheeze rather than gallop with me."

" 'Twill be a near thing. Eating her head off, that's all she's been doing since his lordship was hurt."

Arielle smiled at Geordie's back. She felt wonderful. The afternoon was warm and sunny, the morning shower having left the grass smelling unaccountably greener. She hoped Burke wouldn't overdo. He'd left with three of the men to search for the "damned and blasted" Hannibal, laughing loudly. Still, it had only been two weeks since Dorcas had stabbed him. He seemed fine, his energy, particularly in bed, more than adequate for such a physical man. She gave Geordie a wicked grin and let him toss her onto Mindle's back.

"I shan't be gone long. Tell his lordship, if he returns before I do, that I've joined the hunt. No wringing any necks, now. I begin to think that for Christmas dinner we'll have crimped salmon."

"I think I should come with you, Miss Arielle. You know what his lordship said."

She hesitated a moment, then said quite firmly, "I know, but I can't remain a prisoner all my life. Besides, why would either Evan or Etienne have any interest in me anymore? Leave go, Geordie, I'll be all right."

She clicked Mindle into a gallop and headed toward the east pasture. Geordie smiled after her,

heard one of those damnable half-witted fowls raising a ruckus again, and turned, curses already
forming on his lips.

Arielle felt the wind tugging at her riding hat
and lifted her chin. Strands of hair came loose and
whipped across her face. She tried to tuck the hair
back behind her ears. Mrs. Pepperall, of all people,
had informed her in no uncertain language that she
would assist her ladyship until they could decide
upon a maid to train as her lady's maid. But Mrs.
Pepperall wasn't as gifted as Dorcas in arranging
hair. Another pin slipped.

Poor Dorcas. No matter how encouraging Burke
sounded, Arielle was convinced that the old woman
was dead. If she wasn't dead, then where was she?
A crazy old woman wasn't one to simply disappear.
Folk remembered barmy people and talked about
them. Word would have gotten back to the Abbey.

Arielle pulled Mindle in and called to Hannibal.
How, she wondered, grinning to herself, does one
really call to a gander or goose?

There was no answering squawk and no sight of
a single, long, skinny, white-feathered neck.

She gave Mindle her head and continued east.
She didn't realize where she was going, having paid
no particular heed, until she saw the chimney
stacks of Rendel Hall in the distance. Her fingers
curled about the leather reins. She hadn't been back
here since she's come as Burke's wife to Ravensworth Abbey.

A dream or reality?

She thought of her words to Burke the previous
day. If she went to Rendel Hall, wouldn't it prove
that everything she knew now was real? That *she*
was real, and her life with Burke was real?

She straightened her shoulders and galloped toward her former home. It looked neglected, as if it
had been empty longer than just two months. No

one had scythed the front or side lawns. The shutters over the windows made it look as haunted as any child wanting to be terrified could wish.

I won't be afraid, she said to herself. I won't. I'm not a child. Everything is different now. I am different. *But is that real or a dream? You've only been different at Ravensworth.*

Oddly, she felt her hands grow damp inside the fine York leather gloves. She clamped her teeth together and rode Mindle directly to the front doors.

The Hall was obviously deserted. There was no smoke coming from the chimney stacks. No sign of movement from any of the windows. No lights. Nothing.

Rendel Hall would become a derelict if it weren't purchased soon, she thought as she dismounted. She tied her mare's reins to a sturdy yew bush, then patted her nose. "I shan't be long. It's a question of disproving dreams, that's all."

She grinned at her own foolishness. I am an idiot, yes, indeed, but I really don't care. She wanted to face down this miserable house and all its unpleasant memories. Burke would have approved, she knew that. He would have said she was performing a mental cleaning, getting rid of the excess junk that only made for bad memories.

The front doors were securely locked. This was only a temporary setback. She ran her fingers along the edge of the windowsill just outside the library. Sure enough, there was a key. It was rusted and dirty, and she wiped it off on her riding skirt.

The key turned in the front-door lock after some protracted maneuvering, and she stepped into the entrance hall. It was cold, that was the first thing she noticed. Damp and cold. She shivered, backed up a step, then forced herself to stop. She was here, she would stay until she proved to herself that . . . That what? She wasn't terribly certain what it was she wanted to prove. She only knew that if she forced herself to remember what it was like in this house, to face it squarely, she would have succeeded in exorcising the past.

She rubbed her hands over her arms. There hadn't been any dampness before, or this bone-chilling cold. Arielle walked toward the drawing room. The sliding doors were shut and she shoved them open. All the furniture was swathed in ghostly white Holland covers. She looked at the fireplace and saw Paisley standing there grinning at her, that superior grin of his that granted her nothing but what whim allowed. His whim, naturally. She shuddered. She realized that she was standing as rigid as a rock, a captive of fear. She shook her head. There was nothing here to harm her. Nothing at all. Paisley was dead, long dead, his evil with him.

She froze. She heard the sound again. A shuffling sound from overhead. Mice, she thought. Yes, that was it. She didn't want to go up the stairs. She stood at the base, staring up, straining to hear the sound again. The house was starkly silent. She placed her right foot on the bottom stair.

*Oh, God, I'm afraid.*

"Stop it, Arielle." The sound of her own voice brought reason. She was in her old house, quite alone, with nothing more important to do than to see if mice had invaded the upper story. That was all there was to it.

*But Rendel Hall was never your house. It was his. Only his.*

She flung her head back and shouted, "And you're dead, you miserable old bounder!"

She took the steps quickly then, nearly running. When she reached the landing, she turned and looked down into the entrance hall. It was shadowy and grim and silent. A stupid old house with a musty atmosphere because no one lived here.

Arielle turned back to look down the long corridor. Toward the end of it, on the right, was her former bedchamber, and adjoining it, Paisley's master bedchamber. She forced herself to walk down that corridor. She looked neither to the right nor to the left, but she paused every few steps to listen.

Nothing.

Quietly she opened the door to her bedchamber and stepped inside. Again all the furnishings were covered with white Holland covers. The room looked eerie and somehow frightening. If Burke had been with her, it wouldn't be at all frightening. That realization made her angry with herself. She wasn't a weak, helpless fool. No, she was strong. *Only in the dream. Not here. Here it is real, and real is dangerous.*

"Stop it!" The sound of her voice, high and a bit shrill, made her smile. "There's nothing here to be alarmed at. Don't you see, you ninny?"

She walked quickly toward the adjoining door and flung it open, making as much noise as she could manage. She peered into Paisley's bedchamber. It was filled with shadows and bizarre shapes and airless cold. She heard that strange noise again and paused.

"It's just mice, you idiot!"

She stepped into the room. She could hear her heart pounding. God, this room. Such fear, such hoplessness and pain she'd felt in here. But the room wasn't to blame, it was him. Only him. He was the evil. She looked toward the fireplace and saw something there; no, someone was there, someone who was weaving slightly, someone garbed in billowy, filmy clothes.

"Who's there?" Her voice was a thin reed of sound. "Who are you? Who's there?"

The figure moved.

Arielle couldn't help herself. Her hands flew out in front of her to ward it off. She screamed.

The figure leaped toward her and she turned, bent only on getting through that adjoining door and escaping. She felt fingers close over her upper arm and she shrieked again, whirling about to face her attacker.

Before she could even look up, she felt something hard and stiff come down on the side of her head. She saw brilliant flashes of white light then nothing.

She fell quietly to the floor, unconscious.

They hadn't found either Hannibal or his two ladies, but there was still an overabundance of high spirits. Even George Cerlew, normally the most staid and reticent of men, was laughing at one of Joshua's tales of his and Burke's adventures in Portugal. He was spinning it out outrageously.

"So I'll tell you 'tis true," Joshua said, eyeing his appreciative audience to before delivering his final line, "the goat bit him. Bit him right on the butt. Left side."

Burke was still grinning when they pulled into the stable yard. "No luck!" he called to the stable lads. "We'll rest a bit before we have another go at it."

"I don't think we should bother," said Joshua. "By now somebody's caught those fool squawkers and thrust them in the Sunday pot."

George gave another immoderate chuckle.

"Give Ashes a good rubbing," Burke said to Harry, the newest stable lad, a young man with a wide gap between his front teeth.

"My lord!"

"Yes, Geordie. We didn't find Hannibal, if that's your inquiry."

"No, 'tis Miss Arielle."

Burke tensed. "What about her?"

"She hasn't returned yet. She went out to hunt for Hannibal on her own. She's been gone two hours now, and I'm worried about her."

"She went out by herself?"

"Aye, insisted, she did, that who would care a farthing about her now and she didn't want to be a prisoner anymore."

Oh, God, Burke thought. Oh, please, dear God, no. Aloud he said in the calmest voice he could force, "Two hours? Well, I fancy she's simply lost track of time. We shan't worry until—" He broke off, then cursed. "Saddle up Khan, Geordie. Ashes is too blown for further riding."

Ten minutes later, Burke, George, Geordie, and Joshua were riding east.

"You're certain, Geordie?" Burke asked yet again.

"She was riding east, milord," Geordie said firmly.

It was a ghastly smell. Something rotten, something sticky and wet and rotten. She gagged on the stench. It was so close. Arielle opened her eyes. She lay perfectly still, trying to regain her senses. She was lying on a hard, cold floor. Her hands were bound behind her, as were her ankles. She turned her head slowly, aware of the throbbing pain behind her left ear.

She choked down a scream. Hannibal, his throat neatly cut, lay on a table beside her. His long neck and head were hanging over the side of the table. Blood was dripping slowly, rhythmically, landing to splat on the flagstone floor just by Arielle's head.

She moaned and jerked away, to her other side.

"Shush, my baby. It's all right now. Dorcas is here. You're safe again."

*Dorcas.* Arielle didn't move. She felt fear so deep, so paralyzing, that she couldn't speak. Dorcas was on her knees beside her, her fingers stroking through Arielle's hair.

"Dorcas," she whispered. "You're all right. I've been so worried about you."

"I know, I know, my baby. I'm all right. As are you."

The old woman was rocking back and forth over her. Arielle saw that she looked like the most disreputable old hag imaginable. Her hair was filthy and matted to her head. Her body smelled, and her clothes were stained with food and grease. And her eyes were quite vacant. She was mad.

I must reason with her, Arielle thought, but a wave of hopelessness gripped her. Reason with a madwoman? Dorcas had tied her up and dragged her into the kitchen. There were kitchen knives everywhere. Hannibal's throat was cut. She would kill her. Soon, now, just like the gander.

"Dorcas, won't you untie me?"

"Yes, I'll untie you, but I'm afraid of *him*. He might hurt me again."

The old woman rose, looking furtively around her. "I'll see if he's here," she said in a hushed whisper. And she left the kitchen, her steps shuffling and awkward.

She was no longer Dorcas, Arielle thought. And who was *he*?

"Please come back and untie me," she whispered, but there was only silence now, silence and the stench of blood.

Her arms were growing numb. She tried to pull her wrists free. For five minutes she tugged and shifted and pulled. All for naught. Think, Arielle! She needed to cut the ropes. She saw a knife up on a shelf at least five feet above her. She rolled into a tight ball, then jerked upward to her knees. Slowly, trying to keep her balance, she managed to get to her feet. Her ankles were tied tightly; she'd have to hop to the counter. She managed two tiny steps and fell on her side to the floor, the wind knocked out of her. She lay there for a moment, trying desperately to block out the pain in her hip. Once again she managed to get to her feet. This time she hopped three steps before she again toppled. Five falls later, she finally reached the counter. She stretched her bound hands toward the knife.

She couldn't reach it. Three inches. That was what separated her from the damned knife, from freedom. She nearly pulled her arms from their sockets striving for that wretched knife. It was no use. She searched frantically for another knife. There were three, each one farther out of reach than the other. Her chest heaved and she felt a wave of hopelessness wash over her. She wouldn't give up. Burke wouldn't, ever.

She looked back at the table and saw Hannibal. She made a vow at that moment to release all the geese and ganders. They were penned up, with no power, helpless, just as she was. It was silly, but her vow lifted the numbing despair for a short moment.

A sharp edge. Wasn't there a single one in the entire wretched kitchen? She noticed the filth then, the scraps of rotted and rotting food on every countertop, the layers of dust and dirt and grease. Dorcas must have come here immediately. She'd lived her for the past week and a half. Like something that was less than human. Like an animal. Arielle felt her flesh crawl. Then she saw the small paring knife that was wedged between a pot and a skillet on the far counter. She used the edge of the counter to keep her balance as she moved with agonizing awkwardness toward it. She was breathing hard when at last the small knife was within her reach. She grabbed it easily. Her heart was pounding, churning with fear, excitement, hope.

It was difficult to turn the knife so that its sharp tip could slice through the ropes. She cut herself two times in the process. Finally she settled into a rhythm. Back and forth. Back and forth. She felt pains shooting through her wrists, but she kept at it. She felt the ropes loosening.

Then she heard footsteps. These weren't shuffling and awkward. These were firm and quick. A man's footsteps.

She heard a raised voice from outside the kitchen. A man's voice. She stared toward the kitchen door, unable to look away.

# 22

"My, my. And here I thought the old woman was making it up. Hello, my darling girl."

Arielle wasn't surprised, not really. "Etienne," she said, barely moving her dry lips. She felt the ropes begin to give. She held her hands perfectly still, held her body still, afraid that he would suspect, afraid that he would see something in her face.

"What are you doing, if I may ask?"

"Nothing. I couldn't bear to lie there, smelling the blood."

"I see," said Etienne.

"What are you doing here?"

He smiled at her. He knew she was afraid. It became her, that fear of him. He'd thought and thought and schemed until both he and Evan had been blind drunk more times than he cared to count. How to get her? How to abduct her from that armed fortress that was Ravensworth Abbey? And here she was, all tied up, waiting for him in the kitchen of Rendel Hall! He laughed, unable to help himself. He strolled into the room and leaned his hip against the kitchen table, his arms crossed over his chest.

"I've been staying here for several days now. I am conducting what you might call an inventory. After all, my father owned Rendel Hall and all its furnishings, as did his father before him. I will take anything that pleases me. It is only just and fair. As for your half brother, why, I believe that old Evan has given up on getting to you. I have never seen him so enraged as when he came back to Leslie Farm, his nose swollen and bruised. Your husband smashed him up quite well."

"*I* hit Even in the nose."

Etienne looked clearly startled. "You?" He laughed then. "By all the saints, that is wonderful. Well, it is a good thing you are with me and not with you brother. He isn't a gentleman, Arielle, not at all."

"Did you force poor Dorcas to come here?"

"I? Not at all. When I came I discovered she was living here. I didn't mind sharing with her because she gave me ideas and new hope. I hoped you would come here looking for her. I had heard, everyone has heard, that your precious husband has had men out searching for her for the past week and a half. So I let her stay. Not upstairs, she's far too filthy to be that close, but in the kitchen. She does well down here." Etienne looked at the dead goose. "Our dinner, I suppose," he added. "I should tell her to do her killing outside. The smell is offensive."

"My husband will be coming here soon, Etienne. You must release me and you must let me take Dorcas with me. She is ill. She must be cared for."

Arielle tugged again on the ropes. They had slipped down, even looser now. She was nearly free.

"What is this? Pity for that old bedlamite? After she tried to kill you and ended up nearly sending your dear husband to his heavenly reward? Such an overflowing of good and kindly spirits, Arielle. I find it remarkably nauseating, if you would know the truth. No, my dear, I'm not about to let you walk out of here. You will be my guest. Yes, I like the sound of that. My guest. I will ransom you eventually of course. Your husband is a wealthy man. He will pay dearly for you—at least he'd better.

"No! Do you hear me, Etienne? You won't do that!"

"You excite yourself, Arielle. Is it that he has already tired of you? Or does he still enjoy your whore's skills? I have not liked it, knowing that he has been enjoying you, taking you whenever he wished, having you service him at his whim. No, it has infuriated me each and every time I have pictured you on your knees in front of him."

She moaned, then bit down hard on the bottom lip, appalled that she had allowed him to terrorize her with words. That was all they were, simple words.

"Would you like to know, my darling girl, what we will do before I ask your husband to ransom you? No curiosity? Well, I will tell you so that you may accustom yourself to the idea. You will become my mistress, finally. You will caress me and stroke me and kiss me as you did before."

His voice was trembling slightly before he finished his speech. Arielle stared at him. She'd known, deep down she'd known, that Etienne wouldn't give up all that easily. But it made no sense! She said aloud, "I don't understand you! I never in my life did anything to harm you. Your father made me do that to you. I hated it. Why would you be so cruel? Why would you want to hurt me? I repeat, Etienne, why are you doing this?"

He looked pensive, his gray-blue eyes narrowing on her pale face. "I told you once, but I see you didn't attend me properly. My father gave you to me. I will take you and plant my seed in your belly. You will bear my child. He won't, unfortunately, be master of Rendel Hall, but he will be a future earl, a wealthy and powerful man. And you will have been mine, just as my father had planned. Once your husband pays for your return, I will leave England. I believe I've a fancy to live in Naples. Yes, it is warm there, and the women are as lush as overripe fruit, or so I've been told by Evan. He plowed his way through Italy, he told me. I don't know if I believe him, though. Women don't take to your brother. His personality isn't all that is amiable."

"You must let me go, Etienne. Now. Burke will kill you if you don't."

"Burke? Ah, yes, Burke Drummond. Tell me, Arielle, does he appreciate the exquisite training my father provided you?"

"Stop it! Damn you, let me go!"

He straightened and she pressed backward against the counter. He was coming to her, his expression determined, and in a mad effort, she yanked as hard as she could on the ropes. She felt them split open. She was free.

As he reached out for her, she whipped her right hand out, the knife raised. She slashed at him, but he ducked, jerking to the side. The knife cut through his shirt, nicking his upper arm. He feinted to the right, lunged at her, and smashed her back against the counter. He grabbed her wrist and twisted it until she dropped the knife. He kicked it across the flagstone floor.

"You bitch!" He backhanded her. Her ankles were still firmly tied, and his blow sent her toppling to the floor. He slammed down on top of her, his legs straddling her, and he slapped her again. "So you wanted to knife me, did you!"

She didn't make a sound. He'd knocked the breath out of her. Pain shot through her back and shoulder from the crash against the stone floor. Her cheek was stinging from his blows. He raised his hand, stared down at her face, then slowly lowered his arm.

"No," he said, more to himself than to her. "No, not just yet." He rose, pulling her to her feet and supporting her. "Dorcas!" he shouted. "Come here, you old witch!"

Arielle heard the shuffling steps. Dorcas had been standing outside the kitchen door listening to him abuse her. When she stepped inside, she looked at Arielle and slowly shook her head. "It's all right, Miss Arielle. I'll take care of you just as I always did with him. You'll be safe now." Her voice was a croon, soft and without inflection.

"Shut up," Etienne told her sharply. "I want you to fetch hot water. Your mistress needs a bath. I want her to bathe upstairs, in the master's bed-chamber. Do you understand?"

"Aye, I understand."

"Dorcas, wait! Don't!"

Etienne began to squeeze her ribs until the pain swamped her. But pain could be controlled. She'd watched Burke do it. She could as well. She had but to concentrate and breathe deeply. She had to focus herself inward.

"Don't try to escape me, damn you!" Etienne slapped her again. "I want you aware of everything I do to you. I will make you feel, Arielle, really feel, unlike my father. You won't retreat from me; I won't allow it."

He pulled her against him then, clasped her chin between his fingers, and kissed her once, hard. He hefted her over his shoulder, and when she reared up, he slapped her buttocks hard.

Etienne came to an abrupt halt at the foot of the stairs. She heard him curse. "I just remembered—your damned horse! Well, my dear girl, you have a brief respite. I must needs take care of your mare. If anyone comes around, I don't want her within view." Etienne lowered Arielle to the bottom step, pulled off his leather belt, and tightly secured her wrists to the railing.

"Do wait for me, Arielle," he said, patted her cheek, and left the Hall.

Arielle leaned her forehead against her bound wrists. What to do? One tug on the belt assured her that pulling free was impossible. She felt tears sting the back of her eyes. No, that would solve naught. She heard Dorcas's shuffling steps on the stairs above her and forced herself to look up.

"It's all right, Miss Arielle." She felt the old woman's fingers stroke through her tangled hair. "I'll take care of you just as I always did. I wonder what I did with the cream? I must find it. I don't want you to scar. Oh, no."

She moved past Arielle, across the entrance hall toward the kitchen.

Arielle tried to block out her words. She tried to focus on Burke. Surely he would know that she was missing, and he would scour the countryside for her. He wouldn't give up. Would Geordie remember she'd ridden Mindle east?

*And when he finally finds you? And you've been raped by Etienne? Used by Etienne? Will he still want you? What will he say if he learns you're pregnant with another man's child? Will he hate you?*

She felt a low, deep keening sound fill her throat.

"All secure, my dear girl." She didn't look up. Etienne strode through the front doors and firmly locked them behind him.

He rubbed his hand together. He felt excellent, just excellent. At last things were going the way they'd been intended. He walked over to Arielle and lightly patted her cheek. She jerked away from him as far as her bonds would allow.

"I'm not a bad-looking man, Arielle. Surely you'll admit that. Unlike my father, I'm not fat and I don't have any rotted teeth. Women have told me I'm a good lover. Perhaps not as good as you are a whore, but I shan't fail you. Come, now, don't carry on so."

"Let me go."

"We'll see how long your stubbornness lasts." As he spoke, he unfastened the belt from the railing and loosened her wrists. She bent down to the bonds on her ankles.

"Oh, no, my dear, not just yet." He pulled her to her feet and once again hoisted her over his shoulder. "You're light, Arielle. I will soon see if you're too thin. I remember you so well from that night, your body gleaming so whitely in the candlelight. You were very slender but not thin. Ah, and your breasts. I remember thinking they were so full for such a slender girl. And those long legs of yours, Arielle. I dreamed so many nights of feeling your thighs lock about me."

She couldn't bear it. She reared up, smashing her fists against his head. He jerked her down to stand precariously in front of him. "You do that again and you will regret it. Do you understand me, Arielle?" He shook her, and her head snapped back on her neck.

She understood him and she believed him. She sagged where she stood. This time he didn't heft her over his shoulder. He forced her to take short, hopping steps beside him down the long corridor toward the master's bedchamber.

"There, now you can concentrate on not falling on your lovely face instead of taking exception to what I'm saying. Now, where was I? I will tell you again, my dear girl, that I'm not a brute like my father. There will be no question of punishment." He paused a moment, then added, his voice sounding a bit odd, almost dreamy, "Unless, of course, you force me to it."

Again she felt that odd keening sound coming from deep inside her.

"Ah, here we are. I do hope that old crone has prepared your bath for you. You do smell like your horse, my dear. You even have some of the stench from that damned goose."

Etienne dragged her into the master bedchamber. All the draperies were pulled back from the windows. Bright summer sunlight flowed into the room. A copper tub had been placed by the fireplace. This room, unlike the others, had no Holland covers, but there was dust on the wooden floor and the smell of disuse.

"I believe I'll tie up your wrists again. It won't hurt, I promise you. You remember that hook up there? My father told me of how he would fasten you on a long rope from that hook and just look at you. For hours sometimes, he told me. You'd be there, naked, for him and only him."

"No, please, Etienne. No!"

"Finally you speak to me. Well, I should prefer other words from your beautiful mouth. I will do as I wish, Arielle. Accept it."

He found a long thin rope in the armoire. He wrapped it about her wrists, then stood on a chair and tied the top of the rope to the hook embedded in the ceiling. He adjusted it until she was able to stand comfortably, her arms drawn up above her head.

"Now," he said. He bent down and unfastened her ankles.

She felt numbing pain, for Dorcas had tied them very tightly.

Etienne rubbed them until the stinging feeling made her want to cry out. She didn't make a sound.

He leaned back on his haunches for a moment, and without thought, without consideration for the consequences, she kicked out at him, connecting with his groin.

He stared at her for an instant, disbelief in his eyes. Then he howled with pain and fell back. He doubled over, holding himself.

She stared down at him. Fool, a thousand times a fool. She was helpless and she'd still hurt him badly. She closed her eyes and waited.

She hadn't long to wait. Etienne got hold of himself. The roiling nausea receded. He managed to rise, then finally to stand straight again. He looked at her. She realized, he knew, that what she'd done was stupid. He smiled at her.

He walked close and lightly rubbed his knuckles over her white cheek. "Poor, stupid little girl. You kick out again and you will regret it more than you can imagine. I am right now deciding whether or not to take revenge for the pain you caused me. You try to inflict more, and I swear to you that you will be the one howling in agony. Do you understand?"

Her eyes were tightly closed. She made no movement.

"Do you understand?" He grasped her chin in his hand and shook her head until she opened her eyes. "Well?"

"Yes," she whispered. "I understand."

"Good." Then he kissed her. She gasped, trying to pull away from him, but it was no good. He kissed her until he was through. He'd tried to thrust his tongue into her mouth, but she'd kept her lips tightly closed. He stepped back. He looked lost in profound contemplation. "It has been so long since I've seen you. I can't decide which part of you I wish to see first. Have you any suggestions, my dear girl?"

She turned her face away, saying nothing.

"Well, I shall just start at the bottom, then."

He knelt in front of her and pulled of her riding boots, tossing them over his shoulder. "Now your skirt, I think." She felt his fingers opening her riding jacket, seeking the fastenings on her skirt. They came open easily. He drew it down over her hips, downward until he had lifted each foot and the skirt was on the floor. "Charming," he said. He untied the string of her petticoat, and she felt the cool air touch her bare thighs. "Now the stockings," Etienne said. He rolled down each stocking, lightly stroking her legs as he did so. Soon she stood before him garbed in only her short chemise, blouse, and riding jacket.

"A truly exquisite painting you would make. Yes, indeed."

"I found the cream, Miss Arielle."

Both Etienne and Arielle stared at Dorcas. She came into the room at her slow, shuffling pace, holding a jar in her right hand.

"What do you want, you bloody old hag?"

"The cream," Dorcas said in the exaggerated patient tone she'd occasionally used with Arielle when she'd been a child. "I don't want Miss Arielle scarred. You've tied her up. She always hated that, you know. She cried. Always. She isn't crying now. I don't understand."

"Get out, you cretinous old crone!"

Dorcas looked confused. "All right. I'll wait for you, Miss Arielle, in your bedchamber. I've the cream. I'll take care of you as I always did."

Arielle moaned.

"My God, the old fool's batty as a dander box!"

Etienne followed Dorcas to the adjoining door, and Arielle heard him order her to bring in the cans of hot water. She watched Dorcas, her back bowed, lug the cans of water to the copper tub and dump them in. Again and again until the tub was fill.

Etienne then saw her to the door and slammed it after her.

"Now," he said, smiling at Arielle. "I fear, my dear, that I will simply have to sacrifice your blouse and jacket. You shouldn't miss them all that much. My father told me that you were quite used to being with him as naked as the day you were born. You would do fine stitchery, naked, when he wasn't using you, so he could enjoy the sight of you. Don't you remember those times, Arielle?"

"Your father was the insane one, Etienne. He was miserably insane and he was wicked and evil. You told me you weren't like him. But listen to yourself! Please, you must stop this. You must let me go."

"Don't worry that I will treat you as he did. How many times must I repeat myself? Pray say no more on that head. It begins to annoy me."

He went to Paisley's desk and opened the top side drawer. He removed a letter knife. The handle was of the whitest pearl, the blade only three inches long.

Arielle trembled at the sight of that knife, she couldn't help herself. But what he did was simply to slit open her jacket sleeves from wrist to shoulder. Then he slit the shoulder seams and peeled the jacket off. He performed the same operation with her blouse. Finally she was standing covered only with her fine lawn chemise.

He stared at her for a moment, his eyes roving from her face down to her bare toes. Lightly he touched his fingertips to a nipple, stroking it though the chemise.

She sucked in her breath and tried to pull back.

"All right, Arielle. Enough teasing. Let me see you now." And the knife snipped through the lacy straps. He pulled the chemise down slowly, pausing a moment at her waist, then pulling more until it pooled in a soft white heap at her feet. He stood back, rubbing his fingers over his jaw.

"Glorious," he said.

Humiliation. Pure and unadulterated humiliation. It had been so long but the feelings came back with a rush. She was there again, with Paisley, feeling his eyes on her, feeling his hand pat her buttock as he strolled past her to fetch a cheroot, perhaps.

"A pity, but I don't wish you to have to bathe in cold water. I will untie you now, Arielle. If you give me any difficulties, I will be forced to whip you."

He untied her wrists and pulled her to the copper tub. "Sit down and scrub the horse smell from yourself."

He dumped a sponge and a bar of lavender-scented soap in her lap. He walked to the chair by the fireplace, turned it to face her, and sat down, crossing his legs at his ankles.

"A very pleasant sight," he remarked.

She sat huddled in the tub, her arms wrapped around her knees, unmoving.

"Bathe yourself or I will do it."

She forced herself to soap the sponge. Slowly, her head turned away from him, she began to rub the sponge over herself. "Very nice," she heard him say. "Don't bother with you hair. If there is any horsey scent in it, I'll simply spray it with some perfume I found in my father's desk. I wondered if it was yours, Arielle. It's lavender, just like the soap."

He'd changed, she realized. He was more confident, more self-assured than before. He sounded, oddly enough, more like his father. His French accent was nearly gone. She shuddered, hearing him say, "Is the water cold already, Arielle? Would you like me to help you out now?"

She shook her head. She didn't want to look at him or talk to him. She wanted to ignore him so he

would disappear. Foolish, foolish girl, she told herself. She ran the soapy sponge over her stomach.

"Lower, Arielle."

She swallowed and obeyed him. What to do? She
must think of something! To be a passive victim—
no, she couldn't, wouldn't let that happen to her
again. What if she were the strong one? What if
she took control from him?

Slowly, Arielle stood up in the tub. She wrung
out the sponge, letting the water trail over her
breasts. "Give me a towel," she said, her voice as
cold as the water.

Etienne arched a black brow. He rose, fetched the
thick towel from the back of a chair and handed it
to her. He looked at her breasts, at the slick beads
of water, at her soft nipples.

"Get away from me, you stupid fool!"

He jerked back, unable to believe his ears. "What
the devil did you say?"

"You heard me, Etienne. Go away, like a good
boy. I wish to dry myself."

Confused, Etienne retreated to his chair and sat
down. He watched her dry herself thoroughly,
slowly, as if she hadn't a care in the world, as if he
weren't there watching her, waiting to tie her
wrists again to that rope.

"You are such a fool," Arielle said as she drew
the towel around her and knotted it above her
breasts. "At least your father wasn't that. He was
cruel and fat and wicked, but not a fool. You, on
the other hand, are a foolish little boy."

He leaped to his feet, his face flushed. "How dare
you speak to me that way!"

She forced a shrug, boredom clear in her expression. "Well, aren't you? Trying to steal another
man's wife? Trying to have sexual relations with
your dead *father's* wife? Can't you manage to find
a woman for yourself? Do you have to settle for

other men's women? Admit it, you aren't at all well.
England is obviously not a good place for you. It
makes you even more . . . foolish."

He was striding toward her now, his face mottled
with rage.

"Don't you even think to touch me, you miserable little French bastard!"

He drew up short at the utter scorn in her voice.
He didn't touch her. He stared at her. She stared
back. "Yes," she said finally, her voice replete with
contempt, "you are a very sad case, Etienne. Go
back to France. Find your own woman. Or better
yet, find yourself a young girl. You aren't a man,
after all."

Etienne trembled. Evan had called him mad once
when he'd continued to insist that Arielle was his
and no one else's. He stared at her, and saw her
contempt, and felt himself shrivel deep inside. He
pictured clearly that whore's face in Calais just before he'd taken the packet to England. She'd
laughed at him, at his aborted attempt to come inside her.

He wanted to run and never stop. He turned away
from Arielle abruptly, despair and self-disgust eating at him.

Suddenly Dorcas came through the adjoining
door. "Do you need me yet, Miss Arielle? You poor
baby, aren't you dreadfully cold with just that wet
towel about you? Is that awful man making you
stand there like that? He is wicked, I know it, but
I've the cream."

Arielle wanted to scream. She watched Etienne's
face, his body, while Dorcas spoke. He regained his
control. He even smiled. He looked like his father.

"That's right, Dorcas," he said. "I'm making your
poor baby stand here for my pleasure. Soon she'll
do other things as well. She will call you when she
needs you. Now, stay out of here."

"No, Dorcas," Arielle said quickly. "Stay here." But the old woman had already turned at the sound of a man's command.

"So," Etienne said when at last the adjoining door was firmly closed. "Now, my dear girl, what shall I do first?"

# 23

Arielle's bravado faltered, then crumbled. She saw the gleam in his light eyes, saw that he once again knew his power over her, that he couldn't wait to exercise that power, and in the most demeaning fashion possible. He wanted her obedience, her utter subservience. Or he would hurt her. Just as his father had.

She knew now that he was quite capable of revenge. And he saw her attempt to seize power from him as the perfect excuse to abuse her. God, it had almost worked! She had almost cowed him. If not for Dorcas, telling him so precisely that he was the master.

Oh, God.

She stood quietly, waiting.

He said, his voice calm, pleasant, "What, I wonder, will give me the most pleasure? Sit in a chair as my father used to do and simply look at you hanging from that rope naked? What to do first?"

He smiled then. He walked to her, ripped off the towel, and when she began to fight him, he hit her hard. Her head snapped backward, the pain in her jaw intense. She felt his shaking her, then felt him lifting her and carrying her. He set her on her feet and fastened her wrists again with the rope. She felt her arms drawn up over her head. Once she was secure, Etienne stepped back.

"Magnificent," he said. He saw the dazed sheen in her eyes and frowned. "I do hope I haven't bruised your face, my dear. Such a pity if I did. Still, you must learn that you cannot hurt your master, that you cannot defy him without swift and fitting punishment."

Arielle didn't respond. Her vision was still blurred, her mind cloudy. Her head ached and her mouth was dry.

Suddenly she felt his hand on her belly, kneading her, smoothing her flesh. She flinched, and he chuckled.

"Like silk," Etienne said. "And this." He closed his eyes as his fingers moved downward. He found her and started fondling her.

He stopped abruptly, drawing back his hand as he opened his eyes. "No, I mustn't spoil you like that. My fingers give you too much pleasure, don't they?"

"No," she said very clearly. "They make me want to vomit. You are filthy, Etienne. You are—"

"Shut up!" he yelled at her, raising his hand but not striking her. "Just be quiet or I'll hit you!"

He was breathing hard. God, he didn't want to hurt her like this, damn her. But she was driving him to it, forcing him to behave like his father. He moved away from her, pulling a chair over and sitting down. He was facing her now, his legs stretched out in front of him. Arielle watched him steeple his fingers and tap his fingertips rhythmically together.

"You are lovely like this. I can see why my father arranged for you to display yourself for him. Naked, vulnerable, so beautifully helpless. I shan't give you any more pleasure with my fingers. And no, don't tell me you found my touch repellent. I won't believe you. I told you that I know women and I am a good lover. I know what makes you want to beg me for it."

Arielle marveled at his now blatant belief in his masculine talents. Just a while before, he'd been so uncertain, so bewildered, unsure of himself as a man. She wanted to laugh, but she was too afraid. She said nothing, made no movement whatsoever. Let him talk. Let him carry on with his bragging until he rotted. Burke would come.

"Nothing to say, huh? Well, silence is refreshing in you, Arielle. You've become much too independent for a woman, too shrewish, too demanding. I liked you much better before. You knew then what you were, what you were supposed to be, what you were supposed to do. No, this new you isn't to my liking, but I think I can help you push back the months. I'll make you the way you once were, my dear."

She *had* changed. Burke had helped her become a different person. She mustn't forget that, no matter what. No matter what Etienne made her do.

"It is the woman's sole duty to please the man. I think I wish you to please me now, Arielle. I want you to take me in your mouth and caress me and kiss me."

She looked at him then. If he wanted that of her, he would have to release her. Her hands and her feet would be free. She could have a chance . . .

"Are you thinking that you will hurt me? You could, of course. I suppose I must make you understand that if you attempt anything with me, you will regret it more than you can imagine. If you try to hurt me, Arielle, I will whip you with a riding crop. A riding crop raises ugly welts, I'm sure you remember. And the pain, if again you remember, is most remarkably acute. I remember your screams, you know. Now, what do you say?"

"I won't hurt you, Etienne, for the simple reason that I refuse to touch you."

It was obvious to Arielle that he hadn't considered her outright refusal even a possibility. He glared at her, enraged. Then he looked temporarily unnerved. He didn't know what to do. She waited, not moving a muscle.

"You will," he said, his voice petulant.

"No, I will not touch you. I want you to release me."

He jumped to his feet. It took all her courage not to flinch from him.

He walked over to her, grasped the thick knot of hair at her nape in his fist, and pulled back. She closed her eyes against the pain.

"Look at me, damn you!"

She opened her eyes. They were watering from the stinging pain in her scalp.

"You will do as I tell you, or I will bring out that riding crop right now!"

"You are a coward, Etienne. You would beat me simply because I'm tied and helpless. Only a coward would do that. Not a man, not an honorable man."

She thought he would strike her again, but he merely tugged once more, viciously, at her hair, then pushed away from her. She thought for a moment that she'd won. But just for a moment. He walked toward the armoire in the far corner of the bedchamber. Too soon he was coming back to her. In his hand he held a riding crop.

"Damnation! I don't bloody well believe this. Where is she? Where could she have taken Mindle?"

"As I told ye, milord, I saw her riding east," Geordie answered.

Burke shook his head. He was frustrated and

afraid. Something had happened to her, he knew it, he felt it in his gut. He didn't consider distrusting his feelings; they'd held him in too good stead in the army. He and the men had been searching for nearly an hour now. Not one damned trace of her.

The going was slow. If she'd been thrown, she could be lying in the midst of bushes, unconscious. Or worse.

He cursed softly as Joshua, to Burke's far left, took up calling Arielle's name.

Suddenly Burke thought of Evan Goddis. He drew Ashes to an abrupt halt. "We're going to Leslie Farm," he shouted, then wheeled his stallion about an headed in the opposite direction at a gallop.

Not long after, Turp, the Leslie Farm butler, stared hard at Burke, striving desperately to place the dusty-clothed gentleman in his mind.

"Is your former mistress, Arielle Leslie, here? Well? Quickly, man!"

"No, my lord, married I heard she was, to the Earl of Ravensworth, to the north, in the big house. She hasn't come here in a long time, just once I recall after the viscount's death, and she didn't stay long."

"I am the Earl of Ravensworth and—"

"And you seem to have lost your bride, my lord? How very careless of you. Or perhaps my dear little half sister simply tired of you and sought out new . . . amusements?"

Evan Goddis stood in the doorway of the drawing room, his stance negligent, his look amused. "Well, why else would you be here?"

Burke's rage and anxiety were barely contained. "Yes, my wife is missing. You haven't seen her, Goddis?"

"I, my lord? What would I want with that little . . . well, no, certainly not."

Burke called to Geordie, George, and Joshua over his shoulder. "Search, quickly!"

"My lord!" Turp cried as Joshua unceremoniously shoved him aside and strode toward the stairs.

"I should call you out for this!" Evan said, so furious that he'd turned pale.

"It would be my pleasure," Burke said, his eyes narrowing.

After the brief search, it became evident that Arielle wasn't there.

"Where is the Frenchman?" Burke demanded.

"He left last week. I sent him away. He was becoming quite tedious."

"Unfortunately, my lord, I saw no evidence of another male in the residence," Joshua said.

"All right," Burke said. He turned to Evan and said very softly, "If you have lied to me, Goddis, I will kill you. I swear it."

Etienne flexed the riding crop, then he kissed her hard. "I wonder if I should first take you standing up. Should you like that?"

She said nothing.

"I remember that my father never whipped you while you were hanging there. It gave him more pleasure to see you on your hands and knees, trying to cover yourself, trying to scurry away from him. He like to watch you cower."

Etienne put down the riding crop and unfastened the rope about her wrists. "You will behave as you did with my father."

She spit at him, full in his face.

Etienne jerked back, fury filling his eyes. But he held to his control. "Will you pleasure me now?"

"I will kill you now, Etienne."

He backed up one step and flayed the riding crop at her. She ducked, jerking to her left, and it barely touched her arm.

"Get down on your hand and knees, damn you! Plead with me. Cry!"

"You go to hell, you worthless bastard!" Arielle threw herself at him, her fingers curved like claws. Etienne jumped away from her and swung the riding crop again. Still she came at him, yelling at him, kicking at him.

She heard the hiss and snap of the crop, but when it did strike her, she barely felt the sting across her flesh. He managed to grab her arm in his left hand and fling her to the floor. But she was up in an instant screaming at him.

Her fingernails caught his neck and she felt the tearing of his flesh. He yowled, striking out yet again with the riding crop. "I will master you!" he screamed at her. Why wasn't she cowering? Why wasn't she obedient, pleading, begging with him as she'd done with his father? Slowly, inexorably, he was backing her up against the wall. She ducked sideways, her eyes on the adjoining door, but he quickly cut off her avenue of escape. Soon he had her trapped. The muscles in his arm burned. Finally, instead of attacking him, she covered her face with her arms.

He didn't strike her again. He tossed the riding crop to the floor and lowered his arm. He was breathing hard. He pressed her against the wall, pinning her with his hands on her shoulders.

He gulped in deep breaths. "Now, Arielle? Will you do as I wish now? I won't hit you again if you just do as I wish. I'm not an unreasonable man. Just say yes."

She slowly lowered her arms. Then she fisted her hand and struck his jaw as hard as she could. He fell back, tripped on the riding crop, and landed on his knees.

She was gasping for breath as she stared down at

him. "I'll die before I become anyone's victim again. Do you hear me, Etienne?"

She eyed the riding crop beside him and wondered if she could grab it before he could stop her. But no, he picked it up, and he stood now, painfully, his hand rubbing his jaw. He held the crop close as he strode to the adjoining door, flung it open and yelled for Dorcas.

She heard Dorcas's shuffling step, heard the old woman cry out, "Oh, dear, oh, dear! You've hurt her again. You miserable old man! Oh my poor baby."

Dorcas's thin arms went around her, and Arielle felt herself being hugged and rocked. She felt defeated, and she realized suddenly that she hurt. But she mustered the strength to wrench free of the old woman. Etienne suddenly grabbed her and dragged her into her old bedchamber. He tossed her onto her old bed, her face buried in the pillow.

"Damn you, Arielle! I didn't want to hurt you! I didn't hurt you very much. You didn't ever strike my father, did you? Why me? Why, damn you?"

She managed to raise her head just a bit. "Because I'm strong now."

He looked at her, baffled. "See to her," he said to Dorcas. Then he strode from the room.

Dorcas was crooning all the while. "Now, my baby, Dorcas will care for you. I won't let you be scarred. You just lie still and I'll bathe you. Then the cream, my baby. You will fell better soon. He is a cruel man. Ah, the welts aren't so very bad, thank God. If you like, I could kill him for you again."

Arielle was drifting in and out of the cloud of pain. But she heard Dorcas's final words. She shook her head. "What did you say, Dorcas?" she whispered.

"I said I would kill him for you again if you wanted me to."

She tried to keep her voice low, reasonable. "Paisley choked to death on a herring bone."

"Maybe he was chewing on a herring bone at the time, but no, 'twas I who gave him a nice little dollop of arsenic. I saved you from him and I can do it again. I just don't understand . . ."

Arielle felt the old woman's fingers rubbing the cream gently into the welts. "What don't you understand?"

"He didn't die. He's here again, hurting you like before. Evil, I suppose. Yes, evil reigns. It doesn't die like it should. A pity."

Arielle closed her eyes. It was too much. Much too much.

She realized something before she slipped into unconsciousness. She hadn't given in. She knew now that she would never give in again. She wouldn't ever again allow herself to be a victim. Not ever.

She would kill Etienne herself.

Arielle awoke with a start. It was nearly dark in the bedchamber. Dusk outside. How many hours had passed? How long had she been asleep? Or unconscious? She didn't know which it was. Her body ached and throbbed.

Suddenly the soft flame of a candle shone down on her face.

"How do you feel?" It was Etienne, his face shadowed, his voice soft.

"I hurt. What do you expect, you miserable little worm?"

He sucked in his breath. "I didn't want to hurt you. I wanted to love you, to make you mine. You forced me to do it, Arielle, you forced me."

She saw the nail slashes on his face, his throat,

and she was pleased. She'd hurt him, perhaps as much as he had her. She tried again. "Etienne, listen to me. I am married. I am married to a man I love, surprising as that may sound." But it didn't surprise her. It was true. She did love Burke. It was odd and made her feel warm and strong.

"I don't care! I came to make love to you. I can't wait."

"Listen to me, Etienne. If you touch me, I will kill you. I promise you that."

He laughed, albeit it was somewhat of a nervous sound. "Don't be a fool, Arielle." She watched him set the candle down on the small table beside the bed. The candle was next to the jar of cream. She watched him take off his clothes.

She felt his hands on her upper arms, felt him pull down the single sheet that covered her. "You are so beautiful," he said, and he eased in beside her. She felt his naked body pressing against her side, felt his fingers curving under her chin, pulling her face toward him.

"Don't touch me!"

He kissed her.

"Shush, don't fight me. I don't want to hurt you. Please, Arielle, just hold still."

He jerked her onto her back. He was pushing her legs apart, bending her knees. She saw him rising over her. She was trying desperately to gather her strength, to kick him off her.

Suddenly she saw Dorcas behind him. She was holding a knife high, poised over Etienne's back.

Arielle screamed. "Dorcas, no! Etienne, behind you!"

She saw the knife go into his back. Etienne stiffened. He opened his mouth. His lips worked, but only a gurgling sound emerged.

He fell forward, his head landing on her breasts. The knife stuck obscenely out of his back.

Dorcas said softly, "Now we will see if he comes back yet again. Evil, so very evil. I knew you hated what he was going to do to you. You always hated it. I didn't want to see you suffer anymore. You don't deserve it. Married off to this wicked old man by that evil half brother of yours. Evan Goddis is another work of Satan. He—"

"Dorcas, help me get him off me!"

"No, I must make certain he's truly dead. I'm glad I didn't use poison this time. I like how the knife feels. Flesh is so soft, you know, my baby. So soft, it sinks right in. But he must be dead. I should stab him again. He's so evil—"

'Please, get him off me!"

She knew she was going to be ill. In a spurt of strength she didn't know she still possessed, Arielle managed to heave Etienne's body away from her. She slipped off the bed onto her knees on the wooden floor. She jerked the chamber pot toward her. She vomited until there were only dry heaves racking her body.

It wasn't a question of a dream or reality anymore. It was the darkest pit of hell. She rolled over onto her side and drew her knees up to her chest. Dorcas was calling to her, but she couldn't make out her words. She couldn't have answered her in any case.

It was Burke who saw the smoke.

"Hold a moment," he called to Joshua and Geordie. It was dark now, but there was, thank God, a full moon.

He pointed. "Look. That's Rendel Hall, isn't it?"

His question was purely rhetorical. In the next instant, he kicked his stallion's sides. Joshua and Geordie were quickly beside him.

Burke felt cold inside. Cold with fear. The flames

grew steadily brighter, slashing across the sky. The hall was on fire.

He knew without a doubt that Arielle was there. And she was inside. And she could die.

He flattened himself against the horse's neck and urged him to greater speed.

As they approached the house, the heat slapped them like a living thing, but Burke didn't hesitate. He jumped off the stallion's back and ran up the front steps to the Hall. The flames were leaping out of the upper story, thick dark smoke gushing out of the windows.

"My lord! Wait, I'll go!"

Burke paid Joshua no heed. He flung open the door and ran inside. Smoke filled the entrance hall. He threw back his head, shouting, "Arielle!"

No sound.

He ran toward the stairs. Suddenly he tripped over something in his path. He regained his balance and stared down. It was a dead goose. He shook his head and bounded up the stairs.

He shouted her name again and again. He heard the men pounding behind him. At the head of the stairs, he directed them down the western corridor and he took the eastern.

Suddenly a woman tottered from a room, bent over, coughing.

"Arielle!"

But it was Dorcas, and in her hand was a blood-stained knife. He felt a twisting in his guts, such a deadening fear that when he heard the broken anguished cry, he knew it had come from him.

He ran to her. "Where is she?" He yelled at her, shaking her like a rat. "Damn you, where is she?"

Dorcas raised her watering eyes. "I knew evil wouldn't die. I tried, you know, twice I tried, but here you are again, back to hurt my baby. I won't let you! I won't let you!" She jerked out of his grasp, then came at him with the knife. Burke reacted instinctively. He slammed his fist into her jaw. The knife slipped from her bloody fingers and skittered across the corridor floor. He left her unconscious on the floor and ran into the bedchamber from which she had come.

First he saw Etienne's body, lying half on the floor, half on the bed. There was an ugly gash in the middle of his back. He was naked and he was quite dead.

Then he saw Arielle. She was on her hands and knees, coughing violently. He saw the burning pile of rags in the master bedchamber just beyond.

Had old Dorcas been trying to destroy the evil by burning the room? The house?

"Love," he said and quickly grabbed a blanket to wrap around Arielle. "You're safe now, I promise you. Come, we must get out of here."

Arielle raised burning eyes to his face. "Burke?"

It was a thin thread of a sound. But at least she was alive. He lifted her in his arms.

"It's all right, sweetheart."

"I knew you would come. I knew."

"Yes, I came. It's all right—now it's all right."

He strode out into the smoke-filled corridor. He bent down to look at the mad old woman. She was dead.

He shook his head at the waste of it all. He kissed his wife and held her tightly against him.

"I was strong. Burke, I was strong."

# EPILOGUE

London, England
September 1814

"Thank God that's over!"

Burke grinned at Knight, who had just wiped a singularly beautiful handkerchief across his brow.

"It wasn't you, Knight. Why are you sweating like a pig? Are you feeling like a fox with the dogs on your scent?"

Knight looked pained. "The overflowing good *spirits* scare the hell out of me. It's really a man's last stand, and what happens? Just look at Percy. The fellow succumbs with a vacuous smile on his face. It's enough to make a man lose all hope."

"Your turn will come, you'll see. You'll *want* it to come."

"I will not be domesticated like my aunt Sally's obnoxious cat. It freezes the soul even to contemplate it. At least you should be well pleased, Burke. Lannie and the girls are no longer you responsibility."

"I'll miss Virgie and Poppet." Burke then looked a bit surprised. "Actually, I'll even miss Lannie."

"Where is your beautiful wife?"

Burke had been wondering that himself. "I think she's upstairs with the new bride." He wasn't sure.

He hadn't let her out of his sight since that ghastly night some three weeks earlier. It still made his blood run cold to think about it. He could still picture the violent orange flames, still see the roof of Rendel Hall collapse inward as he was riding away, Arielle clutched against his chest. He could still see his wife's pale face, her pain-filled eyes. He'd asked her no questions. He'd simply kept her beside him, saying nothing even as he'd taken care of her. He'd wondered briefly if Etienne had raped her before Dorcas had plunged the knife into his back. If, indeed, that was why Dorcas had stabbed him.

He hadn't asked her about that either. It didn't matter. All that mattered was that she was safe, no thanks to him, her so-called protector.

And she was strong. She'd told him so over and over that night, even as he'd bathed her and gently rubbed in the cream on the myriad welts.

"You want to try some of Corinne's champagne punch?"

Burke brought himself back to the present and shook his head at Knight. "First let me locate Arielle. If she is with Lannie, she's probably exhausted from all the chatter."

"Look at poor Percy. He appears uninhabited in his upper stories. Marriage does that to a man, you know. Makes him numb in the brain. Like you, Burke. All you can think about is Arielle."

"It isn't a distasteful affliction, Knight," Burke said easily. "Indeed, it is altogether pleasant." And terrifying, he wanted to add, and painful, particularly when one failed the other and the other was hurt because of that failure.

"I can get all the pleasantness in the world with my mistress. Incidentally, Laura misses you. She told me so herself."

"That's nice," Burke said absently, and Knight just shook his head sadly.

"She said I was the better lover."

"Remarkable," Burke said.

Knight laughed, clapped him on the back, and walked over to where Percy stood, surrounded by friends, his fifth glass of champagne punch in his hand. Burke had offered to keep Virgie and Poppet with him at Ravensworth Abbey while Percy and Lannie went on their wedding trip, but Corinne had insisted the girls stay here in London with her. Perhaps, Burke thought, he should take Arielle on a wedding trip. A change of scene, far from the blackened ruin that had been Rendel Hall, far from Evan Goddis, far from all the painful memories.

It had taken nearly three weeks for her body to heal and for the welts and bruises to disappear. She hadn't wanted him to see her, and he hadn't insisted. It was only two night ago that he'd finally seen her naked, in the bathtub. She was so white and soft-looking and so beautiful he wanted to touch her and plunge into her and hold her. But he hadn't. Her body might be healed, but he wasn't certain about her mind. He realized he was afraid. Afraid he might rush her, afraid he might push too hard and hurt her.

He sighed and headed for the stairs. He was deep in thought when he heard her soft voice.

"Hello, Burke."

He smiled from ear to ear at the sight of her. "Are you numb from all Lannie's chatter?"

"No, but she is terribly excited, you know." Arielle walked down the stairs and placed her fingertips on his arm. He searched her face for signs of strain, fatigue, even pain. "You're all right?"

"Yes."

That was always her reply. He had no idea what the truth was. What do you expect? he asked himself silently. He hadn't been forthcoming about his thoughts with her, so why should she be any less reticent with him?

"I should like some champagne punch. I think Lannie imbibed freely and she, I promise you, is feeling top-o'-the-trees."

"Much like Percy, I suspect."

She chuckled and touched his cheek with her fingertips. Without thought, he kissed her. She became very still.

"Burke . . ."

He kissed her again, lightly, not trying to force her in any way, but the possession was there. He knew it and couldn't control it. He wondered if that was what worried her so profoundly.

"Don't sound so wary," he said, softly stroking his knuckles over her jaw. "It's just a kiss. From your husband. He's that man who's inordinately proud of you. That fellow who thinks you're so wonderful he wants to shout it to the world."

He heard a harrumph and saw his sister standing on the stairs behind Arielle. "Hello, Corinne. Everything is splendid. You've done marvelously well."

"You two are as bad as Percy and Lannie! I declare, it is more than a body can stand, a body that's lived with the same man for twenty-two years, that is."

"Twenty-two years," Burke repeated, smiling at his wife. "Will you still be interested in me in two decades?"

Arielle returned his smile, but hers was forced, nervous.

"You two come and mingle now." Corinne said, and with sublime assurance that her orders would be obeyed, she strode forward, not looking behind her.

"My sister is a martinet," Burke remarked. "Come, love, and I'll fetch you some champagne."

It was another fifteen minutes before Burke managed to speak to Arielle alone. She was sipping her punch, standing in the shadow of an overly large potted palm imported for the wedding.

"Are you all right?" he asked again.

"Yes," she said.

That *yes* was the one that tipped over the scales. His voice was filled with sarcastic anger as he said, "Of course you would say yes. And frankly, I'm tired of your continually saying 'Yes, Burke' to me!" He paused but got no response. He controlled himself. His outburst was altogether out of proportion to any provocation. "I wanted to speak to you, Arielle. Would you like to take a wedding trip?"

He was watching her closely. He saw her pale, saw her close her eyes for a moment. He said very quietly, "Please tell me what you're thinking. Don't shut me out anymore."

She remained silent.

"I love you, Arielle. I am your husband. You don't have to be strong all on your own. You can lean on me; you may use me."

"Use you? I believe I have used you, innumerable times. The last time, you saved my life. If you hadn't arrived, well, I would have ended up like poor Hannibal the goose."

"Stop it!"

"It's true."

"Dammit, some help I was when it took me long enough to find you! If only I'd been thinking more clearly, if only I hadn't gotten diverted to Leslie Farm, if only—"

Her fingers touched his lips. "There was no way you could have known I was at Rendel Hall. No way at all. You came. That is all that is important. You saved my life."

He abruptly took the champagne glass from her

hand and poured its contents into the potted palm. "We're going back to our hotel."

"I should like that," she said. He hadn't bothered opening up the Drummond town house for their brief visit to London. They were staying at the Pulteney in Piccadilly, in the suite Czar Alexander's sister, the Grand Duchess of Oldenburg, had used during the summer.

Arielle said polite good-byes and let her husband lead her from the Kinnard town house.

Burke hailed a hackney.

He remarked on the unseasonably cool weather, the interesting cloud formations moving east toward Purfleet, the comfortable gait of the swaybacked mare. Nothing of any importance until they were alone in their suite.

He leaned against the closed door. He looked at her and said very quietly, "I can't bear this anymore, Arielle. I know you've been hurt, terribly hurt, but if you will only tell me, I can help you bear it. At least I can try. Can you not like me enough for that?"

Like him? She laughed, a raw, hoarse sound.

Her hands slashed through the air. "I like you, Burke. I love you, as a matter of fact. I told you, long ago, it seems."

She'd spoken quickly, her voice high. Still, he wanted to hear her say it again. "What?" he asked. "I didn't hear you."

"I said I love you! Far more than that silly fifteen-year-old girl who stared at you with stars in her eyes! Oh, yes, she worshipped you, thought of you as a brave warrior god who through some unexplained miracle deigned to recognize her existence. She believed she was blessed when you smiled at her."

She stopped, infuriated by his slow, mocking smile. "All that?" he said. "Here I thought I was the one who was infatuated by that fifteen-year-old girl. I thought I was the one incredibly blessed when she smiled at me. I had no idea she worshipped me. It makes sense, of course, but I was too enthralled with her to notice."

"She was a guileless twit!"

"And I was beguiled by her, twit or no."

"Oh, be quiet! *She* is not the one who is here today. Her infatuation for you was nothing at all compared with what I feel. You wretch, I love *you*— Burke Drummond—a man who is fine and good and—" She ground to a halt, threw her hands up in the air, turned, and walked away.

He strode after her, grabbed her arm, and swung her around to face him. He pulled her to him tightly and pressed her face against his shoulder. "You foolish woman. I could spend two lifetimes with you and not have enough."

He kissed her then and the possession in his touch filled her and she accepted it willingly.

"I've missed you terribly, Burke." She stood on her toes, fitting herself against him.

He held her tightly, stroking her back. Everything he'd wanted to tell her poured out of him. "You are so beautiful and soft and sweet. I nearly failed you, and I've hated myself for it more than I can tell you. I get cramps in my belly and sweat like the most cowardly soldier under fire when I remember that night. I will try my damnedest never to be apart from you again. Merciful heavens, I need you, Arielle."

She pulled back in the circle of his arms, looking up at him, a frown on her face. "You need me? That sounds so strange, Burke."

"Why? Do you believe me invincible? So removed and remote?"

She pressed herself against him and felt his manhood, strong and swollen against her. "No," she said, "not remote."

He grinned then. "You are a coquette and I will make you pay for it." He swung her up in his arms and carried her into the large corner bedchamber, a room so impossibly opulent that Arielle had simply stared at it for a good five minutes when she'd first seen it.

When he was finally lying naked beside her on the bed, he said, his voice low and intense, "You're the strongest woman I know. You're proud and you're brave. You have so much to give, so much to teach me and our children. Will you come back to me?"

"I never left you." She looked directly into his eyes. "Never. It's just that I left myself for a while."

"Can you translate that, please?"

She laughed self-consciously. "It sounds odd, even to me. But there was so much to consider, Burke, so much to resolve inside me. What saved me with Etienne, what helped me be strong, was you. It was you who helped me become what I am now. You who helped me to stop being a victim. And I wasn't. I hurt him, you know. If it hadn't been for Dorcas, I would have controlled him. It was the oddest feeling, that I had power over him and that I was the victor—until she reminded him that he was the stronger, that he was the master and I was naught but poor, helpless Arielle."

She stopped and closed her eyes tightly.

He said nothing, merely waited. His fingertips stroked over her jaw, her ear, smoothed back the hair from her forehead.

"I didn't mean to close you out or act as if you weren't important to me, Burke. You were and you always will be. It's just that—"

"You had to go away for a while."

"Yes. Etienne didn't rape me," she added. "He

tried and he would have succeeded because I hadn't the strength left to fight him. It was then that Dorcas stabbed him."

"It's over."

"Yes. Finally."

His fingers moved downward as he spoke, and she interrupted him with a small cry. He looked at her face, saw her desire for him darken her eyes, and grinned. "Does that mean you've come back to me? You want me? You want me inside you, caressing you until you shatter in my hands?"

"Yes. That's about it, I expect. In addition to being fine and good, you're also beautiful and I want you. At least for the next two decades."

"You won't leave me again?"

"Only if you don't tell me what Montrose did to get that pony, Victor, away from you."

He stared at her blankly.

"Don't you remember all those wonderful stories you told me when I was ill? You told me about Victor, your pony, and how Montrose wanted him and how the pony wanted Montrose."

"You're thinking about a damned horse from years ago when I want to make love to you?"

"You won't tell me?"

He struck an attitude, one he trusted looked seriously thoughtful. "I will tell you . . ."

"Yes?"

"If you'll remove your hand from where it is. It's making me perfectly frantic."

"Ah," she said and let her fingers slide down his taut belly to touch him and caress him. He sucked in his breath. She smiled, lightly nipping his chin. "I think I like you frantic, Burke."

"Don't you want to know about Victor?" he asked, knowing he was at the very edge.

"Later."

He kissed her then, slowly, thoroughly. He paused a moment, his eyes on her breasts.

"Perhaps at breakfast," she said, her enjoyment clear. "Victor and a rasher of bacon."

"That sounds vastly romantic, Arielle."

"That sounds," she said, "like a long time away. There is much, Burke Drummond, that you must accomplish before breakfast."

"Yes," he said, looking at her from her forehead to her toes. "Now hush, for I am a thorough man and have no wish to be distracted."

"All right," she said and pulled him down on her.

# The Timeless Romances
## of New York Times Bestselling Author

# JOHANNA LINDSEY